INTRODUCTION

A Back Door Ministry by Christian Author, Brandon J Rosenberg, presents his Suspense and Thriller Series, "Cedar Creek County." Brandon has the unique craft of combining Christianity, the World, and Politics into a compelling fictional story on how God can change anyone's life, including those of Presidents in Corporate America and Washington D. C. Politicians. His stories are filled with intrigue, mystery, humor, and flirty romance that will inspire you to the last page.

THE D.C. MANDATE

Enjoy reading all his books in the

Cedar Creek County
Suspense Series

Book One: Rachael's Dilemma

Book Two: The Embezzlement

Book Three: The Picnic Table Heist

Love, Hope & Faith: Gift Collector Hardbound Set

Enjoy reading all his books in the

Cedar Creek County
Thriller Series

Book One: The Year 2035 - The D.C. Mandate

Book Two: The Year 2037 - The D.C. Scandal

(releasing early 2022)

Visit his website for additional details www.cedarcreekcounty.com

"Leading the unsaved to Jesus Christ."

Cedar Creek County, A Christian Thriller Series
Featuring Pastor Rachael & Friends

THE YEAR 2035:
THE D.C. MANDATE
BOOK ONE

BRANDON J. ROSENBERG

This is a work of fiction. Names, characters, places, historical events, and incidents are either the product of the author's imagination or used fictitiously. Any resemblance to actual persons, living or dead, business establishments, or locales is entirely coincidental.

Book cover design by Brent Spears
Editing by Sherri Davis

ISBN 9781-7361013-4-6 (paperback)

Light Morning LLC.
P O Box 9206
Greenville, TX 75404
www.cedarcreekcounty.com
books@brandonjrosenberg.com

A Word From The Author
Brandon J Rosenberg

The Book Series Cedar Creek County is a *"Back-Door Ministry."* Leading the unsaved to Jesus Christ through words written on pages. Prayerfully, my Christian fiction novels will encourage and inspire those with severe addictions to seek the Lord. God can heal and free you from the shackles of addictive bondage. It is my prayer that you will walk the path inviting Jesus into your heart. May the stories of Pastor Rachael and her friends give you direction as to how

God can change anyone's life, including yours.

MY GUARANTEE

Some books offer quick weight loss
Some books offer unbelievable ideas to get rich quick
Some books provide travel tours beyond anyone's imagination
My books offer none of these,
but <u>my guarantee</u> is that if
You declare with your mouth the sinner's prayer
You will be saved!

The words alone will not save you, but it is
the sincerity from your heart that you believe
and will be saved.

Say the words below with someone or out loud to yourself

"Dear Jesus, I Need You. I Am Humbly Calling Out to You.
I'm tired of Doing Things My Way. Help Me to Start Doing
Things Your Way.
I Invite You into My Heart and Life to be My Lord and Savior.
Fill the Emptiness in Me with Your Holy Spirit and Make Me
Whole. Lord, Help Me to Trust You, Help Me to Live for You,
Help me to Understand Your Grace. Help Me to Understand
Your Mercy and Your Peace. Thank You, Lord Jesus, Amen"

If you have prayed this from your heart sincerely, write your name by it along
with today's date as a reminder that you have come to Jesus Christ as a New
Born-Again Christian trusting Him as your Lord and Savior.

If you're still not sure, it is my prayer that the characters in my stories will
help you find a way to really know Jesus, invite Him into your heart, and be
saved.

May God Richly Bless You,
Brandon J Rosenberg

THE RIVER

If you know someone who is burdened with any type of addiction, they are not alone.

The River's mission is to impact people worldwide by providing healing and restoration through Christ-centered resources. In addition to their in-person recovery meetings, they utilize technology including Zoom, YouTube, Facebook, and Facebook Live.

The River provides six open recovery meetings and classes which address addiction and its root causes from a Christian standpoint. They also offer five closed recovery classes and group meetings that focus on the family, including the community juvenile drug court. The River features a live broadcast entitled "Life at The River," where they cover various topics related to and impact the community and culture. Their YouTube channel, The River Philly, offers an assortment of testimonials combined with a robust evangelistic outreach.

For more information visit their website: theriverphilly.org
You can also contact them via email: theriverphilly@gmail.com

ACKNOWLEDGMENTS

To my wife, Mariann, who's a godsend, and without her encouragement, my efforts would have been futile.

To my daughter, Sherri, whose copy editing is heaven-sent, without her expertise, my stories would never get to print.

My grandson, Dennis, a genius with social media, has been a tremendous help in getting the word out.

To Ehren, my web designer and whose creative magic has produced an excellent website.

To Brent, my genius graphic illustrator, who's creating covers that sizzle.

I want to thank each of you for enabling me to continue writing the stories of Pastor Rachael and her friends and how Jesus impacted their lives.

CAST OF CHARACTERS

Rachael Zellner .... pastor of the Jerusalem Tree Church
Darrell Zellner.......................... associate pastor and Rachael's husband
Bernard .... the Angel of the Lord
Irving & Helen Duike.... managers of the George Kogan Rehab Center
Phillip & Terri Dorfman .... Rachael's attorney and accountant
Rabbi Yosef ....friend of Rachael and Darrell
Dolan & Natalie Kogan .... professors, friends of Rabbi Yosef and
Rachael/Darrell
Hughes Reyna ....Owner of Country Club & Funeral Home
Klaus........................ Hughes right hand man-prints counterfeit money
Donna Trice ....Hughes's girlfriend
Giovanni & Lorenzo ....casket tailors
Sergio & Nicolao......alteration tailors in Manhattan's Financial District
Lucinda.. Sergio's girlfriend
Carlo...Italian tailor customizing men's suits
Cambria...........................Carlo's wife selling cosmetics in Manhattan
Richard Filburn.. Retired Sheriff
Agnes Filburn............................hobby of historical cemetery markers
Lawrence Filburn .... son of Richard & Agnes
Kellie Filburn .... wife of Lawrence
Mustafa & Eryman ....semi-drivers
Dr. Wesley Drew .... mortuary school professor
Dr. Amir Korcha .... County Medical Examiner

TABLE OF CONTENTS

THE D.C. MANDATE

CHAPTER ONE

ELECTION NIGHT-NOV 2032

The Reformed Communist Party had rented the new 120,000 seat sports arena for the President's victory speech this evening, November 2, 2032.

"Thank you, thank you, thank you very much," states the newly elected President amidst the roaring noise of over one hundred thousand.

"I want to thank my loyal Comrades and Americans all across the USA, and especially the nation of China. This victory would not have been possible without the unwavering help from both of you. Thank you."

The crowd cheers and chants, "Red, Red, Red. China, China, China!"

"I will not disappoint. I will keep my campaign promise to shutter every church and police department. My administration will confiscate every gun and Bible in America. If congress doesn't pass the D.C. Mandate in my first term, I will sign an executive order. You have my word!"

The crowd roars with cheers. The stadium noise could be heard throughout the city. Everyone was celebrating, in the streets, in the bars-everywhere! The President won the popular vote by over one hundred million against his four rivals. Indeed, his victory was a land-slide-a mandate!

TWENTY-SIX MONTHS LATER-JAN 2035

"The rapture is near!" Pastor Rachael Zellner affirmatively shouts out to the congregation as she begins her message.

She continues, "Is your heart ready to meet the Lord? But understand this, that in the last days there will come times of difficulty. People will be lovers of self, lovers of money, proud, arrogant, abusive, ungrateful, unholy, and heartless. Plus, slanderous, without self-control, brutal, not loving good, treacherous, reckless, swollen with conceit, lovers of pleasure rather than lovers of God, having the appearance of godliness but denying its power. Avoid such people."

"Right here, in Cedar Creek, we can see signs all around us of these traits in people. We must strive to seek the Holy Spirit to lead us appropriately in ministering and showing them God's love. Unfortunately, the addiction to the love of money and power will drive many to be heartless and arrogant, just like those ruling in Washington D. C."

Pastor Rachael continues, "And because lawlessness will be increased, the love of many will grow cold. In the colonial days, in the infancy of America, politics was preached from the pulpit. Today, in the Winter of 2035, the politically correct crowd dares us, pastors, to teach and preach the truth. So, help me, God, as long as I have breath, I will not succumb to these pressures. I implore you, congregation, to stay awake at all times, praying that you may have the strength to escape all these things that are going to take place and to stand before the Son of Man. To the one who endures to the end will be saved."

The associate pastor and Rachael's husband, Darrell Zellner, walks up to the pulpit and makes a quick announcement. "I invite all of you to attend our Wednesday night Bible study. I'll be teaching from the book of Revelation. As my wife articulated moments ago, the rapture is near. We both believe that one-hundred percent. You'll want to know how, what, where, and when things occur. With the reckless lawlessness happening daily in D.C. and even locally, here in Cedar Creek, you'll want to be sure your heart is ready to meet the Lord."

Darrell closes out the morning service with an altar call for those who were touched by the Holy Spirit during church service to come up and invite Jesus Christ as their personal Lord and Savior and become newborn-again-Christians. The worship team sings, "Just as I am," while Darrell and the other associate pastors lay hands upon the people standing around the altar. Many invite Jesus into their heart and become newborn-again-Christians.

After the service, while having lunch at their hotel café, Rachael reminds Darrell that they're invited to attend the open house later in the month at the new country club recently renovated and opened in Cedar Creek.

"Yeah, I'm sure curious why it took two years to reopen. The earth-moving machinery and construction teams seemed to be busy day and night, for two years-really?" Darrell replies with a question in his tone.

"I've heard from others, but don't know how true it is, that the owner, Hughes Reyna, bought the foreclosed property for only ten percent of market value and invested another three million for renovations," Rachael also states with a question.

"Well, sweetheart, I can't wait to attend the open house and see for ourselves!" Darrell shouts.

CHAPTER TWO

OPEN HOUSE-JAN 2035

"Good afternoon, folks! Welcome to my open house! My name is Hughes Reyna, and I look forward to personally meeting with all of you during this event," Hughes announces as the crowd flows into the clubhouse. His business neighbors, seven miles down the road, attending are Rachael and Darrell Zellner, pastors of The Jerusalem Tree Church in Cedar Creek. Rachael, a former fashion tycoon, had the initiative to combine preaching with beautiful models displaying her designer fashions from lingerie to wedding gowns. It indeed was a new concept ahead of its time but became accepted and successful.

"Mr. Reyna, I'd like you to meet my husband, Darrell, and I'm Rachael. We're pastors at the church down the road a bit. You certainly have an imposing establishment here," Rachael replies.

Hughes Reyna is Cedar Creek Country Club's new owner, having a funeral home, cemetery, and mortuary school. This unique golf course and cemetery enterprise combined creates a peaceful setting for those that have passed while simultaneously offering two 18-hole par- 4 golf courses.

"Thank you, Rachael. It took two years to complete the golf courses, pro shop, clubhouse, guest cottages, funeral home, mortuary school, and cemetery on the new life and death concept. I take great pride in my team who have accomplished this major project in record time," Hughes flatly disclosed.

"I can't help but notice how similar your innovation is to ours when we first began our new venture," Darrell states.

"Yes, I've briefly heard about your unique business model. Congratulations! When time permits, I'd be interested in hearing the entire story," Hughes politely imparts.

Rachael excuses herself to greet their friends, having just arrived.

Darrell replies, "Rachael and I would love to have you over for dinner sometime soon. We can then chat and share about our ventures. I'll check with her and get back to you."

"I would like that," Hughes concurs.

"Hey! There you guys are!" Shouts Rachael. "Hughes, I'd like you to meet our friends. Helen and Irving, managers of the George Kogan Rehab Center, Phillip and Terri, our attorney and accountant respectively, Dolan and Natalie, professors at the Conservatory of the Hebrew History and Arts, and College of Music."

"Very nice to meet you all, and welcome to my open house. Please, help yourselves to appetizers, champagne, wine, and, if you must, coffee."

"By that remark, I take it you don't drink coffee," Helen quips.

"This may sound sad, but it is part of life. I do drink coffee, but only when I'm embalming at midnight."

They politely and nervously chuckle. The concept of playing golf around the deceased still seems awkward, but all are willing to keep an open mind.

Hughes politely excuses himself momentarily and disappears into his back office of the clubhouse. Hughes calls his cohort, "Amir, have you been able to generate the unclaimed body certification for the John Doe we buried last week?"

Amir Korcha is the county medical examiner for Cedar Creek County and, on the side, provides Hughes with false death certificates whenever he needs them.

"Great! No name! No family! Indigent! I'll put the records to rest on this one," Hughes pats himself on the back.

"You know, Hughes, it's getting a little dicey over here at the county office. You need to slow down on your elimination process when you find a bad apple in the bunch," Amir admonishes Hughes weakly.

"Need I remind you, Amir, that my company comes to the rescue of your office whenever there's an unclaimed dead body. Plus, we bury the deceased at no charge, saving the county thousands of dollars annually."

"Maybe so, but you use the deceased as embalming practice for your mortuary school students. So, who's doing who a favor?"

"Listen, Amir! If it were not for me, you and your wife wouldn't have that luxurious lifestyle you're enjoying. So, keep your staff unsuspecting, and continue providing those false certificates whenever I need them!" Hughes shouts.

"Sure, as you say. But, try to limit your deceased count to ten a year instead of twenty."

As far as Hughes was concerned, he wasn't about to decrease his body count of elimination. Whenever the situation became a convenience, he would simply add to the John Doe section of his cemetery.

Hughes hangs up and calls Mayor Brady, "Listen, when you win re-election, appoint a new county coroner. Amir's loyalty to the cause is unraveling rapidly."

"It would take some public disinformation, but I could make the switch now during this term if you want?"

"Thanks, but I'll make it work. Heck, we only have some twenty-plus months before the election, and you're a shoo-in, Mayor."

"I wouldn't have won without your assistance, Hughes. I don't know how you did it, but I'm forever grateful you're my campaign manager."

"You and I have the same goals. Whatever it takes, I aim to win!" shouts Hughes with bravado.

Hughes hangs up and quickly makes his third call to Klaus, the mathematician at Hughes Casket Manufacturing in the outskirts of Buffalo, New York. "Do you have the shipment ready for tomorrow's delivery, including the counterfeit packets?"

Hughes is a genius- a mastermind at counterfeiting ten-dollar bills. The unobvious counterfeit never checked for flaws. He designed a secret zippered pocket hidden in the casket's lining with cunning ingenuity: the perfect place to hide one-hundred-thousand dollars in fake bills for each container. His two tailors, intricately by hand, sew both sides of the caskets' lining with secret pockets.

Klaus replies, "I do, boss. Forty caskets as scheduled for weekly delivery to our eight affiliated partners. As usual, we're delivering with only one casket containing the hundred grand counterfeit to each funeral home."

Hughes has an addiction to money, large amounts of money. Nothing will stop him from accumulating millions, not even murder.

Hughes returns to the clubhouse's festivities, mingles with the guests for a while, and shortly announces. "Those of you who would like to visit our pro shop and funeral home, the tour will commence in ten minutes."

Rachael and her friends walk the short distance and are surprised and somewhat shocked to see three casket models on display upon entering the pro shop.

"This is a unique and different marketing scheme that grabs one's attention," Phillip states.

"I think it's rather distasteful," Terri exclaims.

"If it weren't for God saving my life numerous times, I would have been in one of these long time ago," Irving states solemnly.

Helen shakes up the atmosphere and shouts, "Praise the Lord! As a Christian, I know my soul will be with Jesus the moment I pass from this life. My body will be in one of these, but my soul and spirit with Him-Hallelujah!"

Rachael inquires, "Hughes, where is the funeral home, and are there any chapels?"

Hughes invites them to see for themselves. "Let's walk through the archway to the back of the pro shop, and I'll show you."

Walking through the archway, they were amazed to see three chapels, two embalming chambers, multi offices, and a showroom displaying more caskets, urns, markers, and other funeral items.

Dolan and Natalie have been silent all this time, observing this new concept when Dolan asks, "I don't see any pine boxes. Will you be incorporating Jewish funerals here?"

"I'm glad you asked that; I've meant to invite the Rabbi over so we can discuss the best way to honor those in the Jewish faith," Hughes replies.

"If you like, when I see the Rabbi next, I'll ask him to give you a call," Dolan offers.

"Much obliged; I would like that, thanks."

Phillip remarks, "I've noticed a sign on the cash registers indicating that if your purchase is less than fifty dollars, please pay in cash. Isn't this rather odd for good customer relations?"

"That, my friend, saves the company thousands annually in credit card fees. Our employees simply ask if they have the cash instead of using their card. Some do, some don't-no pressure."

With this tactic implemented, whoever handles the cash register, will eventually give a fake ten-dollar bill for change unknowingly to the member. Hughes has the ten-dollar bills stacked, two valid to one fake. The two main cash registers at the bar generate over seven thousand dollars circulated monthly in counterfeit ten-dollar bills.

Natalie spots a large monitor on a pedestal by the archway and softly inquires, "What is that?"

Hughes, eager to brag on his newest techy item, shares with the group. "This young lady is the topographical map of each golf hole depicting every cemetery plot. Each section and gravesite have a unique number assigned to it. We have over ninety-four thousand sites available."

Irving comes up with a one-liner, "so, I can choose where I'll spend the rest of my life."

Hughes states. "yes, you can, and when we expand to our third course, there'll be another forty-seven thousand gravesites."

Bernard, the Angel of the Lord, hastily appears. Irving had encountered Bernard last year when the gang of six discovered the *Jerusalem Tree Picnic Table* in the grove of trees not far from the Cedar Creek Clinic. Bernard's appearance didn't ruffle Irving anymore.

"Irving!" Bernard shouts to get his attention. *"No one else can hear or see me, only you. I trust you were joking with that statement. As a Christian, you know where you'll spend the rest of your life, and it won't be in one of those ninety-four thousand gravesites."*

"Yes, I do know. My old self of kidding around sometimes gets the best of me. The truth is, somebody will bury my deceased body, but my spirit and soul will be with Jesus in heaven. I do know this with all my heart."

"Irving, you never know who's within hearing of your voice. Some people may not be saved, so it's always good to state the truth regarding heaven. Keep up the good work, my friend." Bernard vanishes.

Terri is intrigued beyond reason, "My quick math shows it'll take over two-hundred years to reach capacity. Hardly, a profitable enterprise at the first blush."

"You're the accountant, right?"

"Thanks for not saying bean counter. I hate that line."

"You're welcome, Terri. We cater to forty independent funeral homes in four populated states not affiliated with any cemetery. The baby boomers will be dying rapidly soon. Pending who's left to take care of their final event, be it children or grandchildren, neither will be inclined to attend a graveside service. The deceased will be lucky if their relatives attend the memorial service in their local funeral home."

Phillip declares loudly, "So! In the grand scheme of things, how does this explain why you have ninety-four thousand sites?"

"You're the lawyer, right?"

"Thanks for not saying, legal beagle; I hate that line."

"You're also welcome, Phillip. To answer your question, I own the manufacturing for the caskets. The membership and green fees pay for the gravesites. I pass the savings onto the customer. A lifetime club membership of two thousand includes two family funeral services. Non-membership is three thousand each."

"Are you expecting families to travel hundreds of miles to attend their loved one's funeral?" Helen curiously asks.

"No, not at all. We ship the caskets to the local funeral home. Of course, they take care of the embalming and have the family's memorial service if they want. Then they drive the deceased in their hearse to our cemetery. We provide a video of the gravesite service and final resting place to all family members. Included are printouts of the golf hole and marker. By my estimates, due to our extremely low-cost funeral service, we should reach capacity in less than five years."

Phillip retorts, "Is all this legal?"

"Yes, I'm glad you asked. Our business model meets and exceeds all state and federal regulations. You won't have to lose any sleep worrying about my services," Hughes replies.

Rachael lightens the subject and asks, "What's your favorite food dish, Hughes?"

"All of them! I was just joking. But I guess it would have to be Italian if I had to pick one. Why do you ask?"

"Darrell and I would like to have you over for dinner next Tuesday. When you walk in the front entrance, ask the receptionist for directions to the Italian Restaurant. We look forward to sharing a delightful meal and conversation."

"How many restaurants do you have in the complex?" inquires Hughes.

"Darrell and I will share our complete story with you over dinner. You'll have to wait until then, and we'd like to hear more about your enterprise-it sounds intriguing."

They all thank Hughes for his hospitality and say their goodbyes. On the way out, Phillip acknowledges his uneasiness with the gang.

"Did any of you feel uncomfortable when Hughes broke the news that I wouldn't have to lose any sleep worrying about his business?"

Irving replies, "That's just a figure of speech. Everyone uses that line from time to time."

"Maybe so, but it's weird when someone has to tell a lawyer they're not crooked."

Everyone comes back at Phillip and shouts, "Lighten up a bit! No one intended to harm anyone, just a one-liner joke."

Phillip drives the gang home, but inside his gut, he has a feeling that not everything at the golf course is harmless. As he and Terri walked into their house, Bernard, the Angel of the Lord, shows up.

"You're correct, Phillip, in being concerned about Hughes. If I may suggest, you and Terri should become members, have lunch there several times, pay cash, and circulate your change around town. Then see what happens!" Bernard vanishes quickly.

Phillip and Terri weren't frightened by the appearance of Bernard. They had met him last year at the Jerusalem Tree Picnic Table and always enjoyed his unannounced visits.

CHAPTER THREE

SATURDAY BRUNCH-FEB 2035

Rachael and Darrell invite their friends over for an early Valentine's Day Brunch at their hotel. The scheduled agenda will highlight, among other things, rumblings of the President getting ready to sign the D. C. Mandate, effectively shutting down churches, deleting police departments, confiscating all guns and Bibles throughout the USA.

Everyone in the inner circle had a day off this Saturday in February 2035, including Irving and Helen, Phillip and Terri, Dolan, and Natalie. After walking around the buffet table and filling their plates, they all meet in Rachael's private dining room.

Darrell starts the dialog by reviewing the beginning of the downward spiral. "Like you, I remember all too well, fifteen years ago, in 2020, when some states virtually shut churches due to some left-wing fabricated pandemic and brought in the radicals and their socialist ideology to riot and destroy cities."

Phillip adds to the problem, "I was involved with several court cases during that year representing several local churches, including the Jerusalem Tree Church. Even though Cedar Creek is 375 miles N.W. of New York City, the state treated our village and its churches as Manhattan. After filing several lawsuits, the state finally agreed to allow our churches to be at 25% capacity. But that was 15 years ago! Now, with a liberal, socialist administration and another election in less than two years, we better get ready for the worse and pray for the best."

Rachael continues, "That would be the rapture, Phillip. The best for all Christians, but we can't stick our heads in the sand and pretend this problem doesn't exist. The President is about to issue the D. C. Mandate he has threatened since elected."

Helen interjects, "Does anyone have a plan to overcome this calculated attack on the churches? The D. C. Mandate specifically states every church nationwide must cease all public religious activities. The government has already banned all broadcasts of religion in every media, social, T.V., radio, and internet. The actual church service is the last fortress for all Christians. Can we fight this mandate?"

Terri's answer surprises everyone. "Eventually, the church will need to go underground, like meeting in our homes in small groups of six. I'm also working on a matrix for all the Bible verses to be memorized. I'll report back to this group at our next quarterly meeting on my findings."

Rachael concurs, "The Holy Spirit is really in this place. He has touched Terri and me mightily because my message tomorrow will be about memorizing scripture. Christians must get serious about the Bible and behold its precious words close to their heart before they disappear."

Darrell was about to dismiss the meeting with prayer when unforeseen, Dolan stood up to speak.

"The conservatory may become our best camouflage. The Hebrew History and Arts college could be the platform for memorizing Bible verses by our young college students. It would be fairly easy for them, only 31,102 Verses in the Bible. Memorization would be in Greek, Latin, and Hebrew by one-third of the students, respectively. No one would notice what they were reciting, including the government."

Darrell solidifies Dolan's idea, "You may be on to something there, but best, if we all pray on that and seek God's will. Do you think, Dolan, that worship music and singing will be allowed in the College of Music?"

Dolan replies, "They, the government, may shut down worship service, music, and the message in the sanctuary, but they can't shut it down in the conservatory. It's a school."

"Good afternoon, my Christian friends." Bernard, the Angel of the Lord, appears out of the blue.

"I rejoice you're all preparing for the what if things get worse before they get better, scenario."

Everyone at the luncheon knew Bernard, having met him last year, and always welcomed his visits with pearls of heavenly wisdom he'd share often. Today was extraordinary, though.

"I have a suggestion, especially to Rachael and Darrell. Also, Phillip and Terri pay close attention to what I say. Prayerfully, this idea will work. Why not beat them at their own game. No pun intended. Apply for league sanctions for college basketball and hockey teams as part of the Conservatory curriculum. Once granted, convert your church sanctuary into a college sports arena. Complete with private boxes and arena seating for about 3,000."

Rachael asks the obvious question, "How does that help us overcome the D. C. Mandate?"

"Wish I could take credit for this genius idea, but the heavenly hosts of angels created the plan. Remember, I'm only the messenger. Record your worship service and sermon in the Conservatory College of Music, even at midnight if necessary. Then have your congregation 'rent' rooms during the games and watch church on the hotel's T.V.s."

Darrell shouts with excitement, "That's an excellent idea, Bernard! What a genius plan! Hotels still have T.V.s in the rooms, and nothing prevents us from sending a private broadcast."

"I'll be sure to share your excitement with the heavenly board. The hosts of angels always rejoice with positive feedback."

"You're right, Bernard. We'll beat them at their own game," Rachael smiles as she ponders the frustration this will give the government.

"You're welcome." Bernard disappears.

"Phillip and Terri, would you look into all aspects of this development? First, is it legal? What time frame for league sanctifications, and lastly, at what cost?" Rachael inquires.

All her concerns were answered immediately.

"League sanctifications, less than a year," Dolan reports.

"Legal, yes. It's a business deal. Just need permits, feasibility studies, and final city approval." Phillip reports.

"Probably in the range of three million. At a quick blush, your payback could be less than two years." Terri reports.

Helen shares her thoughts. "It hurts me deeply to say this, but the government will love you for this renovation. Eliminating public church service without being forced into it. They'll happily allow you to have a divided church service in the hotel rooms. Sadly, the church will never be the same again."

"I share your thoughts, Helen, but I believe being proactive will get us a lot more mileage than being dictated to. So, then, let's proceed!" Rachael affirmingly states.

CHAPTER FOUR

THE UNDERGROUND-FEB 2035

Thursday is officially Hughes's day off at the golf course. He quietly leaves at 2 a.m. heading out to the casket company in Buffalo. Once arriving, he drives into the manufacturing facility on the upper street level, which doubles as the employee entrance and raw materials delivery. Hughes parks his car and takes the freight elevator to the sewing and storage chamber, on the lower street level, where the finished caskets are ready to receive the counterfeit monies and prepped for delivery. Exiting the elevator, he walks over to the far end of the room and unlocks a large double door, revealing a secret box on the wall. Hughes opens the box and pushes a red button. Immediately but slowly, the entire wall slides to the right, revealing a much larger freight elevator. Finally, arriving at the printing bunker, 100 feet below the storage chamber, he is greeted by Klaus, having finished a batch of counterfeits, but continues with the task.

"Hey! Good morning boss!" shouts Klaus over the noise of the printing press.

Klaus immigrated from Germany with a degree as a mathematician in high-speed printing. He was going to work at the U.S. Treasury when Hughes made him an offer he could not refuse.

"How many batches have you completed so far?"

"Almost done, boss, only one more to go." Klaus prints five batches of counterfeit daily.

"Okay. I'll grab a pallet and take the completed batches up to the sewing chamber. When you are finished printing, meet me there with the rest of it."

Once in the chamber, Hughes fills each casket with a hundred thousand in counterfeit, slipping them into secret zipped pockets hidden in the lining on both sides of the casket. In addition to Klaus, only the four Italian tailors know of this entire scheme and are sworn to secrecy or death if revealed. Two years ago, Hughes brought into his inner circle Giovanni and his cousins, Lorenzo, Sergio, and Nicolao.

Hughes also brought in two semi-truck drivers who immigrated from Turkey. Mustafa and Eryman, however, are not part of the inner circle.

Finally, the trucks are loaded with counterfeit packed caskets, but unknown to Mustafa and Eryman, and they promptly take off for their deliveries.

Hughes calls a quick meeting to the four in his inner circle. "Come on over to the break room, guys. I brought some doughnuts, and the coffee is on," shouts Hughes so they all can hear.

"So, Klaus, have you heard from your brother recently, Gunter, in Germany, regarding the shipment?" inquires Hughes.

"Yes, I have. We will be receiving one pallet of specifically created paper and ink needed for our work here. Should be arriving at Port Newark in New Jersey later this week."

"Please, tell your brother we appreciate his undercover work, and his pay will reflect our appreciation."

"I will. Still curious, boss, you want me to tag along with Mustafa when we pick up the merchandise?"

"This trip being made once a year shouldn't arouse any suspicion on his part, but to be sure he doesn't get any fancy ideas, you best tag along."

Klaus gives Hughes assurances, "We'll depart next Thursday morning after the counterfeit loaded caskets are placed in the trucks. Eryman should be able to cover deliveries for Mustafa that day. "

Hughes turns his attention to Giovanni. "So, how are your cousins doing in New York's financial district? Are they securing any new clients?"

Giovanni answers, "Last week, they made agreements with five new wealthy gentlemen who will order monthly, two custom suits each. It seems the very wealthy love our suits stuffed with counterfeit cash as they walk out our store."

Hughes, in addition to manufacturing caskets, has another clandestine counterfeit operation going. A storefront in Manhattan selling custom businessmen suits. The suits are imported from India, and Hughes's tailors, Giovanni and his cousin Lorenzo sew hidden secret pockets inside each jacket. Once a business suit is sold and the illegal arrangement is solidified with the client, Sergio and Nicolao make any necessary alterations and fill the secret pockets with counterfeit money. The buyer walks out of the store, wearing his new four-thousand-dollar suit, unsuspecting to anyone.

Hughes continues the meeting, "Listen, each of you. What I am about to say is extremely important," He lowers his voice to equate the importance. "This operation is about to celebrate its first anniversary. As you all know, I bought and completely renovated the Cedar Creek Country Club taking two years to finish. With the implementation of ninety-four thousand burial sites, each of us will be able to retire as millionaires in about five years."

"More importantly, listen up, guys! I'm financing Mayor Allen Brady's re-election campaign. He won by some seven hundred votes in the last election and will be running against his former rival again. So, I expect this cycle to be close also. Mayor Brady will be hitting former Mayor Alderman on his Jewish heritage and his favorable alignment with the police department, possibly creating a police state in the Village of Cedar Creek. If we can continue Mayor Brady's liberal agenda, not only will the police department vanish, but also a complete shutdown of churches and confiscation of guns and Bibles! We won't have to wait for our timid President to sign anything!" Hughes shouts so the guys will unmistakably hear the importance.

Forthwith, over the T.V. in the break room appears President Avci making an impromptu announcement. "Good morning, Comrades and Americans! Even though the D . C. Mandate isn't signed into law yet, I feel it's of the utmost importance to implement the American

Sheriff Squad Office. Today, I'll be signing the executive order creating one-thousand sheriff positions whose sole duty will be to visit every church in America. Their first visit will be friendly, allowing the pastors and church leaders to get acquainted with some of the rules outlined in the D. C. Mandate. This cabinet post will be headed on an interim basis by Ms. Grace Palmer. Thank you, and I'm not taking any questions at this time," President Avci states as he walks off the podium.

Mayor Brady and Hughes have a burning vengeance toward the police, the church, guns, and Bibles. Deleting all four would satisfy the New Reformed Communistic Party and its base of loyal supporters.

"Well! How about that! Our timid President actually made a decision!" Hughes rejoices relishing in one small victory.

Nevertheless, Lorenzo butts in, selfishly stating and ignoring everything Hughes noted about the next local election's importance and the President's announcement. "Forgive me, boss, but allow me to ask the question if you printed twenty-dollar counterfeit bills, couldn't we retire in half the time?"

Hughes shouts, "Our operation wouldn't make it another year! We would all end up in the slammer. Patience is a virtue, my friend. Lorenzo. Are you having trouble making it on one-hundred grand a year?"

Before Lorenzo answers, Barnard appears. *"Gentlemen, and I use that term loosely, I am Bernard the Angel of the Lord, and I have come to help."*

Klaus, Giovanni, and Lorenzo are bewildered and frightened, not knowing what is occurring. Hughes shrugs it off as nonsense like before.

"It's you again. You have a knack of showing up at the most inopportune time."

The other three guys shout, "You know this guy!"

"He's a pest like a mosquito that won't leave you alone, always biting."

"You expressed patience, Hughes. I have over 2,000 years of patience and will stick around until all you guys curtail this very illegal operation."

Klaus shouts back, "And give up this yearly twenty-five-million-dollar golden goose? Not a chance, buddy!"

"You called me buddy, how nice. I want to be your friend too, but I can only befriend those that love Jesus. Alas, I'm afraid you all lack much in that category."

Bernard disappears.

Not missing a beat, Hughes turns to Lorenzo and again asks if he can make ends meet with one hundred grand a year.

"Sure, Boss. I just get tired of sewing zippers in casket linings and secret pockets in men's suits."

"Maybe a week's vacation at the golf course would clear your head; then come back and focus on what's important."

"I would like that, boss. Thanks"

"You can ride back with me next week after your shift. I'll put you up at one of our guest cottages on the course. You'll live like a king for a week."

The following Thursday morning, Klaus tags along with Mustafa to pick up their merchandise from the port. They leave Buffalo at 4 a.m., hoping to arrive by 11 a.m. and avoid gridlock at the freight yards. Klaus and Mustafa's conversations take longer than usual, each with a heavy dialect, German and Turkish, but manage to understand after a few minutes.

Klaus asks Mustafa a question hoping to strike a friendly conversation. "So, how do you like working for Hughes and delivering caskets?"

"Oh, it's okay, but certainly under tight security. Every funeral home I deliver to has its own key to unlock the truck's back doors. If I ever got pulled over, I would not be able to open for inspection. This overkill on security makes me uncomfortable and suspicious. Am I not delivering only caskets?"

Klaus, dumbstruck, but keeps his composure and replies, "If you ever get pulled over, you call me, wherever you are. I'll unlock the doors for the officer."

"I guess I'm not trustworthy. Heck, I am not going to steal a casket! What else am I delivering to these funeral homes? Money?"

"Whatever would make you say something like that? We manufacture and deliver caskets only. That's all!"

Mustafa replies, "Last year, when I made this trip myself, a dock worker accidentally tore a portion of the wrapping over the pallet. I recognized the special paper used for printing counterfeit. My family in Turkey had a similar operation. So, with my expertise, I feel I should receive a promotion to a different position with the company at least double the pay."

Klaus wanting to subdue any turmoil for the remainder of the trip, slowly replies, "I do understand, Mustafa. Tell you what, when we get back, I will inquire with Hughes if you can have a private conversation with him. Would you like that?"

"Certainly, Klaus. Thank you."

The rest of the day was uneventful. They picked up the load and headed back to Buffalo, where Mustafa anticipated a promotion after meeting with Hughes.

Upon arrival at the plant, Klaus invites Mustafa to follow him. They walk over to the far wall of the storage chamber, and Klaus presses the secret panel on the far wall, which opens to a large freight elevator. Taking it down 100' below to the underground bunker, as they exit the elevator, Mustafa shouts, "So this is how the fake money gets printed. I knew you guys had a thing going but couldn't figure out the whereabouts."

"Follow me!" Klaus demands. "We're going to walk over to the other side of this bunker. There is a small tunnel leading to Hughes's private office. You will need to duck your head. I will turn the light on so you can see. There it is! The door to his office. I will let you in, and you wait inside. I'll let Hughes know you're ready," and Klaus slams the door shut tightly.

It was so dark inside the so-called office that Mustafa could not calculate the room size, only 5' by 6' by 6'. He kept feeling the walls for a light switch when, without warning, he smelt gas and succumbed to his death.

Klaus walked back the steps through the tunnel and hi-fived Hughes, waiting at the shut-off valve. "Nice job, guy! your timing to turn the gas on was perfectly tuned."

"Much better than bullets, no stained blood anywhere for evidence. The gas should be gone by now, Klaus. Go ahead and remove the body. I will call Amir for an unclaimed dead body certificate. I'll take the deceased tomorrow in a plain casket and turn it over to the mortuary school so the students can practice their embalming technique. When finished, the cemetery crew will bury him in the John Doe section of the cemetery."

"You got it, boss."

Hughes's brilliant mind charges students attending $800 monthly for the two-year funeral home certification. Hughes offers the county free funeral services for their unidentifiable deceased, so his students never run out of practice corpses. In addition to the marker reading 'John Doe,' the student's initials performing the embalming are also etched in the marker.

On Friday morning, Hughes departs for the Cedar Creek Country Club, taking Lorenzo for his one-week vacation at the golf course. As they are driving, Lorenzo inquires, "Why the casket in the back of the truck?"

"For display purposes. Need this one for the low-budget funeral."

Upon arrival at the club, Lorenzo checks into the guest cottage. An hour later, he decides to lounge out at the pool, where he strikes up a friendly conversation with a beautiful gal. They chat for a moment when she invites him to her room.

"Sure, I'm on vacation. Why not!" Lorenzo shouts.

She walks quickly on the path below the elevated 4th tee, with Lorenzo following a bit behind. Unforeseen, Hughes playing a round of golf with Klaus slams the golf ball low off the tee hitting Lorenzo directly in the head, killing him instantly.

She calls the school's doctor and teacher, Dr. Wesley Drew, who pronounces him dead, and he sympathizes with Hughes, "It was a terrible, freak accident, I'm so sorry this happened off your tee shot. You do know, you'll need to take a one-stroke penalty, but I'm sure in time, you'll recover from the emotional drain that is sure to incur."

Hughes replies, "Thanks, doctor, for those kind words."

"If there isn't anything else I can help you with, Hughes, I best be on my way back to my students at the school."

"Thank you, doctor. Oh, by the way, I'll bring the deceased over to the school shortly and need you to call Amir for the fake death certificate."

"Yes, of course. Consider it done. Also, I believe it's Stan Ramsey's turn to perform the embalming." Dr. Drew jumps on his cart and leaves the scene.

"Klaus, help me with the deceased and lift him to the back seat of the golf cart, strapping him in sitting up. I'll drive over to the mortuary school and drop him off. You call the maintenance crew and have them clean up the blood on the golf cart path. Also, in the next hour or two, take this golf cart to the fire pit, and burn the blood-stained evidence to the ground," Hughes barks out commands like a Sargent.

"Not a problem, boss!"

Pronto, Barnard appears. *"You two are the scum of the earth—filthy rags consumed with greed and addiction to the love of money and power. You have no shame committing two more murders. But, as I've imparted before, I'm here to help."*

Klaus replies, "How do you intend to help us? Doesn't the word state, God helps those who help themselves? We are true to that word; we're helping ourselves."

"You have everything inside out, upside down. I'm here to help you confess your sins, to invite Jesus into your heart and be saved from the ravishes of evil, and to be ready for the rapture that is soon to come."

Hughes retorts, "The only saving I need is twenty million in my swiss bank account."

"Money will not buy your way into heaven," Bernard replies.

"I don't believe in heaven, hell, or the rapture. Therefore, you can save your breath of trying to convince me otherwise," states Hughes.

"You two are going to be a challenge. I've worked with other harsh, to the nth degree men before, but you two will be tough." Barnard vanishes.

"Hey, Hughes, on your way to the school, mind dropping me off at the pool?'

"Sure, Donna, hop in, and thanks for the lure and bait thing you did."

"Not a problem; anytime you need anything, just give me a ring, ding dingy."

Hughes drops Donna off at the pool, and he continues driving to the mortuary school with Lorenzo strapped to the back-seat golf cart-sitting up-dead!

CHAPTER FIVE

DINNER INVITE-MAR 2035

As Tuesday evening rolls around and Hughes drives up to the Jerusalem Tree Church, he gets confused and calls Rachael.

"Hello, Jerusalem Tree Church. This is Rachael."

"Yes, this is Hughes. I don't see your Restaurant, just your church."

"Your attitude and tone toward the church are hostile, Hughes."

"How did you get in my car?" demands Hughes.

"I'm the Angel of the Lord, Bernard, remember? I simply appear, and I have come to help you. I possess all knowledge."

"I don't need any help, especially from a fake angel."

"I've meant to talk to you about those fake $10-bills you have printed. You're breaking the seventh commandment big time-thou shalt not steal."

"I don't buy into any of that stuff, church, Bible, heaven, and hell. By the way, what makes you think I print anything illegal?"

"I watch Klaus sometimes when he's in the underground bunker printing. I hope you don't mind; I helped myself to one of the bills from a packet. Here, go ahead; you can keep it."

Hughes hastily grabs the bill from Bernard and states, "You're trying to trick me into something I didn't do. I'm not confessing to anything!"

"You don't know it yet, but one day you'll confess the Lord Jesus Christ." Bernard vanishes.

Hughes brushes aside the imaginary encounter as nonsense and gets ready to meet Darrell and Rachael for dinner.

Rachael replies, "No problem, just walk into the church lobby, turn right into the long hotel corridor, and the Italian Restaurant, *Italiano,* will be the second door. See you in a few minutes."

Even though Hughes has a hardened attitude toward the church and God, his heart skipped a beat as he walked into the church lobby and saw the Glass Rotunda housing the Jerusalem Tree Picnic Table. He pauses for a few moments, then continues his walk on the thickly carpeted long hallway and opens the second door to *Italiano.*

Rachael graciously welcomes him as he enters. "We're so glad you could make it, Hughes. Come, let's walk over to our table, and we'll start with some wine and appetizers."

"That would be great, just a bit confusing, navigating the inside of your complex. By the way, what's with the picnic table inside a Glass Rotunda?"

"I'll let Darrell explain. He does a much better job on it than I do," Rachael softly states.

"Well, the short version is that the picnic table is over 2,000 years old, and part of the table is made from wood coming from the cross that the Romans crucified Jesus on. Therefore, it is officially an ancient artifact protected by high-tech security around the clock."

"I took religion class during my last six years in a parochial school and am familiar with the death and resurrection of Jesus Christ. The two of you have done a fantastic job of honoring His sacrifice. Praise the Lord!"

They make a toast and begin to order dinner when Hughes states. "Okay, you two, I can't stand the suspense any longer. Tell me all about your enterprise here."

Darrell glances over at Rachael and detects she wants him to explain.

"Believe it or not, Hughes, this used to be a casino. When the Feds shut it down, this and the sister casino in Erie sat abandoned for about eighteen months. For many years, Rachael was a sought-after high fashion model and designer of lingerie and wedding gowns. She eventually sold the company to an Asian conglomerate, and with the proceeds, bought both properties."

"Talk about success! I have to hand it to you guys. You hit it out of the park! So, what's all in here?"

Rachael takes her turn to explain. "Foremost, the Jerusalem Tree Church has a 10,000-seat sanctuary, which usually fills. The complex has five restaurants, two banquet halls, and two hundred and twenty hotel rooms."

"You have done yourselves proud, and I might add, God is also proud of your accomplishments," Hughes states, which seemed like genuine sincerity. He continues, "I don't know if I should bring this up now or not? It may be too sensitive for both of you to discuss. But, what are your thoughts on the President's D. C. Mandate that he's about to sign into law?"

Darrell answers first, "It's a punch in the gut, Hughes. Rachael and I have spent several years ministering to our congregation in this church. Now, with the Reformed Communist Party in his hip pocket, the President has declared war on the church, guns, the Bible, and the police."

Rachael answers next, "Sometimes I cry myself to sleep pondering how quickly America has become a Communist nation. The quest for a one-world government racing to delete the word 'God' from everyone's lips. But, don't worry, Hughes-Darrell, the board, and I are thinking day and night on how to resist the D. C. Mandate."

Rachael and Darrell don't have the slightest clue that Hughes is part of the Communist wealthy elitists living in Cedar Creek. A circle of like-minded angry liberals secretly advocating shutting down all churches, confiscating all guns and Bibles, and eliminating all police departments.

Hughes keeps the niceties coming, "I'd like to invite you two over to the club for lunch next week, and maybe we can brainstorm together on how to resist this D. C. Mandate?"

Rachael and Darrell walk right into the trap, "That would be delightful, Hughes, appreciate the hospitality," Rachael gleefully replies.

"We may also have a surprise for you, Hughes," Darrell shares. "A friend of ours from Italy left us an old but beautiful white hearse with gold trim. I wouldn't recommend using it as such, but maybe, park it out front as silent advertising. It's yours for the taking if you want?"

"What a great surprise, I would love that! Does it run, or do I need to have it towed on a flatbed?"

Darrell replies, "Probably the flatbed. Better to be safe than sorry."

"I would like to return your generosity if you'd allow me. Often at gravesite funerals, the family doesn't have time or know of a pastor to officiate. Would you two do me the honor of presiding at these services? There would be about twenty a week, and I'll pay two hundred for each service."

Rachael and Darrell glance at each other, and she replies, "Mr. Reyna. Do you realize Darrell and I have three full-time ministries? Plus, five restaurant managers, two banquet managers, and three hotel managers we meet every week? Twenty funeral services are more than we'd be able to handle."

"I'm sorry, Rachael. I wasn't aware of the hectic schedule you and Darrell have. I should have known it takes superb management skills and time to operate an enterprise like you two have."

"Darrell and I want to be good stewards of a family member's last event, but that would leave us only Saturday to conduct our other responsibilities."

"I understand, believe me, but that does place me in a pinch. Do you have any suggestions?"

"I do. Resurrection Rival Church in Erie has a Bible College on campus. I'll ask the Dean of Students to call you. I bet you'll be able to get all the pastoral students you'll ever need for your graveside services."

"Wow! You're terrific, Rachael. How can I ever repay you?"

"Don't worry about that but pay the students at least one hundred for each service. I'm guessing the dean will only allow each student one day per week. So, your generosity will benefit each greatly."

"Consider it done!" Hughes shouts with bravado.

"Praise the Lord! Rachael shouts. "On a side note, Hughes, will we see you in church anytime soon?"

"You had mentioned the sanctuary fills up when you're preaching. I prefer a smaller crowd; which service would that be?"

Rachael chuckles. "I'm the smaller service about seven-thousand attend. But when Darrell teaches on Sunday and Wednesday evenings, this place fills up and rocks. The folks love his style and message."

"A quiet giant in our midst that God is using mightily. I'll make it a point to attend each of your services as my schedule allows," Hughes trying to wiggle out politely.

Rachael replies, "We'd love to see you here for church. I also hold a couple's seminar once a month on Saturday afternoons. It's three hours of teaching couples, married or engaged, on having a fantastic, sizzling marriage, biblically. The afternoon ends with a fashion show from my designer's wardrobe. These seminars are a hit. The entire crew working these seminars are role models; each couple is married. However, our policy is only married or engaged couples are welcome to attend. Would you like to attend, Hughes?"

"I'd love to-sounds exciting. But, my wife died a few years ago. She had a horrific final event. The funeral home handling her service dropped the casket taking it out of the hearse. Then, adding humility, the ground crew standing nearby rushed over and carried her to the gravesite."

"Oh, my goodness, Hughes, I'm so sorry for your loss and shoddy service. That's when you decided to open your own, I'm guessing?" Rachael softly shares.

"Yes, it is. I made up my mind that I would never allow that to happen to any family-ever again!" Hughes answers with anger in his voice.

Darrell tries to bring the conversation back to a joyful dinner chat, but to no avail. "Would you care for some dessert, Hughes? We have the best of the best in town."

"I'm sure you do, but I'll take a rain check if you don't mind. I must be getting back to my business and check the various schedules. Thank you for the lovely dinner, conversation, and the hearse."

Hughes wasn't kidding when he revealed he had to check his various schedules. The printing of counterfeit money, the sewing of the casket's secret pocket lining, the corrupt affiliate funeral home partners, the underhanded men's custom suit store in Manhattan. Plus, the golf course, cemetery, and a money-making mortuary school. Indeed, Hughes was busy in all his illegal affairs. His severe addiction to money, holding no limitations to any legality, blinded his eyes and heart to know and do what is right.

"You're welcome, Hughes. Hopefully, we'll see you soon," Rachael states as he is walking out.

Exhausted from being cornered into explaining his wife's death, Hughes slumps into the driver's seat for a spell to collect his thoughts.

"You must be a chameleon, Hughes. Changing characters for whatever the occasion requires. Even lying to get your way."

"Oh, it's you again. How do you keep getting in my car?"

"Remember, I'm the Angel of the Lord, Bernard. Don't need to use doors, just appear. I'm still here to help you if you want?"

"No, thanks again. I'm okay, don't need your help."

"You need to get rid of your anger at the church, God, and funeral home regarding your wife's death. Have you considered giving it to Jesus?"

"All that schooling on religion was for naught. My wife died anyway."

"You're missing something here, Hughes. Attending religion class doesn't guarantee anyone anything. You spoke so well in there, sounding like a holy roller. If they only knew what a rotten apple you are and how conveniently you didn't share your part of the D. C. Mandate movement. How horrible!"

"I'm not admitting to anything. Heck! I'm not so rotten as you state."

"You don't think? Then how about all the murderers you've committed? That is beyond rotten. You don't know it yet, but someday you'll be confessing all this to a magistrate." Bernard quickly disappears.

CHAPTER SIX

CHURCH VISIT-MAR 2035

Hughes decides to visit the Jerusalem Tree Church this Sunday morning and brings Donna along virtually for showing off purposes. They look like the perfect millionaire couple. Hughes, handsome, sophisticated, and extravagant. Donna, gorgeous, charming, and a millionaire widow.

As they walk in the church's lobby, momentarily gazing at the Glass Rotunda, Rachael walks across the lobby floor, approaches, and welcomes them to the church.

"So, I see you made it, and who is this beautiful lady you brought along, Hughes?"

"I would like you to meet my friend and confidant, Donna Trice," Hughes beams with pride.

"It is so lovely to meet you, Donna, and thanks for convincing Hughes to attend church today."

"Well, I must confess, it is Hughes who convinced me to sacrifice my pool sunbathing ritual and join him this morning. I'm glad he did. You have a beautiful, lovely church, Rachael, and it would be a shame if the government shut it down? I certainly hope that doesn't happen." Donna spews politeness camouflaging her contempt for the church, guns, Bibles, and police.

"Thank you, Donna, for those kind words. The prayer team and I are praying unceasingly, asking God to intercede. But, If you'll both excuse me, I see the worship team is walking up on stage. I best join them. Hopefully, we can chat after the service. Can you stick around for a while?"

"Instead of sticking around, I would like to invite you and Darrell to join me and Donna for brunch at the Country Club, say 2 p.m. Will that work for both of you?"

"I'm sure it will. Darrell's been anxious to sample the club's cuisine, which will be a delight for both of us. Would you mind if I bring a couple of my friends from out of town along?"

"Of course not! The more, the merrier!" shouts Hughes

"I appreciate that, thank you. But, I must run, got a message to preach. See you guys at the club," Rachael shouts as she's quickly walking toward the stage.

Darrell makes a few announcements. "First, I would like to address the possibility, as I'm sure you've all heard numerous times, that the government may shut down all public religious activities. You can be assured that the church board, Rachael, and I are looking at every legal angle to maintain a vibrant ongoing church. Secondly, if the Lord doesn't tarry, be sure to attend Wednesday night Bible Study. I'm teaching on the Book of Revelation. You need to be aware of what occurs before the rapture and be certain your heart is right with God. The sanctuary fills up fast on Wednesday evening. If you can, be here early."

Rachel proceeds with her sermon on the book of Esther this morning. Her powerful message delivered an awakening to the congregation.

"Do you realize that God has placed all of us where we are today for such a time as this? Esther risked her life to save her people-her Jewish people.

Because of Queen Esther's courageous act, she saved an entire nation. To those sitting in the pews this morning, let me ask you a question. Are you seizing your God-given opportunity to make a difference in today's world? I challenge you to open your heart and look for ways to save a person's life-just like Esther did-Amen."

Rachael closes out her message with prayer, and the worship team sings while the congregation slowly walks out of the sanctuary.

Hughes and Donna quietly slip out of the church, strolling along with the crowd unnoticed. Once inside their car, they slightly slump into their seats and glance at each other perplexed. Promptly, Bernard appears.

"Pretty darn good message…huh? Especially the one on saving a person's life…huh?"

"Hughes, who is this, whatever, doing in the back seat?"

"Allow me to answer, Hughes. I'm the Angel of the Lord, Bernard, Donna."

"How did he know my name, Hughes? You know this guy?"

"He keeps showing up and harassing me to follow Jesus."

"You don't believe in that nonsense, right?"

Before Hughes could answer, Bernard, interjects. *"I have come to help those who are lost, which includes you two and the rest of Hughes's gang."*

Donna, getting aggravated, shouts, "I'm not lost! I know exactly where I am!"

"My dear lady, I'm referring to a spiritual lost, not knowing Jesus, and not being ready for the rapture. You're also an actress, huh? Telling Rachael, you hope her church doesn't get shut down. You could care less, just like Hughes. "

"I don't need to know Jesus, or whatever you say, the rapture. I'm living my life to the fullest and set in my ways. I don't need Jesus or a church to live my life."

"It is so sad; it is always harder for the wealthy to accept Jesus and to know him. It is my prayer and encouragement that one day, you both will see the light." Bernard vanishes.

James, Donna Trice's late husband, was a successful Wall Street Investment Banker, leaving her millions. Before James' death, Hughes, a widower living on Long Island in the same cul de sac as the Trice's, became friends with James. They joined the same country club, playing golf every Saturday. The three of them, James, Donna, and Hughes, became tightly knit friends doing the country club scene always as a threesome. Before James's tragic and sudden death, Hughes had moved to Cedar Creek to scope up the deal of a lifetime buying the five-hundred-acre golf club and funeral home property. Donna, independently wealthy now but without an escort to hobnob with, contacted her friend, Hughes, and purchased a half-acre estate above the ninth green, building an exquisite two-story villa.

"You have got to do something with that pest, Bernard," Donna shouts at Hughes as they're driving back to the club.

"Princess, he's an angel; no one can kill him like the others you and I have done."

"If you're insinuating I had something to do with the death of my husband, I didn't. He had a heart attack, probably due though, to our constant bickering and arguing over our issue if we should have a family or not."

"Well, how about the recent Lorenzo incident?"

"I was innocent, merely strolling to my room. Can't a girl walk in her bikini from the pool to her room without getting in trouble?"

"You are anything but innocent, Donna. Now let's join Rachael, Darrell, and their out-of-town friends at the club for brunch, shall we?"

Hughes and Donna arrived at the club without a minute to spare. Immediately following them were Rachael and her friends.

"So glad you could make it, Rachael and Darrell," states Hughes. "If I may ask, who are your lovely friends accompanying you?"

"Donna and Hughes, I'd like you to meet Richard and Agnes Filburn from Milwaukee, WI. They had been watching my church services until the government banned the broadcast of live streaming a few years ago. They were so impressed, they decided to visit us."

Richard and Agnes are a delightful African-American couple. He a retired county sheriff, and she dapples in genealogy.

"Princess Donna, would you do the honors and lead us to our reserved table," Hughes kiddingly states.

As the group walks to their table, Richard shares, "You know, Hughes and Donna, my wife and I enjoy Rachael's preaching and the worship team's ministry in song and music, it would be a shame if the government really shut it down."

Upon hearing the loyalty Richard and Agnes have for the church, Hughes decides to snare them into his trap along with Rachael and Darrell.

"Perhaps, you and Agnes would like to join the four of us next Tuesday for lunch here at the club. We'll be brainstorming on how to resist the President's D.C. Mandate."

"We'd be delighted to. What a great idea!" answers Richard.

Once seated, Hughes orders appetizers and wine for everyone. They chat for several moments when Donna inquires with Agnes, "So, genealogy is your hobby? What kind do you explore?"

Agnes, a petit bubbly lady, always having a spirit of joy about her, explains, "I do cemetery genealogy, basically historical headstones and markers. I've also journalized some fairly new graves if they look interesting."

Donna virtually chokes on her appetizer but quickly gains her composure. "What a lovely hobby you have, Agnes. I'm certain at times, it must be fascinating when you stumble across a unique marker."

"It is, and whenever you'd like, I'd be happy to show you some of my journal photos of markers from cemeteries around Milwaukee."

"I'd be delighted to. Will you and Richard be visiting here for a while?"

Darrell jumps into the conversation. "Richard shared with me that their kids moved in this area three years ago, and now Richard and Agnes are thinking of staying and buying a place here."

"My wife and I would like to be closer to our grandkids. We're both retired, so why not?" Richard states.

Hughes inquires, "Are you looking for any particular area or neighborhood? I have connections with some knowledgeable realtors, be happy to give you their number."

Richard replies, "This may surprise you, and I understand if it does, but I like to play golf, lots of golf. So, my wife and I were wondering, how do we go about joining your club and building an estate villa like your friend Donna has?"

Hughes clears his throat and slowly replies, "I can share the membership easily, but I haven't purported to offer any other estate villas, except for the one Donna has. The cemetery allocation doesn't allow for any acreage conducive to home building."

Richard retorts, "You have thirty-five greens left; why not carve out a half-acre above each one. Possibly a two-story, 4,000-7,000 square foot home?"

"If I may ask, Richard, how do you know so much about land development and home building?"

"I have a little education, and while county sheriff for thirty years,

I invested in Wall Street conservatively. Fortunately, those investments became our retirement fund and then some. After leaving the sheriff's department, I formed a group of four like-minded men. We bought a golf course and built custom homes above each green. That was three years ago. Last year the course sold, and each member profited handsomely."

Hughes doesn't miss an opportunity, "I'd be ecstatic for you and your wife to become members of our club. I'll also ask the land development committee to take another look at having green homesites. Can you both stop by my office on Monday afternoon, and I'll get you squared away as members?"

"We certainly can," Agnes replies. "Also, wonder if you could do me a favor for Monday morning?"

"Sure, what's that?"

"Would you provide Richard and me a golf cart to tour your cemetery and golf course?"

"Of course, I'd be glad to!"

After brunch and after the Filburn's left, Hughes mutters to Donna, "I bet they're using the golf cart to scout out homesites. I wasn't planning on developing estates for another year, but I'm going to play hardball if they want one now and fetch top dollar!" Hughes angrily states.

CHAPTER SEVEN

THE MEMBERSHIP-APRIL 2035

Phillip and Terri take the advice of Bernard and join the country club.

"Congratulations!" Hughes bellows out as he shakes their hand. "You now have full privileges of the country club. Enjoy them whenever you can."

"We intend to and look forward to attending many of the scheduled events here. I understand you've snatched one of the top chefs in New York," states Terri gleefully.

"Yes, I have. Chef Reynolds, his reputation, proceeds to Cedar Creek Country Club for, hopefully, the most sought-after venue in the area. Listen, I need to apologize. I always join new members for lunch, but I have to run to an urgent meeting. Can we take a rain check?" Hughes asks.

"Certainly," Phillip replies. "Terri and I will have lunch at the bar. Not a problem, Hughes. You take care of business. We'll catch up to you later, and I'm sure with Reynolds on board, you'll do fabulous."

"Thanks, guys. I appreciate the confidence." Hughes, being late, walks quickly to his meeting.

As they stroll over, Terri whispers to Phillip, "We never sit or eat at a bar. Why now?"

"I need a bird's eye view of the bartender making change. So, let's sit over here, the perfect angle of the cash drawer. Hughes' hasty meeting certainly became convenient for us," Phillip boasts.

"Good afternoon, folks, and I understand congratulations are in order," states Josh, the bartender.

"News travels fast around here, I guess," Phillip politely replies.

"Your picture came up on my phone as new members, so your first drinks are on the house."

"Well, thank you," Terri states. "I'll have a glass of rose wine." "Make mine burgundy," Phillip shouts.

"Are you also ready to order?" Josh asks.

"Yes! We'll have two of your 19th green specials. The BLT hamburger on grilled sourdough."

After Terri places the order, she whispers to Phillip, "Let's see what Chef Reynolds can do with a lowly BLT and hamburger."

While Josh electronically places their order in the kitchen, Phillip watches the other bartender across the bar make change and notices the cash drawer doesn't have any twenty-dollar bills.

When Josh returns with their order, Phillip inquires, "I couldn't help but notice the other guy's cash drawer doesn't have any twenties in it. Is there a reason?"

"Yup! Mr. Reyna believes people will spend a ten-dollar bill in their pocket faster than a twenty. He states that an abundant money flow is good for the local economy and wants to do his part. Hence, we give change in tens."

"Well, Josh, give me back seven tens and four singles so I can pay for my lunch; you keep the four as your tip." Phillip hands him a hundred-dollar bill.

"It isn't counterfeit, is it?"

Philip was caught off guard and had a blank look.

"You know, the hundred-dollar bill you just gave me."

Phillip was about to answer when Josh shouts, "Just kidding!" and hands him the change.

As they were leaving, Terri whispers to Phillip, "So, is there any way you can check them out, the seven tens you received?"

"Yeah, I think the ex-sheriff may be able to help in this matter.

Remember, Rachael introduced Richard and his wife, Agnes, to us last Sunday after church service. "

"Yes, I do. A very delightful couple. If Richard finds any bad ones, you think he'll let us circulate them as you plan?"

"When he understands my thinking on how to smother this possible counterfeit operation, I believe he'll go along with the idea. By the way, wasn't our lunch absolutely delicious, Terri?"

"It sure was. Mr. Reyna outdid himself by hiring one of the best chefs in New York state, Chef Reynolds. We'll need to let him know next time we see him."

Meanwhile, back in the kitchen, Chef Reynolds and Hughes are shouting and yelling at each other.

"You promised me that if I agreed to work for you, I'd have more help in the kitchen than in my previous stint at the New York hotel!"

"I gave you two! How many more do you need?" shouts Hughes.

"At least two more, or I walk out! I walk out right now!" Reynolds demands stubbornly in his European dialect.

"Chef Reynolds!" Shouts Hughes. "I will not tolerate any more outbursts of this nature. You're a professional chef, so act like it! I will increase your kitchen staff budget by two hundred thousand annually. You hire who and how many you need in this kitchen. But next time you pull a stunt like this, I'll shut the kitchen down and serve milkshakes until I hire your replacement. Do we understand each other?" Hughes firmly throws the verbal gauntlet down.

Chef Reynolds realizes he's been defeated big time and agrees to the new terms. They shake hands, and Hughes walks out to the dining room and notices that Phillip and Terri had already left, unbeknown to him, to meet with Richard and Agnes.

Later that afternoon, they agree to meet at Rachael's hotel café, and Phillip shows Richard the seven ten-dollar bills. So, what do you think, are any phony?"

Richard studies each for a long while, holding them up to the window's sunlight, and finally states, "These two are, but probably the best printing of counterfeit I've ever witnessed."

"So, only a trained eye of thirty years would notice?" Terri compliments.

"I would say so. The ordinary business person would never catch the one flaw, but an FBI agent would."

"I'm glad you articulated that, Richard. My thinking is we should flood the local market with these phony bills, and eventually, there will be so many complaints, the operation will be forced to shut down."

"I like your plan, and I'll plant the seed of doubt at various merchants as these phonies appear. Once the area is saturated with these, I'll announce the flaw at a press conference, so everyone will be watching."

Out of the blue, Bernard appears. *"Good afternoon, everyone. I rejoice in the Lord you've figured out a way to stop this operation."*

"We owe it all to you, Bernard, for suggesting we join the country club," Phillip states.

"Awe, shucks, it was nothing. Just doing my job. But, be careful! Hughes is smart as a fox, don't count your chickens just yet."

Phillip, perplexed by Bernard's statement, asks, "What do you mean?"

"Well, when one chicken coop shuts down, a smart fox finds another elsewhere or smells a trap and avoids getting caught."

"So, I wonder how smart Hughes is," Phillip mutters. "Will he move his operation or shut it down?"

"Just be alert to all things! Have a great day, everyone, and keep up the good work for the glory of the Lord." Bernard vanishes.

Unforeseen, and for no apparent reason, maybe a gut feeling, the next day after the encounter with Chef Reynolds, Hughes stops the cash-register scheme. It took Phillip and Richard two weeks of lunches to figure out there weren't any more phony bills in the cash drawers.

As they were walking back to the car after their last lunch, Phillip apologies to Richard, "Well, at least we had some terrific lunches, so all is not lost. By the way, what was the one flaw you noticed?"

"Ah! It's obvious as the hand in front of you, but no one would ever notice. On the backside of the ten-dollar bill where it's printed, "In God We Trust." In between the words 'God' and 'We,' the flag is facing left instead of right."

"Whoever did the original plate engraving goofed big time. Shouldn't we alert the authorities on this find, Richard?"

"A public broadcast would alert the counterfeiters. So, we'll let it play out and see if they shoot themselves in the foot."

CHAPTER EIGHT

JOB SECURITY-APRIL 2035

Hughes and Klaus are meeting in the underground bunker, strategizing how best to replace Mustafa and Lorenzo. The other men in Hughes's inner circle knew that loyalty to Hughes meant life or death. They never questioned why Mustafa or Lorenzo was never around anymore.

"Klaus, have you been successful in contacting anyone in your circle to fill these positions?" asked Hughes.

"Yes and no. I have located this young man, Lucas, who has a legit CDL. He immigrated from Germany a year ago and now lives in New Jersey. My contact states he's reliable, trustworthy, and single."

Hughes brings only single men on board, much more conveniently creating a John Doe death certificate if the need came up.

Klaus continues, "It's been two weeks since we've had these vacancies unfilled. Giovanni can't keep up with the demand. Sewing secret pockets in custom men's suits and secret zippers in the casket linings."

"Yes, I know. Be sure to award Giovanni for all his overtime. What do you have in mind?"

"I think we need to hire two tailors. Allow me to expand. First, I've found this tailor, a single Italian guy, Jacopo, working with this group in Chicago. They owe me a favor, and he's ours if we want him. He can work with Giovanni exclusively for the casket lining section. Secondly, we need to farm out crafting the secret pockets in men's suits to the financial district. We have a back room in the storefront, and the new tailor I'm thinking of hiring, Carlo, would work in there. Sergio and Nicolao would continue generating new clients as they have been while catering to our regular esteemed clients."

"Wouldn't this new guy realize our counterfeit scheme? I'm not sure I want to bring in two new hires at the same time."

"I understand, boss. But our network is getting antsy about the delayed shipments of caskets and suits. We need to fill these positions soon, and very soon," explains Klaus.

"If we can install a door, between the back and front of the store, with Sergio and Nicolao, the only ones with the key, I'll go ahead and hire this guy. How soon can he start?" inquires Hughes.

"There's one other problem, boss. He and his young wife got married eight months ago."

"I cannot! I will not hire a married man! It is too risky. It's too complicated. His wife could bring the house of cards down. I don't trust married couples."

"Boss! I have an idea. We could tell him the secret pockets are for our clients to hide their small guns. You know, concealed license. If we do not hire him now, we'll lose over two million next month."

Hughes ponders for a long moment, not liking the analogy of concealed guns, but finally agrees to the plan. "Yeah, sure, let's go ahead with the hire. But check out his wife's background, what she does, where she works? Find out as much as you can and place a security detail on both for a while."

Klaus agrees to the plan and puts everything in motion. Hughes exists the bunker, leaving Klaus alone, getting ready to print a counterfeit batch when Barnard appears.

"Hello, Klaus. Before you turn on the printing press that creates such an unbearable noise, I need to talk with you. You do remember me, Bernard, the Angel of the Lord?"

"Yeah, I remember you, but not interested in anything you're selling."

"I'm not selling anything tangible but hope in the Lord Jesus Christ. He

isn't visible like the one-million-dollar batch of fake bills you're about to print. That's why one needs faith to walk with Jesus. He's invisible."

"As I explained, I'm not interested. So, if you'll excuse me, I have work to do."

"Same here. Talking with you and Hughes is more work than I ever imagined. Klaus, I have come to encourage you to accept Jesus Christ as your savior and be saved from the sins of evil and to be ready for the rapture that is to come soon."

"Maybe some other day, not now! I have a deadline to keep, Bernard; I'm turning on the printing press. See you later, Bernard!"

"Okay, I'm leaving and will continue praying for you, Klaus."

After meeting with Klaus, Hughes retreated to his office and called Mayor Brady, "So, what are your thoughts on the President's announcement the other day?"

"I think it's great! I received a call from the President's administration office yesterday. They shared that I may be a candidate to head up The American Sheriff Squad's office when the President wins re-election!" Shouts Mayor Brady.

"Would you have to move to D. C.?" Inquires Hughes.

"Yes, I would. But foremost, I'd be part of the old Political Privileged Society Club."

"That's great, Mayor! First, let's get you re-elected! Then when President Avci wins his second term, you'll be qualified and available. Last question. Have you considered who could be your replacement as Mayor once you leave?"

"Yes. It's been solidified by the President's administrative office. Ms. Grace Palmer. I understand she loathes churches and all they represent. As a matter of fact, she used to live here in Cedar Creek for about twenty-four years.

"I wasn't aware. Did she move somewhere?" Hughes questions.

"Yes, and interestingly, get a load of this- I've been informed Grace Palmer has spent the last fifteen years traveling in Europe. By chance, our Vice-President, Ms. Firuzeh, met Ms. Palmer at a restaurant she was hosting in Portugal. They got to talking, and before you know it, Ms. Firuzeh persuaded President Avci to give her the interim position. The caveat being that Ms. Palmer was to run for Mayor of Cedar Creek in 2036, of course, that is just a formality."

"I'll seriously consider financing her campaign also, just like I have for you, Mayor. Not a problem," Hughes speaks with bravado.

Hughes will be in for a rude awakening when he tries to manipulate her. Grace Palmer isn't a push-over like Mayor Brady and can't be bought, even though she's a true-blue liberal advocating the demise of all the churches, guns, Bibles, and police nationwide.

*****

The next Monday afternoon, Richard and Agnes show up at Hughes' office to sign up for membership.

"Welcome, come on in, good to see both of you again," Hughes eagerly greets them.

"Good to see you again, also," replies Richard. "By the way, thanks for letting us use the golf cart the other morning. We toured the entire 36-holes and pretty much like the 6th green on the blue course for our homesite."

"You certainly are persistent, Richard. I haven't had the chance to discuss this with our planning committee yet. I'll need at least a month for approval."

"You also are persistent, Hughes. Tell you what, approve the homesite this week, and I'll pay double over the asking price. Agnes and I love that view. I'll also have my crew start building within the month. What do you say?" Richard puts the squeeze on Hughes to decide.

"Well, I am the owner and director of this complex, and your offer is outstanding. Consider it done!" Hughes accepts the offer, having played hardball with Richard and Agnes and coming out victorious.

"This is a cause for celebration. Would you and Donna join us for lunch tomorrow?" Richard throws out the invite.

"Now, I'll tell you what," blares Hughes. "You're writing to me two checks this week. One for the club memberships, by the way, includes two full funeral services and gravesites. Plus, a second check for the homesite. Lunch will be on me; that's the least I can do!"

Agnes gingerly replies, "That will be nice. We'll accept. But I have a question for you, Hughes. Richard and I drove the golf cart about four hundred yards past the 10th and 12th greens on the Blue Course. While touring the golf course, I noticed way off in the distance a sign reading, John Doe Cemetery. Once arriving at the cemetery, I was shocked to see forty-four gravesites marked John Doe, and each one had a different initial etched. Do the initials represent someone or something? Also, how can you have so many in only one year?"

Hughes replies with a grin, "Yes, I agree, it seems odd, but my funeral home aids the county and takes in all unclaimed dead bodies. We don't charge for this service and saves the county several hundred thousand annually. The county, in essence, is providing our students with embalming practice. It's a win-win situation for both the mortuary school and county."

"Oh...I see...thanks for the clarity," Agnes softly states. "But, what about the initials on the markers next to the words, 'John Doe,' what do they represent?"

"You've probably seen four different ones on the various markers. The initials represent the student's name that performed the embalming. It's our discreet way of tracking students' skill sets, just in case there was ever a need for a disinterment."

Richard inquires, "How many students are currently enrolled?"

For the school's first year, we stopped admissions at four. Hopefully, next year we'll be able to teach a total of eight. You may have noticed the initials 'S.R.' on several gravesites. Those belong to Stan Ramsey, who is our top student. I don't doubt in a few short years he'll be a funeral home director." Hughes shares with pride.

"I'm happy for you that the school's first year is doing well. By the way," Richard inquires, "I noticed close to the maintenance shop trash is burned in the massive fire pit. Were you aware someone burned your golf cart down to the cinders? Hardly anything is left of it. I suppose a forensic technician could come up with the cause?"

"Yeah, that episode. We've had frequent vandals steal onto the course at night and cause some major and minor property damage. Luckily, the insurance paid for those damages. Since that occurrence, we've hired roving guards to secure the golf course 24/7."

Agnes replies with a sigh, "Good to hear that, Hughes. We don't want to be living in a crime zone."

"I understand, and you have my word that around the clock, you and Richard will be fully protected."

"Thanks again; we'll see you and Donna tomorrow for lunch," Agnes states.

"Say!" Hughes shouts. "Why don't you two stay at one of my guest cottages while you build your home? It'll be my treat. You could move in after lunch tomorrow. I'll let you have the house next to the four guys enrolled in our school. I'm sure they'd like to have some adult conversation after their studies."

"We'll accept your generous offer once our home building commences," Richard replies. "Until then, we're staying with our son and his family about twenty miles up the road. Thanks again, Hughes; we'll see you tomorrow."

Hughes peeking out his office window, sees Richard and Agnes chatting away, holding hands like their second honeymoon. As they drive away, Hughes thinks to himself, *are they for real?*

As Richard pulls into the driveway of his son's house, Agnes confides, "It seems strange that any cemetery would have that many John Doe's in one year. Do you think the mortuary school is a valid reason?"

"I'm not sure. After we move in next to the students, let's have them over for breakfast and ask some questions."

"I like that idea, Richard."

"You know, it also seems strange that vandals would only burn a golf cart and only in the fire pit. I didn't see any other property damage during our tour, did you?" Richard puzzlingly inquires of his wife.

"No, I didn't," Agnes replies. "They must have been nice vandals. When we return tomorrow, let's ask to use the golf cart again after lunch and take a closer look at the two courses. "

"Yeah, I agree! Let's do that, but for now, we best go in, visit our kids and have dinner!"

When Richard and Agnes open the front door, a small welcoming party greets them.

"Hey, mom and dad, so good to see you guys," Lawrence gives each a hug, and his wife, Kellie, also hugs them.

Lawrence continues chatting, "It's been three years since we left Milwaukee and seen you last. So, are you for sure moving here?"

His mom answers, "Yes, we are. Your dad and I wanted to be closer to the two of you and our grandkids. We just signed a contract to build on the 6th green over at the Cedar Creek Golf Club."

Lawrence, a handsome African-American man that stole the heart of Kellie, a beautiful blonde, seven years ago and had two children with one on the way.

"Good for you guys," Kellie states. "You guys deserve it. By the way, I'd like you to meet our friends from Brooklyn. Mom and dad, this is Carlo and his wife, Cambria. Carlo began his new job last Monday in the financial district, sewing custom men's suits."

"You Italian men are the best tailors in the world. I know you'll have success in your job," Agnes shares.

"Thank you, Mrs. Filburn," Carlo states.

"You'll stay with us for a while, mom and dad?" inquires their son.

"Yes, until the home construction starts. We'll be here for about two weeks and then move into one of the guest cottages on the course," Richard states.

"That will be great! Debbie and Donnie will have two weeks of fun with grandpa and grandma," Kellie shares with joy.

"So, Cambria, what type of work do you do?" Agnes asks.

"Oh, I work at the cosmetic counter in one of the major stores in Manhattan. Carlo has joined me taking the train together since he started his new job. It's so nice sitting next to each other for almost an hour."

"I take it you two recently got married."

"Yes, we did, about eight months ago, and hope to have beautiful children like your grandkids someday," shares Cambria.

"Thank you for the compliment, dear."

The doorbell rings, and Lawrence shouts, "Must be the pizza; let's eat!"

Over dinner, Richard inquires of Lawrence and Kellie, "So, what do you two think of the proposed D. C. Mandate President Avci is about to sign?"

Larry replies, "Unlike you two, mom and dad, Kellie and I don't attend any church, so it makes no difference to us if the churches stay open or not."

Agnes can't believe her ears on the words coming from her son's mouth, and she replies, "Your dad and I raised you in a Christian home, and you were highly active in the youth activities at church. What happened, Larry?"

"In a nutshell, college professors and Kellie! Virtually all my professors persuaded me, and I believe them that I am my own god. So, Kellie and I are atheists."

"You may not know, Richard and Agnes, that Larry and I met during college at a meeting of the Communist Young America Party. We immediately realized our beliefs were the same, and well, the rest is history," Kellie shares.

"We are shocked beyond words," Richard exclaims. "Why haven't you two ever mentioned that you're both atheists?"

"Dad! Kellie and I thought if we shared that you and mom would never move out here. Don't be angry at us. We love you both and hope our individual religious beliefs won't prevent us from being friends and having good fellowship."

Agnes, listening to all this, can't stand the pressure any longer and bursts out, "What about the grandkids? How are they being raised?"

Kellie and Larry glance at each other, and finally, Kellie shares. "This was a difficult decision for Larry and me. At first, we considered our children to participate in Sunday School and Youth Church until they reached thirteen. But realizing the reality of today's liberal, communistic social lifestyle, we felt our children would be better protected by being atheists as we are."

"We don't want our kids professing Jesus Christ and getting shot for doing so," Larry states loudly.

"So, we ask that you respect our decision and not share Jesus in any shape or form with your grandkids," Kellie states with a deep tone.

"Wow! This isn't the life we envisioned as grandparents," Richard states loudly. "Cambria and Carlo, what are your thoughts on all this?"

"Richard!" Agnes shouts. "You shouldn't be asking strangers to get involved in a family affair."

"Oh, it's all right, Mrs. Filburn. I've been friends with Larry and Kellie all during college, and their religious stance doesn't upset me at all. My Catholic faith doesn't have room for prejudice," declares Cambria.

"I attend church with Cambria, and like her, I'm not bothered by their atheist's beliefs," Carlo shares.

Richard glances at Agnes momentarily and firmly states, "Yes, of course, we'll be friends; we're family. However, we'll be checking into a hotel for the next two weeks. We'll visit the grandkids during the day, in your home, so there won't be any question if we're brainwashing them with Jesus."

"Dad! I didn't mean it to be like that! You and Mom can take the kids with you wherever you want to go. We're family, as you say. We trust you to raise our children according to our wishes. That's all!" declares Larry.

Mom, being quiet by nature, speaks up. "It's better this way. Visiting your children in your home while you're here will take the risk out of Satan dividing this family."

Kellie gets upset. "There you go! We don't believe in God, Jesus, or Satan, and we don't believe in heaven or hell either!" Kellie is angrily shouting. "I think you're right, Agnes! It's best if you two only visit during the day!"

Post haste, Bernard shows up.

"Don't be frightened! I'm Bernard, the Angel of the Lord, and I have come to help. Certainly, seems to be a lot of commotion this evening. If I may offer some clarity, there is a God, and God's Son, Jesus Christ. I have met them both and have spoken with them both."

Larry and Kellie laugh loudly, "Seriously, this has to be some sort of joke. There aren't any angels. This angel thing must be some computer image floating in the air," Larry shouts.

Cambria intercedes, "Sorry, guys, but there are angels all around us. Each of us is assigned an angel for protection. I learned this in Catechism

54   THE D.C. MANDATE

for twelve years. I never thought I'd be alive and witness an actual angel in all my Catholic learning years."

"You have told this correctly, Cambria. God, your father in heaven, is mighty proud of you. Are you still memorizing Bible verses?"

"Yes, I am, but I wish to do more. I've asked my new husband for us to memorize together. We're starting out slow, but, prayerfully, we will get better soon."

"Hark! A warning to all of you. Time is precious. Use what you have left to memorize as much as possible. The rapture is near." Bernard vanishes.

Kellie jumps in immediately, "Oh, I forgot! We don't believe in the rapture either!"

Carlo takes a stand. "This evening has had some challenges. I think we all need a bit of time to cool our emotions. Larry, I know you picked us up in Brooklyn and offered to drive us back this evening. But, under the circumstances, I'm going to ask Richard and Agnes if you would consider driving us back? I know I'm asking a lot and realize this will considerably put you out of the way. But, I believe it's best."

"You and Cambria don't worry about that for one moment," Agnes states. "Richard and I will be most happy to accommodate."

They all finish their cold pizza in virtual silence and awkwardly say their goodbyes.

"Son, your mom and I will be in touch in a couple of days. Don't worry; we're family." Richard assures him.

So, Richard and Agnes drive Cambria and Carlo back to Brooklyn to their apartment. Richard and Agnes check into a hotel nearby for the night.

The next morning, Saturday, Cambria invites Richard and Agnes over for breakfast.

"Sure was interesting last night, wasn't it?" Cambria asks out loud.

"It is our hope and prayer that Larry and Kellie will have a touch from the Holy Spirit, so they come to an individual Jesus meeting in their hearts," Agnes shares.

"Thanks for driving us back, Richard. I really appreciate that. We'll still be friends with Larry and Kellie, but last night would not have been the ideal situation had you not brought us home. Thanks again," Carlo shares from his heart.

"You're welcome. It was our pleasure to help."

Agnes's curiosity compels her to ask, "Carlo, so, you're sewing custom suits all by yourself?"

"In a way, yes. I work in the backroom while Sergio and Nicola are in front, altering to fit. I met them last week for the first time when they hired me, and they seem like two great guys."

"Let me understand this; it sounds like you customize the inside of the suits, and they alter accordingly?"

"Yes. The suits in various sizes are waiting for me when I arrive every Monday at the store. The magic of these suits is customizing secret pockets to carry small guns concealed. I sew eight pockets inside the jacket and two in the pants lining. It's a pretty clever idea if I say so myself," Carlo boasts.

"Now! You have me curious," Shouts Richard. "As an ex-sheriff, it sounds like these designer suits are perfect for smuggling drugs or other contraband. How much are these suits selling for anyway?"

"Eleven hundred dollars."

"Listen, Carlo, you best be careful. Take my advice, don't ask any questions, just do your job. Maybe I should stop in someday and order a suit?" Richard boldly declares.

"Good luck with that. It's by appointment only, and you need a unique phone number. The door is always locked until the client arrives. The heavy metal door between the front and back of the store is locked, with Sergio or Nicola only having access. So, in a way, I do work alone."

"I assume you enter through the back door. How do you deliver the suits when finished?

"I knock on the security door, one of them opens, and I hand them the finished suit."

"If I may ask, what are you getting paid for your talents?"

Carlo answers, "One-hundred and twenty dollars per suit-cash, and I sew seventeen a week."

"Agnes!" Shouts Richard. "Somehow, we need to investigate this. Carlo and Cambria, you kids, be careful. As I voiced before, don't ask any questions, Carlo! Say, are you allowed to leave the store for lunch?" Richard queries.

"Sure, I can have a quick thirty-minute lunch. There's this hot dog wagon not far from the store. I eat there at least three times weekly-the dogs are fantastic!"

"Terrific! I'll meet you there next Tuesday at 11:30 a.m. After devouring those dogs, as you say, I want to walk in front and back of the store, sort of scope it out."

"Sure! That would be great!" exclaims Carlo.

"Let's take an extra measure; you kids call me if anything, I mean, anything is going wrong. I'll give each of you my card. Both Agnes and my number are on them."

Carlo and Cambria thank Richard, and everyone finishes their breakfast. Shortly after, Richard and Agnes head back to Cedar Creek and accept Hughes's offer of living in the guest cottage.

"I was wondering if you two were going to change your mind. I'm guessing six people living under one roof got too crowded, huh?" Hughes, trying to extract some damming information, failed again.

Richard calmly replies, not shedding light on anything Hughes was hoping to obtain, and states, "Yeah, I guess you could say that."

CHAPTER NINE

THE LUNCHEON-MAY 2035

The following day, Tuesday, the foursome has a splendid lunch. Richard and Hughes discuss the upcoming construction project and, of course, their next tee-time for a round of golf. Unfortunately, Agnes and Donna are bookends. Their conversation is awkward at best, but they do manage to share their love for antique shopping.

Donna brings up the invite, "So, Agnes, while the guys are playing a round of golf on Saturday, why don't you and I go into town and do some antique shopping?"

"I would love that, Donna, thank you."

Hughes, being a bit curious, asks, "So, Richard, have you decided on the design for your home yet?"

"Yes, Agnes and I chose a two-story circular home. The ground-level garage will be directly under the elevated second floor. The second floor will be 5,000 sq. ft with floor-to-ceiling windows overlooking the entire blue course."

"Well, congratulations! It sounds like your home will be magnificent," Hughes commends.

"Thank you. Say, Hughes, I was wondering if Agnes and I could borrow a golf cart again so we can roam the course and see the sights?"

"Why don't you and Agnes follow me outside for a second? I have a gift for both of you."

They step outside and are amazed at what they see. Parked looking like a million dollars is a golf cart designed like a Rolls Royce with seating for six and four golf bag slots. A polished bronze exterior is dazzling in the bright sunlight.

"Thank you so much, Hughes," Agnes walks over and hugs him.

"This is mighty generous of you, Hughes. I appreciate the gift immensely. Agnes and I will remember this day for a long time. Also, I would like you to be my first guest on the cart when we play Saturday."

Hughes gratefully states, "I'd be honored to ride with you."

"Well, if you'll excuse us, Agnes and I will hop on this Rolls Royce beauty and roam the sights."

They take off, and Hughes whispers to Donna, "I will be able to see them wherever they are on this course. The sun's reflection will spot them anywhere. I'm keeping my eye on those two."

As Richard drives off toward the first tee, he mentions to Agnes, "This cart is a sneaky ploy on the part of Hughes. He'll know our every move. The bronze exterior will shine like a bright beam wherever we are on the course. With the completion of our new home, we'll also get a plain cart, a lot less noticeable."

So, for the remainder of the afternoon, Richard and Agnes take turns driving their new toy covering the entire 36-hole course. An uneventful ride as far as Hughes was concerned.

Later that evening, Rabbi Yosef calls Hughes.

"This is Hughes Reyna, Director of Cedar Creek Funeral Home." Hughes doesn't recognize the number when his cell phone rings and answers in a business tone. "How may I help you?"

"Mr. Reyna, you don't know me. I'm Rabbi Yosef. Dalton Kogan suggested I give you a call regarding Jewish Funerals."

"Yes, he and his lovely wife attended my open house a few weeks ago. I'm so glad you called. As you can imagine renovating the entire property has kept me busy, and I apologize for not calling you earlier."

"No apology necessary, but I do want to chat with you on some of the conditions required if I'm going to refer your cemetery."

"Yes. I'll be interested in learning those. Are you available for lunch tomorrow?"

"I am," states the Rabbi. "Would you mind if I brought Dalton and Natalie with me? As you may remember, they're professors, and we both may need some advice. Who knows?"

The next day, Wednesday, Rabbi Yosef, Dalton, and Natalie meet with Hughes for lunch.

Rabbi Yosef starts the luncheon congratulating Hughes. "Mr. Reyna, you have created a most beautiful resting place for loved ones that have passed on. Combining it with a golf course is, in my opinion, the best use of the land that God has given us. I would like us to toast your achievement."

All three lift their glass, touching Hughes's, and congratulate him on the completed renovation.

"Thank you, everyone, thank you, I'm humbled. Rabbi, allow me to deviate and ask you a question. What is your take on President Avci's D. C. Mandate?"

"The Jewish synagogue will probably need to go underground same as most Christian churches. Plus, now residing in Cedar Creek brings me a double whammy."

"How so?" asks Hughes.

"Mayor Brady won his first election by attacking the former mayor on his Jewish heritage. Seems his tough stance resonated with the electoral in this village. I'm no longer as comfortable living in Cedar Creek as I was fifteen years ago."

Dolan agrees, "I feel about the same way as Rabbi Yosef does. However, Natalie and I don't plan on moving. We both have good jobs, a nice home, a beautiful twelve-year-old daughter, and a smart eleven-year-old son."

"Mr. Reyna, what are your thoughts on all this?" Natalie asks with a baiting tone.

"Simple! I prefer a wait-and-see approach. If the D. C. Mandate bill ever gets signed, I suggest a strong resistance, as I shared with Rachael and Darrell. You may want to consider doing the same Rabbi."

"I've had discussions with the synagogue board members, and we're more inclined to go underground as a group. If I understand the mandate bill correctly, the government will pay for the building and property if surrendered voluntarily."

"There certainly are two sides to this equation, Rabbi. I admire you and the board members for being decisive. Those who waver, not knowing whether to resist or sell, may be setting themselves up for a tremendous loss," Hughes expounds.

"What do you mean," Dolan inquires.

"Well, I'm not sure if Washington D. C. will give churches warnings or how many. But, surely, the day will come when the military marches in during service and clears everyone out. Then, on that day, those who resist will probably be shot and killed. Once the building is void of people still alive, the church building will be burned. These are the rumblings I hear coming from my contacts in D. C."

Hughes wasn't about to disclose that he receives the information from Washington D. C. via Mayor Brady.

"Oh! How awful!" Natalie shouts with a screech.

"Well, we better get back to business, Rabbi. You had mentioned over the phone something about requirements. I'm curious. Can you expand on that?" Hughes asks.

"One more thing I'd like to mention before we discuss the business at hand. I've heard President Avci is pushing hard to add more judges to the Supreme Court," Rabbi Yosef declares.

"I understand he's reaching for twenty-one judges on the high court," Natalie shares as confirmation.

"Yes!" exclaims Rabbi Yosef. "as a reformed rabbi, I believe twenty-one is too many. Why not leave it at the current number of seventeen judges? Fourteen years ago, nine judges were sitting on the bench. In 2024, the newly elected president adds four more, and likewise on his reelection in 2028."

"Packing the court is the beginning of tyranny," Dolan shares. "But, in addition to a crowded Supreme Court, I've heard President Avci wants to make prostitution and marijuana legal in all states, under the disguise of generating new tax revenue. If those two bills are passed into law, the USA, as a country, will have signed its death sentence. God, in my humble opinion, will not allow rampant sin to take over. Surely, Christians worldwide will be raptured at this point in time."

"You guys are full of doom and gloom this afternoon. I hope our conversations get a tad better as we continue." Hughes didn't want a rapture discussion tossed about any further and changed the tone back to business.

"As you were about to share requirements for our funeral home to serve the Jewish Community, Rabbi, please, go ahead." Hughes smoothly slides out of a jam.

"Sure, it's rather simple. You always need to keep an inventory of thirteen pine boxes. You also need to have thirteen grave sites ready to be prepared at a moment's notice. Unlike other faiths, the number thirteen is significant in the Jewish religion. Therefore, all burials, the next day after death, must be by the thirteen fairway. Is your team able to handle those requirements, Mr. Reyna?"

"I can assure you that my staff will honor the Jewish requirements at all times. You have my word. If you weren't aware, membership includes two full services for any member of the immediate family. The lifetime country club entry fee is two thousand per couple. Without a membership, funeral services are three thousand each.

Dalton interjects, "Mr. Reyna, would you consider hiring two Jewish cemetery workers who have experience with all the rituals of a Jewish funeral?"

"If that what it takes, I will. You have my word."

"Mr. Reyna, I believe Dalton and I owe you some clarity," Natalie states. "Before our marriage thirteen years ago, Dalton and I were both Jewish, but as Dalton says it best, liberal Jews. Today, we follow the Christian faith but are very dear friends with Rabbi Yosef. We wouldn't want any of our Jewish friends to be uncomfortable in the handling of their family's funerals at your cemetery."

Hughes replies softly, "Natalie, Dalton, and Rabbi Yosef, I assure you that my funeral home and team will do everything humanly possible to make everyone comfortable. Both the deceased and surviving family. If any of you have contacts that I could interview to handle the Jewish funeral rituals, please let me know."

Rabbi Yosef joyfully answers, "I was hoping you'd say that sometime during our luncheon. I've brought a list of five names, and they're all qualified. I know chemistry is essential when being on a team, so take your time, interview each one, and hire the two that best fit into your company culture."

"I cannot thank you enough and appreciate your efforts immensely. When I finish the interview process, may I call you with my final decision, Rabbi?"

"Yes, that would be good, thank you."

Dalton excuses himself and Natalie, "My wife and I want to thank you for lunch, Mr. Reyna, and the conversation, but I need to get back to the Conservatory and get ready for my afternoon class. My wife also has homeschooling lessons for our daughter and son this afternoon."

"You're most welcome, Dalton and Natalie, and stop by anytime. I'd love to chat some more with you regarding the Conservatory."

As Dalton and Natalie walkout, Hughes asks Rabbi Yosef if he plays golf.

"I did hit the ball around a bit twenty years ago. Now I probably wouldn't be any good at the game, a little rusty. If I did play, it couldn't be on Saturday, our Sabbath."

"I'll make you a gentlemen's casual wager. The course is closed on Mondays to the public and members. Typically, it's reserved for employees to enjoy and for maintenance to keep everything operating. We'll play nine holes, and if you break a hundred, I'll buy you a bottle of wine. If you don't, you buy me one. Do we have a game on, Rabbi?"

"I can't resist the offer. I trust you'll provide me with golf clubs for the day?"

"You got it. See you next Monday!"

The following Monday, Rabbi Yosef and Hughes start at the first tee, and the Rabbi states, "Why don't you go ahead, Hughes, and tee off first, after all, it's your golf course."

"Okay, I'll show you how to play this game of golf." Hughes drives his tee shot 220 yards leaving an easy five iron for a possible birdie.

Rabbi Yosef tees up and drives his shot 240 yards leaving an elementary six iron for a birdie.

Hughes realizes what just occurred. "I thought you hadn't played golf for twenty years. It looks like you're hustling me, Rabbi."

"Well, it has been twenty years since I played, and I wasn't sure if I still had it. Guess my college golf trophy still shines."

"So, you won a championship? Maybe we should play the lowest score wins a case of wine?"

"I'll be a sport about that, and you're on!" Rabbi Yosef exclaims.

Interestingly, they both shoot 4-under par at 32 and tie. Hughes treats the Rabbi to lunch, and they enjoy their golf chatter. After Rabbi Yosef leaves and Hughes is alone in his office, Bernard shows up.

"You have done it again this time, Hughes."

"What's that?" Hughes feints innocence.

"You're a fake. You're a fraud. You're Mr. nice guy to all the people all the time, and not even running for political office."

"So, I'm a nice guy. Is that so bad?"

"Need I remind you of all the hideous things you've done and still are doing?"

"I'm declaring innocence; what things?"

"You're virtually impossible. But, I'm not giving up on you or any of your comrades in crime. I know you don't think you're lost, but you are...very lost. Jesus is the way, the only way to be assured you'll be in heaven upon passing from this life. God forbid you're still alive here on earth when the rapture occurs. You'll face multiple calamities for the rest of your life.

"As I've clarified before, Bernard, I don't believe in that stuff."

"So, how do you in good conscience make arrangements for funerals when you don't believe?"

"I don't; I have my staff conduct the funeral arrangements. But if I had to, I'd simply fake it, no problem."

"Your bragging is repulsive. You have no shame. The emptiness in your spirit is shallow. Hughes, I pray that the Holy Spirit will come upon you someday and touch you with the love of Jesus." Bernard vanishes.

CHAPTER TEN

THE SUIT-MAY 2035

Carlo and Cambria return to work next Monday, taking the train together. Carlo gets off first, and Cambria at the very next stop, about four blocks down. Unlocking the tailor shop's back door and walking in, Carlo notices a ten-dollar bill lying on the floor next to the divider door.

He knocks on the door and asks, "Did you or Nicolao drop this?"

Sergio answers, "As you know, we enter the store the same as you do, by the back door. Nicolao must have missed his pants pocket after buying breakfast."

"Oh, okay. Glad I could help. Oh, Sergio, could I ask you a question?" Carlo states, unassuming.

"Yeah, I guess. Don't take long; I need to get back to work."

"Have you and Nicolao ever considered making custom-tailored suits for women?"

"Absolutely not! We are an exclusive custom men's designer suit store."

"You two don't have any creative imagination. Look! All these pockets! Women could carry all their whatnots in these pockets, taking the place of a purse. For the executive businesswoman, these designer suits would be a smashing success." Carlo's enthusiasm is extinguished quickly.

Sergio shuts down the conversation. "This discussion is closed. We're hired to be extraordinary tailors, not to think on wild ideas. You best get back to work. Today will be busy with five orders coming in throughout the day."

"Mind if I take one home for my wife to see?"

Sergio reaches the end of his patience and shouts, "Okay, but bring it back in the morning, or else you may get fired."

Carlo didn't scare and labored throughout the day, customizing five suits paying attention to every detail.

On the train ride home, Cambria asks, "What's in the bag? Did you buy yourself a suit?"

"I have a surprise for you. Not a gift to keep, but I want your opinion on this idea I have."

"So, I'll be modeling a suit for you?"

"Something like that."

When they get home, Cambria delays dinner and tries out the custom suit. "What do you think, a little big on me, huh?"

"For sure, but I'll make you a bet you can't find the secret hidden pockets under three minutes. Hint, you won't find them wearing the suit."

Cambria takes the suit jacket off and finds four and none in the pant legs.

"Okay, you win. Where are the other pockets?"

"Four more pockets are sewn in the jacket's back, and the pant legs have a double cuff. Easily accessible for quick retrieval of a small, concealed handgun."

"This is amazing! Who thought of this?"

"I guess some bigwig sitting in an ivory tower with nothing to do except think of wild ideas. But my wild idea was to market these custom suits to women, and Sergio shut me down before I spoke my last word."

Cambria continues to encourage her husband on his idea, states, "I'm guessing, sweetie, maybe a busy executive lady would find these as a time-saver. She wouldn't have to hassle with her purse. Everything would fit in these pockets. I suppose her after five evening wear could be stored in the jacket's back pockets. Her money, credit cards, lipstick, and makeup would easily fit in the front jacket pockets, and as you mentioned, her small gun and pepper spray in the pant legs."

"So, what do you think, would you buy it for eleven hundred?"

"If I were rich, probably so."

"I have to return it in the morning. Otherwise, I may get fired. Wonder if we should call Richard and get his nickel's worth on this idea. It's 7 p.m. now, and it'll be midnight before he arrives. What do you think, Cambria, should we call him?"

"Well, he's a very successful businessman; it certainly wouldn't hurt getting his thought on your idea."

Carlo calls Richard and explains the custom suits' concealed pockets and his idea of marketing those to women.

"Listen, Carlo, you can call me anytime. Agnes and I are retired, not on a robot schedule working the assembly lines. As you indicated, we'll be at your apartment about midnight. If we can sleep on your couch, Agnes and I will also take you up on that lunch tomorrow you raved about."

Cambria overheard the conversation. "That's nonsense; you and Agnes take our bedroom for the night. We're younger than you two, and sleeping on the couch will be, well, snuggly."

"Okay, you win. We'll see you, kids, in a few hours."

Richard and Agnes arrive shortly after 11:30 p.m. Cambria models the suit for their benefit and challenges them to find the hidden secret pockets.

Richard blows them away and finds the pockets in a minute.

"How did you do that?" shouts Carlo.

"Well, you told me to find ten pockets, and so I did. Remember, I was sheriff for thirty years, and not too much will get by me."

Carlo then asks, "So, what do you think?"

"I think it's time for bed. Ha Ha! Gotch you!" Richard is teasing Carlo. "It would be a costly undertaking. You'd need a garment factory with all the right equipment. Then, advertising and marketing with no guarantees of success."

"Darn," Carlo is disappointed but faces the reality of Richard's take on the idea.

"I believe you mentioned that these suits come from India. Your job is to sew in the secret hidden pockets."

"Yes, twenty-four boxes arrive every Monday morning. I'm tasked with completing seventeen suits each week with the secret hidden pockets.

The other seven suits are reserved for supposedly walk-in traffic. They still have to call the number on the door and make an appointment."

Richard comes back with a zinger. "Listen, kids, no one is going through all this trouble and clandestine operation for nothing. I'll bet my last ten dollars that some criminal activity is going through those doors."

Cambria asks, "Will Carlo be safe continuing to work there?"

Agnes helps out, "Quitting would be a smoking gun; safer to work there. Carlo, as my husband uttered before, stop asking questions. Just do your job. If shenanigans are going on there, they will usually reveal themselves eventually."

"She's right," Richard underlines her statement. "I have an idea though, Carlo; let me take some pictures of these pockets and the suit. Agnes and I have been following our favorite preacher for several years, Rachael Zellner. She used to own a garment factory creating attire exclusively for women. Later, she added men's evening attire. Rachael sold the company a few years ago but today conducts seminars on marriage life with her fabulous team modeling the entire fashion line. When I see her next Sunday at church, I'll show her these pics and get her thoughts on them."

"That would be great! Thanks, Richard!" Carlo shouts with glee.

As agreed, Richard and Agnes sleep in the master bedroom while Carlo and Cambria snuggle on the living room couch. The next morning all four ride the train into Manhattan. Agnes tags along with Cambria for the day, and while Cambria works, Agnes window-shops but does meet her for lunch. Richard follows Carlo to the back door but doesn't go inside. Instead, he walks around to the front and stakes out the activity.

Richard was disappointed; only two clients showed up in the morning. He continued looking for a clue that would shed some light, but no luck. So, Richard and Carlo walk over to the hot dog wagon for lunch.

"Mr. Zee, I'd like you to meet my friend, Richard. He used to be a sheriff in Milwaukee, Wisconsin, recently retired, and is planning on living in Cedar Creek," Carlo boasts.

"Well, a friend of Carlo is a friend of mine. Welcome to Manhattan, and I'm sure you'll enjoy my famous hot dog."

"I'm certain I will. Nice to meet you, and have a great day," Richard politely states.

As soon as they leave his hot dog wagon, Mr. Zee calls his wife, Zeela. "Call Hughes and let him know Richard is with Carlo today. Probably snooping around, so best you get here quickly and spy on them."

While walking back to the store, Richard inquires, "So, how was your morning, Carlo? How many suits did you customize?"

"Today is extra busy. I did three suits this morning, with two more for the afternoon. I assume there'll be three more clients showing up later."

"Well, that's great, but I'm not having any luck. It seems this operation is airtight. The front sign is a bit ambiguous, intentionally, I suppose. It reads M & N Men's Custom Suits, by appointment only. Plus, the massive front door is steel with a large security lock. Is this place Fort Knox or something?"

"I've never walked out to glance at the front. Interestingly, the divider door is also steel, but on a smaller scale. Maybe this is Fort Knox, the New York version."

"Let me ask you, Carlo, besides Sergio and Nicolao, who else do you know is involved in this business?"

"No one, those two are the only ones. They hired me."

"By the way, did you return the suit?"

"Yes, I did, but Sergio didn't seem interested when I knocked on the divider door to hand it back."

Richard inquires, "Did he take it?"

"Very hurriedly. I'm guessing I interrupted Sergio and Nicolao's workflow in front of the store."

Indeed, he was; Sergio and Nicolao were busily filling the pockets of four suits, each with four thousand in counterfeit money.

CHAPTER ELEVEN

THE WHITE HOUSE-JUNE 2035

In the Spring of 2029, Congress passed several bills overhauling the American election process. 2028 was the last election with a two-party system. No longer did a President or Vice-President need to be a natural-born citizen, nor a citizen of the U. S., nor have a term limit on time in office. The electoral college was eliminated, paving the way for the top five candidates after primaries to run for President with the highest popular vote-winning.

The election reform opened a window of opportunity for anyone. As fortune would have it, Mr. Avci and Ms. Firuzeh, both from the Middle East, were in the right place at the right time. The election of 2032 catapulted Mr. Avci to the office of President with over one hundred million votes. His closet rival had a petty forty-million votes.

Tuesday morning, April 3, 2035, President Avci calls a meeting with Vice-President Firuzeh, The Speaker of the House, and The Senate Majority Leader.

"In seventeen months, I'll be up for re-election. We must pass the D. C. Mandate bill now! I must keep my campaign promise!" President Avci shouts. "Before the end of this year!" He shouts again.

The Speaker of the House shares, "Mr. President, 100% of your loyal supporters in The House favor this bill but are concerned that their constituents back home do not, and if passed, they may lose re-election."

"I could guarantee passage if the D. C. Mandate bill was tied to an amendment raising the individual $1,000 monthly check to $2,500 for everyone in the USA," declares the Senate leader.

"What are your thoughts, Ms. Vice-President?" asks Avci.

"You all know what my stance is on this. I prefer a hefty tax on churches versus shutting them down. My tax proposal would automatically delete about 80% of the churches in America and simultaneously bring in projected tax revenues of one hundred and sixty million over four years. However, having disclosed my cause, I unequivocally support President Avci 1,000% in his quest to pass the D. C. Mandate bill. Mr. Speaker, do you feel you could muster a bill through the House raising the monthly individual check to $1,500?"

"I certainly believe it can be done!"

"Very well then! Congress! Go to work! Pass the monthly individual guaranteed check of $1,500 before the December recess. By the way, I'm not concerned about the Senate re-elections. We're safe there. On the other hand, the House is more sensitive. So, I'll guarantee every member that my administration and the state governors will cover their vote total by 12%. Mr. Speaker, please convey that message in your closed-door meetings."

"I will, Mr. President."

Bernard, the Angel of the Lord, is sitting in a corner chair, invisible to everyone, listening to all the ramblings, and thinks to himself. *I believe I know what I can do to avert a major church calamity in the United States. The timing has to be perfect, though.*

He prays silently, '*Father God Almighty, bless me with wisdom and clarity to know what to do at the exact precise time.*'

CHAPTER TWELVE

TRAIN RIDE-JUNE 2035

After a full day of working in high heels selling cosmetics, Cambria suggests she and Agnes take a cab to meet with Richard and Carlo at the train station. Agnes shopped all day in Manhattan and was exhausted, so the cab ride was a treat. They sat facing each other on the return train trip to their apartment, and Richard whispered his observation.

"Don't look back, gals, but I think we're being followed. The same couple is four rows behind you, as was this morning on the ride into work."

Cambria replies, "Hundreds of people commute to work; how can you determine they're following us?"

"No explanation, just a gut feeling. Let's see what occurs when we get off at our stop."

Sure enough, the couple followed the foursome about one block behind. But arriving at the apartment, the spy team stayed on the ground while the others walked the three flights and went inside.

Oscar tells his wife, Leah, "We best call and update our status."

"Hey, Klaus. We've followed the couple for a week and can't report anything unusual except an older African-American couple joined them two days ago."

"Well, is there anything in their behavior that sticks out? Did the young couple make any contacts during the week?"

"Not necessarily. The young couple went to work as usual. The older lady stayed with the gal, and the older man walked with the guy to the back door and then stalked the storefront watching the front door intently."

Leah jumps in for her report. "Two days ago, the young man working at the tailor shop walks out with a garment bag but returns with it the next day. Is this anything noteworthy?"

"I'm not sure, but I will let Hughes know. For the next week, I want you two to split assignments. Leah, you follow the gal, and Oscar, you tag the older man. His interest in the storefront alarms me a bit."

"You got it, Klaus," and Oscar hangs up.

Leah's week following Cambria was dreadfully dull. All she did was work, hold hands, and kiss her husband on the train rides.

Oscar's week was eventful, starting on Sunday morning following Richard and Agnes into church service. At first blush, Oscar was mesmerized at the vast auditorium and lobby. Rachael walking through the entry on the way to meeting with the worship team, notices he might be confused.

"Can I help you find something, sir?"

"No, I was just taken aback at the spacious surroundings. I'll find a seat in a while, but thanks for asking."

"You're welcome, and I hope you enjoy the service." Once on stage, Rachael noticed that Richard and Agnes were in attendance, and the man she spoke with, sitting three rows directly behind them.

After service, Richard and Agnes follow the crowd out as everyone is getting ready to shake hands with Rachael and Darrell. Once they approach Rachael, Richard softly states, "Can we visit you for a few moments?"

"Sure. Darrell, you mind finishing as I step aside?"

"Not a problem, go right ahead."

The three-step aside, and Richard shows Rachael the suit's pictures and the hidden secret eight pockets on his cell phone.

"May I have your cell phone for a closer look?"

As he was handing her his phone, Oscar, standing six feet away, runs in between Richard and Rachael grabbing the phone and quickly disappearing into the parking lot. His run knocked Rachael to the floor.

Darrell rushes over, "Are you alright, honey?"

"Yes, I'm okay, maybe a few bruises here and there, but I'll be alright."

Darrell asks out loud, "What was that all about?"

Richard gives his expert opinion. "Sorry, you had to get bruised, Rachael, for the truth to be exposed."

"I'm a preacher. I love the truth. Please share."

Richard and Agnes take turns sharing with Darrell and Rachael the activities of last week. Richard sums it up, "This bold daytime theft confirms my suspicion that some type of criminal activity is going on at William street."

"I have an idea, Richard. My ten-second peak at the suit and secret pockets gave me a good look. I'll contact the Asian garment factory and inquire if they could make a few mockups of the same, but for the ladies in several colors."

"That would be great," Agnes states. "Will you keep us informed on the progress?"

"I certainly will, and if they can create a few designs, I'll showcase them at our Saturday afternoon seminars. The reaction from the ladies will be a true indicator if this style sells. If they do, I'll work out a license agreement with Carlo, no worries."

"Thank you so much, Rachael. I'll let Cambria and Carlo know. I'm sure they'll be excited," Richard shares joyfully.

Meanwhile, Oscar had driven out of the church parking lot in a flash, drove ten miles, and pulled over to examine Richard's cell phone. Once seeing the photos of the suit and pockets, he calls Klaus.

"I stole the phone from the older man, and he has pictures of the suit and pockets. How he got them, I have no idea."

"Probably from what your wife observed. The young guy with the garment bag had our suit in it, took it home, and the older man took the photos. This is serious, Oscar. Drop the phone off outside our factory in the box, and I'm assigning you to Boston, Massachusetts, immediately. We have a funeral home there with some problems. I'll fill you in while you're driving."

"How about my wife? Does she join me in Boston?"

"Not for another week. I'll continue having her watch the honey-mooners. I'll keep you apprised."

The next day Klaus shows Hughes the photos on Richard's phone. Hughes throws a tantrum, picks up his phone, and calls Sergio.

"What were you thinking, giving Carlo the okay to take a suit home, even overnight?"

"He was driving me crazy asking all kinds of questions if we ever considered making these suits for women. Nicolao and I were behind on the counterfeit stuffing, so when he asked if he could show his wife the suit, I blabbered, okay."

"You have a peephole in the front door of your store. I'm sending you a photo of Richard and Agnes Filburn. Check every hour and see if they're lurking outside. We may have to relocate if they keep snooping. Also, as a precautionary measure, I'm having Zeela, Mr. Zee's wife, keep an eye on the area."

"Yes, boss, and sorry for my error. It won't happen again."

"Yeah! Be sure it doesn't happen again!" Hughes roars into the phone.

Klaus inquires, "So, boss, what do you want to do with Richard and Agnes?"

"Well, I can't kill them! Within a week, the police would connect me to the crime. Maybe some type of accident would solve the problem. I don't know, just keep a close eye on their activity, and hopefully, they'll finish building their dream home in record time. I'd rather have them in my sight than elsewhere."

Bernard promptly appears, *"Good morning, gentlemen, and I say that with tongue in cheek. You're both at it again, thinking of ways to kill your adversary. You remind me of the time two-thousand years ago when the people screamed to crucify Jesus."*

Hughes implores, "Are you ever going to leave me alone?"

"Sounds like I'm wearing you down, big boy. I'll make you a deal. Confess your sins, invite Jesus Christ into your heart, and then turn yourself in to the authorities for all the crimes you've committed. Then, I'll leave you alone!"

"I'd rather hang from the gallows than do any of what you demand."

"Ouch. One needs to be careful of what one wishes for; it wouldn't be

pretty watching your 300-pound body and legs flapping around trying to catch your last breath."

Klaus tries to intervene on Hughes's behalf, "Bernard, don't you have anything else to do besides torment, my boss?"

"My torment is soft and gentle compared to the sting of fire in everlasting hell. If you two don't make right with God while living here on this earth, you'll be sorry. Trust me on this. Hell is no joke!" Bernard vanishes.

Monday morning, Richard walks into the phone store and buys a new phone. As the sales rep is finishing the sale, Richard comments, "My phone was actually stolen, in broad daylight, right out of my hands!"

"That's terrible! I'm sorry for all the hassle the theft caused you, but you'll be okay. In a month or less, you'll love your new phone with all the new high-tech features included."

"Yeah, I'm fairly sure you're right. Thanks for the help and have a good day."

On the way out, Richard calls his old phone number to see if anyone would answer. Hughes, sitting in his office, hears Richard's old phone ring, captures the new number, but doesn't answer.

CHAPTER THIRTEEN

THE TRAP-JULY 2035

Hughes invites Rachael, Darrell, Richard, and Agnes over to the club for lunch so they can brainstorm on how to resist the upcoming D. C. Mandate law.

"Since we last met and discussed, briefly, on the best way to rebuke this supposedly, soon-to-be signed bill into law, I've come up with an idea," Hughes voiced firmly.

"You seem to be frustrated on the lack of speed by President Avci?" Darrell suggests.

"I may not agree with every policy on the President's plan, but I have never seen any President so timid on making tough decisions. It would be better to make a wrong decision instead of waiting for Congress to decide," Hughes flatly states.

Darrell comes back, "He did make a decision on that American Sheriff Squad executive order, didn't he?"

"Yeah, but I think he was caving in to his Communist Party backers. A decision, yes, but just pretty frosting on the cake," Hughes feigns an anti-socialist stance.

"Maybe he doesn't want to ruffle any feathers," Agnes shares.

"Maybe so. But, more importantly, Rachael and Darrell, do the two of you consider yourselves risk-takers?"

Rachael answers, "Only if the Lord directs us too."

"Well, let me ask you in another way. Are you willing to fight for your church not to be shut down?" Hughes begins to set the trap.

"My heart and soul are in this place, and I don't want to lose it without a fight."

"I wholeheartedly agree with her," Darrell affirms.

"Let me ask you a question, Hughes. Is this idea you have involve any risk?" Richard boldly inquires.

"As you well know, being a former sheriff yourself, anything good or bad, involves a certain degree of risk. Look at all the criminals you arrested. Their element of risk to reward was on the downside."

"Okay. Now, you have me curious, Hughes, what is your plan?" Richard inquires.

"Let me ask one more time. Rachael and Darrell, are both of you certain you're willing to risk virtually everything to save your church?"

They both answer, "Yes!"

"Okay then. If you're absolutely positive you want to put up a fight and can convince your congregation members to support you, then I have an idea."

Agnes softly and carefully asks, "What is it?"

Hughes lays out the steps. "The sanctuary must be filled to capacity; standing room only is better. Conduct church service as usual. The government isn't going to arrest 10,000 people at once any time soon. As the first layer of precaution, hire about twenty security guards for the parking lot. Local, state, and federal governments will ignore vandalism to vehicles, probably by insurance companies too. The second layer of caution, lock the doors once service commences. I know the Fire Marshall won't approve, but you don't want a protest mob invading the sanctuary. Think you guys can handle this type of resistance?"

"Do you really believe it could come to something like this, Hughes?" Richard asks.

"The radical element in today's society wants what they want no matter how they get what they want," Hughes rattles off those words intending to sound like he's on the side of the church.

"Before we answer, I'm giving Phillip, our lawyer, a call," Darrell briefed.

"I agree. Good Idea," Hughes concurs.

"Phillip, Darrell here. Let me ask you a question. If Rachael and I and 10,000 church members resisted the D. C. Mandate, how many would get arrested and how long in jail?"

"That's a tough question, Darrell. The bill isn't law yet, and no one knows all the intricate provisions that will be hidden in the D. C. Mandate. Suffice it to say, 10,000 people won't be arrested, but the church leaders, probably."

"Ouch! I was afraid you were going to say that," Rachael exclaims.

Richard jumps in with a question. "How long would they be in jail before you could get them released?"

"Again, I don't know. The bill hasn't been finalized. As a matter of fact, all the politicians in D. C. have been unusually quiet on the facets of this bill. This does disturb me a bit. However, usually for a misdemeanor, arrested jail time is two days. But, it could be up to 200 hundred days! It's up for grabs!"

Rachael looks at Darrell, he looks at her, and both shout, "We'll do it!"

Rachael affirms, "Keeping our church open is worth 200 days in jail if it comes to that."

Hughes shakes their hands and states, "Congratulations, I know it was a tough decision, a very tough one indeed. So, moving forward, implement the plan as soon as possible. Practice each step of the plan so that when the day of evil comes, you can take your stand and protect your beloved church!"

"If you guys need any help, Agnes and I are here at the ready. Just tell us what you need to be done," Richard shares.

"That also goes for Terri and me," Phillip shouts through the phone.

"Thank you so much, all of you. Darrell and I are most appreciative," Rachael sincerely states.

After they all leave the club, Hughes places a call to Grace Palmer on her direct line, "Congratulations Grace!, Allen has informed me that you're now the official Director of the Sheriff Squad."

"Thank you, Hughes. President Avci decided I'd be more instrumental here in D.C. than the mayor of Cedar Creek. I'm certain when the president wins re-election, he'll find a position in the belt-line for Allen Brady. So, I'm thinking you have an update for me?"

"Yes, I do. The trap is all set. Whenever you want to implement the church invasion, it's yours for the taking."

"You indeed are a smooth deal maker, Hughes. I'm glad you're on my side. Hey, when you speak with Allen next, tell him to stand firm, and his day will come."

"You got it, Grace, later."

CHAPTER FOURTEEN

SATURDAY SEMINAR-JULY 2035

Rachael receives word from the Asian garment factory and makes a call immediately.

"Hello, Richard here."

"This is Rachael, Richard. I have good news; I just received word from Asia that they can create a few mockups of the ladies' suit!" Her tone is full of excitement.

"Well, that's great, Rachael! Any idea when you'll receive a shipment?"

"Usually, it takes five to six weeks. I've ordered suits in sizes eight and ten, in five different colors for each. As promised, I'll showcase them at my next monthly Saturday seminar. You, Agnes, Cambria, and Carlo have a standing invitation."

"I'll pass the word, and I am certain everyone will be excited to attend."

Rachael has an idea and calls Hughes.

"Cedar Creek Funeral Home, Hughes speaking."

"This is Rachael, Hughes. No, I'm not calling to buy a casket or cemetery plot, not yet anyway. I'm calling to invite you and Donna to my next Saturday afternoon seminar."

"That's very generous of you, but if I recall your rules, a couple has to be married or engaged. Donna and I are neither ones, simply good friends."

"Yes, I did state those words. As like you, Hughes, I'm the CEO and can make a one-time exception. I'm bringing out a new fashion line for women, and I'd like to get Donna's honest feedback. The two of you would be doing me a favor. What you say, Hughes, will you attend?"

"I'm sure Donna would love an afternoon show of women's high fashion. Go ahead and count us in; let me know the date when you can."

Rachael didn't want to push her luck any farther and intentionally didn't mention the one-hour Biblical teaching before the fashion show.

After hanging up with Hughes, Rachael calls her husband at his office.

"You didn't forget, we're going to visit and pray for Alice at the hospital?"

"No, not at all. I'll get the car-meet me out front."

As they're driving, Rachael shares her frustration, "I don't understand why so many elderly are abruptly dying in our county? You have any idea, Darrell?"

"No, I don't, sweetheart. From what I've heard, most are ninety or older, and sadly, last month over one-hundred died from this unknown illness in Cedar Creek County alone!"

"I hate to say this, Darrell, but you think this could be an intentional repeat from fifteen years ago?"

"I'm not certain. But, I'm convinced all governments are capable of imposing any calamity intentionally whenever they want."

"I'm convinced the rapture is near," voiced Rachael. How much longer will God allow rampant lawlessness to increase?"

"Like you, dear, I pray the rapture happens soon. But, as an example, I think it was about five months ago in February that the government shut down a church in our county, declaring the preacher told the congregation that abortion and same-sex marriage were a sin against God. That shutdown was intentional! It seems President Avci is getting restless waiting for Congress to pass the D. C. Mandate bill."

"Yes, I caught that on the news, but I'm not backing down. I'll continue to preach the truth from the Bible!"

"You do know, honey, that I'm backing you up 100%. We need to preach the truth no matter what.""

"As long as God's word gets out to our congregation, I'll do whatever it takes. Now, let's go visit Alice."

As they enter the hospital and take the elevator to Alice's room, Rachael and Darrell can't help but notice the hallways' quietness. Rachael asks one of the nurses walking by, "Why is it so quiet in here? There's no activity going on; what gives?"

"We just had five more patients die this morning. All over ninety, though."

Rachael is taken by surprise, "You state that so casually. Isn't every life worth living?"

"Yes, it is. But having lived to ninety and beyond, one assumes they had a good life. So, not so bad after all."

As they walk toward Alice's room, Rachael whispers, "Did you catch that, Darrell. Now the hospital staff has been indoctrinated to accept hundreds of elderly suddenly dying as normal."

"Yes, I did."

"Alice, it's so good to see you. We miss you in church," Rachael softly speaks as they sit by her bedside.

"I miss being there also. The doctors want to put me on a ventilator, but I refuse and will make this breathing mask sufficient."

"We have come to pray for you, Alice, anoint you with oil, lay hands on you, and speak in tongues over the illness that has attacked you," Darrell firmly states.

"Oh, those words are so comforting, thank you."

Darrell and Rachael stay for over an hour, anoint Alice with oil, lay hands on her, and pray in tongues believing that God can heal her. As they walk out of the room, Rachael and Darrell ask her nurse about the 'real' condition of Alice's health.

"As the saying goes, She's a tough old bird, and with the two of you praying over her, I believe she has a good fighting chance."

"Thank you, nurse, for your truthfulness," shares Rachael.

Three weeks later, Alice shows up in church by the miracle healing power of God. When Pastor Rachael sees her from the pulpit, she announces the blessing, and the congregation gives God applause of appreciation and shouts Hallelujah and Amen.

However, after service and shaking hands with the flock as they leave,

Rachael and Darrell are approached by a man, and it's obvious to them he's not a regular.

"Good afternoon. Are the two of you pastors of this church?"

Rachael and Darrell have an uneasy feeling this wasn't going to be good.

"My name is Walter, Walter Smith. I'm one of the thousand new federal government sheriffs assigned wholly to pastoral and church activities. I'm handing you this letter, signed by the Director of the Sheriff Squad, Ms. Grace Palmer, that you are ordered to cease and desist visiting any patient in any hospital and praying over them. Failure to abide by this summons will result in arrest."

Darrell loudly speaks, "So, you're going to arrest me in a hospital hallway? How would you even know what I was doing or that I was even there?"

"Our government nurses would contact me, and before you vocalized an 'Amen' in your prayer, I'd have you arrested. I trust the two of you will heed this warning as real and not test the waters. Please, have a good day."

As Walter leaves, Rachael guesses it was the first hallway nurse who contacted the Government Sheriff Office. Darrell and Rachael stare at each other, not believing that Grace Palmer actually summoned them with a cease-and-desist order.

Fortunately, Bernard shows up.

"Be of good cheer; all is not that bad. You can pray for those in the hospital virtually anywhere, but not in the hospital. You do know the government had all chapels in hospitals closed down nationwide just three weeks ago?"

"Wasn't that the same time we visited Alice, Darrell?"

"I believe it was, sweetheart. Seems Washington D.C. is on the warpath to destroy the church and prayer."

"Do not be dismayed. All this and more must occur before the end times."

Thank you, Bernard, for your pearls of wisdom."

"You're welcome, Darrell. But, I must be going now. I'll chat with you two later." Bernard disappears.

Rachael turns to her husband, "It's a good thing we met with Hughes last month and have our resistance plan in order. Sounds like it could get dicey very soon."

Meanwhile, Oscar reports to his new assignment in Boston, the

Oceanview Funeral Home, and Chapel. The funeral director, Hudson McDermont, was behind two months of receiving caskets filled with counterfeit bills from Hughes Enterprises.

Oscar walked in unannounced and was greeted by an attractive middle-aged lady. "Good morning; how can I help you?"

"I'm here to speak with the funeral director, Hudson McDermont."

"May I tell him who's calling?"

"Oscar Klein from Hughes Enterprises," he answers in a stern tone.

She comes back momentarily and states, "Mr. McDermont will see you in his office. I'll walk you there."

"Thanks." Arriving at the office door, Oscar opens it quickly, for the shock effect, but to his surprise, Oscar only sees this small, timid man sitting in a wheelchair behind the desk.

"Are you Hudson McDermont?" Oscar inquires hesitantly.

"I can see on your face that you were expecting a bigger-than-life person sitting here instead of this frail funeral director."

"I'd be lying if I mentioned something differently."

"Well, to tell the truth, I've been sick, really sick with cancer the last six months. The doctor states I have, at most, three more months. I'm not surprised you're here; figured the boss man would send someone eventually."

"This may sound cold-hearted, but I'm here strictly on business. Let's chat about the future of your funeral home. Is there anyone in your family that would take over, and do they know about the side business?"

"Hardly! My estranged son, whom I haven't spoken with for over twenty years, lives in Cincinnati and works high-tech. Doubt he'd ever change careers to a funeral director. My wife died several years ago, so what you see is what you get."

"I understand and am sorry for your loss, but under the circumstances, Hughes Enterprises has no choice but to take over your operation. We'll buy you out equal to the cost of your medical bills, hospice, and funeral. We'll also bring in a new director within a few days. Upon his arrival, you can retire to your home and be comfortable."

"Thank you. I'll probably convert my home to a hospice stay and hopefully alleviate some of this ongoing pain in my body."

"Hudson, I'm staying in town until our new director arrives. If there's anything you need, call me on my cell," Oscar hands him his business card.

"Thank you, and yes, I'll call you if I think of anything. I'm sorry I haven't ordered any caskets for two months. My failing health has caused the business to drop considerably. Oh, by the way, there are two caskets in storage with the counterfeit remaining in the lining. I haven't had the time or strength to retrieve them or to distribute the monies."

"Does your middle-aged receptionist know anything about this?"

"No, she works in the front only, been here about six months. When I hired her, she divulged that she had worked as a receptionist at some high-tech firm in Cincinnati but preferred living here in Boston."

Upon hearing Hudson's confession, Oscar marches to the storage area, opens the caskets, and unzips the secret lining. Sure enough, each coffin still had the original hundred- thousand in fake bills. Oscar was in a jam. He couldn't risk bagging the money and taking it with him to the motel. So, he padlocked both caskets until he called Klaus for instructions.

At the motel, Oscar calls Klaus in somewhat of a panic tone.

"Klaus, we have a problem." He explains the jam in detail and waits for Klaus's response.

"We can't take any risk whatsoever. I'll send our fill-in funeral director over tomorrow. When Hudson retires to his home for his hospice stay, I'll have our home healthcare nurse accidentally overdose him with morphine. I'll have our driver take those two caskets and deliver them to another funeral home. I think I have you covered all around. Now, get some rest, and we'll talk tomorrow."

Bernard immediately shows up in Oscar's motel room.

"Be not afraid. I am Bernard, Angel of the Lord, and I have come to help you."

Oscar, overcome with anxiety, didn't realize he was talking to an angel. "Good, I sure could use some help with this crisis I'm in over my head at the funeral home."

"I'm referring to spiritual help, Oscar, not the mess the illegal operation has found you in."

"By the way, who the heck are you?" Oscar finally realizes he's not speaking with a human.

"My name is Bernard, the Angel of the Lord, and I'm here to help you find your way to Jesus. He can give you life eternal. Simply confess your sins, invite Jesus into your heart, and you'll be saved."

"If things don't go according to plans, I'll need to be saved. You can help me?"

"Sorry, Oscar. I'm not here to help you avoid consequences humanly manifested. But, I'm here to encourage you to seek Jesus in your life and to be ready for the rapture that is soon to come." Bernard vanishes.

The next morning, Oscar gets up earlier than usual, still wondering about the conversation with Bernard. Nevertheless, he puts it out of his mind and drives over to Oceanview. No cars were in the parking lot, a bit early for the receptionist to arrive, but Oscar tries the front door anyway. To his amazement, somebody left the door unlocked. He slowly walks in, turning on the lights.

"Oh, gracious me, lobster crab cakes!" Oscar shouts to himself. There in the lobby was Hudson McDermont, sitting in his wheelchair dead. Someone beat him to the punch, taking out Hudson with the morphine drip bag still attached to his wheelchair. Oscar panics and runs to the storage room.

"Dirty rats!" Oscar mutters. Somebody busted the padlocks on the caskets, the lids were left open, and the secret lining left unzipped. "Money has gone, all two-hundred grand," Oscar sadly whispers to himself.

He calls Klaus and fills him in on the details. "Don't call the authorities yet. My driver should be there shortly; those caskets need to be removed quickly. Any idea who took the dough?"

While on the phone with Klaus, Oscar, just for giggles, glides his hands through the linings of both caskets. To his amazement, he feels a piece of paper in each. Pulls them out and reads the notes to Klaus.

"Thank you for the fake money. Don't bother; you'll never catch me. Sincerely, your middle-aged receptionist. And, oh, by the way, you're welcome. I did the dirty deed for you, taking out Hudson. "

Klaus shouts back, "I don't suppose you have her name as if that will do any good."

Oscar fumbles through her desk in the receptionist area and finally finds business cards bearing the name "Nancy Bouvier. Hey Klaus! I just found another business card in her desk drawer. The name is Brad McDermont, software engineer, Rascals Inc., Cincinnati, Ohio." Oscar relates.

Klaus comes back, "I'll bet the farm he's the estranged son of Hudson. It looks like Nancy and Brad teamed up to take advantage of his dad's failing health. How low can one go?" Klaus states in disgust.

Oscar affirms, "That is despicable, having your girlfriend kill your dad."

"I hope they're smart. Pulling off a theft like that takes brains and gusto. If they get caught or spend that money lickety-split, we're in a master jam. So, we're shutting down this operation in Boston. Only clean caskets to be shipped there, no more counterfeit at this funeral home -starting now. Has my driver showed up yet?"

"As you speak, Klaus." Oscar sees the truck backing up to the storage area.

"I assume you'll be taking the caskets back to the factory and reusing them for another funeral home."

"Yes, that would be correct. Listen, Oscar. You need to disappear quickly. Let's see, where does the operation need you the most? Yes, I got it! Drive over to Cleveland, Ohio, and I'll have your wife meet you there. You two take a few days off until your next assignment, and, don't worry, our new funeral director will take care of the situation at Oceanview."

"Got it; I'll talk to you in a few days."

The new funeral director didn't have any problem with the authorities, blaming Hudson's death on the mysterious receptionist. The storage room was void of any caskets. Oceanview was clean and ready to start a new business without a hint of any illegal activity.

Nancy Bouvier, driving cheerfully to Cleveland to meet her boyfriend the next day, has no worry in the world. Eavesdropping the other day didn't hurt Nancy beating Oscar at his game. Not only did she steal two-hundred grand, but for the last six months, since day two at the job, every week when Hughes Enterprises delivered a casket, she'd steal the money. Hudson was too sick to pay any attention. With three suitcases stuffed with two million dollars in counterfeit money conveniently placed in the trunk of her car, Nancy joyfully continues driving to Cleveland. Getting hungry, she stops at a freeway restaurant for lunch.

At full-tilt, Bernard is walking with her.

"Who are you?" Nancy shouts.

"I'm Bernard, the Angel of the Lord. No one sees or hears me but you, and I have come to help."

"Is this a joke? I don't need any help. My boyfriend and I have this all figured out. You can stop walking next to me now," Nancy shouts again.

"It must have been easy for you to kill Hudson with that hardened heart of yours."

"I have no idea what you're talking about, and now, stop following me!"

"I'm not giving up on you, Nancy, but as you wish, I'll stop." Bernard disappears.

Nancy, unfazed, continues driving to Cleveland, daydreaming about all the possibilities that she and her boyfriend will do with the jackpot she stole.

*****

Six weeks have passed since Rachael called Richard inviting him over for the Saturday afternoon seminar. An ensemble of two couples plays soft music while folks are continuing to walk in the auditorium. Standing on the platform, Darrell and Rachael notice Hughes and Donna walk in, taking a seat about three rows behind Richard and Agnes.

Precisely at 1 p.m., Darrell welcomes everyone with an opening prayer, and immediately following, Rachael begins her teaching on Godly marriages. Forty-five minutes later, Rachael closes her teaching seminar with prayer and then announces. "Ladies and Gentlemen, without further ado, please welcome our fashion team models!"

Rachael describes each luxurious and modestly sexy wear for both women and men. Shortly after that, the fashion team members showcase the wedding gown and tux fashion line. The audience shows their appreciation, stands to their feet, and gives the team three minutes of applause. The crowd's enthusiasm could have brought the roof down.

Rachael walks up to the mic again and states, "I'm leaving the best to last. It's a new design for ladies' business suits. Each model will walk out with her husband, and I'll expand on this upcoming trend. As they walk out, I'll announce the colors. First is peach, followed by yellow, burgundy, white and royal blue. As our peach model opens the jacket, six hidden secret pockets are sewn inside with enough room to stow all the things a lady would have in her purse. Furthermore, the pant legs offer a secret pocket enabling our business lady protection, hiding a small gun and pepper spray out of sight, but readily available in a moment's notice."

Upon hearing and seeing all this, Hughes is seething mad that his suit design was stolen. Donna senses his anger and whispers, "Try to calm down. I assure you that your enterprise won't cave in over this one item."

He whispers back, "Okay, thanks."

The ladies in the crowd show their appreciation with roaring applause on the new trendy business suit. Rachael returns to the mic, "As always, any fashion item you've seen today is 20% off. I also have a surprise. Ten ladies will receive one of these suits free! The only caveat is you'll need to report weekly on your likes and dislikes. First, I'd like to show my appreciation to the wife of the guy who thought of this idea. Cambria and Carlo, please come up to the stage."

Ralph and Agnes give them a standing ovation as they walk onto the stage.

"So, Cambria, what color and size would you like?" Rachael asks.

"I'll take the peach in size eight, thank you."

Rachael turns to Carlo and asks, "So, Carlo, how did you come up with this idea?"

"Well, I'm a tailor by trade working for a private company, and one day this idea just hit me. Most women always struggle with their purse, so why not design a ladies business suit with secret pockets that would delete the need for a purse."

"I think it's a great idea," Rachael shares. "We'll know more after the test run. The next couple I'd like to introduce is the new owner of Cedar Creek Country Club and Funeral Home. Hughes Reyna and his partner, Donna Trice, won't you two come up to the stage, please?"

They reluctantly make their way up, but once there, all smiles and oozing with confidence.

Rachael gives them a free promotion, "If some of you aren't familiar with the many services Hughes's Country Club has to offer, I encourage you to visit their facilities soon. I'm sure you'll be impressed as much as I was."

Rachael turns to Donna, knowing fully well, she can't refuse a free suit now. "So, Donna, what suit would you like?"

"Thank you, Rachael; your offer is so generous. I'll take the royal blue in size ten, please."

Rachael announces the other eight winners while Hughes and Donna walk off stage and make a beeline to Carlo and Cambria.

"Congratulations on your winning design, Carlo. By the way, I'm Hughes Reyna, and this is my friend, Donna Trice." Hughes waxes with politeness but still fuming with anger in his gut.

"Good to meet both of you, and this is my wife, Cambria, and my friends, Richard and Agnes."

Hughes chuckles as Carlo introduces Richard and Agnes. "Long time no see, huh?"

Richard explains to Carlo that he and Agnes are building a house on Hughes's golf course and that the four of them are luncheon friends.

"Oh, I didn't know that," Carlo states. "I've been so busy at work, Cambria, and I hardly have any time to visit with our friends and keep up with them."

"So, Cambria, are you excited about testing out the new lady's business suit?" Donna inquires.

"I am, and it should be a hit with the ladies at work. Rachael informed me that we could take pre-orders at 20% off and still receive a 10% commission. That's exciting!" Cambria's joy is contagious, except for Donna, who's a millionaire not needing 10%, delicately responds.

"That is exciting! I hope you get lots of orders and enjoy wearing the new trendy lady's suit."

Agnes politely interrupts, "Well, Hughes and Donna, it's always nice chatting with you, but we must excuse ourselves. We need to drive Carlo and Cambria back home to Brooklyn; it's about a four-hour drive. We'll probably stay overnight at their apartment."

On the drive back to the country club, Hughes shares with Donna.

"I need to coordinate with Klaus and keep a tail on Carlo, and especially Richard. He's already taken photos of the suit and secret pockets. I wonder what else he has in mind?"

Donna comes back, "You did say that Richard was a former sheriff; you best be careful."

"I am. I'm taking all the precautions necessary if the resistance plan I shared with Richard and Agnes never comes to fruition. However, when the D. C, Mandate passes, everyone calling themselves Christian will be arrested," Hughes boasts with confidence.

CHAPTER FIFTEEN

CLEVELAND RENDEVOUS-AUG 2035

Arriving mid-afternoon and hoping to see Brad's car at the motel, Nancy backs her car up to the motel room door for safety measures. Disappointed he's not there, she calls Brad. "Hey, hon, when are you going to be here? I'm getting nervous with the loot in the trunk."

"I got stopped for a speeding ticket about fifty miles south of Cleveland. Should be there shortly, sweetie."

Nancy getting restless, decides to place the three suitcases inside the motel room until Brad arrives.

Taking longer than expected, Brad finally arrives, fuming mad he got stopped for speeding. "I offered to buy the officer a hundred-dollar lunch, but he refused, giving me a two-hundred and fifty-dollar ticket instead."

"Sorry about that, but what do we do with all this money, hon?"

"Two million dollars in those three suitcases, huh?"

"Yup, that would be correct."

"I think we should trade our two cars in for one big SUV and pay the difference in cash. Eventually, the police will mark our cars. We need to make them disappear, and fast!" Brad speaks with urgency.

"Are you crazy? The dealer will inform the Feds on our cash purchase, and when it's discovered the cash is fake, we end up in the slammer."

"Sweetie, we can't be the only crooks in town. We need to find a seedy used car dealer that would love to have a cash windfall, and we'll make it worth his while. I'll ask the motel owner if he knows of any shamelessly used car dealer who's looking to make the deal of a lifetime."

Nancy inquires, "So, hon, about the other idea you had. When do we start the shakedown?"

"After we switch vehicles. From the report you were able to generate from Oceanview, it looks like Hughes Enterprises has forty affiliate funeral homes in his network."

"Let's make sure I have this correct," Nancy rehearses, "We walk in unannounced, ask to speak with the funeral home director, and offer them annual insurance for twelve thousand for keeping their counterfeit operation; quiet."

"You got it, babe! In two months, we'll have almost a half-million in real money!" Brad's ecstatic.

The same afternoon, Brad and Nancy drive around the questionable town area for an hour and finally find Mitch's Used Cars, the car lot the motel owner suggested. Brad gets out and walks to the shanty-looking office.

"Are you the owner of this car lot?"

"Yup, I am. They call me Mitch the Magician because I make things disappear like magic. I can get your old vehicle to disappear and get you into a newer appealing vehicle faster than the blinking of an eye."

"Mitch, I think we can do business today. Hey sweetie, come on over; I'd like you to meet our hero."

Nancy walks over, and the three chat for a while when Mitch states, "You fine folk didn't stop here to only chat with me. What's on your mind?"

Brad lays out the plan. "We'd like to trade in two cars for that SUV over there and pay you the difference in cash. Our cash is a bit funny, though, all in ten-dollar bills. So, for your trouble, we'll pay you three times the cash difference."

"I only see one car; where's the second?"

"At the motel. We'll make the deal here, pay you half, then drive you over, and pay you the other half. You drive the second car back. Do we have a deal?"

"So, let me get this straight, you're trading in two cars, and the trade difference would normally be thirty thousand, but you'll pay me ninety thousand in counterfeit ten-dollar bills. Do I have that correct?"

Nancy yells out, "How did you get so smart?"

Mitch comes back, "This car lot looks like a junkyard, intentionally. I'm the frontman for the biggest counterfeit ring in the region. Mitch Kearney is the name. Nice to meet your acquaintance."

Nancy is shocked and embarrassed, while Brad takes it all in stride.

"So sorry about my English, Mitch. Sometimes it comes out wrong like it just did."

"No worries. But I do have a question. Creating a ten-dollar fake bill is clever. I'm guessing neither of you geniuses printed that and most likely stole the bundle. How I'm doing?"

Nancy confesses, "You are smart, Mitch, indeed."

"Now, I have a deal for both of you. I'm guessing you have more than ninety thousand. Whatever the amount is, somebody will catch you if you don't know what you're doing. I hope you didn't pay the motel in cash?"

Nancy concedes, "Yes, I did, for two weeks, five hundred."

"What motel are you staying at?"

"Motorway Inn," Brad replies.

"Not a problem. I know the owner; I'll take care of it when we drive over. Now, whatever amount you have left after you pay me the ninety grand, I'll give you twenty percent and magically make your worries disappear."

Brad inquires, "How do we know you won't be giving us fake twenty-dollar bills in return?"

"I'll write a cashier's check. You take it to the bank the same day and cash it. Do we have a deal?"

Nancy stomps her foot and shouts, "Listen, Mitch; I worked hard collecting all that dough. It took me several months to acquire the loot. I'm not in the mood to simply give it away at twenty percent. We have 1.9 million left; you can have it for four hundred thousand. Take it or leave it."

"A woman's scorn has no wrath," Mitch poetically teases her. "It seems, Nancy, your English has improved, magically. Sure, we have a deal."

So, Nancy and Brad drive out in a three-year-old black Hummer. Mitch picks up the second car at the motel, collects the rest of the funny money in three suitcases, and hands them a cashier's check for four-hundred thousand. Before leaving, he stops at the motel office and shakes hands with the owner.

Brad inquires, "What was that all about?"

"As I promised, I made things right with the owner. You two have no worries. But, I do have one last question for you, Nancy; where did you get the fake loot?"

"Oceanview Funeral Home and Chapel in Boston."

Out of the blue, squad cars arrive in the motel parking lot with flashing lights beaming brightly.

Brad inquires, "What's going on?"

"Allow me to introduce myself formally. I'm Mitch Kearney with the FBI, Northern District. You're both under arrest for the illegal possession of counterfeit monies and intentionally passing those monies with the intent of fraud. Nancy Bouvier, you're also charged with the murder of Hudson McDermont, and Brad, you're charged with accessory to murder. Your dad-how despicable!"

As they're being pushed into the back seat of the squad car, Brad asks, "How did you find us?"

Mitch states flatly, "We received a tip last month that an organized counterfeit ring was operating out of the east coast. So, we flagged all out-of-state vehicles. When an out-of-state car stops at a motel, the owner is instructed to contact us and place a bug in the guest's room. When you saw me shaking hands with the motel owner, I thanked him for a job well done."

"One last question, Mitch," Nancy pleads, "How did you know to be at the used car lot?"

"Remember, I had your room bugged. It was just a matter of an hour to set up the sting. You guys walked right into it; congratulations. You'll each have at least room and board free for twenty years. Take them away, Officer!" Mitch shouts.

Meanwhile, Oscar meets his wife in Cleveland at the Flamingo Motel. Both tired from traveling, order pizza in, and turn on the TV.

"Good evening, folks. Kelsey Post, reporting live from the Motorway Motel on the far west side of Cleveland. Moments ago, the FBI arrested a couple for allegedly having possession of counterfeit monies and intent to commit fraud. It's also been reported that the accomplices are being charged with murder. The ironic quirk in this arrest is that the counterfeit monies were all in ten-dollar bills. The couple is being held at the west county jail for further questioning. Kelsey Post is signing off; good night!"

Oscar, hearing this, calls Klaus immediately and goes into detail. Then asks, "You want me to post bail and take care of the problem?"

"Taking care of the problem would be too messy, and you'd probably get connected eventually. Too risky! I'll contact Hughes and get his take on the situation. Stay tuned; I'll call you back in an hour or so."

Klaus decides to walk over to Hughes's office and speak in private. Klaus wasn't too surprised to see Donna as he walked in.

"Good evening, Donna. Are you doing okay?"

She dismisses his greeting; "Hughes and I were going over the layout of the two courses, and it will be feasible to sell one-half acre homesites above each green-same as Richard and Agnes for one-hundred thousand."

Hughes embellishes Donna's idea. "She has an eye for architectural landscape design while keeping the sanctity of the cemetery in peaceful harmony with the homes and surrounding area."

"That's great, Donna! But, Hughes, I need to speak with you in private. It's an urgent matter."

"She's part of the team, Klaus. Whatever needs to be spoken, she can hear and add some valuable insight that you and I might not perceive."

"Okay, boss, not a problem." Klaus continues cautiously, "The gal that ripped off the Oceanview Funeral Home in Boston got arrested an hour ago with her boyfriend. The Feds set up a sting operation and caught them with $1.9 million in counterfeit bills. How would you like to proceed?"

Donna smarts back, "Take them out of their misery!"

Although it seems like Hughes's back is against the wall, he manages to chuckle. Believe me, I would like to, but it's too late. The police are probably interrogating them as we speak. If convicted, they face twenty years but likely will strike a deal with the District Attorney for a plea bargain."

Donna inquires, "You shared with me once about a code to activate if things went south. If I remember, you never had to implement the system. So, Hughes, what are your thoughts?"

"I'm going on the premise of two thoughts. First, the FBI will investigate every funeral home that's affiliated with us. Secondly, my gut tells me the arrested couple will walk with supervision, mind you, as part of the FBI undercover team."

Klaus conjectures, "That means we alert all our funeral directors to implement code H602 immediately, right boss?"

"Yes. Unfortunately, this new plan forces us to print six days versus our typical four days to maintain two million monthly profit margins. You'll need to contact your brother, Gunter, in Germany, for two more pallets of paper and ink. Keep me appraised of the shipment."

"You got it, boss!" Klaus is thrilled to be involved in the strategic planning of code H602.

Hughes stops Klaus short of leaving his office. "One more item, you'll need to double the time of the printing press to six hours daily, six days a week. Conduct maintenance after hours and on Sunday. You'll be extremely busy underground, so I'm having Donna be the contact person for all our field personnel active immediately. Klaus, I appreciate your work, and I promise there will be a hefty Christmas bonus in your stocking."

"Not a problem, boss, and thanks for the bonus. I'll contact Gunter now and let you know the arrival date." Klaus leaves Hughes's office feeling sad and slighted but continues as a team player.

"So, Mr. Reyna," Donna teases him a bit, "Care to enlighten me on this secret code?"

"Sure, but it will take a while. go ahead and grab us some snacks from the kitchen, and I'll pour us two glasses of wine."

Donna comes back with crackers, cheese, salami, and grapes. Hughes is delightfully surprised. They toast their wine glasses, and Hughes commences.

"We'll continue with the secret hidden zipper in the casket lining, but instead of counterfeit there, we'll furnish the funeral home with brochures of Cedar Creek Cemetery, itemized price listing, and other sundry items to help the bereaved family in their decision process."

"How clever," Donna shares.

"My calculated guess is that the Feds will tire after investigating twenty of our affiliates not finding any counterfeit in the linings. But, we'll continue with the code indefinitely."

"So, how are you distributing the monies under this code?"- Donna inquires.

"Well, we'll need to modify the manufacturing process to build the casket bottom four inches taller, allowing us to stow one million counterfeit dollars in its belly."

"So, how are you getting these modified caskets to the local funeral home?"Donna inquires.

"We'll continue delivering caskets, without the counterfeit, weekly to our funeral home partners. But, we'll be asking the local funeral director to push our Cedar Creek Cemetery services at every opportunity. When a family of the deceased agrees, the funeral home will drive their hearse, with the deceased, to our cemetery. After the graveside ceremony, the funeral director will pay me fifty thousand cash in a sealed envelope. The empty casket he's taking back in his hearse will have the one million in fake monies. This transaction will be once monthly, part of their monthly quota for burials here of twelve. Anyone snooping or suspecting won't know which trip of the twelve has the counterfeit money. The authorities would be subject to a lawsuit if they stopped every trip. Hence, none will be arrested."

"Marvelous idea, Hughes. You are a mastermind," Donna leans over and plants a kiss on Hughes.

"Donna, I ran the numbers for kicks, and with forty funeral home affiliates, you think we can live on thirty-three- thousand a day?"

Post haste, Bernard appears, *"Money, money, money, is all you think and talk about Hughes. Sadly, money has become and is your God. Do you really believe this life on earth is the only life you'll have?"*

"You know what they say. One only goes around once in life, so I grab the bull by the horns and take whatever I can to possess all for myself."

"Besides being greedy and ruthless, you're missing one crucial truth. Who told you that you only go around once in life?"

"I guess the world. Growing up with friends of influence and wealth was our way of thinking and living. So, what's wrong with that?"

"In one word, everything. I know you don't believe anything I say but ponder this. God says in the Bible that we all will live an everlasting life after we die here on earth. The life everlasting God is referring to is that our spirit and soul will be with Him in heaven or Hell with Satan. Everyone has that choice. Your current choice is a slippery slope directly to hell."

"Well, let me ponder on that."

"Well, don't wait too long. Time is of the essence. The rapture is near," Bernard vanishes quickly.

Donna walks out of the room to her office in a huff, ignoring the conversation Hughes had with Bernard. She picks up her phone and dials Oscar, assuming her new role.

"Oscar, this is Donna Trice, a friend of Hughes, and he's assigned me the role of field liaison. We're implementing code H602 immediately. Klaus has been assigned to the printing press exclusively. If it's not too late, pretend to post bail for the arrested couple. Maybe you'll find out if they struck a plea deal."

"Donna, Leah, and I took the initiative and drove to the police station while waiting for Klaus to return my call. According to the desk Sargent, the district attorney interrogated for five hours, and eventually, they took the deal. Instead of twenty years behind bars, they're on supervised assignment for two years, inspecting every funeral home associated with Hughes Enterprises. Nancy has the list of our funeral home network, which put the icing on the cake for them with the plea deal."

"Hughes and I aren't surprised. He figured it would pan out like this. How about the murder charges, was there a plea deal on that?"

"You won't believe how bad the Feds want this couple to crack our organization. The district attorney figured Hudson McDermont had one foot already in the grave, so he gave them an additional two years' probation. The caveat they'd be willing and able to assist the Feds anytime."

"Fortunately for us, Code H602 is impossible to crack," Donna gleans with pride.

CHAPTER SIXTEEN

INSPECTION GALORE-AUG 2035

After their plea deal, Nancy and Brad inspected nineteen funeral homes in the Cleveland area with no luck. During the week, they'd walk in, introduce themselves, produce the search warrant and check every casket on the premise. After three hours of futility, they'd thank the funeral director for his courtesy and call Mitch Kearney to report. It was virtually the same outcome for each funeral home they visited.

Upon completing their twentieth funeral home, Brad calls Mitch, "Like the other nineteen inspections, this funeral home is squeaky clean. The kingpin must have alerted his network."

"Let me speak with Nancy." Brad hands her the phone.

"Nancy here; what's up, Mitch?"

"Are you sure Hughes smuggled the counterfeit money inside secret pockets in the casket's lining?"

"Yeah, I'm sure. I helped myself to one-hundred-grand every ten days when Hughes Enterprises delivered five caskets, a minimum order. It was like clockwork. Now, the only items in the lining are brochures and price lists for cemetery services."

"Put Brad on speakerphone, Nancy. Listen, guys, we're going to do a raid on Hughes Enterprises early tomorrow, at 6 a.m. I'll have my team of six with me, plus you two. You guys drive back tonight. Maybe, we'll be able to snare some damming evidence," Mitch having uncertainty in his tone, though.

The FBI wasn't aware that phase two of H602 was getting ready to be implemented. Hughes has a hunch.

Getting the counterfeit out of the affiliated funeral homes undetected was dicey at first, but Hughes, as a liberal progressive, calls his friend in Long Island from the old neighborhood.

"Carman, how are you doing? It's been far too long since we knocked the ball around on the links. We need to schedule a tee time, and soon!"

"I agree, Hughes. But, what's on your mind besides money?" Carman knew Hughes all too well with his insatiable thirst and addiction for more money.

"My call is about you. I have a plan that could make you a million dollars richer."

Carman replies sarcastically, " I don't need your million. I have billions. So, get to the chase. I'm busy."

"I can't help but notice that you're taking advantage of the political unrest in America by keeping all these crazy, brainwashed college kids busy with riots to destroy and burn down cities. You also pay for their bus tickets; how nice of you," Hughes throws in the snide remark.

"Hopefully, if I live long enough, all the churches, guns and Bibles, and police departments will burn to rubble, and this country will become a solid Socialist nation. But, you're going to help me how?" Carman cuts to the chase.

"You have multiple-activism groups causing turmoil throughout America, and you pay these kids. You and I both know these ideological wonders do this only for fun, caring less about money. After all, their utopia is that the government will take care of them from the cradle to the grave. So, why not pay them half? Half in funny ten-dollar bills. They'll never figure it out."

"If you have an easy, squeak-proof plan, I'm listening."

"Yes, I do. Assign 40 of your top managers to visit my 40 affiliated funeral homes monthly. The director will hand each manager a package containing one million in funny money, all ten-dollar bills that will never be detected as counterfeit. They, in turn, pay our funeral home partner one hundred thousand with the real dough."

"What's in it for me?" Carman is getting interested.

"Well, we'll play golf at your club in Long Island four times a year. I'll have $250,000 for your troubles in real money for you in a golf bag. We simply switch during our round of 18 holes. Yes, or no. Are you interested?" Hughes cuts to the chase this time.

"While we're talking, Hughes, I'm quickly analyzing my potential cost savings. It looks like it will be about seven million with your scheme. I'll have my son contact your manager to iron out the details. Who should they contact?"

"Donna Trice, Director of Operations. I'll text you her private number. When will your son contact her, and what's his name?"

"Connor, and he'll call at 12: 30 p.m. tomorrow. We'll talk later, Hughes." Carman hangs up.

Hughes, not aware of the upcoming raid, maintains his calibrated schedule, arriving at 5 a.m. Thursday morning. He immediately takes the elevator to the underground to chat with Klaus a bit before the day's activities begin.

"Listen, Klaus, I appreciate the extra hours you're putting in. It's not by design that you should work so hard and long. Believe me, if it were possible to hire someone trustworthy to help you, I would do so in a flash," Hughes, slightly feeling guilty.

"Not a problem, Boss. Don't worry about it; I'll be okay. By the way, Gunter contacted me ten days ago, and the pallet should arrive tomorrow. Listen, I'm caught up on printing and maintenance. Would you like me to accompany Lucas on the pickup?"

Abruptly, the red flashing light turns on, indicating the front door has been rammed open, an automatic system Hughes had installed for occurrences like this.

Hughes shouts to Klaus, "We have to assume it's the FBI. Shut everything down here and stay until I state otherwise. You have enough air for six hours with the pump off. So, don't panic!"

Hughes quickly takes the elevator to the sewing room, which is on the street level, and arriving not a minute too soon, is greeted by Mitch Kearney.

"Good Morning. I assume you're Hughes Reyna, proprietor of this factory."

"That would be correct. May I ask why your team had to ram the front door open? A simple knock would have gotten you in faster with less effort."

"Maybe so, but the point is irrelevant. My name is Mitch Kearney, FBI Director, Northern District. I have a warrant to search inside all your caskets. Instruct all your employees to stand back while we inspect. Thank you."

Hughes goes on to the PA system. "Listen, all my loyal employees. Stop working for a while and give the inspection team time and room to do their job. I will alert you when it's okay to resume work. Thank you."

The FBI team members searched for five hours, finding nothing, except Brad found something unique about Hughes's caskets, unlike others he's seen.

"Hey, Mitch, come over here and look at this," Brad showing Mitch how the bed mattress quickly pulls out, revealing four bolts, one on each corner.

Mitch shouts at Hughes, "Come over here and explain this!" Mitch thinks they've got Hughes hand-cuffed already.

"Oh, this, the four-bolt platform bed. I must admit one of my better innovations. As you know, America's population is getting more obese each year. Pending on the deceased's weight and size, the funeral director can adjust the platform bed to three different levels. We also include a blue lining below the bed, at no extra charge, if the family wishes instead of traditional white."

Mitch concedes, "Very well, Hughes. We're leaving; thank you for your time. Your employees may resume work."

"Hey, what about my front door?"

"Deduct the expense on your tax return as damaged goods," Mitch sarcastically replies.

Hughes leaves the street level overhead doors open, making sure Mitch and his team drive off. Once cleared, Hughes turns off the red warning light, and Klaus, gratefully, reactivates all the machinery back on.

Hughes takes the elevator to the underground to check on things.

"Are you okay, Klaus?"

"Yeah, but it looks like I had forty minutes of air left. Can we somehow increase that, Hughes?"

"Not really. Once the printing press was installed here, no one but you and I are allowed underground. But I bet I could fit an air pipe flowing out and up from the underground office, with a damper allowing you to open in case of emergency."

"You mean your office, the gas chamber?"

"Yeah, exactly. But don't worry, I'm the only one that can turn on the gas switch. Besides, with the flute open, one would stay alive. Probably get extremely sick, though." Hughes rattles off like any ordinary business deal.

Meanwhile, Mitch, Brad, and Nancy meet at the corner cafe not far from Hughes Enterprises.

Mitch is madder than a hornet. "I could have sworn I had Hughes hand-cuffed when you found that bottom of the casket, Brad."

"I thought so too," Nancy replies softly.

"They must be bootlegging the counterfeit through the bottom of the caskets, but how and when?" Brad questions out loud.

"More importantly, where are they printing the counterfeit? I didn't see any printing presses there," Nancy mentions.

"It must be somewhere in that plant, but I don't have enough evidence to get a search warrant for a printing press anyway," noted Mitch.

"Okay, guys, cheer up; let's try one more time. I'm sending you both to Pittsburgh. Ten funeral homes there connected with Hughes. I'll get you guys another casket search warrant."

CHAPTER SEVENTEEN

FLIRTY ROMANCE-SEPT 2035

Hughes is living a charmed life. The raid didn't dent his operation, and H602 is working like a fine-tuned orchestra. The brochures and price lists stuffed inside the casket's lining paid off handsomely. Cedar Creek Cemetery continues with twenty graveside services six days a week.

Donna retreats to her funeral home office to catch her breath when her phone rings.

"Hello, Donna Trice speaking."

"Well, I didn't know Hughes gave my dad your direct number. It's a delight not having to go through twelve different robot commands."

"Aah, whom I'm talking to?"

"Oh, sorry about that. Connor Bridgewater here. My dad and Hughes negotiated a deal, and you and I are supposed to work out the knicks. You do know about this, don't you?"

"Yes, I do. I was in a meeting the entire morning and forgot you were calling at this time. Sorry about that."

"Say, I know cell phones are great and secure, but I think it best if we met to discuss the particulars. I'm finishing up a meeting in Buffalo shortly. I could meet you at the Edelweiss Cafe, about 5 miles north of your club, in one hour."

"Yeah, I can do that. How will I recognize you?"

"I'll wait in my sports car, royal blue, and will have the top down. It shouldn't be difficult to find me."

"You have a sports car!" Donna shouts.

"Yeah, I picked it up last week. Listen, I have another meeting to attend after our discussion, but, if you like, sometime soon, I'll give you a ride in the gem."

"Yes! I would love to. I had one six years ago and missed the thrill of shifting through the gears, hearing the purr of the engine and the wind blowing through my hair."

"Great! I'll meet you at the cafe shortly."

Donna quickly spots Connor in the parking lot as she drives in. As she parks next to his sports car, Connor hops out and walks toward her. She can't help but notice his tall stature with wavy blonde hair and blue eyes. She's wondering to herself,' *why isn't he surfing at a California beach instead of being here in Buffalo.'*

As Donna opens her car door and steps out, she looks up at Connor, and their eyes momentarily gaze. "I hope you're Connor; otherwise, I'm looking into the eyes of a strange man."

"You're not so bad yourself, beautiful lady. I love that royal blue business suit you're wearing. It matches my car. Shall we go inside?"

They order some appetizers and soft drinks, and Connor asks the first question. "So, Donna, what are your thoughts on the exchange of monies? Have you given it any considerations?"

"Yes, I have. Are your managers available on Sunday afternoons?"

"Yeah, I suppose they could be, but why Sunday?"

"Funeral homes are closed on Sunday; no employees to snoop or ask questions."

"Of course! I apologize; my head is still at the last meeting. My dad and I are trying to build a hotel on the west coast. But we're getting a lot of resistance on the off-ramp."

"I'm sorry to hear that; I hope everything works out for both of you."

"Thank you. Now, how is this Sunday thing going to work?"

"I believe, reasonably smooth and easy. We have forty affiliate funeral homes. You have ten of your managers visit ten of our different affiliates each Sunday. I'll have a schedule printed for you."

"Sounds easy, just as you told me it would be. Are there any other kinks we need to discuss?"

"Yes, have your managers drive into the funeral home garage at 2 p.m. precisely every Sunday. No exceptions! We'll have ten cases ready with one-hundred thousand in counterfeit each. Your manager needs to bring a bag with a hundred thousand of real money to complete the exchange. The program starts next Sunday. Will your managers be ready?"

"Yes, they will, and it sounds like you've covered every angle. Cheers!" Connor raises his soft drink celebrating the success of their meeting.

"Can I ask you a personal question?" Donna teases.

"When can you drive my sports car?"

"Well, that was going to be my second question. Is that your natural blonde hair, or do you help to get it there?"

"Ha! I've never been asked that before. We have a subsidiary office on the west coast, so I spend the winter months there, virtually being a beach bum surfing most of the day. I guess the sun helps my hair stay blonde."

"I thought so! You lucky dog!"

"Well, how should I say this? If you're not entangled in a hot romance, come join me next winter."

"Funny you say that. I'm not in a hot romance but am spoken for as Hughes's full-time girlfriend. He pays me a million a year to be loyal to him. If I even hinted at loving someone else, heck, he'd kill me on the spot."

"Sounds to me, you're in prison. But you certainly look fabulous this afternoon. If you ever get paroled, let me know."

"I will, and don't forget the ride in your sports car you promised me."

"Whenever the situation arises that won't get you in trouble, we'll put the car through her paces-promise."

Meanwhile, Hughes is sitting at his office desk sipping a glass of cognac when, without warning, Bernard shows up.

"Good afternoon, Mr. Reyna. Bernard here, you know, the Angel of the Lord."

"Am I in trouble?"

"Always and probably again. Let me ask you a question. About six weeks ago, God blessed a woman named Alice with a miracle healing. Rachael and

Darrell visited her at the hospital, anointed her with oil, laid hands on her, and prayed in tongues. She became completely healed in three weeks while everyone else her age was dying. Hughes, if you ever became deadly sick, wouldn't you want a miracle as Alice had?"

"As you were sharing, the thought did cross my mind. But, I'd have to give up my empire and confess my sins, as you say."

"That would be correct, Hughes, and to tell you the truth, probably serve time in prison."

"I know you can't turn me in, Bernard, so, if you don't mind, I'll continue with my ways. But, should I ever get deadly sick, I may reconsider."

"I don't wish ill will on anyone, including you, but it is my hope it won't have to come to you almost dying to accept Jesus."

"I've worked my entire life building this empire. I cannot toss it away that easily to accept Jesus. In a few years, I'll reach my goal of twenty million, then I'll walk away! But, more importantly, is making sure Mayor Brady gets re-elected and on his way to Congress in a few short years."

"You may not believe me, Hughes, but Jesus never forces anyone to do anything against their own will. So, if you and your Communist comrades want to destroy the church and America, Jesus will not stop you. For sure, you do have your priorities upside down, but. I will continue praying for you and hope the Holy Spirit tugs at your heart very soon." Bernard disappears.

CHAPTER EIGHTEEN

LADIES DESIGN-SEPT 2035

Cambria has tremendous success selling pre-orders of the ladies' designer suit, mostly to her colleagues. She sells twelve orders in her first month.

Cambria calls Rachael at the church office, "Rachael! I've sold my twelfth suit this morning! I'm so excited!"

"Congratulations on a job well done. You undoubtedly must love these designer suits."

"I do! Any idea when the Asian company will be shipping these orders? Some of the ladies are getting anxious to wear them and will order one of each color after they receive their first."

"I'll call my contact at the Asian factory and let you know. Let me ask you a question, Cambria. Would you be interested in working with me at my fashion shows one Saturday a month?"

"Would I ever, Rachael." Cambria's youth, energy, and enthusiasm are an absolute sweet joy to Rachael. "Say the word, and I'll be there!"

"I may have a Saturday brunch show coming up. I'm going to make some calls and will keep you informed. Will that work for you?"

"I'm fairly sure Carlo won't mind. Besides, once Richard and Agnes get their home finished, we'd probably be able to stay over and then visit your church on Sunday. A win-win all around."

"You're a smart, lovely young lady, Cambria. I admire your zest, and I'll get back to you soon."

"Thank you," Cambria is smiling as she hangs up.

Rachael's next call is to Hughes at the country club. He answers on the first ring.

"Hi, Rachael. I recognized your number. What's on your mind today?"

"Listen, Hughes. I would like you and Donna to consider sponsoring the Conservatory College of Music with a Saturday brunch while simultaneously helping out Carlo and Cambria."

"Why?" Hughes isn't even vaguely interested at this point.

"Carlo and Cambria, friends of Richard and Agnes. Remember, you met them at my last teaching and fashion seminar. He's the young man that created the ladies' designer suit, and his wife called me this morning sharing she has sold twelve pre-orders in her first month!"

"If I say so myself, that is excellent selling." Hughes, giving a polite, nice talk but still angry that Carlo stole his design. "So, how does this involve Donna or me?"

"I thought you'd never ask. I want to hold a monthly Saturday morning fashion show and brunch at your club. The exposure your club will receive from the community will be endless. Hence, I'd like you to donate the proceeds of the brunch to the Conservatory College of Music."

"I like the idea, but let me ask you a question, Rachael. Why are you so in tuned with this Conservatory College of Music?"

"Rabbi Yosef and I hold an annual music competition for our high school juniors. Eight students play piano concertos from world-renown composers of times past. Four students receive a two-year scholarship, and the other four a summer internship at our Conservatory. You and Donna should attend our next competition in July."

"Sounds like we should and see for ourselves how effective our donations will be for these students.

My last question, Rachael. Will you be preaching?"

"Ouch! Don't you like my preaching? So, you do know, Hughes, the Saturday seminars teach married and engaged couples how to keep the sizzle going throughout their years of marriage."

"Yeah, I remember, okay." Hughes doesn't have any inclination to ever getting married, so he shrugs off the teaching portion as a waste of time.

"To answer your question, I won't be preaching or teaching at the brunch but will give a quick three-minute summary of why attending The Jerusalem Tree Church will greatly benefit couples and families. I'll also provide a brief overview of the devious intent of the D. C. Mandate. Knowledge is power, and the residents of Cedar Creek need to be aware of the far-reaching evil arms of Washington D. C."

"I couldn't agree more, Rachael," Hughes continues to set the trap.

"I'll also have Norman and Natalie provide a benefit statement of the Conservatory and the unique studies it offers."

"When do I get to state my thunder?" Hughes, beginning to feel left out.

"Oh, I'll introduce you immediately before the brunch is served, and by the way, Hughes, I'm looking to break even on the ladies' designer suit campaign. I'm channeling all the proceeds to Carlo and Cambria. After all, it was his idea." Hughes, grinding his teeth, unable to say a word to the contrary.

"That is very noble of you, Rachael. Curious, what avenue will you be selling through?"

"Primarily, online sales with some spot magazine advertising. I'll also cover the cost of advertising the brunch event. I only ask of you that you make the best donation to the college from the proceeds of the brunch."

"Yes, I agree. Donating to the college is a worthy cause. So, when are you looking to schedule the first show?"

"The last Saturday of December, pending your club's schedule for that Saturday morning."

"If it's okay with you, Rachael, I'll have Donna coordinate the actual date. I don't see a problem. I like the idea, and it should be a success for everyone."

"Great! I look forward to speaking with Donna."

Meanwhile, Donna calls Nicolao at the suit store early in the morning before it opens.

"Nicolao, this is Donna Trice. You don't know me, but I'm the new Director of Operations assigned by Mr. Reyna. Klaus is working exclusively in the underground, and I'll be your contact moving forward. We've implemented code H602 yesterday and need to make a few changes at your store."

"Okay, I'm listening."

"In about two weeks, we'll be moving you and Sergio to a new store-front in Manhattan. A larger facility with a climate-controlled basement. It's only about three blocks from the current store. The entrance to the basement will be in one of the fitting rooms with a concealed trap door. Your esteemed client will wait in the fitting room while you retrieve his loaded counterfeit suit from the basement. He changes into his new suit, pays you two-thousand dollars, and gives you the one he wore for his next visit."

"Okay. What about Carlo?"

"He continues doing his job at the old store. At the end of his work shift, he'll leave the completed suits in the back. You pick them up in the morning on your way to the new store and place his pay on top of his next work assignment. During the day, call him to answer any questions, and keep him informed on future projects."

"Question, Donna. Now that Klaus is unavailable, who will come around to collect the real money and replenish the fake?"

"That will be me. I'll be there every Monday afternoon. Now that we have a hidden, concealed basement, you'll be able to stash the real money in the safe, and I'll place the week's counterfeit in there also. With the beauty of the new store, with the safe and the client's suits in the basement, we will be able to make the task of stuffing the pockets a lot easier."

"Got it. I'll share it with Sergio. You want us to start the new store via our current clients, word of mouth?"

"Yes, that's the safest and fastest way to continue our fifty-member client base. Plus, as a grand-opening bonus, for every honest referral they give us, we'll add an extra two-hundred dollars in counterfeit for them."

"Okay! When do we start?"

"Start the referrals now, and open in two weeks."

Nicolao replies, "Got it, and oh, Donna, please tell Hughes we appreciate his confidence in us."

After the call, Donna walks over to Hughes's office.

"Well, that hurdle just got finished. By the way, Nicolao and Sergio appreciate you for the new location. Also, are you aware, Hughes, that you're one lucky man?"

"How's that?"

"As much as I don't like Klaus as you do, he did save your butt yesterday when the Feds raided the factory."

"Really?" Hughes never remembers the small stuff.

"Isn't Klaus the one who talked you into hiring Carlo and farming out the sewing of the secret suit pockets to the storefront?"

"Yes, he did now that you remind me. If it weren't for him, the Feds would have seen dozens of cases with men's suits in them. Don't know if I would have been able to explain that to their satisfaction?"

"As I voiced before, you owe him big time, Hughes. If I recall, he inquired if he could escort Lucas when he picks up the pallets of paper and ink."

"Oh my gosh! I forgot all about that with the commotion yesterday. I suppose Klaus forgot it also. What time is it, Donna?"

"10:30 a.m."

"Good, there's enough time. I'll call Klaus now."

Klaus answers his phone from the underground.

"What's up, Boss?"

"You and I both forgot about the pallets at the shipyards. Can you leave immediately? You should get there before they close at 6:30 p.m."

"Remember, I don't have a CDL. Can you call Lucas in the field and have him meet me at the halfway point?"

"Luckily for us, his route today is along Interstate 390 and 86 east. He should have only four more stops, finishing at about 2 p.m. If you leave now, Klaus, I'll have Lucas meet you at the Valley of the Peace Funeral Home in Binghamton around 3 p.m. Leave your truck there, and on the return trip, follow him back to the factory."

"Sounds like a good plan, Boss. I'm leaving now."

Fortunately for everyone, Klaus and Lucas made it to the Newark shipyard with ten minutes to spare. After getting loaded, Lucas drives off with Klaus riding shotgun. As they cross the state line from New Jersey to New York, Lucas gets stopped by a state trooper.

Lucas rolls down his window as the trooper approaches his truck.

"Is there a problem, officer?"

"I need to see your license and insurance card."

The traffic stop occurred at 8 p.m. so, the trooper used his flashlight and thoroughly examined the cards and picture I.D.

"What type of cargo are you hauling other than caskets?" Hughes Enterprises is advertised on both sides of the truck with a casket picture.

Lucas answers straightforward, not wanting any more questions.

"Two pallets of printing paper and ink for our brochures and other printed material for our funeral homes. Here's the Bill of Lading," Lucas states as he hands them to the trooper.

"Very well," The trooper acknowledges as he hands Lucas back his items. "Best you get the left rear taillight fixed as soon as possible. Do drive carefully for the remainder of your trip." The officer walks back to his squad car and drives off.

Pronto, the Angel of the Lord, Bernard, appears, sitting in between Lucas and Klaus.

"Be not afraid, Lucas. I am the Angel of the Lord, Bernard, and I have come to help you."

Klaus interjects sarcastically, "Don't pay any attention to him. He's a bit radical on situations of life."

Lucas is startled and confused and asks Klaus, "Who is this guy? Do you know him?"

Before Klaus can answer,

Bernard shouts, *"Oh yes, he knows me, alright! He and I have had several discussions, Lucas. But Klaus is stubborn as a mule. I'm here to encourage you, Lucas, to follow Jesus."*

"I've heard of Jesus, but I'm not sure what he's all about. You know life is difficult, especially working ten-hour days. There's not much time for anything else."

"Time. You mortals and your time. I have had and will have endless time. But you two don't have the luxury of time. Every day that passes and you don't

invite Jesus into your heart, you're one step closer to living in eternal hell when you pass from this life on earth."

"Oh, don't listen to him, Lucas. He says a bunch of words that don't mean anything."

"On the contrary, Lucas. My words are the breath of life through Jesus Christ. Those who confess their sins, and invite Jesus into their heart, will have everlasting life, and life here on earth, more abundantly."

"Now that you mention this, Bernard, I remember my German grandmother saying stuff like that when I was a boy. But as the years passed, I never followed up on that stuff. Maybe I should go to church on Sunday and find out more?"

"Excellent decision, Lucas. Do yourself a favor. Drive twenty-seven miles south of the factory and attend the Jerusalem Tree Church in Cedar Creek. There you will get good Biblical teaching. They also have an adult class in between services, which I strongly suggest you attend, on the rapture and end times." Bernard swiftly vanishes.

Klaus is exasperated, hearing all this about Jesus repeatedly, and shouts to Lucas. "You seriously aren't going to church on Sunday, are you?"

"Yup, I am, and also the class on the rapture. You want to come with?"

CHAPTER NINETEEN

THE MEETING–NOV 2035

It's a week before Thanksgiving and, Rachael has her hotel chef prepare a light feast for the next round-table quarterly meeting on Friday, November 16, 2035.

Rachael starts the meeting. "Thank you, everyone, for joining and taking time out of your busy schedules. Before we start with the business on hand, I'd like to introduce some very dear friends who agreed to become members of our inner circle. Please welcome, Richard and Agnes Filburn."

The small group gives them a sweet round of applause.

"Phillip, would you start the meeting with an update?"

"I'd be delighted to, Rachael. As you all may have heard, President Avci hasn't signed the D. C. Mandate yet. Congress seems to be wrangling passing this bill while trying not to lose any seats in the House. So, we have time on our side on how best to wrestle with this evil."

"That's great, Phillip!" Rachael shouts. "Listen, everyone! Let's review the other ideas before making a final decision on the resistance plan as our best option."

"Phillip, any updates on the feasibility of converting the sanctuary into a sports arena?" Darrell inquires.

"We caught the Mayor's office off-guard by initiating the idea first.

Now they're back-peddling and stating they won't shut down our church. However, I don't believe them for one iota! I'll keep pressing the issue."

"Thank you, Phillip," Rachael politely states. "Next up, Dolan, would you give us the report on league sanctions?"

"On the first and last go around, the Commissioner for College Team Affiliations turned our request down. He informed me that since President Avci announced his proposed D. C. Mandate, The Collegiate Sports Association isn't allowing any Christian schools into the league. It's obvious, a cloaked, silent, and deliberate elimination of Christianity. We need to take a stand and come up with another idea, I believe."

"Why don't we start a Christian Collegiate Sports Association?" Irving volunteers the question.

"Two reasons why not," exclaims Terri. "First, the undertaking would cost millions for starters. Secondly, we'd need the commitment of hundreds of Christian schools to be effective as a league. This endeavor could take several years, and my prayer is that the rapture would occur first."

Richard stands up and requests to speak.

"Of course, you're more than welcome to share with the group any ideas. With your background as a sheriff, you may be able to shed some light on this dilemma," Rachael hopes.

"While Dolan was speaking, Cambria was whispering in my ear on her thoughts. Before she shares them, I may have discovered a loophole in the D. C. Mandate. Phillip, as an attorney, you correct me if I'm wrong. The Mandate states in particular, 'No Public display of religious activity shall be allowed.' What if we kept the sanctuary, but with No Public display of a church service?"

Helen quips, "How would that work?"

"I'll let Cambria explain. Go ahead; it's your idea," Richard states.

"Thank you, Richard. This plan may have two elements to be successful. Instead of renting hotel rooms for church service via video, why not offer headsets to everyone as they walk in. They select a pew in the sanctuary and listen to church service via headphones."

"It would save millions in not having to renovate to a sports arena," shouts Carlo.

"That is true," shouts Irving. "But what if people are seen praying? Wouldn't that be considered public display?"

"Technically speaking, yes, they could nail us on that one. But, would the politicians actually do that?" Phillip throws out the question.

Natalie tosses an idea with a question. "When the Mandate passes, will the Feds allow shuttered churches to have charity drives? If so, why not offer Bingo games? Parishioners can choose a headset and listen to church service while playing bingo. If they're praying, no one will notice, but only the constant noise of the bingo games. It would be the perfect ruse."

Helen shouts, "You may have something there, young girl. Praise the Lord! This plan would meet the criteria of no public display of religious activity."

"This plan would also save millions from the original sports arena idea," states Terri.

Bernard promptly appears.

"I sort of like this idea, gang. My concern. Wasn't this place a casino when it first opened? Now, you may, inadvertently, be inviting elements of sin to take up residence in the holy of holies, the church? If you implement this plan, be incredibly careful to use it as a charity. Don't let anyone misappropriate funds for their own pocket."

Rachael assumes responsibility, "Forgive me, Bernard. I'm somewhat troubled these days, thinking of ways to continue with church service. My heart and soul are in this place, and I don't want to lose it without a fight. The Filburn's, Darrell, and I met with Hughes in April, and he gave us a plan on how to resist the upcoming D. C. Mandate. I wanted everyone to hear all the ideas before we agreed on the resistance plan."

"You don't know, but I was there in that meeting. I stayed invisible for its entirety to not affect the outcome either way. As you know, you'll be fighting the spiritual forces of evil in the heavenly realms when this takes place, aren't you? The armies of the Lord will fight on your behalf, but you need to cover yourselves with prayer and fasting so as not to make yourselves vulnerable to the attacks of the devil."

"Yes, I'm fully aware, and so is my inner circle group. I've also shared with the congregation, asking for their support. I'm praying for at least an 80% show of support when the day of resistance arrives. I must admit, resistance is not for the weak of heart."

"The church is in a war for survival, and it's outnumbered by the strongarm of Washington D. C. Once the church falls, they'll come after your Bibles. I suggest you have a practice run unannounced. Hire plainclothes men, not the police, storm the church and arrest some of the congregation and the church leaders in handcuffs. After several minutes, declare it was practice. Prayerfully, the result of this practice will make everyone tougher for the actual day of resistance."

"Wow, Bernard!" Darrell shouts. "That is a tall order. I believe Rachael and I will need to outline the necessary steps needed by everyone for our resistance to be successful."

"You're right, Darrell. I'll share with the congregation a preliminary outline before each sermon, and you can do the same at the Wednesday night Bible study," Rachael states calmly.

"I'll be the first volunteer to get arrested!" shouts Irving.

"You're not going without me, dear. I'll be the second," declares Helen.

The Holy Spirit was touching the hearts of everyone in the meeting. They all volunteered to be in the first group to get arrested. Prayerfully, a show of solidarity for the congregation.

"Praise the Lord! Looks like you all have a handle on the situation. Glory be to God in the highest heavens." Bernard vanishes.

CHAPTER TWENTY

BOGUS PITTSBURGH-NOV 2035

Brad and Nancy arrive at the first funeral home in Pittsburgh to inspect. As they get out of their car, Brad shares, "I hope Mitch is right about this operation. It gets boring and disappointing to come up empty-handed every time."

"Yeah, I know what you mean. So, who do we see here at Bethlehem Funeral Home?"

Brad answers, "I believe it's Katy Dodds, the funeral home director of this establishment."

"How interesting, and it's about time," Nancy states, "I've read the national statistics showing that more women are getting into the funeral industry."

"Sure, I agree, it's about time, but, well, let's go inside and talk with Ms. Dodds and see if we can snag some evidence of counterfeit money," Brad articulates. But deep in his heart, he hopes no arrests will be made.

As Brad and Nancy walk inside, their breath was taken aback by this larger-than-life Nativity Scene taking up half of the lobby space. Katy heard the door chimes and steps out front to greet them.

"Good afternoon, folks, welcome, and how can I be of assistance today?"

"I can't believe my eyes on how magnificent your nativity scene is. I bet you receive many compliments," Nancy speaks with sincere joy.

"Yes, my late husband built that several years ago. It's our namesake, Bethlehem, the birthplace of Jesus, and our funeral home."

"I'm sorry to hear about your husband, and he indeed created a masterpiece," Brad wanting to console Katy.

"Thank you. But something tells me you two aren't here to discuss funerals."

Nancy leans forward toward Katy and hands her both credentials for her and Brad. "We're from the FBI and do apologize for giving you this search warrant, but it's our job."

"Oh, my goodness," Katy's breath gets short. "I have to sit down, excuse me."

Brad asks, "Can I get you some water?"

"Small frig in my office, down the hall, you can't miss it. Thank you."

Brad returns with a water bottle, and Katy takes a sip, catches her breath, and shares. "I've never been cited before, not even a speeding ticket in my entire life, and now, at my age, to have the FBI walk in with a search warrant, it took my breath away, unbelievable and shocking!"

"I can assure you that Brad and I will not do anything to harm the integrity of your funeral home. Should there be any questionable circumstances found, we'll address them with you first," Nancy shares delicately to Katy.

Katy replies, "What are you talking about, questionable circumstances?"

Brad replies, "The search warrant dictates us to inspect every casket you have on the premise, including storerooms, chapels, garage, and any place else you may have them."

"Sure, go ahead; I don't have anything to hide. I run a clean, Christian business, with the Lord, Jesus, as my partner. Please don't damage any of the caskets. I carry an upscale line that retail from three to seven thousand."

Nancy inquires, "You don't buy from Hughes Enterprises?"

"No, I haven't since he moved his factory to Buffalo from Newark. Delivery costs were getting out of hand. So, I switched to a local vendor that handcrafts them. My funeral home doesn't thrive on volume, but quality with a decent profit margin."

Brad inquires, "Besides yourself, does anyone else help you in the funeral home?"

Katy gleefully answers, "Yes, my part-time mom who works in the mornings answering the phones and keeping the place clean. My son is the mortician doing all the embalming. I wasn't about to learn that task after my husband passed."

"If I may suggest, Katy. Let's do this," Brad's sympathy cord is working overtime at this point. "Walk us over to one of your caskets and give us a demonstration of the benefits of buying yours. If Nancy or I have any questions, we'll stop you. Fair enough?"

"Sure. Would you prefer the casket supply room or the chapel?"

Nancy quickly answers, "The supply room will be great!" Since attending the wake of her mother, the combination of chapel and casket gives Nancy the chills.

While walking over to the supply room, Bernard walks alongside Nancy.

"So, why are you so afraid of chapels? You know one day; you'll be here also."

"Oh! It's you again! You like being a pest, don't you?"

"On the contrary. I am here to help you, so when that day arrives, and you've been put to rest, your soul will be with Jesus in heaven."

"I appreciate your concern, Bernard, but I must get back to work. Maybe I'll go to church someday. Would you like that?" Nancy blares out simply to get rid of Bernard.

"That could be a good start," Bernard quickly disappears.

Once all three enter the supply room, Katy explains all the benefits of a handcrafted wood casket versus a factory metal one. Upon completing her demo, Brad asks, "Are you able to lift out the bed mattress from its underneath platform?"

"Sure, but there's no reason for anyone to do that. Why you ask?"

"You don't have three levels of support for the obese deceased?"

"No, there's no reason to. No one is too large at death not to fit in a casket."

"How many inches from the ground to the bed are your caskets, Katy?"

"I don't know. I have never been asked. Let me grab a tape measure from the desk here. Looks like about ten inches; why you ask?"

Nancy looks at Brad, then looks at Katy, wondering if she should disclose their inquiry element.

Nancy starts slowly, "Katy, the caskets from Hughes are four inches higher from the bottom with a platform metal plate under the bed mattress with three levels to accommodate any size person."

"There's no reasonable explanation for his caskets to be taller unless he's doing a two-for-one funeral," Katy states.

Nancy looks like she's going to puke, "You mean having a deceased body under the bed mattress as well as a deceased on top? How awful to even think about something like that!"

"Well, believe it or not, burying two people in the same casket isn't illegal. I wouldn't recommend it, but if the family wishes prefer that type of arrangement, I suppose I'd oblige."

Brad glances at Nancy momentarily and then remarks, "I suppose we're done here for today, Katy. Nancy and I need to make our final report to our supervisor later today. Can we call on you if we have any more questions or if we need your help?"

"Sure. As I declared, I have nothing to hide. But you never did tell me what exactly you were looking for, did you?"

Nancy replies, "No, we didn't. We're not at liberty to disclose. Thank you for your time, Katy, and we'll be in touch as the need arises."

After they left, Katy walks to her office, crying, and calls her mom. "You'll never believe what happened to me today. I got served with an FBI search warrant."

"What did they want?"

"I don't know—something about the various sizes of caskets."

"Well, let me pray for you now, dear. Lord Jesus, I ask you'd comfort my daughter during this trial of unanswered burdens. Give her the strength to overcome and let her know that you are with her always, Amen."

"Thank you, mom, and I'll ask Jacob to pray with me also when he gets home from church."

"Does he have any embalming to complete this evening?"

"No, I don't think so, which will give him time to prepare for his message this Sunday."

Katy's son, Jacob, is the pastor at Bethlehem Community Church next door to their funeral home. Jacob, never being married, wholly dedicated to serving the work of the Lord, shares his mom's house directly behind the funeral home.

Meanwhile, Brad and Nancy are sitting in the car, contemplating how to prepare their report for Mitch.

"He's not going to be happy with us," Nancy mutters.

"I'm going to take him up on his suggestion and wear a wire moving forward. At least he'd hear what occurred."

"Brad, when we drove up, I was so focused on our assignment, I overlooked the church next door to the funeral home with the same name, Bethlehem. You suppose that's a coincidence?"

"Well, maybe her late husband was the pastor. I wonder who is now?"

Nancy quickly calculates, "Today is Wednesday, and there are nine more funeral homes to investigate. I think we could be finished late Saturday. Brad, assuming it's part of our assignment, shall we attend Sunday morning church service to find out who the pastor is?" Nancy makes an excuse not wanting to admit anything about her conversation with Bernard.

"As long as you don't get religious on me, I will attend with you," Brad concedes.

CHAPTER TWENTY-ONE

KATY & JACOB-NOV 2035

Sunday morning rolls around. Nancy and Brad didn't back out. They actually attended Bethlehem Church. As she promised, Nancy didn't get religious, but she asked Brad after the service, "What the heck was Pastor Dodd talking about? Some D. C. Mandate?"

"Yeah, from what I gather, the government is proposing to shut down all churches, confiscate all guns and Bibles, and shutter all police departments."

"I don't understand," replies Nancy. "Aren't churches just a place for social gatherings? Why shut them down? Seems unnecessary. They don't cause any harm."

As the pastor was leaving the pulpit area, he approaches them. "I couldn't help but overhear your conversation. Do you mind if I answer your question?"

Nancy replies, "No, not at all, go ahead."

"You're right. The church is a social gathering, but not primarily for fun and amusement, as you alluded to a moment ago. But, it is a coming together for believers to strengthen their faith corporately. It is a unison of voices praising and praying to our Lord, Jesus Christ. Yes, the church will, on occasion, have a potluck. Plus, all kinds of games for the kids, but always with Jesus as the focal point."

"That is a fantastic explanation, Pastor!" Brad lightly shouts.

"So, I'm still confused," Musses Nancy. "What does this D. C. Mandate have anything to do with the church?"

"Well, since 2029, when Congress revamped the election laws and shredded the constitution, the United States has become a Communist Party of one. There is virtually no opposition," shares Jacob.

"So, if there's no opposition, why have this D. C. Mandate?" Nancy asks.

"A true Communist government cannot allow any other god to be worshiped but them. Hence, the shuttering of churches and police departments. More importantly, the confiscation of guns and Bibles becomes a necessity for them to grab sheer control and power," Pastor Jacob explains as best he can.

"Do you have any plans for yourself and the church, Pastor, if this mandate becomes law?" Brad inquires.

"Strength is in numbers. So, we'll join forces with the mega-churches in the area and become part of the resistance movement."

"What's that?" Nancy asks.

"We're hoping to fill every mega-church with at least 10,000 people every Sunday, trusting the government won't arrest all of us. But, if they do, we'll stay in jail as long as it takes to keep the doors open of every church."

"Wow! That's commitment!" Nancy shouts.

Katy Dodds, Jacob's mom, interrupts their talk. "Son, looks like you've met our visitors already. Remember, I shared with you the couple with the FBI giving me a search warrant. This is them!"

"Yes, yes, I do. After you two left, I understand you made my mom cry," Jacob glances over at his mom standing next to him. "She's never received as much as a speeding ticket in her entire life, and for her to experience the trauma of a warrant, well, it was more than she could handle."

Nancy speaks first, "We're so profoundly sorry, pastor. We had no intention of causing your mom any harm."

Brad speaks next, "As we explained to your mom, Nancy and I were only doing our job as instructed."

"I know you guys were doing your job," Pastor Dodd states jokingly.

"Just having a little fun. My mom is okay, and she shared with me this morning before church that if you guys came back and needed us to help you in any capacity, we'd be willing to do that."

Brad looks at Nancy, and she glances at him. Brad explains the looks, "It must be because we're in church this morning. Your timing is incredible. As you informed the congregation this morning in your message, pastor, nothing is impossible with God. Nancy and I received a wire last night from our boss. In their clandestine, mysterious methods, the Feds received a solid tip that Hughes Enterprises is seeking a new funeral home in the Pittsburgh area to be an affiliate in his counterfeit ring."

Katy shudders, "So that's what your search warrant was all about. But, if I correctly hear what you're alluding to, there's no way I would agree to be part of any counterfeit crime syndicate."

"The FBI would give you protection," Nancy tries to give her reassurance.

"Mom, circulating counterfeit money is like bad cancer that continuously causes pain until eradicated. It's our obligation to society and God to stop this evil."

"I suppose you're right, son, but it is scary, at least for me."

"Brad, Nancy, how would this sting be implemented, and tell me the truth, how dangerous?" asks Jacob.

"Well, bad news first. If you were to be found out, somebody could kill you, or would you prefer I lie and tell you everything will be peachy keen?"

"I wasn't sure if you'd tell the truth, Brad, or sugarcoat it. How can you assure my son and I will be protected?"

Nancy jumps in, "I'll ask our FBI Director, Northern District, Mitch Kearney, to give you a call and explain our security plans."

Mitch does call the next day, and after assuring Katy and Jacob, they would be safe in accepting a role in Hughes' counterfeit operation, they agreed to the plan.

However, Hughes always has a potential affiliate partner checked out in person before becoming official. He had Donna call over to the Bethlehem Funeral Home last week to set up the Tuesday interview. All was well until Oscar showed up mid-morning. Nancy was in the front foyer waiting to greet whoever Hughes Enterprises sent. Brad was on alert off to the side unseen, and the two agents were ready, one at each side of the foyer.

As soon as Oscar opened the door and walked in, he sees Nancy and yells, " It's you! It's a trap!" Oscar pulls out his gun from his suit jacket and fires. He misses Nancy, she ducks behind the desk while Oscar fires another shot, but wide left, hitting baby Jesus in the Nativity Set. The first agent quickly fires from the right side of Nancy's desk and shoots Oscar dead.

Hearing gunshots, Katy and Jacob came running from their home, and out of breath, yelling, "What happened?"

Jacob, Katy, Brad, Nancy, and the two agents are huddled around the dead body for a quiet moment when Brad looked up at Nancy and asked, "So, Nancy, you want to tell them, or should I?"

"No, I will. It's okay. I was hoping our friendship would never come to this, Katy and Jacob. Allow me to explain. I used to be the receptionist at a funeral home in Boston. They were part of Hughes Enterprises' counterfeit ring. The director was slowly dying of cancer, so whenever he received a casket with one-hundred-thousand hidden inside, I would simply steal the fake money."

Jacob inquires, "So, how does your theft tie in with this dead man?"

"Hughes sent in his strongarm, Oscar, to investigate why the funeral home was two months behind on casket orders and counterfeit circulation. We met when he walked in, asking to speak to the director. I left the next day with all the fake money and wrote a note stating they'd never find me."

Katy screeches, "And you're an FBI agent? How can this be?"

Brad interjects, "I'm Nancy's boyfriend and part of the big scheme we had in mind but got caught. So, instead of twenty years behind bars, Nancy and I took the plea agreement. We're now working for the FBI on a two-year stint, or more if they deem necessary."

Jacob's reply stunned his mom. "This all makes sense, and I forgive both of you. However, you may want to ask God and His son, Jesus, forgiveness also."

"How can you be so giddy about all this, Jacob? They're criminals, just like the guy that got shot."

"Mom, where is your forgiveness? Ever since Dad died, you've become somewhat bitter. I think it's time for a change. Brad and Nancy, please accept my apologies for my mom's behavior."

"No apology necessary," Nancy states softly. "What occurred this morning can be extremely upsetting to anyone. I need to call the police, and Brad, will you contact Mitch?"

"Sure, will do."

Brad calls Mitch and explains everything in full detail. "I believe Nancy and I can continue with this sting operation. No one at Hughes Enterprises knows that Oscar recognized Nancy. We should be okay to continue, right?" Brad suspects he knows the answer.

"Mr. Reyna is no dummy. He'll realize that his man recognized who he was scheduled to meet and had to take her out. It's too dangerous for us to continue."

"Okay. But, regarding our dead friend here, should I follow standard protocol and have him moved to the county morgue after the police complete their investigation?"

"Yes, and I'll have the police Sargent call at Hughes Enterprises and explain the details on where they can pick up the body."

"Thanks a lot, Mitch." Brad knew he had his work cut out for him and whispered a small prayer as he walked over to approach everyone with the news.

Meanwhile, Donna receives a call, and not knowing the number, she just answers, "Hello."

"Ms. Trice, this is police Sargent Fred. I'm calling from the Pittsburgh Police Department. We found some identification in a man's suit pocket. An Oscar Kleen, and it states, call Donna Trice in case of emergency. That's all the information we have. Do you know this person?"

"Oh, my goodness! He's my vagabond half-brother. I haven't heard from or seen him in years. Is he okay?"

Unfortunately, it seems he got killed in a shootout at the Bethlehem Funeral Home. From our investigation, for no apparent reason, as he walked in, he fired two shots before being hit. You can recover his body at the county morgue. I'm so sorry for your loss, and my condolences."

"Thank you for the call, Sargent. I'll handle it from here," Donna states through fake tears.

Donna, now with no emotion or empathy, walks over to Hughes, sitting at his desk. "Just received a call from the Pittsburgh police. Oscar is dead. He fired two shots before being hit. We can pick up his body at the morgue."

Hughes contemplates a moment before saying anything. "We could sue the department inquiring who shot him, but that process would reveal our enterprise. Oscar recognized who it was when he entered the funeral home and knew they had to be taken out. Do you have the contact's name at the funeral home, Donna?"

"Yes. A Nancy Bouvier. One of the new owners, along with a guy named Brad McDermont."

"Undoubtedly, the entire meeting was a setup, probably by the FBI. I wouldn't be surprised if that Mitch guy were behind this. You do know their next step, Donna, don't you?"

"Witness protection?"

"Right! Only God in Heaven knows where Mitch is sending them. I'm guessing Leah would like revenge for them killing her husband. Donna, will you work with her on your computer, gleaning all the information she'll need to track them? If required, you can hire a private detective to help her in this quest. Of course, once found, all of them will become residents of our John Doe cemetery."

Hughes, once again, narrowly misses getting caught.

Meanwhile, Brad lets everyone know that Mitch decided not to place them in a witness protection program but secretly puts them up at Rachael's hotel indefinitely. However, for their protection, the FBI bought their property to resell to new owners later.

CHAPTER TWENTY-TWO

MORNING BRUNCH-DEC 2035

The last Saturday of the month, December 29, 2035, two days before New Year's Eve. The clubhouse restaurant is packed with over three hundred and fifty guests. Richard and Agnes, who received free tickets, sit in the back row, allowing others to sit up front where all the action takes place. The charity fashion show became a highly coveted drawcard in its first debut, despite Hughes charging two-hundred dollars per ticket. Hughes allocated fifty-six thousand dollars to the Conservatory College of Music from the benevolence of his heart.

As the guests are filling their plates at the buffet line, Hughes approaches the podium.

"Thank you, everyone, for attending our first Saturday brunch fashion show. At this time, I won't bore you with all the services Cedar Creek Country Club has to offer. But I will encourage you to speak with our friendly staff at the pro shop afterward. Now, I'd like to introduce Dalton and Natalie Kogan, professors at the Conservatory, and chairpersons for this event."

Natalie speaks first, "Thank you, Mr. Reyna, for sponsoring this fabulous event and charity drive. I've been told by a little birdie that you, Mr. Reyna, and your co-partner, Ms. Donna Trice, have pledged fifty-six thousand dollars to the College of Music, providing four-two-year scholarships. Please, Hughes and Donna, stand up so we all can show our appreciation."

The crowd politely gives them a nice round of applause while they continue enjoying their brunch as Dalton begins to speak.

"Good morning. I'll keep this brief." The audience humors him by giving faint applause.

"Thank you," Dalton acknowledges. "I'm going to assume that most of you aren't aware that the Conservatory has two schools. The College of Music and the College of Hebrew Arts and History, of which my wife and I are professors. I do see a few of my Jewish friends in the crowd. Thank you for attending this event, and I'll be sure to meet with you afterward. I want to mention the next person I'd like to introduce is a man with a gentle spirit but has a giant heart for music."

Tom Gerrard wears two hats-as the worship leader at the Jerusalem Tree Church and as a professor at the College of Music.

"Tom, please stand up so we all can see you," Dalton graciously introduces Tom.

Tom stands, takes a small bow while the crowd politely gives him a round of applause.

"If any of you in attendance this morning has a son or daughter in high school who loves playing music, be sure to speak with Tom after the show. Now is the perfect time to get your child started in the enrollment process. Okay! Enough of the school talk! Without further ado, I'd like to bring up to the mic, pastor of the Jerusalem Tree Church, and host for this fashion show, Rachael Zellner!"

She receives a sounding applause of appreciation from the crowd.

"Thank you. Thank you, and good morning everyone, and welcome! Did you all enjoy the tasty brunch served up by the finest chef in the area, Chef Reynolds?" The crowd applauds, showing their appreciation.

"I do have one quick announcement to make; we'll show the ladies' designer suit last. I have a surprise for you, ladies, so bear with me. But now, let's give the show model couples a big Cedar Creek round of applause as they showcase the wedding gowns and tuxedo line."

The crowd stands to their feet, cheering and applauding as the lovely ladies and their handsome husbands showcase the wedding lineup.

Rachael begins to speak, "While our lovely couples change into their next attire, I'd like to plug our monthly Saturday afternoon seminars. These Biblical teaching seminars are reserved for married and engaged couples only. The title is '*How to keep the zest in your marriage forever.*' You can register online or call the church office. Also, as always at our seminars, every item you see today is twenty percent off retail. Okay, folks! So, after the wedding is the honeymoon! Please, show your appreciation as our modeling couples showcase our sexy but modest lingerie line, keeping the zest in your marriage forever!"

The crowd goes hysterical, cheering, applauding, whistling, as the couples strut the sexy attire.

"That was exciting, wasn't it?" Rachael gets the crowd to agree by receiving applause and cheers. "Now, for our finale. As I mentioned earlier, I have a surprise for all of you ladies out there. We're introducing two new colors today for the summer and winter editions of our ladies' designer suit. Lilac and purple!"

The audience applauds as Cambria showcases the purple suit escorted by her husband, Carlo, wearing a purple sports jacket with matching slacks but no tie. As she's walking down the aisle showing the secret inside pockets, a man in the audience yells, "I've seen that suit before, but a man wearing it in black. He was walking in downtown Manhattan. How can I get one?"

Carlo glances at his wife, Richard whispers to his wife, and Donna whispers to Hughes, "This is not good. You better say something."

Hughes stands up, sitting not far from Rachael, and begins to speak.

"I'll confer with Rachael and her expertise in fashion design. Hopefully, she'll be able to inquire with the Asian garment factory on the feasibility of creating a man's designer suit. For all those who are interested, please give us your contact information before leaving. Rachael, did I cover everything? Do you have anything to add?" Hughes amazingly squirms out of another potential mess.

"You pretty much covered all the basis, Hughes. I do have a few questions for the men, though. What colors would you like, and what price point do you have in mind? Jot those down along with your contact information; thank you." Rachael walks over to Cambria and Carlo and notices that Richard and Agnes are already conversing with them.

The crowd, lingering after the fashion show, continues small chatter with the modeling couples. While others are placing orders with Rachel's staff, and not surprisingly, several men are giving their info.

As Rachael gets close to Richard, he slightly pulls her by the arm, drawing her closer to the group and speaking in hushed tones. "You know, of course, Rachael, that. Carlo customizes those men designer suits in Manhattan, but he has no idea who he works for."

"What? That sounds crazy. You're kidding me, right?"

Carlo shares, "I'm like locked up in a room sewing these secret pockets into the men's designer suit. When I complete one, I knock on the inside locked door, hand one of the guys the completed suit, and he gives me one-hundred- and twenty-dollars cash."

"Carlo, if you don't know who the owner is, how did you get the job?" Rachael inquires.

"When I arrived in New York a year ago from Italy, I stayed with my uncle and aunt. My uncle gave me some odd jobs to hold me over until I secured a full-time position. Incidentally, my aunt introduced me to Cambria one Sunday after church service. That was ten months ago. Anyway, I posted some seeking work signs in the Manhattan financial district. That's when Sergio and Nicolao contacted me. The rest is history."

Rachael shook her head, states, "That is really strange. I'd be careful if I were you, Carlo."

Richard jumps in, "My exact words, Rachael. I've been there, where he works. It's like Fort Knox. Steel doors front and back. A non-effective business sign. About three clients daily. It seems they call ahead of time, approach the steel door, and seconds later, they're let in. But leave wearing the men's designer suit about twenty minutes later. It's the strangest business arrangement I've ever seen."

"Richard, as a retired sheriff, do you suspect anything?" Darrell inquires.

He was about to answer when Hughes and Donna approach the group.

Donna waxes politely, "Rachael, that was the most fabulous fashion show I've ever attended. You and your staff did an excellent job on that.

I look forward to the next month's show. Maybe you'll have the men's designer suit available by then?" Donna is interrogating secretly.

"We were just talking about that," Rachael remarks. "Did you know that Carlo works in the Manhattan financial district customizing men's designer suits like the guy in the crowd claims he saw?"

"You don't say!" Donna feigns surprise. "So, what company do you work for, Carlo?" Donna is interrogating again.

"I have no idea. When I finish a suit, I knock on the locked steel door, hand one of the guys working upfront the suit, and he gives me one-hundred- and twenty-dollars cash. That's all I know."

Hughes inquires, "So, you happy working there even though it sounds a little weird?"

Carlo shrugs his shoulders, "Yeah, I guess so. It's so quiet in there. I brought my radio in for some music."

"You certainly get paid funny-all cash. Who does that these days?" Hughes is interrogating now.

Richard pipes up, "Carlo isn't a citizen yet but wants to pay his taxes. He's grateful for having a job in America. So, his uncle pays his share of the taxes."

Hughes loudly proclaims so everyone can hear, "That is mighty patriotic of you, Carlo. I'm proud of you for doing the right thing."

Cambria had left the group a few minutes earlier to check in with the staff on the orders and happily returns to the group as a kid in a candy shop.

"Rachael, you'll never guess how many orders we received and the money we took in?" Cambria is all excited, waiting anxiously to share the news.

"I could guess. Let's see about thirty pre-orders for the lady's designer suit, about ten wedding gowns and tux, about fifty lingerie wear, and ten orders for the men's designer suit."

Cambria replies with all smiles, "If you double that, you'd be closer. Look! I can fit all the orders and cash in these hidden secret pockets in my suit," She opens her suit jacket revealing all the goodies. "But when I zip these pockets shut, no one, I mean no one, can see what I have. Pretty neat, huh?"

Everyone glances around, momentarily blind-sided by Cambria's remarks. Rachael breaks the ice, "Of course! That's what the pockets are supposed to do-hide everything a woman would carry in her purse. If our businesswoman wanted extra protection, she could carry her purse as a decoy. No one would be the wiser."

CHAPTER TWENTY-THREE

THE HUDDLE-DEC 2035

The group of six huddles around Richard's car in the parking lot after leaving the clubhouse, and Richard shares his idea on what occurred at the fashion show.

"Listen, this must be kept confidential, but it's my hunch that these men's designer suits are smuggling some type of contraband from their Manhattan store."

Darrell asks, "If you were still working as a sheriff, what's your professional guess?"

"Anything small and lightweight."

"Drugs are the only thing I can come up with," Carlo states, frustrated.

Cambria still has the orders and monies in her suit jacket and shouts out, "How about money?"

Agnes, not wholly into detective games, innocently states, "There's no profit in smuggling money. Money is just money."

Darrell shouts, "Bingo! Unless it's counterfeit!"

Richard joins the discovery, "Yes, of course, counterfeit! Small and lightweight like the two fake ten-dollar bills we received as change at the club three months ago, which Hughes, immediately, shut down."

"Surely, it's not being printed at the Manhattan store or at the country club. But where?" Rachael states out loud.

"If I were still sheriff, I'd have one of my deputies stake out the store for a couple of weeks."

"I know just the persons," Rachael confidently states. "Irving Duiker and his wife, Helen! They're managers at the George Kogan Rehab Center. I'll ask George Kogan, the director of the center, if I can borrow them, with pay for one week."

*****

Meanwhile, Hughes and Donna huddle at his country club office. Once inside, Donna brings out treats, wine, cheese, and crackers, knowing it will be a long session.

Hughes starts the meeting, "Obviously, from what occurred at the end of the fashion show this morning, we need to make some significant changes. Do you agree?"

"I agree, and the first change is my assigned task of driving to Manhattan weekly to deliver the goods and return the other merchandise. We can't afford me being seen anywhere near there."

"I agree. How about this idea? Why not have Leah be the weekly Sunday messenger for the Manhattan store? "

Donna shoots back, "That should work and will allow her to continue searching for her husband's killer."

"Once found, he'll be paying a visit to our cemetery," Hughes smirks.

"Hughes! Bernard shouts. *"There you go again, thinking of ways to snuff anyone out who gets in your way. From what I've seen in the past, only Washington D. C. politicians do that, but you're catching up with them quickly."*

Donna yells at Bernard, "Get out of our office, now!"

"My, my. Such hostility, such anger. If you had Jesus in your heart and life, you'd be calmer and enjoy life a lot more."

Hughes interjects, "Thanks, Bernard, for your pearls of wisdom, but Donna and I enjoy life to the fullest. Heck, with over $33,000 coming in daily, who wouldn't?"

"If you two keep believing Satan's lie that money is the answer to everything in life, well, you haven't seen anything yet. Remember, Jesus Christ is the answer to everything, not money." Bernard disappears.

✶✶✶✶✶

Meanwhile, Sergio takes off an extra hour during lunch to find the perfect gift for his girlfriend. He hasn't told Nicolao yet that he's been dating Lucinda for two months for fear of losing his job or, worst, losing his life. Sergio takes a cab four blocks down to the shopping district, paying the cab driver with a phony ten-dollar bill by mistake.

Once inside the department store, Sergio walks toward the cosmetic counter and is greeted by Cambria.

Cambria cheerfully greets him, "How can I help you today? I'm guessing you're looking for a gift for that someone special?"

"Yes, we've been dating for two months, and I want to give her something, well, nice. Any suggestions?"

"Well, we have perfume in several different fragrances. Do you know what your girlfriend's favorite scent is?"

"Is cherry blossom or lilac a scent?"

"Let me suggest this, so you don't get in trouble with her. How about this gift box of two perfumes? If she doesn't like it, return them, and let her pick out a favorite."

"Okay, I guess. So, how much?" Sergio is getting too embarrassed and shy.

"Only eighty dollars plus tax, and I'll gift wrap at no extra charge."

"That's great! Thank you."

Cambria comes back with the completed gift wrap and states, "That'll be ninety-two dollars, Cash or charge, sir?"

Sergio, nervous to the nth degree, isn't thinking straight and reaches in his pocket and pulls out ten phony-ten-dollar bills. "Huh, I have just enough," he hands her the hundred dollars.

As Cambria hands him the change, she jokes, "Well, it looks like you have enough left to buy a hot dog at the wagon pavilion."

"Yeah, I do, thanks." Sergio briskly walks back the four blocks to the suit store, hoping to walk off some of his nervous energy.

As he enters the old store, Nicolao states, "You took longer than expected. You do know that we have a ton of stuff to do getting ready for our move next week?"

"Yeah, sorry about that. My shopping trip took longer than I wanted."

"Hey! What's that in your hands? A gift? All wrapped? Do you have a girlfriend, Sergio?"

"Please, don't say anything to Mr. Reyna or Ms. Trice; I don't want to get into any trouble," Sergio almost begging.

Nicolao goes along slightly. "Okay, but if you make any stupid mistakes, you're on your own. I'm not losing my life due to any of your blunders like the last time. When you gave Carlo the green light to take a suit home, that was a dumb move. I doubt Mr. Reyna would give you a pass next time. You best be extra careful."

Taken aback, Sergio realizes he had eleven of the phony ten-dollar bills in his pocket from this morning's stuffing of suits. When fake bills look terrible, they pull them from the main stash and return them to the corporate office. Sergio accidentally placed them in his pants pocket, intending to toss them in the return box later in the day.

Sergio is thinking, *'oh my Lord, have mercy on me, help me.'*

Unaware, Bernard appears, *"I have come to help you, Sergio."*

"Who are you, and how did you get here?"

"Didn't you just ask the Lord to help you? I am the Angel of the Lord, Bernard, and I am here to help you. Let me ask you a question, do you know Jesus Christ as your personal savior?"

"Who?"

"Oh boy, this will be another long explanation," Bernard mumbles to himself. *"Sergio, let me say it like this. Jesus Christ is the Son of God. He paid for your sins on the cross of Calvary, shedding His blood to pay for your sins. Once you accept Jesus into your heart, you will be saved from eternal damnation and have everlasting life in heaven with Jesus. Would you like to receive Jesus now, Sergio?"*

"Will he save me from the wrath of Mr. Reyna?"

"Man's futile attempts at life are vain. Unfortunately, one must bear the consequences of their sins. However, the Holy Spirit can lead you to a way out with the help of Jesus Christ."

"I don't understand everything you say, but, yes, I will accept Jesus as my savior," Sergio, feeling he's at the end of the tunnel having nothing to lose, says the sinners' prayer with Bernard.

"*Congratulations, Sergio! Right now, the heavenly host of other angels are rejoicing in heaven that you've become part of the flock. A word of advice is to be aware of the soft voice of the Holy Spirit as he guides you. Plus, to get more grounded in the word of God, buy a Bible, and read every page.*" Bernard vanishes.

CHAPTER TWENTY-FOUR

PERFUME GALORE-JAN 2036

A week later, **Sergio and Nicolao** move from the old store to the new digs a few blocks down. Donna thought it best to move over the weekend while Carlo is off, leaving him a note they'd be in touch.

The next day, Monday morning, Rachael calls George Kogan at the rehab center.

"Good morning George. I wonder if you could do me a favor?"

"As seeing you married my grandson and his beautiful bride and were instrumental in getting the clinic named after me, heck, I owe you a lifetime of favors. How can I help you?"

"I'm wondering if I could borrow Irving and Helen for a week to conduct some light surveillance in the Manhattan Financial District. I'll pay their expected salary and provide hotel accommodations for them."

"If you're willing to do all that, it must be important. But will this assignment be safe? I personally don't want any more harm to come to Irving or Helen. I think they've had more than their share."

"Yes, that was a tragic incident nine years ago when Irving got stabbed at the hotel-casino. This time, they'll be watching two doors, recording who's coming and going, no contact, surveillance only!"

"Sounds okay to me, Rachael, and I'll continue their pay. You don't have to do that; you take care of the hotel. Fair enough?"

"Yes, that's mighty generous of you, George, thanks. By the way, can they start tomorrow?"

"I'll place them on a conference call, and we'll ask." George presses all the right buttons and connects.

"Helen, I'm glad you answered. I have Rachael on the other line, and she has a favor to ask of you and Irving."

"Hi, Racheal, it's been a while since we've talked. You're always so busy after church, Irving and, I don't want to bother you. We'd rather have you get acquainted with the visitors. So, what's on your mind today?"

"I've made a swap arrangement with a deluxe hotel in Manhattan for you and Irving to stay for a week, and George is continuing your pay, if you two will do me a favor?"

Helen retorts, "It must be risky; you're sugar-coating it before we know what you want us to do."

"Helen, George here. Rachael tells me it would only be surveillance, watching two doors, and observing who's coming in and out. Hardly any risk there."

"Irv is listening on the other phone and shaking his head up and down. He says it'd be like a vacation, so we'll do it. God knows my Irv could use a breather. When do you want us to start?"

"Tomorrow morning, Helen. You and Irving go ahead and check-in tonight at the hotel four blocks down from M & N Men's Custom Suits on William St. Your assignment is to watch both the front and back doors. Record people traffic; if you can identify anyone, that would be great."

Irving jumps into the conversation. "That's all you want us to do; keep an eye on two doors. This task will be like taking candy from a baby-easy peasy."

"Should be. We have a hunch that counterfeit money is being distributed from this store. You won't have to encounter anyone, just observe. You guys okay with that?" Rachael questions.

Helen immediately expresses herself, "as long as observing is the only requirement, Irving and I are okay with the plan."

"That's the only requirement," Rachael ensures. "But, as a side note, and more importantly, the hotel you and Irving are staying at is amid the most fabulous department stores. You two will want to avail yourself to maybe a nice shopping spree while there?"

"Now that you mention it, Rachael, I'm sure Irving will be eager to take me shopping," Helen plants the seeds for Irving to hear.

George jumps in, "Hey, everyone. I've been listening and have an idea. Irving and Helen, you two are the most dedicated employees I've known in a long while. Unfortunately, they don't make them like you two anymore—honest, loyal, and non-complaining. I'm going to give you a thousand-dollar gift card to spend on whatever you desire. I want you two to enjoy that shopping spree."

Before Helen and Irving could reply, Rachael comes in, "I almost forgot an essential item during your stay there-food! As I mentioned, I've made a swap with the hotel, five nights, and up to a thousand dollars in meals. So, you guys, enjoy?"

"Thank you, thank you, thank you." Irving and Helen can't say enough about how much they appreciate the mini-vacation, as they call the trip to Manhattan.

They all hang up, and Bernard appears amid Irving and Helen.

I'm so happy for both of you that you're getting a well-deserved mini-va-cation. Just be on the lookout. Sometimes things don't go exactly as planned.

"Bernard, are you hinting at something?" Helen softly inquires.

There's a possibility, a strong possibility, that Satan will come after those who are aware of the counterfeit scheme. But the other angels and I will protect the innocent." Bernard disappears.

Helen glances at Irving and verbally reflects, "I know Bernard is true to his word. I have no doubt that we'll all be protected. How I don't know, but the grace of God will be with us always."

During the first two days of their surveillance, nothing extraordinary occurred. Starting at 6 a.m., Helen watches the front door, and Irving stares at the back door. Irving sees a guy come in the back door at 7:30 a.m. and leaves shortly carrying looking like seven garment bags. At 8:30 a.m. Irving sees a guy come in the back door, stays there till lunch, returns, and then leaves again at 5 p.m.

That evening over dinner, Helen and Irving discuss their strategy for the next day.

"Watching the front door is boring," Helen confides. "I feel guilty about taking all this money from George and Rachael. We're not doing anything."

"We still have two days left. Hopefully, we won't earn our keep. We'll thank George and Rachael again, and to make it up to them, maybe we could volunteer for some community service."

"I like that idea, Irv. Praise the Lord! So, what do you have in mind for tomorrow, Thursday?"

"The guy that arrives at 8:30 a.m. I assume he works there. But the guy that shows up at 7:30 a.m. and leaves with garment bags each day and walks with them to where I don't know. But it can't be far. So, I'll follow him tomorrow. Can you watch the back door for me?"

"Sure, but Irv, you be careful. You don't need to be a hero again."

Precisely on time, Nicolao shows up at 7:30 a.m., retrieves the garment bags, and walks three blocks to the new store, followed by Irv. Sergio arrives for work at 8:30 a.m. and begins his daily routine of customizing three business suits.

Meanwhile, at his office in the casket manufacturing plant, Hughes reconciles the return box of bad phony bills and discovers a discrepancy of $110. He calls over to the new store, and Nicolao answers.

"Hey, Nicolao! Do you or Sergio have a stash of $110 in bad bills you forgot to return?"

"Not that I know of, boss."

Hughes retorts, "Let me talk to Sergio."

"He went to an early lunch. Nicolao wasn't about to cover for Sergio, not this time. Something about taking his girlfriend to the department store to exchange some perfume he bought her last week."

Hughes is raging mad; he calls two of his on-call hitmen stationed in Manhattan. "Be ready, and I'll have work for you in about five minutes. Walk over now to our new store, go inside, and stay close to your phone!"

Meanwhile, Helen decided to watch the front door of the old store again for no reason. Out of the blue, an attractive young girl shows up, and in a few moments, she's embraced by a handsome Italian guy. He's holding something that looks like a gift box, and they walk together four blocks to the department store. Helen follows.

Meanwhile, Carlo, working by himself now with no expressed super-vision, decides to surprise his wife, Cambria, and take her out to lunch. He walks the four blocks, enters the department store, and walks toward the cosmetic counter, and says, "Surprise!"

"Oh, my gosh! What are you doing here?"

"I wanted to surprise you and take you out to lunch."

As Cambria was about to say yes, Sergio and his girlfriend show up at her counter.

"Hi, I was here last week, and you helped me pick out some perfume for my girlfriend. She would like to exchange it if possible."

Meanwhile, Hughes orders his two hitmen to take out Sergio and anyone near them. They run furiously to the department store where Cambria works with guns drawn and Irving frantically running, trying to keep up with them. People on the sidewalk are screaming and scampering, not knowing if they are plainclothes cops, detectives, or hired by politicians.

Cambria leans over the counter and whispers to Sergio, "You were the guy with the phony ten dollars bills. I remember you from last week. My register was short one hundred dollars. I don't want to embarrass you, but I need to call my manager. I'm sure it was a big mistake, and we'll be able to rectify the matter in no time."

Helen standing far left of the perfume counter, falls to the floor for safety when, without warning, one of the hitmen charges in and aims at Sergio. The gunman trips while firing his gun, and the bullets crash the counter glass with all the perfume bottles.

Cambria and Carlo take cover on the other side of the display case when the second hitman aims but shoots too wide to the right and knocks out the perfume counter over there. Sergio and his girlfriend, Lucinda, are crawling on the floor, hiding behind whatever they can find.

Irving spots Helen also crawling on the floor and quickly runs to her defense. The first hitman shoots but misses again. Irving is covering Helen with his body while they both continue to crawl for safety.

The second hitman spots Sergio and Lucinda behind another perfume counter, coils around the backside with a direct aim, but slips on the perfume running all over the floor as he shots, missing them but taking out another perfume counter. By this time, the department store is reeking with the blended fragrances of over a thousand perfume bottles, plus shattered glass everywhere. Before the police arrive, the hitmen sneak out unidentified but left their guns behind in their haste to escape.

CHAPTER TWENTY-FIVE

THE HIDEAWAY-JAN 2036

Cambria, Carlo, Sergio, and Lucinda continue crawling on the floor, not knowing if the gunfire is over, when they bump into each other behind one of the display cases still standing.

Carlo shouts out, "Sergio! What are you doing here?"

Cambria asks Carlo, "You know this guy?"

"Yeah, he hired me, I sort of work for him."

Sergio fesses up, "Listen, guys, I'm in big trouble. I work for Hughes Reyna, and I need your help badly."

Carlo shouts out again, "So, that's who I work for, Mr. Reyna. I'll be darn."

Cambria calculates, "You're in trouble because it has something to do with the phony ten-dollar bills?"

"Maybe like something around three-hundred thousand a month circulating," Sergio shares.

Carlo promptly realizes the truth, "Oh, my goodness. I've been sewing secret pockets so they can distribute counterfeit money."

Sergio teases Carlo, "Yup, you're guilty."

As the police captain approaches behind the display case cautiously, not wanting to frighten them, he assures them.

"All of you are cut up badly from the broken glass, but it doesn't look life-threatening. I have ambulances taking you to the hospital. After initial treatment, we'll be needing a statement from each of you. My guess is you'll be there for two or three days for observation."

Irving and Helen are also taken to the same hospital. Upon arrival, Helen asks the nurse to dial Rachael's number.

Rachael answers on the first ring. "Are you guys okay? I've watched this on the news. I didn't know if the shooting directly involved you in the situation or not."

"Irving and I are at the hospital somewhat cut up, but we'll be okay. I think the intended target and his friends are also here."

"We'll be right over. Hang in there!" Rachael calls the others, and they arrive about an hour later.

Upon entering their room, Rachael and Darrell rush over to Irving and Helen's bedside, followed by Phillip and Terri.

Irving speaks first, "I think we've earned our keep."

Helen deciphers his statement. "We felt guilty on the first two days of our assignment with nothing happening. We thought of maybe volunteering for some community service to make up for all the money you and George paid us."

George happened to walk in, hearing Helen's compassion. "You guys don't owe Rachael or me or the community anything more than you've already contributed."

"I agree," states Rachael.

No sooner had Rachael spoken when Richard and Agnes arrive, and Richard announces, "I've had conversations with our friends, Cambria and Carlo, in the other rooms. It seems the guy that hired Carlo was the intended target. His name is Sergio. He'll need a place to hide and a good lawyer."

Darrell softly states, "Phillip is a good lawyer."

"Thank you for those kind words, Darrell, but I'd need to interview him first before I take another step in helping him. What room is he in, Richard?"

"Come on. I'll walk you all over. The four are sharing adjoining rooms, so we'll be able to ask everyone their recollections on what occurred."

The nurse was applying the last of bandages to Sergio when the group arrived in his room. As she was leaving, she whispered out loud, "It could have been worse. They're all badly cut up but will heal in time."

Agnes asks, "How long you think it will take?"

"Oh, probably five days in the hospital, and then one month or longer to completely heal. They'll need rest mostly after they leave here."

Phillip glances over at his wife and asks gently, "Terri, would you mind going with Rachael so she can speak with the girls while Richard and I stay here and talk with the guys?"

"Sure, I'd love to."

As they walk into the adjacent room, Rachael immediately goes over to Cambria, "The nurse says you'll all be fine in no time at all. So, do you remember anything about the incident?"

"I was speaking with Sergio about the counterfeit money he used to pay for his girlfriend's perfume last week. Then, at full-tilt, gunshots all around, glass display cases shattered, perfume bottles exploding. Carlo and I were crawling on the glass-strewn floor, trying to escape. It was horrible, Rachael," Cambria begins to cry.

"It'll be okay, Cambria; try getting some rest. I'll go ahead and speak with Sergio's girlfriend now. Do you know her name?"

"Yes, it's Lucinda."

Rachael walks over to her bedside and shares, "What a pretty name. If I had a daughter, I would name her after you, Lucinda. Let me introduce myself; I'm Rachael Zellner, pastor of the Jerusalem Tree Church in Cedar Creek and friends of Cambria and Carlo."

"Nice to meet you. Are you here for my last rites?"

"No, no, my dear. Nothing like that. I've spoken with the nurse, and she states, you should be good to go in no time at all. Is it okay if I ask you a couple of questions?"

"I already told the police all I know."

"And what was that, Lucinda?"

"You won't believe this, but Sergio and I met at his relatives' funeral during the celebration service. You know, Italian families are prominent in family and celebrations. I had no idea he was dealing with counterfeit money while I was dating him."

"Well, don't be too quick to judge; there may be more to this than you realize. You get some rest now, and we'll talk later."

Rachael and Terri walk over to the next room and meet up with Phillip and Richard. Terri asks her husband, Phillip, "Any new developments?"

"One word, Shocking! The mastermind of this elaborate scheme starts by hiring single men only from Eastern Europe. He virtually shackles them into working his counterfeit ring. Arriving in New York, broke, alone, and scared, they're easy targets for his manipulation."

Terri inquires, "So, does Sergio know who this person is?"

"Are you ready? Hughes Reyna."

Rachael flops down on the edge of the bed, trying to catch her breath. Darrell comes over, "Are you alright, honey?"

"Yes, I'll be fine. But I don't understand. I always read people well. I had not one lousy vibe that Hughes is a bad apple."

Darrell consoles her, "You weren't the only one. He had all of us fooled. Hughes is a good actor with a brilliant mind. Unfortunately, all for the wrong reasons."

Richard pipes up, "Even with Sergio's testimony, we'd still need proof of the counterfeit printing. Also, Hughes's big guns will continue going after Sergio to eliminate his voice. Sergio needs a well-camouflaged hiding place. Any ideas?"

Agnes shares, "He could stay at our son's house, but they have little children, too risky, and they're atheists. It would be like oil on water."

Rachael also shares, "I was thinking of my professor friends, Dolan and Natalie, but they have two pre-teens. Also, too risky."

Terri shares, "Phillip and I are empty-nesters, but a lawyers' house, if suspected, will be the first place to shoot up. Also, too risky."

The proverbial light bulb goes off for Rachael. "I have an idea. My worship leader and professor of music, Tom Gerrard, is single. Sergio could stay with him. It'd be the last place anyone would suspect. Sergio, do you play any type of musical instrument?"

"I used to play the accordion when I was twelve at all the family weddings. You know, Italian families and any excuse to have a celebration."

"That will work; you'll immediately be the devoted student learning classical piano under the tutelage of Tom."

"I'm not sure, at my age, if I could learn classical piano."

Richard adds his voice to the equation, "Practice like your life depended on it because it does. All of us will do everything we can to protect you and bring this counterfeit crime to its knees. But you'll need to do your part."

"I understand and will do that. What about Lucinda? How's she doing?"

Rachael looks at Darrell, speaking with her eyes as he understands what she's about to do.

"Lucinda will be staying with my husband and me, at least till this thing is resolved. We have a five-bedroom apartment on the third floor of our hotel. She'll be safe, no worries, Sergio."

"Will I be able to talk with her or see her?" Sergio implores.

Richard attempts to console him, "As an ex-sheriff, Sergio, for the sake of your lives, that's the very last thing you ought to do. Wait till this is over. Besides, you'll be busy healing and learning the piano."

Sergio is getting a bit jealous. "I guess you're right, but what will Lucinda be doing?"

"Oh, I'll have her help me with church things, or maybe in fashion design. We'll see," Rachael assures Sergio that Lucinda will be watched over with care.

As they're all about to leave, Terri explains, "We'll be taking turns visiting each day, and you have a 24-hour police guard. So, rest peacefully. We'll see you tomorrow."

While the group is walking to the hospital parking garage, Rachael shouts, "How will we converse with Hughes now?"

Agnes softly suggests, "You and Darrell will need to get down on your knees and pray that the Holy Spirit will guide you each second of every day."

Terri adds, "Rachael, you were a fashion model in your youth. I bet some of that was acting. You may want to ask the Lord during your prayer time to give you that gift back. Temporarily, of course."

"Okay, then. Darrell and I will pray and seek the protection of Jesus Christ and the guidance of the Holy Spirit."

Pronto, Bernard appears in the hospital room of Irving and Hellen.

"Be of good cheer and blessed healing," Bernard joyously shares.

Irving replies, "What's there to be so cheerful about?"

"Well, you're both still alive, a bit banged up, but you'll both heal soon."

"We're grateful, Bernard, for you and the host of angels covering our back," Helen knows what really occurred.

Unfortunately, Irving doesn't get it. "What are you talking about, dear? We got shot at and have glass bits here and there all over our bodies. What's there to be grateful for?"

"Sometimes! I take it back, actually, all the time, you're a puzzle, Irving. Allow me to share how the host of angles and I protected you, Helen, and everyone else. Remember, I broke the news that Satan's big guns would be coming after everyone?"

"Yes, I do now."

"Well, When the hitman tripped, aiming right at Sergio's head, it was my foot. When the next hitman missed far right, it was the angel's hand that bumped his hand. When the first hitman missed hitting you, Irving, he slipped on the wet floor. Likewise, when the second hitman missed a direct hit on Sergio and Lucinda, he slipped on the wet perfumed floor. The host of angels protected all of you from getting killed-Amen!"

Irving is embarrassed that he hadn't figured out the Lord's hand and His protection and was remorseful.

"I'm so sorry, Bernard. My thinking isn't what it used to be since that knife wound incident nine years ago. Please forgive me."

"That's okay, my friend. You two rest well. I must go and visit the others," Bernard vanishes.

"Lucinda, you're the only one that can see and hear me. I am the Angel of the Lord, Bernard. I have come to help you."

"Are you taking over Rachael and Darrell's help?" Lucinda, still drowsy from the medications, hasn't realized she's speaking with an angel yet.

"No, they are the help you need now, but I have come to help you spiritually and emotionally."

"Other than the cuts all over my body, I seem to be okay."

"Yes, you will heal soon, physically. But you have a cut in your heart that needs healing. An emotional cut."

"You can see through to my heart?"

"Yes, I can, and I speak the truth. You had an abortion three years ago and haven't forgiven yourself. Your heart is in constant turmoil. Until you forgive yourself, you won't have a pure life nor be a pure wife."

"How do you know all this? It's unreal that I hear this from… who are you, now?"

"I'm Bernard, the Angel of the Lord. I'm here to help you confess your sins and invite Jesus into your heart. He will forgive you of that abortion, make you clean and pure as white as the newly fallen snow."

"I haven't told anyone, no one! I've kept it a secret until now, I guess."

"Lucinda, our conversations are private. No one will know unless you tell them. I'm aware that you've been dating Sergio for only two months. It would be good if you became a new Christian like Sergio. Should you two ever marry each other, it's best to be equally yoked."

"Marrying him has crossed my mind, but my past haunts me. Should I tell him or not, and if so, when?"

"That's even more reason to come to Jesus, confess your sins, and invite Jesus into your heart. You will have joy in your soul once again." Bernard disappears.

Lucinda ponders the words of Bernard for a while and doses back to sleep.

CHAPTER TWENTY-SIX

TACTICAL STRATEGY-JAN 2036

Donna is in Hughes's office as she calls Nicolao, "I'm implementing plan HH604 immediately! We're shutting down the old store completely; with Sergio and Carlo no longer working for us, there's no need to keep it open."

"What you want me to do with all the suits I have here?" Nicolao inquires.

Donna replies, "I'm having one of our drivers take them back to our country club cemetery. We'll be burning the remaining inventory at the fire pit. Virtually all evidence will go up in smoke."

"Great! So, what do you want me to do for work then?" Nicolao sounds exasperated.

Hughes answers, "We're changing our new store to a little specialty shop both for men and women. Casual and business attire. Donna has hired a lady to sell exclusively to women while you continue with the men. The only difference now is our private clients will receive a two thousand dollar ready-to-wear sports jacket twice monthly, while we continue the operation at full speed with more profit."

"Will I still be doing alterations, or is the new line ready to wear off the rack?" Nicolao is hoping.

Donna answers, "Ready to wear! You'll be busier now than ever-no time for alterations. Hughes hired a contractor to remodel the inside over the weekend. The new fashion line should arrive Sunday afternoon. I had it expedited so we could open Monday morning."

Hughes speaks jovial, "Nicolao, I'm aware you're usually off on weekends, but I need you to stay with the contractor this weekend, and I'll pay you overtime."

"Wow, since Sergio is gone, you've become more generous. I like it, and of course, I'll be here. Thanks for the overtime, it wasn't necessary, but I do appreciate the offer."

"Well, my friend, you'll be earning every dollar of that overtime pay. Even though our store will be new and exciting, with a new name, 'Wall Street Flair,' every federal agent and his relatives will be snooping there. Be sure the trapped door in the men's fitting room leading to the basement is sealed tight. However, if a punk agent discovers it, show him to the basement and our inventory. If they inquire about the safe, they'll need to produce a search warrant. But, they'll only find real money in there."

"So, where are we hiding the phony money if not in the safe?"

"Great question, Nicolao!" Hughes shouts. "I've made arrangements with the owner of the doggie wagon, Mr. Zee, at the Hot Dog Pavilion. Leah will drop off every morning five packets of counterfeit, each with two thousand dollars. After you make a sale, walk over with our client to the pavilion and buy him a doggie. Mr. Zee will hand him a paper bag with the fake dough, which the client places inside his sport coat."

"But, can this guy be trusted?"

"Absolutely! He's worked for me before and is willing to do anything I ask. I'm also paying him a bonus if he brings in any new clients."

"By the way, Nicolao," Donna jumps in the conversation, " Mr. Zee's wife is the sales lady I hired, and she goes by Zeela. I'm certain you'll love working with her. She'll be your added protection. No one would ever guess she can shoot a target the size of a dollar coin from twelve feet out."

"Wow! I hope Zeela won't have to use her weapon while working here. The sound of gunfire scares the jeepers out of me."

Donna tries to console Nicolao. "As long as you hear the gunfire, it means you're still alive."

Nicolo changes topics quickly, not wanting to talk about guns and stuff. "I thought you guys didn't like married couples working in the inner circle. What gives?"

Hughes comes back with a roar, "Taking care of the business at hand is more important than any of my original rules. I need our new store and counterfeit operation to run smoothly without any hitches. I believe Mr. Zee and Zeela will help us accomplish that goal."

"Anything I can do to help?" Nicolao decides getting on the wrong side of Hughes could jeopardize his life.

"No, just keep the store running profitably in all aspects. Work with Zeela; she's there to help you. By the way, every day at the store's closing, you place the day's haul, the real money, in the basement safe. Leah will retrieve the loot each morning while she's visiting Mr. Zee before any Feds show up."

"I got it, boss. No problem!"

Hastily, Bernard appears.

"Nicolao! You're neck-deep in sin!"

"Who the heck are you, and what are you?" Nicolao is mystified.

"I'm the Angel of the Lord, Bernard, and I'm here to help you."

"I'm doing extremely well, thank you. I don't need any help."

"You're thinking of doing very well is camouflaged by the lies of the devil. Continuing your current employment with Mr. Reyna has and will muddy your thinking on what is right and what is wrong."

"Having left Italy three years ago and arriving in New York alone and frightened, Mr. Reyna gave me work and hope. I am loyal to him, and nothing you say can change my mind."

"Nicolao, every day you live on this earth, you're making a daily decision on right and wrong. Do you realize that even one wrong is a sin in God's eyes?"

"I don't believe in this stuff you call sin. I may have done some bad things in my life, but sin? I don't think so."

"The Bible says everyone has sinned. That includes you, Nicolao. No one can escape the penalty of sin unless they confess and invite Jesus into their heart."

"When I was a child, my parents would take me to this monstrous church. We'd go and kneel at the altar, pray out loud, confessing our sins.

I had no idea what that was about; it didn't do anything for me. So, if you'll excuse me, I have work to do. I'll stay loyal to Mr. Reyna."

"I will continue to pray for you, Nicolao, that one day, your eyes and heart will open to the salvation message of Jesus Christ."

"I'll stay with Hughes as my inspirational leader. You go with Jesus or whoever you follow."

"In a way, Jesus is my boss. I've been following Him for over 2,000 years. I pray that one day you'll see and understand the way of life and Jesus Christ.

"Whatever! As I articulated before, I don't believe in that stuff. Now, if you'll excuse me, I have work to do."

"I will continue praying for you, Nicolao." Bernard vanishes.

Later in the afternoon, a man walks casually into the store pretending to buy some clothes when, without warning, he grabs Nicolao around the neck, pointing his gun at Nicolao's head, and looking directly at Zeela. "Give me all the cash on hand, and no one gets hurt."

Zeela, exceptionally calm, standing about twelve feet away, states, "Of course, no one is going to get hurt. I need to grab the key to the safe; it's in my pant leg cuff."

"Sure, go ahead, but no funny stuff or your buddy will be checking out prematurely."

As she reaches inside the cuff, she grabs her baby pistol. She shoots from a kneeling position, hitting the would-be robber directly in Adam's apple, immediately stamping his check-out ticket.

Nicolao is breathless, shaking, his entire body trembling. Finally muttering, "I could hear the sound of the bullet passing over my shoulder. You could have killed me, Zeela."

"Yeah, could have, but I didn't. Chalk it up to twenty years of competition at the gun range. You'll be okay in a while. Take a break in the basement, and I'll call the police."

Zeela closes the store for the afternoon's balance and answers all the police's questions to their satisfaction. The first responders remove the body and take it to the county morgue. Nicolao returns from taking a break and asks Zeela, "You want me to call Hughes, or are you going to?"

"Don't worry about it, I will. You best take the rest of the afternoon off. Nicolao. Before you go, grab a new shirt and clean up a bit. You look like a Halloween freak and will scare everyone that sees you."

"Yeah, that is a good idea. I didn't think of that, thanks," Nicolao still rattled. As he wanders to the bathroom, he's thinking, *'why did she say I look like a Halloween freak?'* Nicolao screams when he sees himself in the mirror, not realizing he had blood splatter all over him. After cleaning up and putting on a new shirt, Nicolao tells Zeela, "Now that I'm thinking and feeling better, I want to thank you for saving my life. I know the situation could have been worse."

"That's why Hughes placed me here. I spoke with him a few minutes ago, and he's going to place two security guards at the store starting tomorrow. Listen, Nicolao, I don't want you walking home alone, so my husband, Mr. Zee, will drive you. But, before that, he'll treat you to one of his famous New York Dogs. Now, get out of here, enjoy and relax, and I'll see you in the morning."

As Nicolao walks to the Hot Dog Pavilion, Bernard shows up.

"That, my friend, was a close call. Your soul could be in Hell right now if Zeela's shot was off just a smidgen."

"Why you say my soul would be in Hell?"

"Because you haven't confessed your sins or invited Jesus into your heart. Right now, you're doomed to Hell as most of the world is, but it doesn't have to be this way, Nicolao."

"Listen, Bernard, I'm still rattled a bit. Let me grab my hot dog, get a ride home, and I'll think about what you are saying tonight while I'm watching TV."

"Don't wait too long. As the saying goes, time is of the essence. Especially when it comes to matters of Jesus Christ and your eternal soul." Bernard disappears.

Unfortunately, Nicolao doesn't give any thought to Bernard's heed and falls asleep while attempting to watch TV.

✶✶✶✶✶

Meanwhile, back at the funeral home office, Hughes answers Donna's question. "

I'm curious, why did you close the fake-bill bar operation at the country club?"

"Heck, that was a no-brainer! After Phillip and Terri became members, they had lunch at the bar and received seven-ten-dollar bills as change, with at least two of them being phony. I knew it'd be a matter of time before the entire area would be flooded with counterfeit ten-dollar bills. So, rather than being caught, I shut it down. But, it was my fault. Had I not visited with Chef Reynolds in the kitchen, and instead invited Phillip and Terri to join me for lunch at a table, my treat, as I always do with new members, the entire situation would have been avoided."

"So, I'm guessing you need to make up that annual $84,000 shortfall and then some."

"You're getting good at this; I'm impressed."

"Any idea how you'll do this?" inquires Donna.

"Oh, I'll simply charge the affiliated funeral homes an extra two hundred monthly for the cost of doing business. It shouldn't be a problem. They love my golden goose."

"Have I told you lately that you're a genius and that I adore you?"

"Yes, you have, and I appreciate your love, Donna."

"By the way, simply curious, Hughes, how are you planning on finding Sergio, his girlfriend, Lucinda, Carlo, and his wife, Cambria?'

"That should be relatively easy, but how to implement the process of elimination will be the ultimate task."

Donna is puzzled, "Easy to find, how?"

"I'm sure they're in our backyard. We'll attend church this Sunday, have dinner there, and probably bump into Rachael. She'll reveal their whereabouts."

CHAPTER TWENTY-SEVEN

THE CONFESSION-FEB 2036

Meanwhile, Brad and Nancy are in Cedar Creek, still working for the FBI and discussing their strategy on filing the report for Mitch when Bernard appears out of the blue.

"You so conveniently left out when confessing to Jacob and his mom that not only did you steal the money but killed Hudson."

"Well, I didn't want to alarm anyone. Besides, the FBI cleared me of all charges."

"That doesn't make it right with God. Nancy, one day you'll need to confess your sins to Jesus and ask His forgiveness. Also, you'll need to tell the truth to Jacob and his mom. Nancy, this is the right thing to do." Bernard vanishes.

"I guess he might be right, Brad, but it will be so difficult to do. I'm not ready for any of that yet," confesses Nancy.

Brad shares his thoughts, "I whispered a little prayer back at the funeral home after the shooting. That situation brought the realization of how short one's life can be. So, I would like to invite you, my friend, to join me this Sunday at any church we can find and walk up to the altar and invite Jesus into our hearts. Think you can do that, Nancy?"

"If I can hold your hand tightly while we walk up and confess. I will."

Meanwhile, they need to call Mitch, file a report, and update him on their activities. Brad starts out with the good news of him and Nancy.

"Mitch! Nancy and I are planning on attending church this Sunday and inviting Jesus into our hearts."

"I thought you were going to say the two of you were getting married. Why do you want to do something like inviting Jesus? What does he have anything to do with your life?" Mitch asks annoyingly.

"You see, I've been talking with this angel, Bernard."

Mitch yells, "You've been what?"

"Yeah, this guy, Angel of the Lord, Bernard appears to Nancy and me flat out, anywhere, anytime. He has us convinced that we need Jesus Christ in our lives to be certain our soul is in heaven with Him when we pass from this life on earth."

"You don't say? Brad, I think you've been working too many hours. Why don't you take off for an entire day tomorrow?"

"Oh, don't worry, I'll be okay. But did you forget Jacob is a pastor? He, Katy, and Doris will want to attend church on Sundays. So, will it be okay if we all attend the Jerusalem Tree Church next to the hotel you have them sequestered in?"

Mitch talking from his office in Albany, New York, is abruptly startled by Bernard's appearance.

"So, you don't believe in angels or Jesus. How sad."

"Oh, my goodness. Have I died and gone to heaven?"

"Hardly, Mitch. You would need Jesus Christ as your personal savior to be with Him in heaven. Before arriving in your office, I examined the Lamb's Book of Life, and sadly, your name isn't written there."

"I need to know if you're real. May I touch you?"

"Sure, you can, but I have a glorified body; your hand would simply go through. But my words have wisdom and truth. Mitch, you've been doing this line of work for how many years now, twenty or twenty-five?"

"Going on twenty-five next month. Five more, and I can retire at the young age of fifty with a full pension."

"You humans and your almighty pension. That only gives you financial security-maybe. Undoubtedly, you've seen a few of your agents get killed in the line of duty. Some knew Jesus. Most did not. The real security in life is knowing Jesus, so when you die, you can be assured that you'll be in heaven with him and not in hell with Satan."

"I hear what you're saying, but I don't necessarily believe in hell or Satan. Surely, God wouldn't send anyone there. Ever since I was a child, I always heard that God is all-loving."

"Sorry, Mitch. Whoever told you that, parent or pastor, didn't share the entire truth with you. Yes, God is all-loving, but He is also a just God."

"What do you mean by that?"

"First, you have to accept the number one truth in the entire universe. Everyone has sinned. If you don't believe that, you're missing the whole point and will go straight to hell. A just God demands that all sin must be repented and paid for; hence, He sent his only begotten Son to pay the penalty for all of humanity's sins. Then whosoever believes in Jesus will be saved from eternal hell."

"You make it sound so dramatic and real. I've never heard anyone talk like you do. What can I do to learn more about this Jesus, heaven, and everlasting life?"

"Buy a Bible, a good study Bible. Then attend a church that preaches and teaches from the Bible. I recommend you visit the Jerusalem Tree Church in Cedar Creek for a while. It's only a three-hour drive. I bet you could set up a temporary field office there. You may find some great truths while visiting." Bernard disappears.

Mitch ponders his conversation with Bernard for a moment and wonders what he meant; *'you may find some great truths while visiting.'*

"Mitch, you still there?" Brad asks.

"Yeah, still here. I must have been daydreaming for a few seconds. Tell you what. I'll join you all in church next Sunday, and for extra measure, I'll bring two security agents with me."

"That will be great! What changed your mind?"

"I'm visiting out of curiosity, that's all."

"Have you been talking with Bernard, Mitch?" Brad had a hunch.

"I'll never tell. See you in church Sunday, Brad."

CHAPTER TWENTY-EIGHT

BIBLE PREACHING-FEB 2036

It seemed like everyone living in the area wanted to attend this Sunday morning. The Jerusalem Tree Church was packed; people arriving late stood in the lobby, willing to watch the service on TV monitors. Pastor Rachael Zellner, a zealous preacher, never apologized for speaking the Word of God's truths when delivering her message.

After last week's message, Rachael shared with the audience, "Next week, I'll be making a major announcement that will impact the essence of life. Be sure to invite your friends. You won't want to miss this truth from the word of God."

Ten minutes before service, Rachael and her husband, Darrell, are in her church office praying, imploring the Holy Spirit to anoint the message and to move upon the congregation. In attendance, this morning are both familiar and unfamiliar faces. Sitting close to the front row center is Richard and Agnes. Directly behind them are Carlo, Cambria, Irving, and Helen, who recovered well from the incident three weeks ago. Hughes and Donna, Lucas, and Klaus decide to sit in the right front row, virtually opposite the others.

Tom Gerrard, the worship leader and music professor at the Conservatory, walks out on stage with Sergio playing the piano and Lucinda singing a solo.

Promptly, sitting up straight, leaning forward to get a better look, Hughes whispers to Donna in a hushed surprised tone, "That is Sergio playing the piano-is it not?"

"It most certainly is; I didn't know he could play any musical instrument. My understanding as a poor immigrant, he was lucky you gave him a job as a tailor."

"Well, somehow, the college discovered his hidden talent. So, you see, as I revealed before, Donna, our targets are right in our backyard."

"What do you plan to do about this situation? It seems as long as they're in church, they're protected."

"Remember, no one is connecting us with the hitmen shooting up the department store. So, play it cool. Eventually, Sergio and his friends will leave the premise, and my other hitman will be ready."

"Speaking of shooting things up, did you bury Oscar in the John Doe section of the cemetery after Stan embalmed him?"

"Yes. I had Klaus pick up his body the day after you received the call from the police Sargent. I also had Amir issue a false death certificate, not wanting Oscar's name anywhere on the cemetery grounds associated with the country club. By the way, are you working with Leah trying to find our other target?"

"Yes, we've made some progress, but not much. I did hire a private eye to help with the search."

"Great! Now we have a 50% chance of locating them. Hope we get lucky!"

After Lucinda's solo, accompanied by Sergio playing the piano, Tom leads the orchestra and choir into a beautiful music and song ensemble. Mitch Kearney and his friends walk in late but find a seat four rows behind Hughes, not knowing he's there. Hughes is also unaware that Jacob, Katy, Doris, Brad, and Nancy were part of Pittsburgh's sting operation that got Oscar killed and sitting five rows behind him.

Darrell walks out on stage and makes a major announcement. "Pastor Rachael, the church board, and I thought it best we informed you, our beloved congregation, that in the next few weeks, we'll have a practice run on our resistance plan. When President Avci signs the D.C. Mandate bill into law, we must be ready for whatever may come, including getting arrested. We don't want to alarm you, but prayerfully have your heart prepared to do the Lord's work." Darrell then opens the service with prayer before his wife comes up to share the word of God in her message today.

Rachael walks up to the podium and speaks into the mic, "Let us pray. Dear heavenly Father, I ask that your son, Jesus Christ, will anoint me with the blessings of the Holy Spirit and that He will give me the words to utter, that the gifts of the Holy Spirit will prevail over the congregation. I ask for a mighty move of God in the sanctuary this morning, Amen."

"If you have your Bible with you, please turn to the Book Of Deuteronomy, or you can see the verses on the big screen behind me. Reading only the 6th and 8th commandments, I want to share with you for a few moments the truths of God's word."

Hughes and Donna begin to squirm a bit in their seats as they listen with apprehension.

"I'm going to share the 8th commandment first. 'Thou shall not steal.' The word stealing covers a broad spectrum. It can be anything from a pencil you took at the company you work for, or at the other end, your boss's car. I'm confident the latter would get you caught in no time at all."

The congregation emits a soft chuckle.

Rachael continues listing various sins, "There's the sin of stealing money, robbing, embezzling, printing and circulating counterfeit money. All are considered stealing under the law, but in God's eyes, a sin." Rachael's tempted to glance at Hughes but doesn't.

The 6th commandment, 'Thou shall not murder,' is the one I want to spend more time on this morning. Murder is a hideous sin. It is intentional. Completely different from one, say, being killed in a car accident. Murdering someone comes from anger, selfishness, or believe it or not, from convenience."

Hughes and Donna continue to squirm in their seats, but Rachael never glances their way, keeping focused on her message.

"Yes, I uttered convenience. Murdering someone because they may snitch on a criminal activity you've committed would be convenient. But, let's talk about the other convenient murder...abortion!"

A quiet hush enveloped the sanctuary as Rachael vocalized the word abortion.

"Allow me to expand. This is contrary to what some politicians say. It has been proved, by medical science, without the shadow of a doubt, that a baby, the second it's conceived in the womb, is a living human being. From the time the baby is conceived to the time, it is born, they are a living human being, and no one has the right to murder that baby boy or baby girl!"

About 80% of the congregation stand up and applaud for a few minutes.

"The political landscape in America has supported abortion for the last sixty-three years. Women of all ages and backgrounds have been brainwashed-that it's their right. But, I have news for you; this morning-God never gave you that right! Instead, He gave the breath of life!"

This time, the entire congregation stands up and applauds.

"In this vein, my husband and I and the church board are starting a new ministry titled, 'Adoption- not Abortion.' We're setting aside twenty hotel rooms for this program. Any young girl not knowing with certainty how to handle her unwanted pregnancy, but would consider offering their baby for adoption, can stay with us!"

The crowd stands and applauds once more.

"We will have a medical team available for these girls, including nurses and counselors. We will cover all costs associated with birth and adoption. I ask that you pray and seek God's will if He would want you to become a partner in this ministry. You'll see envelopes in front of you on the back of the pew. If the Holy Spirit is nudging you to participate, be obedient with a cheerful heart. Nothing is more precious than the life of a human being, especially a helpless baby."

As the ushers walk the aisles collecting the offerings, Tom comes on stage with Sergio's piano accompaniment, and Tom sings a familiar old hymn.

Rachael returns to the podium. "I'll be just a few more minutes. If anyone knows of a young girl interested in participating in this program, have her contact the church office and speak with Lucinda. Say, Lucinda, come out here so everyone can see you, and wasn't that a beautiful solo she sang?"

The congregation gives her a solid round of applause.

Lucinda gracefully walks to Rachael's side, and Rachael begins to share, "Lucinda came to us recently in one of God's mysterious ways. She'll be heading up our program, 'Adoption-not Abortion.' I believe she is qualified beyond measure to help others. Please listen to her message. Lucinda, the mic is all yours."

"Thank you, Rachael. I'm a bit shaky, so please, everyone, bear with me while I get through this emotional tragedy in my life. Three years ago, I had an abortion."

The congregation sits spelled-bound, hardly able to consume her words.

"My background was probably no different than most girls. My mom was a single parent, working two jobs to make ends meet. During my senior year in high school, I got pregnant with my boyfriend of four years. I was confused, afraid, frightened. My boyfriend repeatedly yelled at me to get an abortion. Finally, I visited one of the abortion clinics in town, and they quickly convinced me this was the right thing to do. I've never told anyone this, not even my mom. Had I known then what I know now, I would have placed my baby for adoption. Today's laws allow the birth mother to continue communication with her baby while they're growing up. I have had a tough time forgiving myself. I've asked God to forgive me, and I know He has. So, if you're confused and distorted about your pregnancy, come, talk to me, and together, we'll sort out your best options. Thank you for listening."

The entire house of God stands and applauds for seven minutes. During the celebration of God, Darrell comes up on stage and begins to speak.

"Wasn't that a great message? Okay, give God another round of applause." The audience does so appreciatively when someone in the balcony begins to speak in tongues. After forty seconds, Darrell interprets.

"The Lord of Hosts says, 'consecrate your babies, your children, all of humanity unto me. Do not murder, for their blood will be on your hands unless you humble yourselves, confess your sins, and invite my son, Jesus Christ, into your heart. Then I will restore your soul.'

Darrell shouts, "Amen, Amen, Hallelujah! I feel the presence of the Holy Spirit moving in this place. I sense some of you need to make right with God. I'll be making an altar call in a few moments. If Jesus is tugging at your heart, come on down to the altar. We won't embarrass you; come on down right now. Yes, yes, hundreds are lining up in front of the altar. If you haven't made your way down yet, stand in front of your pew, reach out your hands, as I say the 'sinners' prayer.' The words alone won't make you a Christian, but what you believe in your heart will transform you into a newborn-again-Christian. I'm asking everyone within the sound of my voice to repeat after me."

"Dear Jesus, I need you. I am humbly calling out to you. I'm tired of doing things my way. Help me to start doing things your way. I invite you into my heart and life to be my Lord and Savior.

Fill the emptiness in me with your Holy Spirit and make me whole. Lord, help me to trust you. Help me to live for you. Help me to understand your grace. Help me to grasp your mercy and your peace. Thank you, Lord Jesus, Amen."

If you have prayed this from your heart, sincerely, remember that this is the day you became A New- Born-Again Christian."

"Before you all leave, Rachael and I would like to give those of you who became a new Christian a small pamphlet titled, 'How to live for Jesus.' Girls line up with Rachael and guys with me."

As Rachael is handing out the pamphlets, she hugs each girl and says, "God bless you."

They, in turn, say, "Thank you, and God bless you too."

The next voice she hears, "Rachael, thank you so much for inviting me to share my testimony. I feel unshackled and have also given my heart to Jesus. What do you think Sergio will say?" Lucinda asks softly.

Before Rachael could answer, Donna shows up. "Listen, Hughes is in the lobby waiting for me and doesn't know I'm speaking with the two of you. But, here, take this check for your new program. It's from my equity account, and please, can we keep this private, ladies?" Donna quickly does an about-face and sprints up the aisle toward the lobby, not wanting to arouse Hughes' suspicion.

Rachael opens the envelope and reads the note inside. *'twenty years ago, I had several abortions. I murdered my babies. As a result, I became cold, callous, holding hatred in my heart, and even evil. Please use this money to adopt as many babies as you can".'*

Although Donna never had any children, her biological mother instincts kicked into high gear. As evil as she was, she didn't have the heart to see a baby in the womb get murdered, not anymore.

Rachael looks at the ten-thousand-dollar check and shares it with Lucinda. "This check is our seed money for the program. However, we must honor Donna's wishes and keep it private."

"Yes, of course, I will. Now, about my question on Sergio," Lucinda anxiously waiting for Rachael's answer.

"Yes, Sergio. Why not ask him during dinner? I believe it's safe now. Darrell and I are inviting both of you over for a celebration at our Italian restaurant. Think you can make it by 7 p.m.?"

Lucinda gives Rachael a tight hug and whispers, "Thank you."

"There's someone else I think you'd like to meet. This lady, whom I've never met, is standing behind you, bawling her eyes out, and you look like her daughter."

Lucinda turns around and shouts, "Mom!" They hug, cry, and hug and cry some more. Shortly after a few moments, they stroll over to one of the pews and talk.

"Mom, how did you know I'd be here?"

"For whatever reason, I thought I'd visit in person today. So, glad I did."

"Me too, mom. Listen, I'm so sorry I walked out on you three years ago. I was barely twenty-one and didn't dare to tell you I was planning on having an abortion."

"I didn't even know you were pregnant when living with me. You hid it very well."

"It wasn't tricky, mom. You were working two jobs, hardly paying any attention to me. I moved in with my boyfriend, and we stayed together for about a year after the procedure."

"I couldn't help but overhear the pastor. You have a new boyfriend now?"

"Yes, I do! One day soon, I'd like you to meet him."

"That would be great."

"Say, mom, it's still the lunch hour. So, let's grab a quick bite! They have a cute café here. I'll treat, and we can catch up on the years we missed. Would you like that, mom?"

"Yes, I would like that daughter."

Meanwhile, Darrell is busy handing out hundreds of pamphlets when he suddenly feels a tight handshake grip causing him to look up.

"Pastor Darrell, you don't know me, but I just invited Jesus into my heart. My name is Mitch Kearney, and I love the message preached here today."

"I take it this is your first visit."

"Yes. You won't believe it, but an angel told me to come here today."

"I do believe that. We have angles all around us. Some are even assigned to us. Did this angel have a name by chance?"

"Yes, funny, you ask. His name is Bernard."

"I'm not surprised. From what I can gather, Bernard has been assigned by God to encourage people in our community to invite Jesus into their hearts. It looks like that miracle happened to you today, Mitch."

Before he could answer, they both hear a booming voice coming from five rows up in the pews. Hughes left Donna standing in the lobby when he saw Mitch speaking with Darrell.

"Well, well, now. If it isn't my favorite FBI director, Mitch Kearney," Hughes boasts loudly with the sanctuary virtually empty.

Darrell inquires of Mitch, "You know Hughes?"

"Unfortunately. My team and I raided his casket factory in Buffalo last month looking for evidence of fraud but found nothing."

"That's because, my friend, there isn't any, nor will there ever be. You're welcome to stop in any time and pay a visit."

Mitch disregards his statement and asks, "You attend here often?"

"To be honest, occasionally. It's close enough, though; I should attend more often living up the road only seven miles."

"Isn't that close to the Cedar Creek Country Club?"

"That's me. I own it along with the funeral home, cemetery, and mortuary school." Hughes goes boasting again.

"Darrell, maybe you can help me set up a temporary field office in your hotel. Think I'll stay awhile and visit the surrounding area. Maybe even play a round of golf."

"Sure, Mitch. I catch your drift. You're welcome to visit the country club anytime. I'll even buy you lunch. Now, if you gentlemen will excuse me, I hear my wife calling for us to leave. I guess we're running almost late for a wedding engagement party." Hughes walks up the aisle and holds Donna's hand as they leave the church building.

CHAPTER TWENTY-NINE

FIRE PIT VISIT-MAR 2036

Living in the guest cottage for a few months now, Richard and Agnes got acquainted with the four guys next door and had them over for breakfast. But the discussions went weird on the different embalming techniques, and Agnes wasn't too thrilled to hear all those medical terms, especially over breakfast.

As three of the guys hurriedly left for class, Stan stayed back to thank Richard and Agnes for their hospitality. "I hope we can do this again soon. It was mighty fine talking with you folks this morning. Guess I better get to my first class and meet my new cadaver."

"You're welcome, Stan. You guys come over anytime," Richard shouts so Stan can hear as he's running to catch up with his pals.

Agnes suggests, "Richard, let's ride out on the golf cart and visit the John Doe section of the cemetery this morning. I'm curious if any new burials have occurred lately."

"You know, Agnes, I simply can't put my finger on it, but something terrible is going on here, and it frustrates me that I can't figure this out. Maybe, I'm getting too old for this detective stuff?"

"No, you're not too old, my charming sheriff, but I'm glad you didn't wait for us to move into our new home before buying an ordinary golf cart. If Hughes inquires, we'll simply state the bronze cart needed to be charged. Hopefully, our drive around this morning will be unnoticed."

They hop into their cart and drive off toward the John Doe section. Once there, Agnes notices a new marker.

"Look, Richard, a new marker and burial. It has the initials of 'SR.' Stan must have performed the embalming on this guy." But they had no clue it was Oscar.

"How can you tell it's a new burial?"

"Simple! The dirt is fresh, and the grass hasn't had time to germinate. So, this can't be any more than a week old. It looks like there are over 100 gravesites here now. It seems our students have been extremely busy lately."

"Yeah, I agree with you-strange so many burials in less than a year. Hughes states he accommodates the county by doing this as a free service. As I recollect, counties pay for the cremation of their unidentified deceased. So, why is Hughes spending an extra thousand dollars and exercising a casket burial? Is it solely for the mortuary school?"

"Richard, I have an idea, but we need to visit this area every day. I'm hoping we'll see multiple new burials within a week. Then we ask the County Sheriff to secure rights to disinterment," Agnes states flatly.

"That, my dear, will be extremely challenging to accomplish. We'd need to prove some sort of suspected criminal activity or have cause to identify the deceased," Richard dumps on her idea.

"My second idea then, as an ex-sheriff, my dear, is that you could invite the local sheriff and other police officials to a round of golf with you. That could perk Hughes's attention."

"What a great idea, honey! But let's do one better and ruffle his feathers. I'll invite them as you suggested, and I'm sure, in today's hostile environment, each will bring at least two uniformed bodyguards."

They slap each other with high-fives, jump into the cart and drive over to the fire pit for a look-see. The fire pit is still smoldering due to Donna having a hundred suits burned a few days ago. Richard gets out of the cart and slowly walks up to the area.

"Hey, honey, look at this," as Richard bends down on one knee and fingers the ashes. "This soot doesn't feel like paper or usual rubbish, but almost like a fabric material. What do you think?"

While examining, Agnes digs a little deeper in the ashes and quickly shouts, "Richard, I think what I have in my hand is cloth." She holds up a tiny piece about a one-inch square.

"I think I'll walk around the area. Maybe we'll get lucky and find some valid evidence on what was burned here and why?"

"Okay, I'll work this side," Agnes anxiously starts her investigation around the fire pit.

"Bingo!" Richard shouts. "I believe this will be valid."

"What is it, dear?"

"I'm guessing when the flames were at their peak, some of the material blew off the pile and scattered. What I have here, my love, is the hidden zippered pocket that Sergio sewed into the suit jacket."

"I can't believe it!. Incredible! That piece stayed intact without getting burned!" declares Agnes.

"I wonder if the flames betrayed any more evidence. Let's look around some more," Richard suggests when they hear a voice.

"Hey, you two, what are you doing here? This area is private property."

"Oh, we live here and occasionally drive around this beautiful course taking in all its beauty," Richard answers without blinking.

"Okay, not a problem. I'm one of the four-person security that patrols these grounds. I just want to make sure you're both okay, but you should leave the smoldering to the maintenance crew for your safety."

Agnes replies, "We saw smoke billowing a few yards away and thought it best to check it out. Luckily, it seems harmless at this point. Thanks for stopping; we appreciate your concern."

"Not a problem, that's what we're here for, and please, enjoy the rest of your day."

As the security patrol drives away, Agnes asks, "Do you have the evidence?"

"Yes. I stuck it in my pocket when I heard the voice. We now need to contact Sergio and get his opinion."

Still standing at the fire pit, Richard calls from his cell phone, not trusting any calls made from the cottage. As a precaution, he calls Rachael on her direct line.

"What's up, Richard?"

"Agnes and I may have found some evidence. We're at the firepit at the northeast corner of the golf course. Can you contact Sergio and ask him to meet us at your café tonight?"

"I trust your judgment, Richard, but we need to be careful. Sergio is practicing with Tom at the conservatory this evening. It would be better if you slipped into his music practice than for Sergio to be walking across the parking lot to the café."

"I agree. What's the best time for me to be there?"

"He and Tom finish at about 8 p.m."

"Okay, I'll be there."

"Richard, one more thing. Use the side employee entrance; you'll be less noticeable. I'll contact Tom, so he'll be expecting you."

"Thanks, Rachael."

Later that evening, Richard drives over to the conservatory and notices only one car parked in the employee area. Richard guessing it's Tom's car, parks next to it and walks about 15 steps to the side door.

Once inside, Richard hears, "Over here, we're up on stage," Sergio getting his attention.

With no concerts scheduled for a week, the auditorium was empty of chairs and seemed like an open football field as Richard walked across to the stage area.

Finally, for what seemed like five minutes, Richard walks up the steps and greets Tom, "How are you tonight, and Sergio, thanks for meeting with me."

Tom, not entirely comfortable meeting with Richard under these circumstances, quickly states, "Rachael told me you had an urgent need to speak with Sergio. What's up?"

Not wanting to waste any time, Richard digs out of his pocket the smoke-stained fabric he found earlier.

"Do you recognize this, Sergio?"

"Yeah! It's one of the pockets that I used to sew into the jacket lining. Gosh, it smells like smoke. Where did you find this?"

"The fire pit area at the golf course."

Sergio ponders for a moment, then states. "I'm only guessing that Hughes closed the old store I was working in and decided to scuttle the remaining inventory of jackets with the eight hidden zippered pockets."

Unforeseen, the side door opens, and a voice screams, "You forgot to lock the door!" Stepping one foot inside, a fully masked man begins shooting at the stage some hundred yards away. He fires six shots and immediately leaves.

It happened so fast Richard didn't have time to draw his gun.

"Are you guys alright?" Richard asks.

"Yeah, I'm fine," Tom states. "How about you, Sergio?"

"I crawled under the piano, and I think one of the shots hit its side. I could hear the zing as the bullet hit."

Tom inspects the other musical instruments and sadly states, "those shots damaged the drum set, some horns, and guitars. Looks like no concerts for a while."

"Tom, will you call the police while I check the outside perimeter?" Richard asks.

"Sure, but be careful."

Richard opens the side door cautiously with his gun drawn. He peers out the door slightly and assesses the area is safe. He then walks over to the cars for further inspection.

"Gosh, darn!" Richard shouts. He walks back in and locks the door behind him.

Tom inquires, "Everything okay?"

"No, not really. You would think six shots would have been enough, but the shooter slashed all of our tires also."

Sergio trying not to show he's shaking, states, "I guess we're stuck here for a while then, huh?"

Richard tries to calm Sergio by stating some humor. "You thought your life was upside down living with Tom and practicing classical piano. Sergio, you haven't lived like anything you're about to experience."

Tom catches the drift, "Hey! It's not so bad living with me, is it, Sergio?"

"No, but Richard, what are you really saying?"

"I'm guessing you and Tom will be living in Rachael's hotel with 24-hour bodyguard security for a while."

Tom inquires, "I can't live in my home. Why?"

"It won't be safe. Scrawled on our windshields with what looks like blood are the words, *'next time, my aim will be better.'*

Tom sits down on the piano bench next to Sergio and takes deep breaths, hopefully trying not to faint.

Sergio, gaining some composure, asks, "How long will we have this security and hotel living?"

"Don't know, son. I wish I could give you a definite answer. Much will depend on the police investigation and all the parameters involved in a crime scene like we experienced tonight."

CHAPTER THIRTY

POLICE INVESTIGATION-MAR 2036

Four squad cars arrive at the conservatory within three minutes after Tom's call. Leaving his hotel room, Mitch Kearney shows up at the scene also.

He walks over to one of the officers, "Are you the lieutenant in charge of this crime scene?"

"May I inquire who's asking?"

"Mitch Kearney, FBI Director-Northern Region," Mitch shows his badge.

"Lieutenant Kace, good to meet you, sir."

"Has your team developed any preliminary analysis of the shooting yet?"

"Some. It's early in the investigation, but we have this much figured out. The shooter missed hitting his targets intentionally. This wasn't amateur night at the music hall. We're dealing with a professional. Also, I'm having the vehicles towed on a flatbed for further examination—especially the scrawling on the windshields and the origin of ink used."

At that moment, Agnes shows up, driven over by police, to join her husband.

"Richard, are you okay? I freaked out when the police showed up at my door. Are you okay?"

"Yes, dear, I'm okay." Richard nods his head toward the policemen that drove his wife over. "Thanks for bringing her, officer. I appreciate your kindness."

"My pleasure, sir,"

Moments later, Rabbi Yosef shows up with Darrell and Rachael. She runs over to Tom and Sergio, still sitting on the piano bench, numb but alive.

"Are you guys okay? Tom, I am so sorry I got you involved in this mess. I had no idea it would get so tragic. You're both staying at my hotel indefinitely until this situation is resolved!"

No sooner had Rachel uttered those words when the police lieutenant walked up on stage and approached Tom.

"Are you Tom Gerrard?"

"Last time I looked in the mirror, I was."

"Well, you may not be aware, but part of a police investigation encompasses inspecting all property concerned with a crime. You and your roommate were the probable targets. Our team just left your home, Mr. Gerrard. I'm sorry to state it's currently uninhabitable. It seems like nothing is destroyed or missing but ransacked thoroughly. Sadly, the same words on the windshields were also on your bathroom mirror. *Next time, I won't miss.*'

Tom looks over at Sergio, then Rachael, and profoundly states, "Rachael, we will accept your offer; what's are our room numbers?"

Mitch Kearney walks over to the group. "I got off the phone with the police captain moments ago. The department is providing both of you 24-hour police security for as long as needed."

Mitch turns his direction to Richard and Agnes. "It seems the cottage you're living at hasn't been compromised. You weren't the target, Richard. Nevertheless, at least for a while, the captain is also providing you 24-hour security. The two of you may return home if you like or stay overnight here at the hotel?"

Darrell jumps in, "Richard, Agnes! Don't be silly, and it's late! You'll be our guests for tonight. Rachael and I won't accept 'no' for an answer."

Agnes accepts before Richard declines. "Thank you, Darrell; we appreciate your concern for our safety."

Rabbi Yosef walks over to Rachael, "May I speak with you for a moment?"

"Sure, if it's important."

"When you called me on this tragedy that occurred this evening, I thought it best to drive you and Darrell over. I'm thinking of safety for everyone. It's vital to me. I know you're rattled; it's to be expected. But, have you given any thought to the pregnant teenage girls in your 'Adopt-not Abort' program staying at your hotel?"

"Oh! My goodness, gracious, I haven't!" Rachael is horrified, not remembering.

"If I recall, there are three girls currently registered in your program. Naomi and I would be glad to take them into our home for a spell if that would give them more security than staying here."

"I appreciate your compassion, Rabbi, but I think they're safe staying in the east wing. The conservatory is on the west side of the hotel where the shooting took place. But, let's ask Mitch and the lieutenant."

Conveniently, they find Mitch and Kace huddled, going over the incidents when Rabbi and Rachael approach them. Rabbi Yosef explains the conundrum he and Rachael are facing.

Mitch takes a second before answering. "It would be more dangerous to move them than if they were to stay here. Lieutenant, could your department provide them 24-hour security also for a while?"

"I'm sure we can. I'll call the request into Captain Sullivan and let you know."

Mitch replies, "Thanks, Kace."

Rachael confides to Rabbi Yosef, "As long as you're here, I have this concern, more so than ever before now. For convenience and, most importantly, safety, especially after tonight's horror. The conservatory needs an elevated walkway from the hotel. It would allow students to walk in safely versus having to span the parking lot. What are your thoughts on that idea?"

"I agree, but that will need to take a backburner to something more relevant. Do you realize there could be some fallout from this incident? Several parents will retract their student's enrollment, at least for the semester."

"Although I'm rattled, as you state, I have given that some thought. I think the school of music can continue in the church lobby. God knows it's big enough to hold a football game. Plus, we'll refund the one-semester cost. I believe that should ebb any parent's concern."

"Okay, I like your thought process on that problem. How about church and security?"

"Darrell and I will hire and triple our security force during church services and school sessions. Prayerfully, this will console any trepidations our parishioners may have."

"Rachael, don't ever tell my wife I'm saying this, but, 'Praise the Lord!' I believe you have all the speed bumps knocked down as best as possible."

"Why, Rabbi Yosef, you never cease to amaze me. Tonight has been emotional, and you're allowed to express your heart's feeling out loud. I'm sure Naomi would understand your praise. Give it a try, share with her, and let me know how she feels."

The police were wrapping up the investigation for tonight when the lieutenant walked over to Mitch.

"Regarding the 24-hour security for the expecting young girls, Captain Sullivan will provide all necessary uniformed police. It seems nepotism does have its rewarding side. It turns out one of the girls is his granddaughter. Unfortunately, her parents kicked her out of the house when she confided she was pregnant. The captain and his wife can't take her into their home-too much danger. So, 'Praise the Lord' for this church embracing life, pro-life, and giving these girls a place they can call home."

Meanwhile, Tom enters his hotel room and is greeted by Bernard.

"*Good evening, Tom. I'm Bernard, the Angel of the Lord, and I have come to comfort you in your time of distress.*"

Tom isn't fazed one bit by the appearance of Bernard. "Thank you. I could use some comfort. You have any suggestions or advice to calm me down?"

"*You should call room service and order a pot of tea, and then read the Book of Psalms. Those two will give you comfort and calm.*"

"That's a good idea, and I will. I also need to call Sergio before he retires for the evening and sees how he's doing."

"I'm proud of you, Tom. You handled the situation rather well this evening. Two years ago, had this occurred, you'd have been a basket case."

"I know. I thank God for giving me the strength to keep on going no matter how dark and bumpy the road of life may be."

"All the angels and I have everyone covered; I can assure you. Oh, I hear a knock on the door. It must be your room service and tea. Enjoy, get some rest, and we'll meet up soon." Bernard disappears.

Tom opens the door and is surprised, not expecting the royal treatment. All decked out in his English uniform is the hotel waiter standing in the back of a silver cart. On top is an elegant carved English teapot. Next to it on a silver-lined tray are lemons, sugar, and spices.

"May I roll the cart in, sir?"

"Yes, sure, by all means. Thank you." Tom is speechless by this gesture of kindness, and he reaches into his pocket, about to tip the waiter.

"No, sir, but thank you, anyway. Tonight's room service is on the house, gratis Darrell and Rachael."

As the waiter leaves the room, Tom reaches out and shakes the uniformed policeman's hand watching both doors. Sergio's and his.

"Thank you, officer. You have no idea how much I appreciate the unselfish service the men and women in blue give to the community. On behalf of Cedar Creek, I just want to say, 'Thank You.'"

"You're welcome. It's my pleasure to serve. I wish the new mayor would feel the same as you do, sir."

"I recently moved to this city and wasn't aware the voters elected a new mayor."

"Yes, our previous mayor presided over our city for three terms. He did a fantastic job, but it seems several of the citizens got their feathers ruffled when his challenger campaigned against Mayor Alderman's Jewish heritage. Now, we have a liberal attorney as the mayor. His background is in bankruptcy law. Together with his wife, they operate a law practice in town, and her specialty is family law. "

Tom, trying to look on the bright side of life, asks, "is it so bad the new mayor knows bankruptcy laws, officer?"

"Yes! The mayor and the council are in virtual tandem with President Avci and his D. C. Mandate. They, too, want to defund the police department, shutter all churches, and confiscate all guns and Bibles. I'm afraid what you witnessed tonight, sir, will be common. God help us, but it looks like sin is taking over my beloved city. Mark my words, there will be a rash of businesses filing bankruptcy due to the destruction caused by the ongoing riots. Incidentally, those bankruptcy filings will line the Mayor's pocket very nicely. How convenient."

"Oh, I see." Tom is trembling again, and all he can muster is, "I will pray for you, the police department, and the city. Good night, officer." Tom closes the door and slumps into bed.

CHAPTER THIRTY-ONE

GOLF OUTING-APRIL 2036

The following morning, Hughes makes his usual rounds checking out the golf course and cemetery when he bumps into Jax.

"Hey, good morning, Jax. Are you and the other three members of the security patrol team handling everything okay?"

"Yes, sir. The golf course and cemetery are looking good. Sadly, I can't say the same about the auditorium and musical instruments. I shot them up fairly bad last night."

"Your marksmanship is beyond approach. Your military stint as a sniper has come in handy as a second career. Good job, and Tom's house?"

"A total mess; it'll take a month of Sundays to restore it. Especially the bathroom mirror, I used pig's blood to write my messages."

"Oh, yes, your infamous writings. Eventually, they'll figure out the windshields, and the mirror will need to be replaced. Good job, again, Jax. Have a good day,"

"Thank you, sir."

Hughes drives over to the 6th green on the Blue Course and checks on Ralph and Agnes's new home's building progress. He walks over to the project superintendent, "Hey, when do you estimate the completion date for this home?"

"Twenty to twenty-five days, and the new owners should be able to move in. When completed, it will be a shining light on top of a hill with all the wrap-around windows."

Hughes replies, "Very impressive. This home will be one of five models I'll make available to all future home buyers. Thank you and have a good day."

"You too, sir."

Hughes drives off to the John Doe section of the cemetery and calls the new mayor on his direct line. "Good morning, Mayor Brady. Have you been able to resolve those nasty conflicts permeating the city council?"

Allen Brady and his beautiful wife were the first African American couple to occupy the mayor's Cedar Creek office. His priority campaign promise was to decrease costs for the city, especially religious parades that encompassed extra police and double time.

Six years ago, the Jerusalem Tree Church sponsored, in part, a parade moving the historic antique picnic table from the grove to the church's lobby. Rachael and Darrell paid for half the costs of additional police and overtime. Nevertheless, the new mayor has a vendetta against God and secretly loves nothing more than to see all the churches in Cedar Creek close their doors.

"No, not yet!" Angrily shouts the mayor. "There are two members of the eleven-member council that are adamant about not defunding the police department. They predict that Cedar Creek will become a city in turmoil and chaos constantly if we lose 25% of our police force."

"Remind them that reduction will save the city over two million dollars, and that's the reason you all got elected."

"Maybe I should propose a 40% reduction and compromise on 15%?" Mayor Brady suggests with exasperation in his voice.

"Settle for 25%!" Demands, Hughes. "Text me the names of the two. I'll invite them over for a round of golf and lunch. Maybe my kindness will persuade them to vote your way, Mr. Mayor."

"Sure! You got it, and thanks! Good luck!"

Hughes is thinking to himself, *I don't need luck; I make things happen.*

Meanwhile, Richard and Agnes return home to their cottage after a goodnight's rest at Rachael's hotel.

"So, my dear, Richard, are your nerves still shaken from last night's incident?"

"I don't think so, but to be sure, I think a round of golf will calm me down."

"Yeah, I agree, you should. Who's going to play with you?"

"I'll give the police captain and lieutenant an invite and see if they have time for a quick round of nine holes."

"In that case, I'll take the other golf cart and inspect the progress of our new home. I'll leave you the bronze six-seater cart."

"Yeah, good idea, thanks."

The captain and the lieutenant were thrilled with the golf invite and showed up at 5 p.m. for the scheduled tee time. As Richard drives up in the bronze beauty, everyone was impressed with the Rolls Royce-style golf cart.

Captain Sullivan inquires, "Where did you get that gem, Richard?"

"A gift from the owner of this course and cemetery, Mr. Hughes Reyna. My wife and I are building a home here above the 6th green, which was his way of saying thanks."

Lieutenant Kace faces Richard, "I hope you don't mind, but we brought three of our uniformed policemen as security while we play. After last night's shooting, no one can be too careful."

"I don't blame you. Good thing I brought the six-seater cart. It also has room for four bags. I see you have an extra golf bag, but there are only two of you playing. What's in the third bag?"

Captain Sullivan answers, "Machine guns."

"I told my wife that if I played a short round of golf, it would calm my nerves. Now, I'm not so sure."

"Don't worry; we use that artillery as the last weapon of defense, only if our lives are on the line," Sullivan replies.

Richard is shaken by the thought of machine guns riding in the back and takes a bogey on each of the first three holes. Lickety-split, as the threesome walk over to the fourth tee, Hughes shows up in his golf cart.

"Good afternoon, gentlemen. I'm wondering how a sixsome became the new norm to play a round of golf?"

Richard answers, "You haven't heard about the shooting that took place at the conservatory last night?"

"I can't say I have. What shooting?" Hughes feigns innocence.

"Tom, the music director and professor, his protégé, the young classical pianist, and I were shot at while standing on stage rehearsing. Thank God the shooter hit none of us, but he did manage to cause major damage to several musical instruments."

"I'm glad you're all okay, and I'm confident insurance will replace all the instruments. So, I take it the three men in uniform are bodyguards for whom?"

"Oh, sorry about that, Hughes. Let me introduce Captain Sullivan and Lieutenant Kace. They're part of the investigation team, and after last night, I figured nine holes of golf would be relaxing for each of us," Richard shares the facts.

"Good to meet each of you, and hopefully, your guards will be bored to tears with nothing to do while watching you guys play golf," Hughes's little sarcastic remark didn't go unnoticed.

As Hughes drives off, the captain and lieutenant simultaneously state, "He doesn't like the police. His tone has a deceptive loathe."

Poor Richard, his idea of a relaxing, calm golf game became the worse game he played since he was seventeen. He lost the junior high tournament on the final day, bogeying every hole for eighteen over par. Today was slightly different. He double-bogeyed the ninth hole for a ten-over par.

Richard takes his lousy day on the golf course in stride and invites the guys to the clubhouse for some snacks. Sullivan and Kace accept.

Once inside the clubhouse, they noticed several members had their eyes on the TV. As they approached closer, it was apparent the news wasn't right, at least for them.

"Mayor Brady, would you share with the citizens of Cedar Creek what took place at the council vote moments ago?' The reporter asked.

"Sure, it would be my pleasure. Two city council members abstained from voting, so we had a unanimous vote of nine to reduce the police department funding by 25%, saving its citizens over two million a year. As a result, the city won't be hiking taxes in the next two budget years."

The reporter comes back, "You've kept your campaign promise, decreasing the city budget. Now, how will this affect the police force?"

"All of our men and women wearing the blue uniform have had stellar years with the department. We'll be offering several with early retirement, and others, we'll assist with job replacement. Our office is committed to honoring those who have served our fine city for all these years."

"Thank you, Mayor Brady, and now back to our studio."

Captain Sullivan glares into space, annoyed by what he just heard. Finally, turning to Richard and Kace, "That press conference was nothing but sugar frosting. Reading between the lines, except you, Richard, we're all fired and looking for another job."

"I thank God I was able to choose my retirement," Richard states appreciatively. "Listen, guys. Darrell and Rachael are tripling the security teams at church and college. Consider applying. Darrell and Rachael are good people; you won't go wrong being part of their Godly team."

All five members of the police squad state they will, even tomorrow.

Captain Sullivan stares at the four men in front of him and shares the unspeakable. "You all know what this means, don't you?" Kace shakes his head, but the others haven't done the math yet. "When Kace and I are gone, the police department will drop the investigation of last night's shooting and Tom's house ransacked. Convenient, huh?"

"Funny, I was just about to say something similar, " Richard states. "I wonder who or what got this vote to be accomplished so quickly?" Richard snaps with a persnickety tone.

Kace catches on quickly, "Are you alluding to our wonder boy who owns this course and loathes police?"

"Precisely."

Meanwhile, Hughes is back in his office when his private line rings.

"What can I do for you, Mayor?"

"I think you already have. Your persuasion was quicker than I had anticipated. What did you say?"

"Simple, I suggested if the two members abstained from voting, I'd gift them with a lifetime club membership. If not, I assured them they'd have a lifetime of never being able to swing a golf club ever again."

"I sometimes wonder how I ever would have won the election without your back-office assistance."

"Don't wonder; just do as I say."

Without warning, Bernard appears in the mayor's office. *"Do not be afraid. I am Bernard, the Angel of the Lord, and I have come to help you find the truth of life."*

"Who are you? How did you get into my office?"

"More importantly, Mayor Brady, is why did you sell your soul to the devil. Simply to win an election?"

"No, you have it wrong. I didn't sell my soul to anyone."

"The devil has a tight grip on Hughes, and you're following in lock-step."

"He only helped during my campaign, nothing more."

"You conveniently forgot Hughes's last phone call to those two members, threatening to break their arms."

"Hughes carves out his daily agenda. I don't tell him what to do."

"The truth is, mayor, you're his puppet. Hughes is the master puppeteer tugging at your strings constantly."

"I wanted to win the election regardless of costs. It didn't matter the price I had to pay."

"The truth is, mayor, if you don't cut the strings soon, the price you'll pay is your soul lost to damnation forever and ever. It would be better to give your soul to Jesus, knowing you'd have eternal life with Him in glorious heaven."

"About that, Jesus's stuff. I don't believe it, and I don't like it."

"It seems you don't like the police either. What goes on with you, mayor?"

"Back in the day when my granddaddy was alive, the country church he attended was pastored by the county sheriff. In those days, everyone wore at least two hats. Anyway, the sheriff treated my granddaddy very mean. I don't need a sheriff or a church to fulfill my life. Hughes's desire to decrease the police department is a reality, and my goal to close church doors is a work in progress. I contend that partnering with Hughes will give both of us a power grab unheard of only by the politics in Washington, D.C."

"You have anger festering in your heart, mayor. I contend, instead, you should partner with Jesus and allow Him to touch your heart. It is not too late, mayor, to change your heart and mind and have a meaningful relation-

ship with Jesus Christ. The path you're on will lead your soul to everlasting torture in the lake of fire."

"But, you don't understand, Bernard, or whatever your name is. The path I'm on will surely lead me to the United States Congress."

"That, Mr. Mayor, is a lie of the old serpent, the devil, keeping you on the path of sin. God will not have mercy on your soul if you become a career politician and don't repent your sins. God is just and cannot and will not accept any sin-stained soul into His heaven to join His Son, Jesus Christ.

"Listen, Bernard, I have another news conference to attend. Enjoy the rest of your day, and hopefully, our paths won't cross again."

"One day, you will pray that I will be with you." Bernard disappears.

CHAPTER THIRTY-TWO

HOTEL LOCK-DOWN-APR 2036

Three weeks have elapsed since the department store shooting, and all the victims involved have healed better than expected.

Irving and Helen weren't the intended targets, so Mitch Kearney, the FBI Director, allowed them to return home and manage the rehab center.

Just as important, Mitch schedules a post-incident meeting in the hotel's conference room. He invites Rachael and Darrell, Tom, Sergio, Lucinda, Cambria, and Carlo. He also scheduled Rodriquez, one of his security guards, to secure the conference room while the meeting was in progress.

"I want to thank each of you for taking the time to attend this meeting. We have several issues to cover, so let me begin with the good news-bad news first. I've discussed the situation with Rachael and Darrell before this morning's meeting. The good news is, you'll all be living in this hotel indefinitely until further notice."

The room is abuzz with chatter and excitement from the announcement.

Tom anticipates Mitch's answer but inquires anyway. "So, when do you feel I'll be able to return to my house?"

"Unfortunately, Tom, yours is the bad news. My team has removed all your furniture and belongings that weren't damaged and placed them in storage. We'll escort you there in about a week so you can retrieve what you need. Your house, Tom, is a marked target forever. No one would ever be safe living there again. Thank goodness your home is in the country with acreage. The Feds will be buying your home at fair-market value, bulldozing it down, and then a year later, constructing an apartment complex on the property."

"I'm not surprised and do feel safer living here. I would like to inquire of Darrell and Rachael if we could generate a lease agreement allowing me to make the hotel room I'm staying in my permanent address?."

"Yes, of course, Tom," declares Rachael.

"We would love to have you as our first full-time resident, Tom," exclaimed Darrell.

"We don't broadcast it, but Darrell and I have set aside ten apartment hotel-style rooms in this complex. As a full-time- employee, we'll lease the two-bedroom to you at 40% off, plus half off on all meals. Will that work for you, Tom?" inquires Rachael.

"I'm so ever grateful. Yes, it will. Thank you."

"It's the least we can do for our worship leader and professor of music. We hope and pray you'll be richly blessed, Tom," imparted Darrell.

"Well, this is a turn of events I hadn't expected and is cause for thanking God on how He blesses when one is least expecting. Praise the Lord!" shouts Mitch.

"Yes, indeed! Praise the Lord," voiced Tom.

"Incidentally, I'm moving the rest of you to the east wing, across the hall from the 'Adopt-not Abort' program," Mitch alerts. "This move will enable our 24-hour security to cover all the rooms on one floor, making it safer."

Rachael speaks next, "Darrell and I shared this next idea with Mitch before announcing, and he approved. So, we would like to offer employment to Cambria and Carlo. You'll both head up the casual suit line-fashions for men and women. The focus and responsibility of your combined positions will be online marketing and fashion shows, primarily in New York City and Chicago."

"I can't thank you both enough. I was concerned about where and what type of work we could do after rehab," Carlo shares. "This is a blessing for Cambria and me; thank you again."

Darrell replies, "You're most welcome.

Mitch speaks next, "We need to discuss personal expenses while you're living here. During your collective rehab, Darrell and Rachael covered all your costs. Obviously, they can't continue with that program. I have good news. The Feds are picking up 60% of all your room and meal expenses. So, each of you has only 40% of the balance to cover."

Tom speaks first, "Lucinda, Cambria, Carlo, and Sergio. You're all about twenty years younger than I. Your 40% responsibility may sound unreasonable at first, but believe me, this is good news! If you're wise and disciplined, you should all be able to save a tidy bundle by the time you're allowed to leave here."

"Thank you, Tom, for those words of encouragement. He's right, kids; if you're here a while, you should have a nice bundle saved up," Rachael shares.

"Before we adjourn, I have some more news," Mitch shares with the group. "Sergio, the Feds need your testimony, and it could be several months before we have enough evidence to go to trial. I'll be escorting you to your room in a moment, you'll grab your belongings, and then we're leaving immediately. Rachael, I'm also checking out. Darrell, thanks for setting up the temporary field office, and I'm assigning Sullivan and Kace to be my liaison at this property. Should you need anything, they will contact me on your behalf."

Rachael is astonished by Mitch's announcement and loudly exclaims, "I thought Sullivan and Kace were with the police department?"

"Believe me, Rachael and Darrell, I don't have anything against God or church, but sometimes it would be good to listen to the news, so you're aware of what's going on-especially in Cedar Creek!" Mitch was kind of giving them a verbal scolding.

Darrell asks, "What do you mean?"

"Yesterday, the mayor and city council voted to defund the police department by 25%. Supposedly, saving the citizens over two million in tax dollars. Sullivan and Kace took early retirement, and I hired them as part of my team. Undoubtedly, the city will fire more officers, and I'm sure several will apply here. The word did get out that you're looking to beef up your security."

"Oh, my goodness gracious," is all Rachael can muster. "I'm so sorry, Mitch. Darrell and I weren't aware. I promise we'll do our due diligence moving forward."

"It's for your good, trust me on that. One more item, and then Sergio and I will be leaving. He'll be staying at my headquarters in Albany, the most secure place at this time for him. This is vitally important. Should you see Sergio or me anywhere, on TV, at the grocery store, don't acknowledge you know us, don't say hi and don't look, simply keep on walking. I trust my message is loud and clear-right?"

Everyone at the meeting agrees.

"Before you all adjourn, I want to announce we'll be continuing this meeting immediately after lunch," Rachael reminding everyone.

Rodriquez steps out of the room as they all leave, walks to the courtyard for privacy, and calls Hughes. "They're having another conference meeting this afternoon, and Sergio will be staying at the FBI office in Albany."

"Thanks, Rod. I'll have my man take care of the conference room situation first and then have him travel to Albany and take care of Sergio."

"If I can help you with anything else, just give me a holler."

"I will, Rod, and thanks."

CHAPTER THIRTY-THREE

DOUBLE-HEADER–MAY 2036

Later in the day, while Mitch and Sergio are heading out to Albany, Mitch receives a call from his detective out of the blue.

"Max, you have never called me on this hot-line number before. It must be urgent. Go ahead. I'm listening."

"It is. This afternoon, twenty minutes ago, I was at the gun range practicing. This guy next to me, slightly drunk already, was bragging about how he would shoot up the 2nd-floor east wing of Rachael's hotel. You best get someone there and fast!"

"I'm halfway to Albany, and my two guys are on assignment. But, don't worry, Max, I have this covered."

Mitch calls Richard.

"Hey, good to hear from you, Mitch. I just sunk my 4th birdie this afternoon."

"Sorry to break up your game, but I'm deputizing you now. I need you over at Rachael's hotel, east wing, 2nd floor immediately! Just got word that Hughes has his hitman there to take out Sergio's friends. I don't have the time to return or round up my deputies. You have to be my go-to man."

"Oh, my goodness, that's on the same floor the pregnant teenage girls are staying. You know, the 'Adopt-not Abort' ministry Rachael started."

"Yes, I remember now. I'll contact Sullivan and Kace to help you out, but don't count on them being there in time. Keep me posted, Richard, and God be with you."

Hughes has Jax do the dirty deed at the hotel, the same guy that shot up the conservatory. Jax takes the back stairway up to the second floor. Spotting one of the cleaning ladies in the hallway, he hits her with pepper spray, drags her limp body into one of the rooms, and steals her master key. A few moments later, he spots one of the security guards and hits him with pepper spray. After changing into the security guards' uniform, Jax, using the master key, opens the doors to all the rooms. To his chagrin, no one is inside any of the places.

Considering his second option, Jax slowly walks toward the second-floor atrium where the conference room is located. Drawing his gun, he places his hand on the doorknob, turns it ever so slowly, swings open the door, and shouts, "Freeze!"

When Jax abruptly entered the conference room with his gun drawn, he startled everyone engaged in the meeting except for Rachael. She states, "God have mercy."

"What did you say?" Jax demanded.

"I blurted, God, have mercy."

"You got that right. You're all going to need God's mercy. I'm going to have a field day this afternoon. It will be like shooting birds sitting on a rail fence."

Rachael shouts back, "You misunderstood. I uttered, may God have mercy on you!"

At that precise moment, Richard enters the room and yells, "You forgot to lock the door," and fires two shots, one each in the arm and leg of Jax.

Seconds later, Sullivan and Kace arrive. "Everyone okay in here?" Sullivan inquires.

Rachael assures him everyone is okay. Kace reads Jax his rights as they haul him out on a stretcher.

"Wait, one second, officer, I want to ask this man why he didn't shoot to kill me."

Richard replies, "I aim to wound so justice can be served. You'll now have the opportunity to testify against your boss or take your chances in prison."

"I have no idea what you're talking about, officer; take me to the hospital. I'm done here."

Rachael, Darrell, Cambria, Carlo, Lucinda, and Tom, take a moment in prayer to thank God for His protection.

Tom walks over to Richard and inquires, "How did you know to arrive at that precise moment?"

"I had alerted Rachael before she started the meeting. She simply had her cellphone on so that I could hear the conversation. Timing and aiming are everything. Praise the Lord!"

Rachael walks over to Sullivan. "I want to thank you for hiding my three girls in the central kitchen. I'll bet they're hungry by now, smelling all those aromas for the last two hours."

"When I left them, the chef sat them at the employee's table and treated them to some of your finer meals, Rachael. It looked like they were eating for two."

"Well, when a girl is six months pregnant, that seems to be the norm."

"Yes, I do recall those days when my wife craved everything we had in the kitchen. Well, I'm glad all things worked for good; thank you, Lord! Kace and I best be getting over to the hospital and asking our suspect some questions."

"I know you won't be able to divulge any information, but I'll be curious if he'll be protecting Hughes or decide it better to testify?" Rachael wondering out loud.

"You're right. I won't be able to tell you anything." Sullivan chuckles as he leaves.

During the ambulance ride to the hospital, Jax encounters the presence of Bernard.

"Do not be afraid, Jax, I am Bernard, the Angel of the Lord. I have come to help you. No one sees or hears me, only you."

"Unless you're a doctor, I don't need any help, whoever you are."

"In the world's vernacular, you're a lucky man. Richard didn't kill you. Do you know why?"

"So, I'd supposedly testify against my boss, which will never happen."

"Well, that's one reason why you're still alive. But, more importantly, so you can confess your sins, accept Jesus Christ as your savior, and be certain you'll have everlasting life in heaven."

"Well, as soon as I heal up from these wounds, I like my life as it is right here on earth. What do I care about heaven, even if there is such a place?"

"Listen, Jax. I am always the messenger of good news, but sometimes, I need to be the bearer of bad news."

"You have bad news?" Bernard got Jax's attention quickly.

"Those wounds are more severe than first thought. You may not have much time left. I don't know if you'll make it to the hospital in time for surgery. Jax, if you were to die in the next three minutes, would you want your soul to be in Heaven or Hell forever and ever?"

"I don't understand everything you're saying, but most assuredly, I want to be in heaven with whoever else is there. Do I need to do anything to be sure?"

"Repeat after me, 'Dear Jesus, forgive me my sins, and come into my heart as my Lord and Savior.'"

Jax repeated those words as the ambulance arrived at the emergency entrance. The attendants were able to whisk him into surgery, and he survived.

Later in the afternoon, Kace and Sullivan visit Jax in his hospital room.

"I hear you had a close call. You almost left us in the ambulance ride. Glad to see you're still alive," Sullivan shares.

"I had this weird experience of an angel talking with me. I believe I accepted Jesus Christ while chatting with him."

Kace shares, "You did, Jax. The angel's name is Bernard. He encourages bad people to confess their sins and accept Jesus, and then, forsake their previous lifestyle."

"Listen, guys. I don't know how to forsake being a sniper. During my stint in the military, I was the best of the best. I feel lucky that Hughes found and hired me. What am I to do, guys?"

Sullivan jumps in, "What if we could get you in the department of special forces with the Feds and provide immunity for you. Would you then testify against your boss?"

"Yes, but only if you give me 24/7 protection while I'm recuperating in this room."

"You got it. I'll contact Mitch Kearney, and you'll probably be flown to another hospital in a short while for added protection."

"Any idea where that would be?"

"Yeah. Albany, New York."

CHAPTER THIRTY-FOUR

DINNER CHAT-MAY 2036

Mitch Kearney delivers an important National News Conference.

"Good evening. I'm speaking from Buffalo, New York. My name is Mitch Kearney, FBI Director, Northern District. I'm proud to announce that members of the FBI teams in Cedar Creek, New York, abated an assassin attempt early today. The assailant was shot and killed during the line of fire. Unfortunately, no identity was found on the person, and, in the last hour, the body was cremated. Currently, I'm not taking any questions." Mitch walks away from the podium and speaks with Richard, Sullivan, and Kace that accompanied him to the press conference.

"When Hughes hears this news, it should solidify his soul that no one is going to squeal on him," Mitch tactfully states.

"Now I know why you're the director, Mitch. That speech was brilliant," Sullivan acknowledges.

"We'll let time unravel the rest of Hughes's empire. My hunch is it will be just a matter of days," Mitch states.

Hughes hears the news of his associate getting killed in the line of evil duty and is relieved he can't testify. He continues with added zeal in his empire-building and takes the call from Carmen, the billionaire zealot whose political ideology is to shutter all churches in America.

"If I'm going to continue funneling your counterfeit monies, you owe me a factory tour. I want to see with my own eyes your operation. My son, Connor, and I have booked two rooms at a hotel adjacent to a church, I guess not far from your country club."

"I wish you would have informed me sooner; you could have stayed at one of my guest cottages."

"The reservation went through my concierge. Something about a swap with the Manhattan hotel I usually stay at, no problem. Pick us up late morning, and we'll have lunch at your club, then head out to your factory," Carmen asserts his will non-sparingly.

Hughes isn't used to having commands barked at him but maintained his composure. "Sure, I'll have my driver pick you up in our limo at 11 a.m."

"Is that the limo you use for funeral processions?" Carmen inquires with a questionable tone.

"Yes, but don't worry, there aren't any dead bodies in the limo. They're only in the John Doe section. By the way, how are you guys getting to the hotel?"

"My son wants to drive his new sports car and supposedly treat me to something exciting. Tell you what, Hughes, leave the limo at your club. Connor and I will drive up in the sports car. After lunch, we'll all ride to your plant in the limo. Fair enough?"

"Sure, that works for me. See you tomorrow."

Meanwhile, back at the hotel, Rachael and Darrell decide to meet with all the employees regarding the afternoon shooting.

Rachael speaks, "Darrell and I want to thank all of you for maintaining your composure during the brief turmoil that took place. We also want all of you to know that we have plainclothes security officers throughout the facility. We assure you, you are all safe."

Darrell adds, "I am aware as humans it will be a challenge not to discuss this occurrence with coworkers, and maybe even guests. For your safety, I highly advise you to keep silent about this. Just do your job as you've always done, and I promise, this ordeal will end soon."

All the employees acknowledge their requests and return to their respective stations for their shifts.

That same evening, Carmen and Connor check into Rachael's hotel.

The desk clerk recognizes Carmen and calls Darrell at his church office after they leave the registration area.

"Darrell, Quinn here. You won't believe who just checked into the hotel!"

"The Madam Speaker of the House?"

"No! Not that bad! But it's Carmen Bridgewater and his son, Connor. You know, the billionaire who's rumored to fund all types of radical unrest in this country."

"Well, Quinn, you know our policy. We honor all guests regardless of their political or religious persuasion. Nevertheless, I'll ask our security to keep an eye on them."

"They inquired which restaurant I'd recommend, and I suggested the Italian. Most likely, they'll be dining there tonight," Quinn voice shaking.

"Not a problem, Rachael and I will introduce ourselves and welcome them to our facility."

Sure enough, at 7 p.m. Carmen and Connor walk into the Italian restaurant and ask to be seated in a far corner facing the front door. The host calls Darrell, "They're here, sitting in the far corner-Godfather style."

"Relax, everything will be fine. Rachael and I will be there, momentarily."

As Darrell hangs up the phone, he's thinking, "Honey, we should dress to impress. I'll wear my tux, and would you consider wearing that white chiffon evening gown?"

"I'd love to, sweetheart. Give me fifteen minutes, and I'll be ready."

Moments later, Darrell and Rachael take the elevator down from their third-floor hotel apartment and stroll over to the restaurant. The host nods in the direction Carmen and his son are dining.

As they approach his table, Carmen stands up to greet them formally. "I see it didn't take long for the rumor mill to work its magic. I take it you two are the charming hosts of this fine establishment."

"Yes. I'm Darrell, and to my right is my lovely wife, Rachael."

"I'm delighted to meet both of you. Allow me to introduce my son, Connor. He's the vice-president of Bridgewater Industries. Please, sit; we're about to order an after-dinner cognac. Would you like to join us?"

"Sure, why not? We'd love to," Rachael replies.

As they sit down, Darrell asks, "So, what does Bridgewater Industries do?"

Connor waits to answer, allowing the waiter to serve the cognacs. "Yes, my dad and I prefer to state our company dabbles in many avenues of commerce and politics. I'm sure you've read the tabloids insinuating that we are involved in certain areas of unrest in this country. But, you can't believe everything you read, right?"

Rachael speaks next. "I find it interestingly strange that two billionaires sitting at this table have wholly different persuasions. One is, should I say, leans left, and the other leans right. Don't you find that interesting?"

Carmen answers, "I'll put your suspicions to rest. If this next election, in November 2036, brings the results we're hoping for, President Avci and Vice-President Firuzeh's re-election, we'll be able to enforce the D. C. Mandate that hopefully, President Avci will sign next month, June 2036. Having secured the return of his loyal incumbents after the 2034 mid-term election, it's only a matter of time when the D. C. Mandate becomes law. Resulting in the closing of all churches and confiscation of all Bibles in America. So, how do you pastors like that idea?"

Rachael ponders and then answers. "I have never witnessed so much bitter hatred toward churches and Bibles. Is your ideology so mighty that churches can't co-exist in your world? Besides, in the six months to the election, lots of things can happen."

Carmen snips back, "Don't count on it!"

Connor answers, "My generation has been brain-washed by college professors into believing America is evil. That was half the battle which the left won, as you say. Our goal is to bring about a one-world government for people in the liberal circle who strongly desire this. When the new government is established, it will become the god for all people. Not the God in a church."

"Prayerfully, the rapture will take place before the saints of God are subjugated to that evil," Darrell states.

Connor comes right back, "The left is winning every skirmish for a liberal society. Regardless of it through the courts or mob rule, or both, we'll eventually win over the world."

Rachael is getting rattled inside but maintains. "I'll pray harder and longer, seeking the hand of Almighty God to prevail."

Carmen comes back, "I admire your faith. I do. But let me give you an example of mob rule. First, I'm surprised your attorney hasn't advised you to place 'No Trespassing-Private Property' signs around the perimeter of your campus. Secondly, your church holds ten thousand. I'm guessing even though you have deep pockets, the weekly offering covers most if not all of the expenses."

"Yes, that's close enough. What are you getting at, Carmen?" Rachael asks with an eerie tone.

"What if a thousand cars came into your parking lot and blocked your members from attending church on Sunday? What if they protested in front of your church with nasty signs and words? One Sunday morning like that, the attendance would be down 50% or more the following week. Besides, the police wouldn't be available to assist. Your mayor and council just defunded the department."

Darrell asks, "Are you threatening us?"

"No, not at all. Now that we've met, you have my assurance that nothing like that would ever occur here. But think about it. The mob rule would demand you have gay pastors and that no one preaches from the Bible and a sundry of other liberal demands. There's nothing you can do about this; the wave of socialism is coming like a tsunami."

Rachael gets up from the table and states, "I think we're done here. Our after-dinner chat was informative. Darrell and I appreciate your insights. You're welcome to stay as long as you wish, and you have our word-you'll be treated with the utmost respect, no exceptions."

Carmen also stands, "I wouldn't have it any other way. But Connor and I will be checking out in the morning. We're driving up in Connor's new sports car to take a tour of Hughes's casket manufacturing facility in Buffalo tomorrow."

Darrell begins to chuckle, "Be careful you don't try one on for size while visiting."

"I'm glad you still have your humor, Darrell. Good to see that," Carmen acknowledges.

"Oh, one more item before you gentlemen retire for the evening. I'm sure you've noticed that we have two of our security men keeping tabs on both of you," Rachael states.

Connor replies, "Of course, it comes with the territory. Dad and I are accustomed to this."

"It's not what you think. Our security is not looking for an excuse to shoot you, but in case some crazy right-winged conservative tries to shoot you, our guard would take him out to save your evil skin. How's that for Christianity?" Darrell questions boldly.

"You're expected to do just that, nothing less! Have a good evening." Carmen and Connor leave the restaurant and retire to their respective rooms.

As Connor enters his room, removing his sports jacket, Bernard briskly appears.

"Good evening, Connor. I am Bernard, Angel of the Lord."

"You are what? How did you get in here? I'm calling security to remove you from my room."

"No one can see or hear me, except you. You'll look like a fool explaining. Security may then remove you from the room into a mental ward. So, are you ready to listen to me?"

"Do I have a choice?"

"No, not really. I'm curious, Connor, why you believe the brainwashing of America's youth is a good thing?"

"Socialistic education is the best method of tearing down Judeo-Christian values and the nuclear family. Our values are based on the Socialist Manifesto."

"Yes, the Socialist Manifesto is the devil's bible, Satan himself. Your collective circle of friends and you are going straight to hell to the devil's den unless you change your beliefs."

"Collectively, we believe in a one-world government where the government is the god for all the people."

"Your end goal sounds like the repeat of the Roman Empire, which eventually did crumble."

"Ours will never crumble. The best minds in the universe will have total control."

"Connor, I hate to be the one to burst your balloon, but God will reign

on the new earth forever and ever. He is the Prince of Peace. Wonderful Counselor. Mighty God. Everlasting Father. I know this to be true, for I have seen Him, and you can actually read about the end times in the Bible in the book of Revelation."

"Shocker alert! I don't believe any of that stuff!"

"One day, you will, Connor, when you face the mighty throne of God and His Son, Jesus. You will give an account of all your actions, deeds, and beliefs. You will be shocked when you hear Jesus say, 'I never knew you, be cast into the everlasting lake of fire.'"

"What you say, Bernard, to me, is all nonsense. Listen, it's been a long day, and I need to get some sleep. My dad and I have a busy schedule tomorrow. I trust you can see your way out."

"Funny guy 'can see my way out.' Anyway, one day when you're bored conquering the world, I suggest you read the Bible. Start with the Gospels of Matthew, Mark, Luke, and John. You say you have a brilliant mind. Give me a shout when you get to the book of Revelation and explain it to me verse by verse." Bernard disappears.

CHAPTER THIRTY-FIVE

FACTORY TOUR-JUNE 2036

The next morning, Connor and his dad drive up to the country club, where they are greeted by Hughes and Donna.

"Welcome to Cedar Creek Country Club!" Hughes bellows. "Carmen, I'd like you to meet my Director of Operations, Donna Trice."

"It is all my pleasure, beautiful lady," Carmen articulated.

As Connor steps out of the car, his and Donna's eyes lock for a split second.

"Thank you, Carmen, for those kind words. Shall we proceed to the dining room and discuss business over lunch? We have a busy schedule this afternoon and must be prompt." Donna assumes her role as director.

As they arrive at the table, Hughes, who has known Donna for several years, frequently forgets to treat her like a lady. But not Connor, He immediately pulls out a chair for her.

"Thank you, Connor, that was a nice touch," Donna states while tossing a glare at Hughes across the table.

As their lunch is being served, Carmen asks, "So, Hughes, how many employees in your casket plant?

"We hover around fifty employees manufacturing 1,300 caskets monthly. Those are exclusive to our funeral home affiliates of forty."

"Your network is working reasonably well for us, Hughes. When we visit your plant operation, I'll be curious if you have any capacity to increase the counterfeit production," Carmen hints at wanting more.

Hughes and Carmen, engaging in nothing but business and money, are unaware that Donna and Connor are flirting. Their eyes kiss across the table while their feet are touching playfully under the table.

Hughes feels he's playing defense by Carmen's remark. "I'll be happy to discuss the capacity level when we get there. You'll see for yourself that we're running at maximum levels."

As they leave the dining room and about to ride in the limo, Connor yells, "Dad, Hughes, if it's alright with both of you, I'd like to take Donna for a spin in my new sports car. She used to have one and is curious about what power these new ones have. So, we'll meet you both at the plant."

"Sure, it's okay with me. Hughes and I have a ton of business to discuss while riding in the limo. Okay, with you, Hughes?"

Hughes felt like he was on defense again but wasn't about to cause a scene, "Sure, no problem, we'll see you guys at the plant."

Connor and Donna hop into the convertible sports car and take off in a flash, leaving the two businessmen standing by the limo.

Hughes has a quiet moment sharing with Carmen. "She used to have one like that years ago. I'm sure she misses it. Guess I should get her one for her birthday coming up next month."

As the two men climb into the back-limo seat and put up the privacy window, Carmen states, "Hughes, I think you're right. You should get her one."

Meanwhile, Connor, showing off to Donna, shifts the six gears through all its paces, hearing the roar of the engine with each shift.

"So, how do you like the ride so far?"

"I wish it would never end. I haven't had so much fun for several years. Are you sure you have a date tonight? Can't you reschedule? Maybe, somehow we could also ditch the meeting at the plant."

"I would love to do that, but my dad would be furious. He wants me to marry this millionaire princess lady, whom I can't stand. But, I also suspect, your buddy, Hughes, would be beyond furious, as you alluded to me a few weeks ago."

"Well then, maybe I could interest you in a warm-up before your date tonight. Trust me. I have an idea."

Connor and Donna arrive ten minutes earlier than the limo. As Hughes gets out, Donna inquires, "So, did you two get all the irons straightened out?"

"Hardly, he wants an additional 10% discount to continue with the operation or switch to printing twenty-dollar bills. The latter is too risky. I'll have to cave in to his demands for the discount. I don't see any other way." Hughes sounds defeated.

"I think if we have Klaus explain the intricate mechanics of printing counterfeit on this press and in the underground, maybe Carmen will understand and relinquish his demand." Donna quickly switches her brain back to business.

"Let's give it a try," Hughes states as they all walk into the casket side of the manufacturing plant.

Hughes waxes with pride as he explains the design he created to smuggle counterfeit within the casket in every detail.

Connor states, "Mr. Reyna! I am impressed beyond measure with your creativity and engineering mind. You're a genius!"

Carmen continues barking orders to the chagrin of Hughes. Carmen obliges, "I concur with my son. Shall we depart for the underground and see the workings there?"

Connor continues to be impressed when they walk over to the far wall, and Hughes presses a code. Pronto, the entire wall slides open, revealing a large freight elevator.

Connor and Donna step in first, followed by the two older men. Carmen and Connor are shocked by the printing presses' immense size when the elevator door opens to the underground.

Hughes starts the dialog. "Welcome to the underground, 100' feet below street level. As you can see, we have a generator, water pump, and an airflow system that maintains the cooling level of the press, and so we can also breathe."

Connor inquires, "How many hours can the press run before overheating?"

"I will let my mathematician extraordinaire explain the details. Carmen and Connor, I'd like you to meet Klaus," Hughes states with flair.

"As my boss already imparted, welcome to the underground. There's enough air in here without the press running for about six hours, but when running at full capacity, four hours. We have pumps drawing the generator fumes to the outside, and likewise, the water also. For every four hours of run time, it takes another four hours of maintenance. A full day's work."

Connor then asks, "Do you work straight through or take a break, Klaus?"

"I work straight through for security reasons. None of the employees know about the underground or printing press, except four. I usually arrive at 8 p.m. and conduct the maintenance schedule. Then at midnight till 4 a.m. I print the monies, bundle them into packages, and get out of here by 6 a.m. before the employees arrive for work."

Carmen inquires, "You're the only one that knows how to operate the press and make all the repairs?"

"Yes, that would be correct," Klaus answers honestly.

Carmen turns to Hughes, "On the limo ride back, we need to discuss that situation."

Being curious, Connor inquires, "What is your plan if the airflow stops down here?"

"That almost happened a few months ago when the FBI raided the casket plant," Klaus begins to share. "I had to shut down all the equipment immediately, preventing any noise filtering to street level. There were 40 minutes left of air remaining when the Feds left."

Donna interjects, "Hughes and I realized that was unacceptable. So, Hughes installed a flute for additional airflow in his underground office."

Carmen looks at Hughes with puzzlement, "You have an underground office? Why you need one down here?"

"I'll show you and explain. But before I do that, come over to the press for a second."

They all walk over, wondering what in the heck Hughes is doing.

"Klaus, would you hand me a few of the fake bills from the press?"

Hughes digs out his wallet from his suit jacket, pulls out a ten-dollar bill, and lays it next to the fake ones.

"Gentlemen, do you see any difference?" Hughes challenges Carmen and Connor.

Both examine all the bills and arrive at the same conclusion, "They look alike!" Connor shouts.

Carmen goes a step farther and states a compliment, "Bravo to you and Klaus for creating such a beautiful masterpiece. Now, about that office of yours."

"Well, since that incident, I installed a flute, inside doorknob and lock, and light with a wall switch, and a cot!"

"I would think an office would have those creature comforts, to begin with. You installed them as an afterthought?" Carmen is extremely puzzled.

Hughes starts his explanation. "Let's walk through this tunnel; you'll need to duck your head. It's only four feet high."

They all walk through the dimly lit tunnel for about fifty feet when arriving at the office door. Hughes explains, "This originally was and still is, the gas chamber, and now doubles as a fail-safe airflow room."

Unsurprisingly, Carmen isn't fazed. Donna and Connor glance at each other momentarily, and she winks at him.

"How many times have you used it, Hughes?" Carmen asks.

"Only once, and he's buried in the John Doe section of my cemetery."

Connor asks, "The fail-safe airflow. Has that been tested?"

Hughes answers, "No, but if somehow, the gas got accidentally turned on, there should be enough air from the flute to allow at least two hours for one person."

Carmen commands, "Let's get out of this tunnel; my neck is hurting."

Once at the other end of the tunnel, Carmen turns to Hughes, "We have some important business to discuss in the limo. I think I'd like to rent your office from time to time if you catch my drift."

"We can certainly do that. Depending on what you have in mind and how the logistics would work, there shouldn't be a problem."

Carmen turns to Connor and Donna, "Would you two mind driving back in the sports car? There isn't any necessity for either of you to hear any business transactions Hughes and I may make."

Connor glances at Donna quickly and states, "Sure, that would be okay. I'd like to stick around and ask Klaus some more questions about the printing press. I may have some ideas on how to improve production without defeating the integrity of the operation."

"If it's okay with Connor, I'd like to drive the sports car back," Donna hints.

Hughes, trying to get back on offense, states to Carmen, "I trust that what you have to share with me is of the utmost vital interest to our combined business deals."

"I can assure you. You won't be disappointed."

"Klaus, when you and Connor are done, be sure to lock up. I'll send the elevator down on our way out."

"You got it, boss!"

Carmen and Hughes make their way toward the limo waiting for them on the street level side. The surrounding area is tranquil, with the plant closed and employees having clocked out three hours ago.

Meanwhile, Connor asks Klaus a question, "Do you happen to have a schematic drawing of the printing press? Once I see the drawing, I'll know if my guess is on target."

"Yeah. All the employees are gone, so it's safe to retrieve it from my locker in the lunchroom. Give me about fifteen minutes. I'll be right back."

The second Klaus closes the door to the freight elevator, Donna grabs Connor's hand, and they dash through the tunnel, fling open the office door, and lock themselves in, kissing and hugging frantically.

Connor asks Donna, "How many hours can you run before over-heating?"

"Twenty-seconds!"

Meanwhile, seated in the limo, Hughes shouts, "Gosh, I must have left my wallet by the printing press when I was showing off our ten-dollar bill. It'll only take a few minutes, Carmen, and I'll be right back."

Hughes walks briskly to the elevator wall and finds it's on street level with the door opened. Hughes is thinking, *Klaus must be somewhere in the building.* Nevertheless, he takes it down and runs toward the tunnel. As he suspected, Hughes hears laughter coming from his underground office with Connor and Donna's voices. Hughes turns the gas on, gets back in the freight elevator, and quickly returns inside the limo.

"So, did you find your wallet?" Carmen asks.

"Yes, I did. Also turned the gas on. You're sure this is what you want, Carmen?

"I expect loyalty, same as you do, Hughes. My renegade son was trying to take over the company with a group of investors. I'll have none of that!"

So, everything is in its place," summarizes Hughes. As the limo driver takes them back to the country club, Hughes asks, "What is it you wanted to discuss with me?"

Meanwhile, Klaus finds the manual, steps into the freight elevator, and takes it underground. As he steps off, he hears faint sounds like pounding on a door. Walking toward the tunnel, he hears voices.

"Help, get us out of here! Help, we can't breathe. Help!"

Flat-out, Klaus realizes the gas is on and quickly closes the valve.

"Thank God I had the dead-bolt key with me," Klaus states as he opens the door allowing Connor and Donna to walk out, gasping for air slowly.

"Why didn't you open the flute or simply unlock the door from the inside?" Klaus is perplexed.

Connor slowly answers, "The flute was stuck, and there's no mechanism to unlock the deadbolt from inside. I don't want to be hasty, but someone wanted us dead."

Klaus asks, "How long were you in there with the gas on?"

Donna, still gasping for air, mumbles, "It seemed like forever."

Connor calculates, "It was maybe seven minutes. The room is so small, I don't know how much longer we would have made it."

Klaus hesitantly asks, "Do I dare ask why you two were in the office?"

Donna speaks one word at a time in between breaths, "Connor had a date tonight, which he missed. But, I just wanted to show him the new wave in hugging and kissing that's taking over the dating scene." Donna's choppy and slow response seemed to be adequate for Klaus.

Connor glances at Klaus and Donna, then states the unimaginable, "It was either my dad or Hughes or both who tried to kill us, Donna."

"Why would your dad want you out?" Donna shouts with unbelief.

"He thinks I'm trying to take over the company. Nothing could be farther from the truth. Regardless of the wealth he's accumulated, my dad is insecure. I've heard rumors that he believes I'm heading a group of investors in a hostile takeover bid to oust him out."

"Sounds like he's paranoid," Donna shares.

"Not to change the subject, Donna, are you always this friendly with men you just met?"

"To be accurate, we met a few weeks ago, and you asked me to join you on the west coast next winter. So, we didn't just meet as you say. To answer your question, I like to flirt, and sometimes that gets me in hot water with Hughes. I must admit, flirting is an addiction that I can't seem to overcome. But, I know I can't go back to my villa, the club, or Hughes. Not anymore; what are your options, Connor?"

"I've lost my title as Vice-President and son, but I still have my life, I think?"

Out of the blue, Bernard shows up.

"Good evening. It's good to be alive, huh?"

"Bernard, it is good to see you," Donna shouts. "I have never come that close to tasting death. I am ready to accept Jesus. Whatever I need to do, I'll listen, Bernard."

"Sometimes, a near-death experience will shake one's core to its foundation, as it has for you, Donna. How about you, Connor? Are you ready to accept, Jesus?"

"If you're willing to take me under your wings, no pun intended, and help me to shed my false thinking of God, church, and Christianity. I would be willing to listen to the ways of Jesus."

"My wingspan is broad, so, yeah, I can do that. You'll be a challenge, but not impossible. Klaus, how about you? Are you ready to accept Jesus, or prefer to stick around and continue working for Hughes?"

"It depends on how this situation is handled. But, I'm thinking, regardless of what I do, I'm probably a dead man walking."

"Listen, it's almost 11 p.m., we don't have much time. Connor, you call Darrell. Donna, you call Rachael. Whoever answers, tell them I'm with you and have them contact Mitch. He needs to call one of you back immediately, if not sooner."

Donna then asks, "What do we say when Mitch calls back?"

This is the part I don't like. It's covering up a bad situation to solve a crime. When Mitch calls back, he needs to bring two dead bodies that look like each of you. Not you, though, Klaus, sorry about that. By the way, I'm taking you under my wings also."

"That sounds gruesome, Bernard," Donna flinches.

"Throughout the hundreds of revolutions this world has witnessed, humble peasants gave up their life sparring the prince and princess of royalty their death. Willing to die is not new under the sun. We're not asking anyone to die for us. They already have on their own."

Connor's phone rings at 11:15 p.m. "This is Darrell; I have Mitch patched in. Go ahead and explain your situation."

Connor puts his phone on speaker, so all three can converse.

"So, if I understand the situation correctly, either Hughes or Carmen tried to kill both of you. You want me now, within two hours, to locate two lookalikes that are already dead, so you two can escape to-where?" Mitch reveals the loophole.

Donna comes up with the clincher, "If we stay here, Mitch, you won't need to find two lookalikes."

"Okay, I get it. I'll make all three of you a deal. It has to be all of you or no bargain."

Connor and Donna glare at Klaus, "Yeah, I'm in also."

Mitch comes back, "Good. If you're all willing to testify at trial, I'll place each of you in my Secret Protection Program."

"I'm not familiar with that program," Connor replies. "Mitch, is it similar to the Witness Protection Program?"

Mitch avoids answering directly, "Sort of. You'll all need to just trust me on this one."

Connor glances at Donna and Klaus. "Our options are limited, Mitch, so go ahead. What are the plans?"

"Connor and Donna, send me a picture of each of you, headshot only. I'll send out a squawk message to the Fed's funeral home directors list. Within the hour, 12:30 a.m., two hearses will drive inside the plant, street-level side. Klaus, will you lead them to the freight elevator?"

"Yes, of course. But what happens to me?"

"Stay tuned; you'll know in five minutes."

"The funeral directors will dress the two deceased lookalikes in the clothes you have on now and bring you a new set of clothes. Klaus, you'll need to make available a Hughes casket for each and leave our two heroes in their new caskets, nearby the printing press, lids closed but not locked. Then, leave a note behind for Hughes, reading. *'I've done your dirty work for the last time. I trust the two deceased will find their way to your John Doe section. For me, I quit. Going to Germany or Brazil.'*"

Mitch cannot provide witness protection for the gang of three, Connor, Klaus, and Donna, due to their criminal involvements. But does offer them protection at Buffalo General Hospital.

Meanwhile, Carmen and Hughes finalize a deal they brokered while riding in the limo.

"So, Hughes, if I get to rent your gas chamber once monthly, I'll waive the extra 10% I wanted. Plus, I'll pay you a hundred grand for each rental over one per month. Assuming you'll take care of the disposal."

Hughes is pleased with the brokered deal and then asks Carmen, "What time is it?"

"About 2 a.m. You think we should turn around and go back. It'll be another half-hour, time we get there. My kid and your girlfriend should be dead by now."

"Yeah, I'm sure. Thanks also for bringing on two new pressmen to operate the printing press and soon to be installing a new ventilation system to double production."

"How are you going to get rid of Klaus?" Carmen inquires.

"Same way. My office gas chamber."

The limo pulls up at the casket plant at about 2:30 a.m. Carmen notices that Connor's sports car is still there.

"Well, that's a good sign," Carmen remarks.

"Yeah, of course. They're both still here," Hughes vocalized. "By the way, Carmen, I will need your help in placing the deceased into two caskets."

Hughes finds it puzzling that the freight elevator is left open on the second floor. "I guess Klaus got tired and forgot to lock this baby up."

When they arrive at the underground and step out of the elevator, Carmen is the first to spot the two caskets next to the printing press.

"Hey, Hughes, over here! It looks like Klaus did our work for us, and he left you a note."

Hughes reads the note out loud and is troubled that Klaus could testify. "If it takes me a year of Sundays to find him, I will."

Carmen opens the lid to each casket and verifies Donna and Connor.

"Well, it's them," shouts Carmen. "They're wearing the same clothes. You want to take them back now or come back later tomorrow for them?"

"Wait a minute!" yells Hughes. I don't remember Donna wearing a bracelet on her left wrist. Look! So is your son."

Hughes picks up Donna's left wrist, turns over the locket, and reads, 'To my forever, Lucy. I will always love you, Keith.'

Carmen does the same for Connor and reads on the locket's backside. 'To my forever, Keith, I will always love you, Lucy.'

Abruptly, reality hits Carmen, "Hughes, we've been robbed! These two lying in the caskets are Lucy and Keith, not Donna and Connor. That only means one thing. They're alive and loose. But how and where?"

Hughes bellows out, "The how is Mitch Kearney, and the where is anywhere !"

CHAPTER THIRTY-SIX

FIELD DAY-JUNE 2036

Stan Ramsey walks over to Richard's home to invite him for a field day trip. Richard opens the door and sees Stan standing there. "Come on in. What's on your mind today?"

"I would like to invite you to join the other students and me on a field day touring the casket manufacturing plant.

"Are you sure you want an old fuddy-duddy hanging out with you guys all day?"

"Yes, it would be an honor having an ex-sheriff as our chaperon. After all, if it weren't for our profession, there would be no need for classy caskets. Plus, we get to see how these caskets are manufactured. So, what do you say, Richard?"

"I would love to! When is the day?"

"In two days, Friday. Dr. Wesley Drew will be heading up the tour. It's technically a class credit, but we know it's a chance for him to get out of classes. He gets exhausted in the afternoons. Don't know why. We do worry about him, though."

Dr. Drew uses the school's van for the 90-mile trip to Hughes's casket plant. The four students and Richard are chatting away when Dr. Drew asks, "Richard, would you mind driving a while? I need to rest my eyes."

"Sure. Not a problem, just pull over when you can." Dr. Drew does, they switch seats, and Richard continues the trip while Dr. Drew sits in the back, relaxing with his eyes closed.

Upon arrival, the group was disappointed to find out the foreman would be giving the tour instead of Hughes, the owner. Of course, they didn't know this foreman was hired by Carmen to be one of the pressmen to operate the printing press underground. But, the group enjoyed his detailed explanations. After a while, Richard whispers to Stan. "This is boring; let's step outside for a bit."

"Sure, I'd like that."

They're walking around the perimeter of the building when Stan, unaware, trips. "Are you okay?" asks Richard.

"Yeah, but what the heck caused me to trip?"

Richard walks back about four steps and sees nothing. Stan begins to crawl on the ground, looking for anything that may have caused him to stumble and fall.

"I think I found it, Richard. It looks like a pipe projecting horizontally from the building, hence causing my fall."

Upon closer observation, Richard shouts, "It's an exhaust pipe!"

Stan questions, "An exhaust pipe for what?"

"Something that runs on gasoline, like an engine," Richard contemplating.

"Or, how about a generator?" Stan exclaims.

"Huh. Like you blurted, for what? Auxiliary power?"

"I suppose. Look! About a foot apart, two more pipes are projecting from the building," Stan shouts on his discovery.

Richard crawls to get a closer look." You won't believe this, Stan, but one pipe is more like a chimney flute, and the other has droplets of water inside."

"Hey! I got it, Richard. Air, water, and power. Three elements to allow something to operate, like machinery, maybe?" Stan impresses Richard.

"Say, there's no school tomorrow. Do you suppose, Stan, you and the other three guys would be willing to return tonight with me and stake this place out?"

"I'm sure they'd be okay with that, seeing it's Friday. Saturday night would be out of the question, though."

Richard promptly gets curious, "Why Saturday night?"

"That's the Funeral Home Directors Bowling League night."

"Stan, you got to be kidding?" Richard exclaimed.

"Nope. It's a nationwide league, and we guys have a blast bowling with the other directors. I bet you don't know what the trophy is for the winning team?"

"Can't say I do," Richard uttered.

"It's a miniature bronze casket placed on top of a white pedestal base."

Abruptly and unforeseen, Dr. Drew is standing in front of them. "Richard, would you and the guy's mind if I called this tour short. I don't feel well, and I want you to drive me to the nearest hospital." Dr. Drew collapses.

"Stan, get the van and the other guys," Richard yells. "I'll stay here with the doctor."

As Richard is waiting, the doctor whispers, "Fake burials, fake certificates," and Dr. Drew passes out.

Richard called the police, and they escorted him to Buffalo General, following the ambulance with Dr. Drew inside. The emergency staff quickly brought Dr. Drew inside and administered various medicines to bring him consciously

Once in the hospital room, Dr. Drew sees many faces, blurry but distinguishable. "Richard, who's the guy standing next to you? He doesn't look familiar."

"Allow me to introduce myself. My name is Mitch Kearney. I'm with the FBI, Director, Northern District."

"Should I tell you what I know before I go?"

"You're not going anywhere. The doctor tells me you forgot to take your diabetes medications, maybe for over a week. You'll get your strength back in no time at all. So, what is it you want to tell me?"

"Mr. Hughes Reyna is a criminal. He kills people and then buries them in his John Doe section. Ask Amir at the county office. He issues fake death certificates. I've been keeping this hideous information a secret for over a year. My conscience won't let me; I can't do this any longer. Will you protect me, sir?"

"Yes. You have my word. You get some rest, heal back soon, and we'll talk again. Okay?"

"Yeah, sure, okay." Dr. Drew falls asleep exhausted.

Richard and Mitch walk out to the lobby area, where the four students are anxiously waiting to hear how their teacher is doing.

"He'll be okay, guys; he just needs a lot of rest," Richard shares. "Nurse tells me he forgot to take his daily meds; that's why you always saw him tired in the afternoons."

Stan asks, "Who will teach our classes while Dr. Drew is hospitalized?"

"Allow me to introduce myself; I'm Mitch with the FBI, and no, you guys aren't in trouble. On the contrary. Let me ask you all a question. How would you guys like to be deputized for the weekend?"

Stan asks, "What does it pay?"

"A thousand-dollar credit on your tuition when classes resume."

"Okay! We're in, and when do we start?"

"Right now, but it's only 9 p.m. Why don't you guys get something to eat, maybe take a nap here in the lobby. At 11 p.m., all of you and Richard will drive back to the plant and observe the building where you tripped, Stan."

"Just us five?" Stan asks.

"Good question. No, I'll have my security team in place surrounding the area just in case."

Richard and the guys drive out to the casket plant arriving at midnight with the security team directly behind.

Astounded, Stan sees smoke billowing out from the pipe he tripped on early. He and Richard walk out to the spot and discover another line to their astonishment.

"Richard is this what I think it is, a gas line?"

"Yup, you're right, Stan. A gas line, but for what? I'm going to phone this into Mitch and get his slant."

"Mitch, this is Richard. We found a gas line in addition to the other lines discovered earlier. What would you like us to do?"

"Return to Buffalo General. I received a call from Donna about fifteen minutes ago. She and Klaus confessed to everything. The John Doe section, the underground printing press, the affiliate funeral homes, the secret freight elevator, and the gas chamber, where she and her friend, Connor, were almost killed. Speaking of Connor, I need to ask him more questions about the bus depot strategy his dad devised. Apparently, college students were being paid partially with counterfeit money to damage several downtown cities. He was still a bit delirious from the gas chamber incident when I spoke with him last."

"I'm surprised about Donna, never could figure her out. But I'm glad she gave you the info you'll need for prosecution. So, what's our next move, Mitch?"

"Set up a tee time with Hughes for Sunday morning at 10 a.m. If he bulks, bet him $10,000, you'll beat him. While we're arresting Hughes, my team will be doing likewise with the forty affiliated funeral directors."

"You got it, Mitch. Glad to help," Richard vocalized.

CHAPTER THIRTY-SEVEN

TEE TIME-JULY 2036

Early Sunday, unable to sleep well the night before, Hughes is in his funeral home office, incredibly upset, and calls Carmen.

"We're in this pickle together, Carmen, and I need you to provide me with two of your best hitmen that can take care of business yesterday!" Hughes shouts.

"Well, I hear you—no need to shout. Klaus isn't a concern to me. His personality type isn't aggressive. Wherever he's at, he probably took a job and will stick his nose to the grindstone. However, your ex-girlfriend and my ex-son need to be a concern to us."

"I know without a doubt that Mitch has them hidden secretly, but where?"

"Well, let's brainstorm for a minute, Hughes. If you were the FBI director, at what place or facility would you secure the witnesses?"

"When you mentioned facility, I'm thinking a major hospital. You can't get more secure."

"Yes, I think more secure than an ordinary hospital would be a research university hospital, especially if any of the witnesses were sick or wounded."

"Excellent deduction, Carmen! The best research hospital connected with a university is in Albany, New York. Can you get two of your men out there quickly?"

"I don't want to sound like a cheapskate, but you own half of the problem. It'll cost you one-hundred grand to hire my guys. Yes or no, Hughes?"

"Yes, I'm in, but remind me not to go into partnership with you again."

"It's too late-I own you! I brought in two new pressmen to take over Klaus and upgraded the ventilation system to double counterfeit production. But, I'll allow you to continue operating the casket plant."

Hughes hangs up and is frustrated, not fully understanding how his control got shifted over to Carmen. He swivels in his chair toward the wine cabinet when the phone rings.

"What do you want now? Another hundred grand?" Hughes answers in a huff.

"Whoops, sorry. Did I catch you at the wrong time, Hughes? This is Richard calling to inquire if you'd be interested in a round of golf later this morning?"

"Oh, sorry, Richard. I thought it was Donna calling again. We broke up the other day, and now we're in negotiations on how much I should buy her villa."

Richard knew he was lying but went along with the spoof. "I'm sorry to hear that, Hughes. You two looked like the perfect couple, but I can assure you, time will heal a broken heart. Any idea where's she's going?" Richard is having some fun.

"Yeah, I think she mentioned something about Brazil, not sure, though. So, about that round of golf, what time you have in mind?"

"If 9 a.m. is too early, will 10 a.m. work better for you?"

"Heck! You are an early bird. It's 7 a.m. now; but, I can meet you at the first tee by 10 a.m. By the way, Richard, if I remember, you're a five handicap to my seven. I'll give you the benefit of the doubt and bet you a thousand dollars a hole. Are you interested?"

"Then make it an additional two-thousand for the winner of the 18-hole round. It'll be fun taking twenty-thousand from you, Hughes."

"On the contrary, It'll be more exciting taking twenty-grand from you, Richard!"

Hughes checks his schedule and realizes he'll need to hire someone to take Donna's place. The twenty daily gravesite burials and the frequent John Doe burials are overwhelming for him. He thinks to himself, *'I'll give Rachael a call and inquire if she can recommend someone.'*

As Hughes was walking out the door, his phone rings again.

"This is Carmen. I located and hired two men from Albany, New York, that will take the assignment. They should be at the University Hospital within thirty minutes. I'll keep you advised."

Hughes is getting a bit antsy but does manage to hop on his golf cart and drive over to the first tee. As he pulls up and walks over, he states, "Richard, I thought this was going to be a match-game just for the two of us? Who are your two buddies? Now we're playing as a foursome?"

"Hughes, I'd like you to meet Phillip Dorfman and Sullivan Bridges. Their handicaps are like yours, and I thought it'd be good for the four of us to have a conversation."

Hughes, perplexed, shouts, "A conversation about what?"

Richard answers, "Whether you should go to prison for life or receive the death penalty?"

Instantly, six squad cars surround the first tee preventing Hughes from making a run.

Richard commences, "If you turn yourself in, Phillip Dorfman has agreed to be your attorney, and Sullivan Bridges, the FBI agent, will handcuff you and bring you in to appear before a magistrate."

"Now, why would I want to do something incredible like that? You have nothing to charge me with."

Richard continues, "As we speak, the FBI agents are arresting all forty of your affiliate funeral home directors. Should I continue?"

"That doesn't prove anything!" Hughes is bucking the allegations.

"Allow me to add to your demise, Mr. Reyna," declares Sullivan. "We have witnesses that will testify against you. Jax, Dr. Drew, and Dr. Amir Korcha."

"I thought the FBI killed Jax?" shouts Hughes surprised. "Besides, you may not have all the witnesses you think you have."

Sullivan continues, "You mean like these three?"

Immediately another squad car pulls up to the first tee, and out steps Donna, Connor, and Klaus.

Phillip speaks up at this point. "Mr. Reyna, I believe it will be in your best interest to turn yourself in. The initial charges against you will be counterfeiting and murder. I'm guessing you value your own life more than others. Turn yourself in now, confess, and you'll be lucky to be sentenced to life in prison."

"What will happen to my golf course and the country club?"

Sullivan states, "It will be forfeited to the County. I've spoken with the District Attorney. If the courts rule in favor, Richard and Agnes Filburn will buy the enterprise."

Hughes glares at Richard first, then at the three witnesses standing by the squad car, and realizes his best option is to surrender, "Very well, then, I'll take the advice of my attorney. What's the next step, Mr. Dorfman?"

"Sullivan will take you to the county jail. You'll see the judge within forty-eight hours, at which time you'll enter guilty."

"If I don't?'

"If you go to a jury trial, there is enough evidence against you for a death verdict. It's up to you, Hughes, a life sentence in prison or other-wise? I'll be at your side during the hearing," Phillip attempts to give Hughes some comfort.

Meanwhile, Carmen's two hitmen arrive at the Research Hospital and inquire at the front desk, "We're friends of the family and came to visit Donna Tish, Connor Bridgewater, and Klaus Weber. What rooms are they in?"

The receptionist replies, "Sorry, those names you stated never checked in. Perhaps you have the wrong hospital?"

The hitmen storm out of the hospital, run to their vehicle, and call Carmen. "The three patients never checked in; what do you want us to do?"

"Make your way to Buffalo. If my suspicions are correct, I'll need you guys to pay a visit to the hospital there."

"Sorry, Carmen. You've paid us only 25%, so we're staying in Albany. You know where to wire the rest of the funds; when we receive them, we'll go back to work for you."

"Forget it! I'll find some locals!" Carmen shouts.

No sooner had Carmen finished that call when his phone rings.

"Yeah! Did you guys change your mind?"

"Dad! This is Connor. Yes, I'm still alive-surprise! Hughes got arrested an hour ago. It would be best if you turned yourself in and plea for lesser sentencing."

"That will never happen! I'm in the underground working, don't bother me!" he shouts and hangs up.

Carmen supervising the counterfeit printing in the underground, directs his pressmen to triple production for the remaining three hours of their shift.

The lead pressman alerts Carmen, "But sir, the extra pressure on the press could be risky. I don't recommend pushing it to the limits."

Carmen retorts, "Look, guys, I'm shutting down this operation forever, and I'll give each a half-million after you print four million. What do you say?"

The two pressmen look at each other and nod knowingly. "We'll forgo our portion to keep the press at a reasonably safe level and print you the three million. Okay, with you?"

"Sure, but you're fools." Carmen decides to rest in the underground office to contemplate his next moves while waiting for his three million.

The press begins to shake vigorously in the second hour, and electrical sparks start to fly everywhere. Without warning, the gas line breaks, and the ensuing implosion caused the entire manufacturing plant to collapse, leaving a crater five hundred feet below street level.

Luckily at 4 a.m., none of the casket employees were present, but a battalion of fire trucks and emergency vehicles arrive momentarily.

The fire chief radios the status to the city manager, "You won't believe this, but the crater has like a lake in it with flaming fire on top. I've never seen anything like this in all my years. What do you suppose the city will do with this monster?"

"You imparted its five-hundred feet deep and two blocks wide. Heck, we'll use it as the new city dump. Our trash will allow the everlasting lake of fire to continue burning for a long, long time."

Meanwhile, Mitch Kearney arrives at the first tee and chats with Phillip first. "So, Hughes surrendered. You think he'll plead guilty, hoping only to receive life imprisonment?"

"Probably, he values his skin too much. So, what are your plans for the three witnesses?" Phillip asks.

Mitch answers, "I'll put them up for a while at Rachel's hotel. You don't know, but I never placed them in witness protection but hid them at Buffalo General Hospital after escaping from the underground. Each will need to go before the judge to determine what involvement they had with Hughes."

"If you like, Mitch, I could handle their case also. My number one goal will be to get leniency for each," Phillip shares.

"I'm confident Donna and Connor can afford the best lawyer money can buy. Probably not, Klaus, though. I'll suggest they hire you as a package deal. Your knowledge of Hughes's enterprise and his manipulating tactics should get each a reduced sentence," Mitch flatly states.

Mitch and Phillip walk over to the squad car, where Donna, Connor, and Klaus patiently wait for instructions.

Phillip addresses the three. "I'm an attorney, Phillip Dorfman. Due to the nature of these crimes, Hughes Enterprises, and whatever your involvement may be, Mitch highly recommends you hire me. I'm your best bet for a reduced sentence."

Mitch addresses them, "I'm placing each of you under house arrest at Rachael's hotel for a few days. It's for your security. I'll meet with you later tonight and expect a decision on your choice of lawyer. Phillip and I are meeting with Hughes at the county jail shortly."

The sheriff's deputy takes the three over to the hotel. While checking in at the front desk, Donna, Connor and, Klaus is stunned, watching the news bulletin announcing that the Casket Manufacturing Plant imploded.

"When I spoke with my dad last, he was in the underground and hung up on me."

"I'm so sorry, Connor. I know you probably have mixed emotions at this very moment. Your heart is in a tough place now. I'm sure in time, healing will take place. Unfortunately, we won't see each other anymore.

I'll be going to prison. You probably not. You take care." And she gives him a soft kiss.

The deputy escorts each to their respective rooms and stands guard until his replacement arrives.

Swiftly, Bernard shows up in Donna's room.

You've had a busy few days, almost lost your life, and now starting at a different experience, you know nothing about."

"Hi, Bernard. It is good to see you. I sure could use some comfort. My life has unraveled big time. I'm so sorry for all the things I've done."

"Let me help you, Donna. Let's go to the Lord in prayer, shall we?"

"Yes, I would like that. You've gathered I don't know how to pray."

"Yes, a long time ago. But it's not that difficult. So, repeat after me, and you'll get the hang of it after praying a few times."

"Okay."

"Dear Father in Heaven. Thank you for your son, Jesus Christ, whom I believe in and ask, Jesus, that you would forgive me for my many horrible sins. I have indirectly murdered two people and know I must pay the penalty. I ask you would provide me with blessed protection throughout my remaining days here on earth."

"I feel better already. Thank you, Bernard."

"One more item, Donna. Have you given any consideration to what you'll do with your estate? You can't take it with you. Of course, you could leave those funds in securities and hopefully have a nice nest egg when you get released in seven to fourteen years. But, there is a better investment you could do that would give life to the innocent. Examine your heart, Donna, and you'll find the reason." Bernard disappears.

Donna goes to prayer again and immediately feels the presence of the Holy Spirit nudging her. "Yes! That's what I'll do!"

She opens her room door and asks the deputy to contact Mitch or Phillip. "I have something important to share; please ask one of them to call me. Thank you, officer."

CHAPTER THIRTY-EIGHT

THE SENTENCING-JULY 2036

As Phillip had expressed, Hughes appears before the judge within forty-eight hours after his arrest. Phillip accompanies him into the courtroom.

The judge asks, "How do you plea?"

Phillip whispers into Hughes's ear, and Hughes states, "Guilty, your honor."

"You realize you give up most of your rights with that plea. What shall say your attorney?"

"Your honor, guilty, asking the court for mercy and leniency in their deliberation," Phillip states firmly.

"What say the prosecution?" the judge asks.

"Your honor. Mr. Reyna has murdered and been involved in over one hundred people killed, all buried in his John Doe cemetery. Also, your honor, Mr. Reyna has printed and distributed over twenty-four million in counterfeit monies. Justice will only be served with nothing less than the death penalty!"

"I appreciate your validation, prosecutor. But, because Mr. Reyna pleaded guilty, the court will show leniency and mercy by sentencing him to life in prison at the Farm State Correctional Institution in upper New York."

*****

Meanwhile, Mr. Zee and Zeela catch wind that Hughes is going to prison and decide to abandon the hot dog and clothing business and flee to London, taking Nicolao with them.

*****

While waiting for the expedition to state prison, the bailiff walks Hughes back to his cell. Phillip adjourns to the courthouse lobby and sees he missed a call from the deputy.

"You called?"

"Yes, I did. Donna has asked to speak with you or Mitch. Do you wish to speak with her?"

"Yes, go ahead and give her your phone, but on speaker."

The deputy knocks on Donna's door. "You may stand in the doorway and speak with Phillip."

"Thank you, deputy. Phillip, I want to donate my entire estate to Rachael's ministry, 'Adopt-not Abort.' You are familiar with that, right?"

"Yes, I am. But, are you sure you want to do something like that? Should you get released early, you'd be penniless out on the street."

"I know you're a good lawyer, but seriously, you think you'll be able to negotiate an early release for me?"

"If you follow my procedure as Hughes did, I don't see any reason why not."

"What did he end up with, if I may ask?"

"Life."

"Oh, dear. I guess better than the alternative."

"Tell you what, Donna. You'll be in that room for a few more days, maybe a week before your hearing. In the meantime, I'll talk with Mitch and Rachael and get their view on your idea."

"Phillip, it's not an idea. It's my heart. Please convey that; thanks."

In the following days, the Judge hears testimony from several others. The first is Dr. Drew, who verified the burials of people Hughes killed, and the scheme he had with Amir.

The judge reads his verdict. "Dr. Drew, due to the fact you were negligent, knowing full well on the murders and burials, I sentence you to three years in the Farm State Prison, with possible early parole in one year."

Amir and Klaus get seven years. Leah receives three years for being an accomplice in Hughes's illegal activities. She's placed in the Women's Correctional, which is adjacent to the Farm State Prison.

The following week, Connor appears in court, and the prosecutor asks to address the bench. "Your honor, we have new evidence that Mr. Bridgewater is not entirely innocent as first thought."

"Go on," states the judge.

"Mr. Carmen Bridgewater, the now-deceased father of Connor, bought counterfeit money from Mr. Hughes Reyna to pay college students to riot and plunder cities across the USA. Connor Bridgewater would meet these students at multiple bus depots, paying them 50% in counterfeit money. In essence, he was paying the students half of what they were entitled to. Your honor, we believe Mr. Connor Bridgewater should be mandated to a prison term."

"I almost agree with you, prosecutor. However, there can be so much pressure on the son in a family rule that he would do anything to gain favor. Therefore, this court assigns you, Mr. Connor Bridgewater, three years of house arrest in Cedar Creek with community service to be determined later. This court is now adjourned."

Phillip turns to Connor, "It could have been worse, like butchering cows at the Farm State Prison."

Unforeseen, Phillip gets a call from Mitch. "I just spoke with Richard, and the district attorney agreed that Connor could live in one of the guest cottages on the golf course effective immediately, but not to leave Cedar Creek."

Phillip shares the stipulation with Connor, and he's exuberant with the news, "So, I can drive my car over there now and get situated?"

"Yes, but check in with Richard first; he'll set you up. Stay close to your phone. I never know when the court will call to assign you to community service."

The following week is Donna's court appearance. Rachael and Darrell attend as spectators, hoping to know why she'd want to donate her entire estate to their ministry before appearing in court for her sentencing.

Phillip and Donna stand, likewise, the prosecutor, as the judge enters the courtroom.

"It is my understanding this is the last hearing on the Hughes Enterprises case. Prosecutor, say what you have," states the judge.

"Your honor, Ms. Donna Trice has a long list of aiding and abetting Mr. Reyna in all of his criminal activities. Counterfeit printing, distributing, and as an associate in the murder of his employee."

"Ms. Donna Trice, how do you plea to these charges? Before you answer, best you consult with your attorney," the judge admonishes.

Donna is seen whispering in Phillips's ear. He first shakes his head, 'no,' but after a few more seconds, he whispers, 'yes.'

"Your honor, before I state my plea, I would like to indulge the court for a few minutes and ask permission to explain my reasoning."

"Granted. Go on."

"The prosecutor has my charges barely half correct." A wave of hushed whispers is heard from the spectators. "Yes, I was involved in the counterfeit thing and the employee murder. But I also murdered three of my babies."

The courtroom fills with noise from the spectators. The judge hammers his gavel and shouts, "Order in the court! Order in the court!"

Everyone quiets down, but not for long when the judge asks, "Ms. Trice, is there anything else you'd like to say?"

"Yes, I want to repeat, I murdered three of my babies."

There were only fifty people in the galley, but it sounded like five thousand spectators at a high school sporting event. The chatter was so loud. The judge was pounding his gavel so hard, sweat was trickling down his forehead. Phillip was shocked, never being confided by her history. Rachael and Darrell go into silent prayer, asking God to give her wisdom.

The judge inquires, "Do you care to clarify your last statement? This court could be interested in what you say."

Donna commences, "During my twenty-year marriage, I got pregnant three times and proceeded with an abortion. It was never convenient for me to raise a child. My husband wanted children and to raise a family.

My selfishness caused many shouting matches between my husband and me. After many years of yelling, shouting, and screaming at each other, he couldn't take the stress any longer and collapsed from an instant heart attack that killed him. I suppose, in a way, I murdered my husband also."

The judge proceeds with some facts. "Your story is emotional, for sure. However, this state does not recognize abortion as murder."

Donna interjects, "But it should, your honor!"

"I don't write the laws. I look at the evidence brought before me. There isn't any prosecutor who would arrest a woman for having an abortion and bring the case to court. They would be barred forever."

Donna continues, "Recently, I had an encounter with an angel named Barnard. I have confessed my sins, invited Jesus Christ into my heart, and am now a newborn again Christian. I've asked my attorney to sell my entire estate and donate the proceeds to a ministry called 'Adopt-not Abort.' After my first pregnancy and abortion, I should have stopped getting pregnant. I didn't want children and hated being pregnant. Nevertheless, I continued getting abortions after each pregnancy. Now, I have a change of heart and encourage people to adopt-not abort."

"I'm calling a thirty-minute recess so all parties can confer on the best approach taking into consideration the confession of Ms. Trice." The judge pounds his gavel and dismisses the court.

Phillip, Donna, and the prosecutor meet in the conference room, hoping to agree on a conclusion worthy of the court.

Once seated, Donna asks, "Would it be okay if Darrell and Rachael were invited to this meeting? Their ministry is an integral part of my plea."

Phillip glances at the prosecutor, and after a few moments, he agrees.

As Darrell and Rachael enter the room, they say another silent prayer asking God to bless the open conversation.

Rachael speaks first, "Phillip, do you have any idea what sentencing Donna may incur?"

"Let's ask the prosecutor. What are your thoughts as we proceed with this trial?"

"The prosecutor's office is impressed with Ms. Trice's request to donate her estate to a ministry. However, we don't know at this time the size of the donation."

Phillip remarks, "That shouldn't have any bearing on this trial. I hope you're not insinuating she buy down her sentence. That would be unorthodox and perhaps illegal."

"We must not forget that every inmate upon release receives a bill for their cost of incarceration. There isn't anything on the books that would prevent a well-funded inmate from pre-paying their estimated costs."

Phillip questions, "What are we talking about here?"

"On average, it's eighty-thousand a year. On a pre-payment, we could issue the bill, say, for seventy-thousand annually."

Phillip talks to the prosecutor, "Can you excuse us for five minutes so I can have a private consultation with my client and her friends?"

"Five minutes, that's all!" He states while leaving the room.

Phillip stares at Donna and states, "With your permission, I want to call his bluff. You can't be charged for the death of your husband nor your abortions. Not now, not today, not ever. However, they could conjure up some frivolous charge while you're in prison just to make your life miserable."

Rachael interjects, "Before we go any further, Phillip, I need to ask Donna what she had in mind for her donation."

"About twenty-million."

"I guessed it would be in the high millions," Rachael shares. "Donna, are you sure you want to do this? You've already donated, and Darrell and I are most appreciative. But, Donna, twenty-million? Are you sure?"

"Yes, I'm sure. Besides, what can I do with it while in prison?"

Phillip's remarks caught everyone by surprise. "You can buy down you're sentencing."

"I thought you noted that was unorthodox," questions Rachael.

"Only if the prosecutor brings it up first. I'm guessing he'd like to sneak in a penalty for the death of your husband and get you 14 years. He legally can't but will try to wiggle around that. I will offer him a pre-payment of $490,000 for a seven-year sentence with an early release of three years. Plus, he won't charge you for any other crimes, and you won't have to work unless you want while in prison."

Donna doesn't believe what's she's hearing but states, "If you can get that on my behalf, go for it. Praise the Lord!"

Darrell shares with Donna, "While you were all talking, I was running some numbers. It's conceivable the proceeds from the sale of your villa will equal your prison bill. You should maintain 20% of your equity fund, so when you're released, you'll have something to support you. Rachael and I will only accept 80% of your fund as a donation."

Rachael underscores what Darrell revealed. "Donna, I can tell your heart is in the right place. Your desire to help young girls and women who seriously consider giving their newborn up for adoption and not abortion is admirable. Darrell and I will open a west coast ministry for our program when you're released from prison and would like you to manage the center. Would that be of interest to you?"

"Oh, my goodness, gracious. I love you guys. I'll be counting the days."

"Well, you may want to start a ladies' Bible study or join one if one already exists. That will help you count the days with joy," Rachael shares.

"Yes, yes!" Donna shouts.

The prosecutor returns to the room and inquires if any terms have been reached.

Phillip shares the facts, and not surprisingly, at least for Phillip anyway, the prosecutor agrees to all the terms. Likewise, also the judge.

CHAPTER THIRTY-NINE

FARM-STATE PRISON-JULY 2036

The insurance company paid two million for Hughes's Casket Manu-facturing Plant that imploded. Richard and Agnes paid one million for the five-hundred-acre golf course and country club, including the funeral home, cemetery, and school. The state seized all the proceeds to pay for Hughes's life-term incarceration.

The Farm State Prison is a self-sufficient enterprise raising cattle and crops to feed both the men's and women's penitentiary adjacent to each other. The women's prison operates the dairy farm for both.

Hughes is assigned to the kitchen as a butcher working in the refrig-erated locker all day. His daily tasks have become boring only after three weeks.

"Hey, guys," Hughes addresses the other two butchers, Sammy and Charlie. "How long you guys been doing this? Isn't it boring? Take a side of beef off the meat hook, slap it down on the table, and then cut it up into steaks or grind it into hamburger. Besides, it's darn cold in here."

Sammy, Hughes's cellmate, answers, "You better get used to this. Everyone working in the kitchen is a 'lifer,' and once assigned a job, it's always your job."

"If I do request a transfer to a different job, what are my options?"

Charlie answers, "The only way you'll get a transfer is when someone dies or gets killed, or if you complain loud enough. But then, you'll get solidarity confinement for thirty to ninety days. So, you see, the options are limited."

"Great! Guess I'll learn to love my job here and walk outside to warm up after my shift."

"Now you're talking, Hughes. It won't be so bad in this locker. Heck, after three years, you'll look forward to your shift," Sammy states as he thrusts his carving knife into the side of beef hanging on the hook.

Hughes strains to maintain composure, not wanting to show any fear, after his cellmate's bold act of intimidation. Every afternoon, when his shift ends, Hughes walks outside in the pasture amongst the longhorn cattle grazing.

"Sure is nice and warm out here, Lord," Hughes surprising himself, begins talking to the Lord. *'Dear God, everything unraveled so fast. How did I get here? I'm so stressed out, and it's only been three weeks. How am I ever going to survive this 'lifer' albatross around my neck?'"*

Unaware, Bernard shows up walking alongside Hughes.

"When are you going to confess your sins and invite Jesus Christ into your heart?"

"Oh, hello, Bernard. I didn't feel your presence. I've been so preoccupied with my internal turmoil; I don't know what I should do."

"Well, I don't want to say, 'I told you so,' but you should have listened to me when we first met. Hughes, this would be a good time to say the 'sinners' prayer' with me while you're wandering the cattle pasture. Do you suppose you're ready?"

"No, not yet. I need a little more time. Speaking with God, I can do it, but confessing to Jesus is a bit scary. Will I see you again, Bernard?"

"Well, isn't that a complete turnaround? Before, you couldn't wait to get rid of me, and now you're asking me to return. Thank you, Holy Spirit, for touching my buddy to search for the truths of heaven." Bernard disappears.

Hughes wasn't aware, but God ordered an angel to stand in front of every longhorn steer, protecting Hughes as he walked and prayed every afternoon in the cattle pasture.

Klaus, Amir, and Dr. Drew meet in the prison lunchroom daily. In the fourth week of their new prison life, they concoct a plan to heap revenge at Hughes for getting them in prison. The next morning, the three sneak into the kitchen at 4 a.m. and pepper spray Hughes as he walks in. They commence dragging his limp body into the locker, tie his hands behind his back, place a gag over his mouth, and prop him up standing on the chair. While Amir and Dr. Drew hold him from falling, Klaus slips a noose over Hughes's head and flings it over the 11-foot rafter. They await a few seconds for Hughes to awake from the spray and shout, "This is what you get for getting us in prison," and they kick the chair out from under him and quickly run out unseen.

Hughes is flaying his legs furiously, trying to scream, but to no avail. His three-hundred-pound body is quickly tightening the noose around his neck. Hughes is about to take his last breath when Sammy rushes in and cuts the rope dropping Hughes three feet to the floor.

While Hughes regains his breath lying on the locker floor, Sammy hides the rope and noose in the locker's back corner for later disposal. Fortunately for Hughes, he gains consciousness.

"Sammy, you got here just in time. I owe my life to you. I will be forever indebted to you. How can I repay you?"

"Listen to me really carefully, big boy. You don't know the secret rules of prison life yet. First, when the correctional officers and warren interrogate you, you play dumb. Simply state, you have no idea how that red mark got attached to your neck. When you woke up, it was there. Secondly, you're going to be teased by the other inmates big time. You're going to sucker punch a few of the guys and cause a brawl. Then you'll go into solitary confinement for a spell. Thirdly, I could have used my butcher knife to slice you up like a piece of meat hanging from the hook, but I didn't. I've been here for ten years and know my way around this place. I've earned the respect of others. I can help you enjoy life here more abundantly, and you can avoid all the mess."

"How's that?" Hughes inquires.

"Simple, be my girlfriend."

That afternoon, Hughes told the correctional officers and warren the same story Sammy coached him on. They didn't believe him but allowed Hughes to return to the kitchen to finish his shift. Later that afternoon, Hughes walks out to the cattle pasture to pray.

"Dear heavenly Father, help me, oh, God. I'm being blackmailed into something I never thought would happen to me. Oh, God, help me."

"Prison life certainly has its moments, doesn't it, Hughes?"

"Where were you when I needed you most? I almost lost my life."

"I was the one that had Sammy rush in and cut you loose. I must keep you alive, Hughes, in the hope one day you'll receive Jesus Christ as your Lord and Savior. However, I can't prevent prison calamities from incurring to you. You only have yourself to blame for being here."

"I know, you're right. I'll survive. About that sinners' prayer, I would like to be a child of God now; I'm ready."

Bernard and Hughes pray together, and the angels in heaven rejoice that another soul is saved.

"You're now a newborn-again Christian, Hughes. Be sure to listen to the soft prompts of the Holy Spirit. He will guide you throughout your prison life. Also, be sure to pray day and night to our Lord, Jesus Christ. You best get back inside. The crew is about ready to do tonight's cattle round-up." Bernard vanishes.

Each evening the cattle roundup crew is randomly drawn. The goal is four heads to be butchered in the morning for tomorrow's meals. Surprisingly, Sammy draws as the lead crew master, followed by Klaus, Amir, and Dr. Drew. It's becoming dusk as the crew walks out to the forty acres. Sammy chases the longhorn cattle into the chute at the far end when, flat-out, the longhorns get spooked and make a U-turn into the crew. Sammy gets gored through the stomach, dying instantly, while the other three get gorged in the legs ending up in the infirmary, but luckily for them, surviving.

Hughes gets a new cellmate that same evening, "Hi, I'm Hughes, and what are you in for?"

"Yeah, I'm Roger, the accountant. I got caught embezzling one million from a funeral home. The sad part is it was all counterfeit. Double jeopardy for me-yeah? What idiot would print and distribute fake money? If I ever get my hands on that guy..."

Hughes pulls his orange suit up closer to his neck and states, "Yeah, that is pretty dumb. How long you in for?"

"Hopefully, less than Seven. My lawyer is working on a reduced sentence. How about you?"

"Well, I'm in for life."

"What the heck did you do?"

"You don't want to know. Now get some rest; I have to get up at 3 a.m."

"Why so early?"

"I work in the prison's butcher shop. Now, get some rest."

Roger decides to sleep with one eye open. From that evening forward, Roger never asked Hughes any more questions.

The women's correctional institute was adjacent to the men. One afternoon, while Hughes was walking the cattle pasture and praying, he hears a faint voice in the distance. As he looks west, he thinks he sees a couple of ladies working in the dairy parlor. As he moves closer to the fence line, the two women also approach the fence.

"Howdy, scumbag! How the heck are you? Thanks for trying to kill me in your office gas chamber," Donna shouts sarcastically.

Hughes didn't recognize her in the prison suit but did know the voice. "Is that you, Donna?"

"Yup, that's me, milking cows all day, every day. But still alive. By that red line around your neck, It looks like whoever tried to hang you missed a golden opportunity. What a shame."

"What red line? Do I have a red line around my neck? I must have woken up with it and have no idea how it got there."

Donna glances at Leah, "Sounds like our scumbag here has learned the rules of prison life quickly. You remember, Leah, right?"

"Sure, yes, I do. You also work in the diary?"

"Yup, just like Donna. But, I regret the day I ever met you, Hughes, ending up in prison carrying out your lame-brained scheme. I agree with Donna; it's a shame you didn't die hanging."

Hughes is out of words for a reply and simply stands there like an oak tree.

Donna breaks the quiet, "Well, we best get back to the cows. We discovered by playing Christian music the cow's milk production is 50% more. They are content for sure, and so are Leah and I as newborn again Christians."

"Oh, by the way, I'm a newborn again, Christian also," Hughes softly states, trying to appease them.

"Really? Unbelievable!" Donna shrugs her shoulders.

Leah shouts back, "You got to be kidding!"

The next day, Mitch pays a visit to Hughes. Mitch and Hughes began their conversation on each side of the glass partition with hard wire phones in their hands.

"So, you've been here how long now, six weeks?" Mitch tries to confirm.

"Yeah, that's right. Six wonderful weeks in paradise!" Hughes states sarcastically.

"Well, that's better living than your buddy Carmen Bridgewater has going for himself. Connor told the investigators when he called his dad that he should turn himself in as you did. Connor also mentioned his dad was working underground and didn't care that Connor was still alive and hung upon him. The next thing occurring was that the printing press began to throw sparks and ignited a gas leak causing an implosion creating a 500-foot crater."

Hughes replies, "I guess my Casket Manufacturing Plant went down in the implosion."

"Yes, and that's not all," Mitch continues. "The implosion caused a virtual circular earthquake creating a lake with burning flames on top. The city has decided to use it as their new garbage dump. This is Carmen's final resting place."

Hughes remembers Bernard's words, *"Which do you prefer, Hughes, Heaven, or the everlasting lake of fire?"*

"So, you see, life imprisonment isn't so bad after all," Mitch tries to encourage Hughes.

Hughes continues, "I've been a bad boy all my adult life, and only good for a few weeks. So, the worldly flesh in me continually fights with the Holy Spirit in me. Mitch, It's complicated and confusing. But, I do pray every afternoon with the longhorns in the back forty."

"And you don't get gored?"

"I'm guessing Bernard the Angel is protecting me?"

"Well, I'm going to shove off, Hughes. While I'm in the neighborhood, I may as well visit Donna and Leah next door. Oh, by the way, I see someone tried to hang you; best be careful, Hughes. "

"I have no idea what you're talking about."

"You learn quickly. It looks like you'll survive prison life after all."

On the way out, Mitch mentions to the guard, "I can't believe that guy walks out in the pasture every day and doesn't get gored?"

"No, not him. He has angels watching over him. But four men did get gored a few weeks ago. One got killed, and the other three gored in the legs."

"You happen to know the names of the survivors?"

"Sure. A guy named Klaus, a Doctor Drew, and a man called Amir."

"Ha! Of course! Those three men worked for Hughes in his counterfeit scheme. His hanging was payback."

"Hughes denies knowing anything about that every day. Those three guys will be on crutches for the rest of their lives. The warren suspected them but decided they already received their penalty. So, we allow Hughes to play dumb, better that way."

CHAPTER FORTY

VOTER FRAUD-AUG 2036

Almost four years to the date from the last election, the quiet village of Cedar Creek hastily became a bedlam of activity. Unaware of the county police department's recent findings, Mayor Brady was bombarded by a horde of reporters shouting questions at him in a flurry.

The mayor's office was jammed with reporters. Nevertheless, one reporter was able to muscle his way through. He shoved a mic in the mayor's face and boldly asked, "Say, Mayor Brady, about an hour ago, one of the county's police officers found an abandoned car virtually buried by tall weeds in a field. When she popped the trunk open to investigate for a dead body, to her surprise, she discovered four ballot boxes instead. The ballots totaled 1,200 votes for your opponent, Mayor Aderman. Surprisingly, that would have given him the win by 500 votes four years ago. Do you know anything about this?"

"Are you sure the ballots are valid? Are they legible? It's been what, four years? Who knows, they could be bogus, smudged, or even rusted? To answer your question, I have no clue whatsoever," Allen states as he walks out of his office for a short three-day vacation with his wife at their cabin in the Adirondack Mountains.

The dozen-plus reporters chase after him shouting questions without ceasing, but to no avail. As Allen briskly walks out to his car and throws his two suitcases in the back seat. He's in a tizzy and fuming inside, wondering why the vehicle and evidence weren't burned as planned.

Allen jumps behind the wheel and drives out on Interstate 90 toward Hoffmeister, New York. He and his wife, Jayna, are planning a relaxing three-day stay in the Adirondacks. During the five-hour trip, Mayor Brady is still agitated and cussing Hughes for not finishing the assignment.

Arriving at their cabin, Brady notices Jayna's already there. Opening the door, he continues to mutter, "If only Hughes finished the job, if only."

Jayna interrupts him, "What's the matter, Allen? You seem extremely upset."

"Some county police officer found the abandoned car with the ballots in the trunk that Hughes was supposed to have destroyed four years ago!. Just hours ago, my office was stormed with reporters asking hundreds of questions! Asking if I stole the election!"

"I see. Well, I guess this is as good of a time as ever," Jayna states.

"Good as a time as ever for what?" Shouts Brady, perplexed.

"It wasn't Hughes fault the car wasn't burned. It was mine. You're a quiet and unassuming man, Brady. You accepted whatever Hughes told you as gospel. You never knew, but I volunteered at the other party's precinct and stole those four ballot boxes. Hughes coached me on the mechanics of the theft. I wanted us to win and did whatever it took to get it done!" Jayna states.

"I don't like the sound of this," Brady mutters.

"I was supposed to destroy the vehicle, but Hughes's driver arrived too soon, so we made a quick exit. I left the evidence there, hoping the field weeds would cover it up and that the car would eventually decay along with the ballot boxes." Jayna states softly.

"When Hughes told me he'd take care of everything, it never crossed my mind that he would select you as the go-to person."

"Well, it wasn't a matter of selecting me, dear. We became close friends during your campaign. One thing led to another, and we've been having an affair non-stop since then, which of course stopped with his prison sentence."

"Oh, my God, that hurts Jayna!"

"I know. So, I'll be filing for divorce. My heart hasn't been in this marriage for a long while. I don't want to pretend anymore. You're a good Mayor, Allen, and I wish you success in your re-election. I did everything for my personal ambitions; obviously, I won't be helping you this time." Jayna walks out the door and drives off, leaving Allen in their cabin and alone to reflect on things of his life.

After her declaration of filing for divorce, Jayna drives almost a hundred miles to Watertown, New York, to visit Hughes at the prison. Once arriving at the prison parking lot, Jayna struts to the main entrance, and the guard immediately opens the door.

"Nice to see you again, Ms. Jayna. How are you this afternoon?"

"Peachy keen if I say so myself. As you know, I'm here to see my buddy, Hughes."

"Yes, of course. Right, this way. I believe he's waiting for your arrival."

Once seated at the security window, Jayna boldly states, "I told my husband that I'm filing for divorce."

"So, with that completed, what are your plans? I coached you on how to steal those ballot boxes without getting caught. Didn't I?"

"Yes, you did. You coached me well. Thank you."

"You still interested in making a run for Congress?"

"Hughes, it's too bad you committed a federal crime. No conjugal visits at this prison. I'm sorry I won't be able to repay you with favors as I used to. But, we must keep our eyes on the goal, agree?"

"Yes, absolutely agree! Besides, you'll run a much better campaign than your husband ever could. You suppose he'll continue being mayor and leave it at that with no further ambitions for Congress?"

"Sure. Once the hurt settles in, I'm certain Allen will be content just being mayor of Cedar Creek."

I agree. Being mayor suits him much better than the Washington D. C. swamp. He'd be eaten alive. So, I'll coach you from here, Jayna. Just continue visiting me twice a month. We'll nail this election also!"

Out of the blue, Bernard appears. *"Vipers of evil, Good afternoon. Relax, Jayna, no one sees or hears me, but you two doers of evil. Hughes! I thought you gave your heart to Jesus Christ. What gives?"*

"Ah, I tried it for a week or two, and it doesn't seem to work."

"Who do you suppose stopped you from being hanged until death? Who do you figure protects you from the longhorns? What do you mean it doesn't work?"

"I'm still in prison, aren't I?"

"No one is responsible for your stint in prison except yourself, Hughes. Believing in Jesus Christ is an assurance that your soul will be with him in heaven everlasting. Also, Janya, if you continue associating with this man, you'll find yourself next door in the women's prison."

"Unlike my soon-to-be-divorced husband, I am strong, never flinching. Hughes and I are determined to thrust me into Congress to support President Avci and the D. C. Mandate bill. Eventually, opening the door for a one-world government!"

"Upon both of your declarations, I declare all heavenly protections are immediately removed from both of you. You have willingly become partners with Satan. However, should either of you change your mind, call out to Jesus." Bernard vanishes.

CHAPTER FORTY-ONE

THE DAIRY PARLOR-AUG 2036

Mitch drives over to the women's correctional facility to meet with Donna and Leah. As he opens the car door, he can't help but notice the dairy parlor's pungent fragrance permeating the air. Mitch is grateful the women's prison is a low-security facility allowing for an open meeting room.

The guard walks Mitch back to the room, "Have a seat for a minute while I get the gals to come in for a spell from milking the cows."

Mitch was patiently waiting, looking around, and was surprised to see this prison allowed the inmates to hug family and friends that were visiting. No sooner had he processed that thought when he felt hugs coming from Donna and Leah.

"Hey, guy, what brings you into our neck of the woods?" Donna asks.

"I was next door visiting with Hughes and thought I'd stop by to surprise you both."

"How's my old boss, the scumbag doing?" Leah inquires.

Donna jumps in, "We met him at the fence bordering the two prisons last week and told him it was a shame he didn't die hanging."

"I understand your hostility, it's to be expected, but I came here to visit you two gals and not discuss Hughes. But, tell me, what's with all these cows? The country air smells like you have a thousand heads."

Leah chuckles, "That's close. Sixteen-hundred, to be exact. We have twenty gals, each milking 40 cows twice daily. Our dairy parlor supplies the milk for the men's prison next door as well as our facility. All surplus milk is donated to the local food bank."

"Wow! I'm impressed with the operation. I think if it weren't for the high walls and barbed-wire fence, this place out in the country could be a decoy for a resort."

"Hilarious, Mitch," smacks Donna. "Live here for a day and tell me again it's a resort."

"Yeah, I know, just joking around. But, the reason I stopped to visit with both of you is no joke. Phillip and the District Attorney found a fly-in-the-ointment sort of speak. There was a flaw in both of your cases, and you'll both be released in your 13th month!"

"Are you serious?" Leah asks.

"Are you joking again, Mitch?" Donna asks. "Because if you are, I'm going to ask the guard to make you muck out the stalls before you go home, and that's no joke!"

"No, no. I'm serious. You'll both be released in about eleven months. Of course, there are caveats."

"Oh, boy! Here it comes!" shouts Leah.

"Donna, remember in your plea deal, you'd be the director of the west coast 'Adopt-not Abort' Center?"

"Yes, of course, I do. Remember, I donated a substantial amount to that cause, which I don't regret for one moment."

"I hope I'm not putting the cart before the horse, but you've never been asked, Leah. Would you be interested in being Donna's assistant?"

"You mean working with Donna, pregnant girls, babies, and adoptive parents? Would I ever! Now that I'm a Christian, it would be the most beautiful act of kindness for me to help save a baby's life."

"On my drive up here, I was praying you'd say something like that. Okay, here's the program going forward. On your release, you'll both be in training for two months at the Jerusalem Tree Church. Lucinda is the director there, and she'll hold your hands through all the steps. After training, she'll fly out to the west coast and stay for two weeks and get you both set up. Any questions?"

Leah softly inquires, "Should I assume that Donna and I will be on probation for the remainder of our respective terms?"

"Normally, that would be correct, but due to the misstep by the district attorney, you'll each be free and clear."

Donna begins to sob with joy, and tears flow down her face. "Mitch, I hear what you're saying. I believe what you're saying. But, right now, it seems it will take over a year living and working on the west coast before reality sets in that I will be free indeed! Praise the Lord!"

"I feel the same way, Mitch," Leah states. "I can never thank you enough nor ever repay your kindness. You're a good man, Mitch."

"You're most welcome, ladies. So, before you drag me in to muck out the stalls, I best be going. I will attempt to visit every two months to keep both of you posted on the progress."

"Hey, before you go, can you share what the status is on the others?" Donna inquires out of curiosity.

"Yeah, I suppose I can. No national security issues here. Well, you may not know, but Richard and Agnes bought the whole shebang! The country club, golf course, funeral home, mortuary school, cemetery, guest cottages, and your villa, Donna."

"How are they operating their new enterprise?" Donna's business acumen kicks in her curiosity.

"Richard is smart. He's leasing all operations to different managers. I haven't told anyone yet, but I will when I return to my office. I'll offer Jacob and his mom, Katy, and her mom, Doris, to lease and manage the funeral home, cemetery, and mortuary school."

Leah asks, "Do they know how to operate these types of businesses?"

"Yeah, they owned a funeral home in Pittsburgh. Jacob is also a licensed preacher, so he'll be able to perform funeral services."

"Who's managing the golf course?" Donna inquires.

"Connor is a natural for this. He'll lease and manage the golf course, country club, guest cottages, and the villa."

"Who'll be living in the villa?" Donna, getting a bit suspicious and jealous.

"It will be leased out to corporations for golf tournaments only. All managers will reside in the guest cottages. It's a win-win for everyone.

Especially Richard and Agnes, they just play golf and count the lease income."

"Wow! What a package! Praise the Lord!" Leah shouts.

"Oh, before I go, one more thing. Like your two cases, all the other verdicts involving a three-year house arrest and community service have also been reduced to thirteen months—that darn-fly-in-the-ointment. Listen, I must run, gals. See you in two months." Mitch drives back to headquarters in Buffalo.

After Mitch leaves, Leah notices Donna sobbing again. "What's the matter, dear?"

"I was hoping and praying after my release that Connor and I would reunite, but I'm not so sure that will work out anymore."

"Now, now, don't be so quick to conclude anything. Who knows, God may order things around, so you two will be together. Keep the faith, my friend!" Leah tries to console Donna.

"It doesn't matter. Connor has a lease agreement, he's staying in Cedar Creek, managing the course and playing golf every day, and I'm starting a new life on the west coast!"

"That's the spirit, girl! We'll be victorious in the Lord!" Leah shouts.

CHAPTER FORTY-TWO

COMMUNITY SERVICE-AUG 2036

Mitch, not traveling this week but conducting business from his Buffalo headquarters, calls Rachael's hotel, where Jacob and his mom, Katy, are waiting it out.

"I have terrific news! You're all released from having to testify. Hughes has been sentenced to life in prison, and subsequently, as it turns out, the FBI didn't need you as witnesses after all," Mitch shares. "So, I'm curious, what would you guys like to do now?"

Jacob speaks first, "My passion is preaching, and my mom's is operating a funeral home."

"I was wondering how long you'd be able to stay away from the pulpit, Jacob. I may have some encouraging news for you," declares Mitch.

"Hey, Mitch, Katy here. What do you have for us?"

"The former sheriff, Richard and his wife, Agnes, bought the Cedar Creek Country Club and all the other businesses on the property from Hughes. The funeral home, cemetery, and mortuary school have been closed for six weeks now and need new management. I can't imagine any other two-some than the two of you operating this enterprise. Are you guys interested?"

"It sounds exciting, Mitch, but I'm not sure we could afford a business in that zip code," Katy states.

"Well, the deal gets better, hang on. Richard is leasing out the funeral home, cemetery, and school. Plus, for the first two years, the FBI will pay 50% of the lease. No down payment or mortgage is required. Now, are you guys interested?" Mitch shouts, asking the question?

"This sounds like a dream come true," Jacob states. "I believe I'm speaking for my mom also."

"Yes, you are, speaking for both moms. My mom, Doris, also. So, Mitch, in essence, we'll be starting a new business. You have any practical advice on a quick start-up?"

"Funny you're asking that, Katy. My two agents, Brad and Nancy, I've assigned them to re-open the forty affiliated funeral homes we shuttered. They'll be securing retired directors to manage the business until you have enough graduates from the mortuary school. They've also secured three custom wood casket makers to replace the now-defunct Hughes metal casket Manufacturing Company."

"You're sweet, Mitch, thank you," Katy softly states. "If I were twenty years younger, I'd be asking you out on a date."

"You're making me blush, but thanks for the pretend invite."

"One day, you'll find your soul mate, Mitch."

"I have one more item, and it seems you forgot about this, Jacob."

"What's that?"

"As a preacher, you'll be able to reside over all the funerals taking place at your chapel and cemetery. Plus, I've spoken with Rachael and Darrell, pastors at the Jerusalem Tree Church. They'd like you to occasionally fill in for them so they can get some R & R. They haven't had more than two days off consecutively in four years."

Jacob is thrilled, "This is more than I ever expected. Praise the Lord! I look forward to getting acquainted with them."

"I'm sure they'll be delighted in getting to know you, your mom, and grandma," Mitch states.

Mitch takes a break from the numerous phone calls and mumbles to himself, *'one down and several to go.'"*

Before making the next call, Mitch ponders what Katy voiced to him about finding his soul mate. *'I tried once, and it didn't work out. Maybe, eventually, I should be more open to dating again.'*

His next call is to Sergio, waiting it out at the FBI headquarters in Albany.

"Sergio, I have good news for you. You're free to come back to Cedar Creek. We won't need you as a witness after all. Nevertheless, I hope you enjoyed the two-month stay at headquarters?"

"Yeah, it was splendid, except for the 24-hour security guards following every footstep I took."

"I'm curious, Sergio, will you continue playing the piano at church?"

"Absolutely! I'm going to ask Tom if he feels I could offer piano lessons as his assistant. And, I can't wait to see Lucinda!"

"I'm sure she'll be happy to see you also. Two months is a long time to be apart, but you're both young and have the rest of your lives to enjoy this journey on earth."

"So, will you be picking me up and taking me back?"

"Yes, I will. I'll pick you up tomorrow before lunch."

"Okay. I'll be here. Can't wait to get back."

Mitch has an idea and calls Lucinda.

"Hi, Lucinda. Mitch here. Are you keeping busy with the Adopt-Not Abort Ministry?"

"I am, but I'm sure you didn't call to adopt a baby, did you?"

"No, nothing like that, but I was wondering if you'd like to join me when I pick Sergio up tomorrow and bring him back to Cedar Creek?"

"Wow! Would I ever!"

"I'll take that as a yes. Be ready by 8 a.m. Sergio doesn't know, so it'll be a surprise. You okay with that?"

"Sure. I'll add to the surprise element and have a small bouquet to greet him with."

"Sergio will get a chuckle from that, I'm certain."

Unforeseen, Bernard shows up.

"That is a mighty fine gesture you're doing, Mitch. Maybe the romance bug has smitten you?"

Oh, I don't know. I've been thinking about taking another chance. Life is short, you know.

"For you mortals, yes, but for us angels, life is an eternity-everlasting. If

I may suggest, Mitch, go, take a chance at romance again. You won't know unless you try."

"I will pray about that, Bernard, and ask Jesus to open doors according to His will."

"You're on the right track. Keep the faith, and good things will come to you." Bernard vanishes.

The next day Mitch picks Lucinda up at church, and they buckle up for the four-hour drive. Arriving at their destination, Mitch shows his badge to security. They commence the long walk through a maze of hallways and finally arrive at Sergio's room. Mitch knocks on the door, and Sergio opens it slightly, always being cautious.

"I have a surprise for you," and Mitch steps aside, allowing Sergio to see Lucinda standing there with a small bouquet of flowers in her hand. Their hugs and kisses were the exclamations of joy seeing each other after two months of silence.

"What a surprise, Mitch. Thank You!"

"You're welcome, Sergio. But before you two do any more hugging and kissing, we best go to lunch. There's a cafeteria in here, my treat. Grab your stuff Sergio, and we'll be on our way."

During lunch, Mitch brings Sergio up to date on the Hughes case and then excuses himself.

"You two have a little catching up. Go ahead and finish your lunch; take your time. When you're ready to leave, I'll be in my office."

As Mitch begins to leave, Lucinda stands up and gives him a gentle hug, and whispers, "Thank you."

During the first hour, Lucinda and Sergio chat non-stop across the table from each other. She scoots next to him during the next hour, and they talk some more in between kisses.

Lucinda sits in the back seat on the drive back to Cedar Creek while conversing with Sergio seated upfront. After an hour of non-stop romantic talk, Mitch decides he's had enough.

"Sergio, would you mind driving the rest of the trip? I'm sort of tired and need to rest my eyes. Lucinda, you sit in the front, and I'll go in the back seat."

"Sure, we won't have to talk as loud then being next to each other"

"That would be great. Maybe I'll even get some shuteye then. Thank you."

Upon arrival in Cedar Creek at the church, they're greeted by Rachael and Darrell, everyone hugging each other.

"Welcome back, Sergio. So, how did you like your surprise?"

As he and Lucinda lock arms, Sergio shouts, "Wonderful!"

Darrell inquires, "Have you made a decision on continuing with the worship team?"

"I have, and it's a definite, yes."

Darrell shouts, "Great! We'll talk more on Monday if that's okay with you?"

"It's not the weekend yet," Sergio mutters. "Isn't tomorrow Friday a workday?"

Rachael gleans with joy. "Lucinda, I'm giving you tomorrow off so you and Sergio can start dating again. Enjoy your three-day weekend!"

"Thank you, Rachael. We appreciate that."

"Sergio, I have another surprise for you," Darrell starts. "Just because you were sequestered for two months, not by your choice, we're paying you the normal salary had you been working. So, enjoy your weekend!"

Sergio reaches out and shakes Darrell's hand and then gives him a brotherly hug. "I can't thank you enough, both of you, for this kind gesture. Thank you."

"You're welcome," Rachael shares. "Now, to help you two get started, Darrell and I have arranged for you two to be double dating with Cambria and Carlo over the weekend. You'll also be staying with Richard and Agnes at their stately home as guests. Cambria and Carlo will be there too, and they have an entire weekend of activities lined up. So, enjoy, and we'll see you both on Monday.

As they start to leave, Lucinda and Sergio give Rachael and Darrell hugs and more hugs. "Thank you again," they shout as they walk to Lucinda's car.

Lucinda drives the seven miles to the country club, navigates the winding curves in the road leading up to the Filburn's house. Arriving just in time for dinner, they're greeted by Cambria and Carlo waiting for them by the front steps.

"Welcome, welcome! It's so good to see you, Sergio," shouts Cambria as she gives him a big sisterly hug.

Carlo grasps his hand and gives Sergio a firm manly handshake,. "It's good to have you back, brother."

"I enjoyed my sequestered stay at headquarters as humanly as possible, but it is so good to be back home with my friends. Thank you for that warm welcome."

Richard steps in the doorway and shouts, "Come on in, guys. Agnes has a special treat for you all."

After a few minutes at the dinner table, the four 'youngsters' wondered why Agnes or Richard wasn't serving the meal yet. Richard poured each a glass of wine, and they continued with small chatter. Still no food. Lucinda, Sergio, Cambria, and Carlo were befuddled. *Do we have appetizers only as our meal*, they thought?

At precisely 7:30 p.m., Chef Reynolds comes rolling out of the kitchen with a country club catered cart loaded with exquisite food. A feast to look upon and taste.

"So, this is the surprise!" Cambria shouts happily.

"I thought you kids would like something extra special to celebrate the homecoming of our brother-in-Christ, Sergio," Agnes shares softly.

Sergio can't express his appreciation enough. "Thank you so very much. You didn't have to go through all this trouble for me. How can I ever repay your kindness?"

"You can never repay us," Richard declares. "It's a gift. Just like the salvation message that we each receive as a gift from God."

Agnes, however, does express a question. "Sergio, do you still play the piano?"

"I do and will start up again with the worship team next Sunday."

"That's wonderful! Richard and I would like you to consider playing soft dinner music at the club on Friday and Saturday evenings, about three hours each. Lucinda can join you and sing a few songs. Are the two of you interested?"

"Oh, my goodness!" shouts Sergio. "If Lucinda and I did this, I wouldn't need to give piano lessons."

"Praise the Lord!" Shouts Lucinda. "I give God all the glory."

They hug each other at the dinner table with joys of happiness but quickly glance at Cambria and Carlo, jokingly ask, "Did you two know about this?"

Cambria speaks innocence, "Carlo and I didn't know anything about this, any of this. The surprise catered dinner, and the offer for you two to provide dinner music and song. We're surprised as much as you guys."

"My wife and I have heard both of you at church. You each have a gift from God, and I'm certain our club members will be delighted to hear your music and singing."

"When do you want us to start?" inquiries Sergio.

'How about next weekend. Will that work for each of you?" states Agnes.

"Absolutely!" shouts Lucinda.

After dinner, Richard shares with Sergio and Lucinda that Cambria and Carlo will be managing fashion shows for the next two months featuring the ladies' business suit.

"How exciting for the two of you!" exclaims Lucinda.

"Yes, it is. This is our first road trip with the modeling team. So, a bit nervous, but Cambria and I have Jesus at our side. So, we know we'll be okay," states Carlo.

"You guys have nothing to worry about," assures Richard. "You both know your fashion line impeccably. Besides, you were coached by Rachael. The best of the best. She fashioned and managed what the two of you are about to embark on as your next journey in life."

Lucinda turns her attention to Cambria. "Rachael tells me you have the entire weekend scheduled for us as a double-date. Sounds like fun. What do you have in mind?"

"It's sizzling summer outside, worse than a sauna, which rules outside actives as a non-starter," states Carlo. "However, gleaning the internet, Cambria found the Indoor Adventure Park, not far from here. They have virtually any activity one would want. Rock climbing, miniature golf, tennis, air conditioning, and a whole bunch more. We can go there tomorrow right after breakfast."

Agnes chides in, "Please don't expect Chef Reynolds for breakfast. It'll be continental."

They all laugh and tease her a bit on why not Chef Reynolds for every meal.

Sergio inquires, "What do you have planned for Saturday?"

"Maybe take in a movie, visit the aquarium, or go back to the adventure park," shares Cambria. "What would you guys like to do?"

"If it's okay with Richard, Lucinda and I would like to go over to the clubhouse and practice our routine for an hour or so. Maybe around 3 p.m.?"

"I think that can be arranged. Actually, we should all go over, give you guys moral support, and then we'll have dinner at the club. Chef Reynolds style!"

"Wow! This is something I can get used to!" shouts Sergio.

"Actually, you and Lucinda can. All employees receive half off on all food purchased when working their shift."

"Thank you, Richard. Not everyone in your position in life is willing to share the blessings that God has bestowed upon them as you do. You're a kind and generous man and have been blessed with your lovely wife, Agnes, next to you at all times," Lucinda shares sweetly.

"My husband has one more surprise for you kids. Go ahead and tell them, dear," Agnes grins while sharing.

"After church on Sunday, we'll all be heading out to the Bills Stadium for a pre-season night game. I was fortunate enough to procure some skyline box seats, and I'm told the view is spectacular!"

The guys high-fived each other and Richard, celebrating a make-believe touchdown. The girls simply give him a hug.

"This is fantastic!" shouts Cambria. "Think I'll wear my ladies' business suit to the game and maybe create some interest."

Agnes shares softly again. "All these surprises are getting me tired. It's getting late anyway, so I'm calling it a day and going to bed. By the way, Lucinda and Sergio, we're treating this weekend like summer camp. Remember when you were young children? Girls bunk with girls, and guys bunk with guys. Besides, I'm sure Cambria and Lucinda have a bunch of girls' talks to chat about."

"Come to think of it, I'm calling it a day also. We'll see you kids in the morning," Richard states as he walks up the stairs.

Agnes was right. Cambria and Lucinda, snuggled in their bunks, stayed up till 2 a. m. talking about everything under the sun. Mostly though, about romance and guys. Sergio and Carlo just talked about sports and fell asleep at midnight.

Friday afternoon at the Indoor Adventure Park was exhilarating for all four. The girls played tennis while the guys did the rock-climbing wall. Interestingly, they all played miniature golf, three games. The girls won all three!

Saturday afternoon rehearsal at the club went fantastic. Sergio and Lucinda blended together as if they had been a duo for ten years. On their last note, Richard, Agnes, Cambria, and Carlo give them a round of applause.

"You two are fabulous in music and song. I'm so appreciative that you're willing to share the talents God has given you," Richard sincerely states. "Now, let's go and have dinner, Chef Reynolds style!"

However, Sunday evening at the football game turned out to be a national crisis, especially for those who attend a church. During the 3rd quarter, with seven minutes left, without warning, on the jumbo monitor screens throughout the stadium, the Vice-President, Ms. Firuzeh, begins to speak.

"Good evening, all Comrades and Americans. I come to you this evening to announce a major breakthrough in negotiations with Congress regarding the D. C. Mandate bill."

A hushed silence falls over the stadium. The players stand on the field, awe-struck.

"Congress and I have persuaded President Avci to delay until after the November elections this year to sign the bill. So, we were able to avert the churches' shuttering and confiscation of Bibles, at least for a year."

Only 30% of the crowd of over one-hundred thousand shout joys of Hallelujah's when she made that statement.

"I am glad to report that Congress, myself, and the President were able to hammer out a compromise bill, called the D. C. Church Tax/ Registration Reform."

Some of the crowd moans, while the majority cheers.

"All churches, regardless of size, will be taxed fifty thousand annually due December 1ˢᵗ each year. I suggest smaller churches merge with larger ones. You'll have ninety days to make this transition or simply pay the tax."

Most of the crowd cheers their approval, as well as most of the players on the field.

"Last but not least. All those who wish to attend the church of their choice must register. The President has ordered the Sheriff Squad's Director, Ms. Grace Palmer, to have officers stationed at each church's main entrance door for the next four weeks. Failure to register will result in arrest with a minimum fine of five thousand and up to five months in jail. The Sheriff Squad will concentrate on a continual random checking of churches. Failure to present your church registration upon entering will result in arrest and appropriate fines also."

The anti-church part of the crowd starts to chant, "Fine them, fine them, jail them, jail them!"

At full-tilt, the anti-church players on the field began to attack the silent minority players. The few security forces available and referees stood on the sidelines watching the attacks unfold. Skirmishes started in the stands, and chaos was about to occur. But, out of nowhere, out of the blue, an angel flew through the middle of the playing field. The crowd was subdued instantly. The angel flew the entire perimeter of the arena several times. Thousands in the stands were slain in the spirit. A total calm enveloped the stadium. The referees called the game a no-contest, and the hundred-thousand exited the stadium in an orderly fashion.

Later in the evening, the Speaker of the House makes a short nation-wide announcement. "Due to the attacks we witnessed at every football game played today or intended to play, we strongly advise churchgoers that they do so at their own risk if they attend a football game or play on a team. Stay in a church where you're safe. We cannot offer you any protection in any stadium from this day forward."

The speaker's statement was a veiled nudge to indiscreetly march all Christians into a church building, getting ready for the military invasion.

Later in the evening, after the game, while at home, the six-some, Richard, Agnes, Cambria, Carlo, Lucinda, and Sergio, were in total shock while watching this unfold on TV.

"I'm sure that was Bernard, the Angel of the Lord, flying through the football stadium early today," Lucinda proposes.

"That incident goes to show that even the anti-church crowd knows about angels. The immediate appearance of Bernard subdued the attacks. Where it not for him at that precise time, many people may have been killed," Carlo states.

"When I return to work tomorrow, I'll ask Darrell how he and Rachael took the message," Sergio shares with the group.

"Lucinda, would you do Carlo and me a favor? Ask Rachael what the protocol is for traveling people. How do they register?"

"I sure will, no problem."

"Well, listen, kids. It's been a long day. Agnes and I are calling it a day. We'll see you in the morning."

"Thanks for everything, Richard and Agnes. You've made my first three days back home memorable. I appreciate everything you've done for Lucinda and me. I guess we'll see you next weekend-Friday and Saturday at the club, and Sunday at church," Sergio speaks fondly.

CHAPTER FORTY-THREE

HOMECOMING-SEPT 2036

Several months later, Donna and Leah, having fulfilled their thirteen-month sentence, are released. Mitch picks them up and drives to the Jerusalem Tree Church.

While driving, he laughingly asks, "Are you both going to miss the cows and all the fringe benefits that come with the milking?"

Donna, sitting in the passenger seat, smartly replies, "If you're referring to the fresh country air, yes. I have grown accustomed to it. When out west, I'll find one of those corporate dairy farms and walk the barns and pasture to remind myself of the country air and my prison stent."

Leah jumps in, "I couldn't have put-into-words any better myself."

Heading west toward Buffalo and passing Syracuse, Mitch stops at his favorite truck stop and treats the gals to lunch. Walking back to the car, Leah whispers to Donna, "It's my turn to sit up front."

As Mitch buckles his seat belt, Leah shares, "I got you a cup of coffee to go. You like it with cream, right?"

"Yes, thank you. That was nice of you." Mitch doesn't understand Leah's gesture of kindness.

Once arriving at church, Darrell and Rachael greet them at the foot of the church steps. Welcoming embraces go all around.

Rachael shouts, "Well, come on in! Let's get you settled, and we'll catch up over dinner."

They invite Lucinda, Sergio, and Mitch to join the group for dinner. After much laughter and sharing, Darrell starts the business discussion over dessert.

"As a quick review, Donna and Leah, you'll be going through training with Lucinda for six weeks now versus the original two months."

Leah inquires, "Why the change?"

Rachael answers, "We've aligned our non-profit organization with several churches on the west coast and have received an overwhelming response to our 'Adopt-not Abort' program. Darrell flew out there six months ago and secured the perfect location and building on reduced lease terms."

Donna inquires, "I thought you were going to use my donation to build a campus-style ministry?"

Darrell replies, "We've earmarked all your funds exclusively for the west coast ministry. You need not worry, Donna. What we've leased is a two-year-old 180 room hotel on forty acres. Unfortunately, the investors didn't get the exit ramp off the interstate for their hotel's success. So, instead of filing bankruptcy, they leased it out for only twenty-five thousand annually."

Rachael adds, "If the ministry succeeds like we pray it will, then we'll purchase the acreage and hotel and add more buildings. The first will be a church to be the beacon of light for the area."

Donna softly replies, "Please forgive me for not trusting your judgment. Working in the dairy parlor for thirteen months is no excuse, but maybe that fresh country air, as Mitch refers it, has caused my brain to be rewired." Everyone chuckles.

The following Sunday becomes a sort of celebration for some at the Jerusalem Tree Church. Richard and Agnes asked Connor to join them, along with Cambria and Carlo. Leah and Donna are sitting with Mitch when Donna's heart flutters, and she immediately jumps an inch off the pew while watching Connor walk down the aisle.

Rachael and Darrell sit on the platform, and she makes an announcement after Tom, Sergio, and Lucinda bring joy to the congregation with music and songs.

"Good morning, everyone! Welcome! It is so good to be in the House of the Lord, Amen! Today we have a special guest preacher that will deliver the message. Before I introduce him, I want you all to know he also excels at burying people," the crowd chuckles hesitantly.

"All kidding aside, Jacob, his mom, and his grandma are the new managers at Cedar Creek Funeral Home, cemetery, and mortuary school. He asked me to share; there's no hurry to take up residence, but you may want to visit for the all-important pre-need. Darrell and I have also asked Jacob to fill in for us occasionally. So, without further ado, let's give Pastor Jacob Dodd a warm Cedar Creek welcome."

The congregation gives Jacob a robust round of applause as he steps up to the podium.

Jacob's message was on the abundance of life using the books of Corinthians, John, and Deuteronomy to underscore his theme.

Jacob continues, "I understand one of your very own church members lives the abundance of life every day. Lucinda, would you please come up here on stage? I want to share with the audience your zeal for living."

She walks onto the platform with the radiance of God's love within her.

Jacob continues, "Some of you may not be aware that Lucinda is the director of 'Adopt-not Abort' ministry at this church. If I understand correctly, you've had seven adoptions so far."

"Yes, that is true. I am so grateful this ministry can reach out to the community and help girls with unwanted pregnancies. Here, women have the opportunity to learn and realize the importance of giving life to a newborn through adoption."

"Thank you, Lucinda. I also understand the ministry is expanding to the west coast soon."

"That is correct, Pastor. The new managers for our west coast facility are in the audience this morning. Donna and Leah, please stand so we can give you our appreciation for the work you'll be doing."

As they stand and the audience gives polite applause, Connor can't believe his ears or eyes. He thought Donna's sentence was up to seven years, and she's here now-*unbelievable,* he thinks.

Lucinda finishes, "Donna and Leah have two more weeks of training here, and I'll be flying out with them to help them get started. Thank you, pastor, for letting me share."

After the last prayer dismissing the congregation, Conner elbows his way through the crowd streaming against him. Finally, catching Donna before she leaves, he taps her on the shoulder.

As she turns around, Connor trips over his words, "I thought you were still in prison. I can't believe you're here."

Donna's words are cold, "Would you like me to be back in prison?"

"No, no, of course not. It's so great to see you!" Connor wanted to give Donna a hug but could sense she was angry about something.

"Yeah, I guess it's good to see you also," Donna intentionally not warming up to Connor. "I understand you're the new manager at the golf course, and I assume you'll be staying here playing golf 24/7."

Connor's response is lame at first, "Probably. No, not 24/7. I have work to do as a manager, can't be playing golf all the time."

Donna tries to warm up to Connor but just can't. "That's nice. I remember you enjoy playing golf. As you've heard, I'm leaving in two weeks and have much preparation in getting ready to manage the west coast facility. So, if you'll excuse me, Connor, I best be going."

Connor tries to grab her attention, "How about us getting together for lunch before you leave?"

"I don't think that would be a good idea. We'll be some 2,500 miles apart. You'll be playing golf, and I'll be delivering babies, sort of. If you want to do something worthwhile, Connor, sponsor a tournament supporting our ministry, 'Adopt-not Abort.'"

"That's an excellent idea, Donna! One-hundred dollars for every birdie and one-thousand for each hole-in-one. You like it?"

"Sounds fantastic, thank you. But, I need to go; Leah is waiting for me, Connor. You take care." She abruptly turns and leaves.

As she's walking away, Connor shouts, "If you change your mind, stop by at the pro-shop. Coffee is always on."

CHAPTER FORTY-FOUR

THE VISIT-SEPT 2036

Lucinda drives over to the funeral home to pay Jacob a visit regarding the ministry. She walks into the front lobby and is greeted by Katy.

"Well, good morning, Lucinda. I'm assuming you're not here to look at caskets or buy a pre-need. So, what's on your mind?"

"I know I should have called first, but I thought I'd take a chance and see if Jacob has a few minutes to discuss the adoption ministry."

"Oh, I'm sorry, he's presiding over a graveside funeral this morning. But he should be back in about ten minutes. Can I get you something to drink?" Katy inquires.

"Sure, that would be great. A bottle of water will do. Say, so how long have you and your son been in the funeral business?"

"My late husband and I started our first one in Pittsburgh fifty-two years ago, right after Jacob was born. We started the business on a shoestring, and I used a casket for Jacob's crib. I never told Jacob, and Lucinda, don't you dare. My husband did remove the lid, so it wasn't as bad as it sounds."

"Wow! That does sound strange, but I'll keep your secret, promise."

Katy looking out the lobby window, swiftly shouts, "Look, here he comes now," and Jacob walks in, surprised to see Lucinda there.

Katy breaks the ice, "Jacob, Lucinda is here to discuss the adoption ministry with you. She has a few ideas and would like your input."

"Sure, I guess I can spare a few minutes. Come on back to my office, Lucinda, and let's hear what's on your heart."

As they walk back to his office, Jacob leaves the door open and motions for Lucinda to sit in the oversized chair while he sits behind his desk.

"So, what are your ideas?"

What he was about to hear coming from a bright, beautiful twenty-four-year-old girl, all the college degrees wouldn't have prepared Jacob for this.

Lucinda begins, "Like you, Jacob, I love God and have dedicated my life to Him. This ministry that God has given me to shepherd over is a gift from above. I can't think of anything more precious than a newborn being adopted and not aborted."

"I agree, Lucinda. What you and God are doing is precious. Is there any way I can help you in this ministry?"

Lucinda drives home the essence of her meeting with Jacob.

"God is good all the time. God is omnipotent. God is righteous. In His infinite wisdom, sometimes He allows babies to be miscarried. Why? We mere mortals will only find out when we meet Jesus in heaven. Both local hospitals in the area have at least four each annually. So, I'm wondering, Jacob, if you would consider setting aside a small part of the cemetery for these babies when this occurs?"

Jacob shares with Lucinda, "That request came from the heart. Praise the Lord! Absolutely Lucinda! I'll have my cemetery ground crew prepare a special place for the precious babies' section

They both begin to cry, and Jacob grabs a few tissues and hands, Lucinda, some. As Jacob's mom hears the cries from the open office door, she softly walks in. Not knowing why they are crying, she nevertheless asks both to join hands with hers and prays.

"Dear Father God, we ask that you hear these cries and pour out your love and wisdom for the answers Lucinda and Jacob are seeking. We thank you in Jesus' name, Amen."

Jacob shares with his mom Lucinda's request, and they both were shocked by her reply.

"Jacob! I've never shared this with anyone. When you were two years old, I had a stillborn. You were too young to realize the happenings, but your sister would have been fifty next month. Jacob, I would like to honor her by placing a headstone in the precious babies' section with her name on it. She's resting in peace at the Pittsburgh cemetery, but her memory lives on."

Jacob and Lucinda are crying again after hearing what Katy shared with them.

Jacob turns slightly to his right and asks Lucinda, "I would like you to speak at the dedication services."

"I would love to, Jacob. It'll be an honor. Is it okay if Sergio joins me?"

"Of course, he's more than welcome. By the way, congratulations on your engagement. Have the two of you picked a date yet?"

"Not really. I've asked Rachael to perform the wedding. So far, it looks like an early fall ceremony, and I hope you don't mind. She has been nothing short of a miracle in my life, and Sergio's also."

"I wouldn't expect anybody else but Rachael to do the honors of uniting you and Sergio as husband and wife."

"Thank you so much, Pastor Jacob. I guess I need to dry my eyes and get back to work. So, I'll see you in church, Sunday?"

"Yes, of course. God bless you."

As Lucinda walks out the door, Katy mentions out loud, "She has a beautiful heart. A heart of God."

CHAPTER FORTY-FIVE

THE SHERIFF SQUAD-OCT 2036

Grace Palmer, the director for the American Sheriff Squad, used to be tightly-knit friends with Rachael sixteen years ago. Grace, at that time, was the director of nursing at a clinic in Cedar Creek. She and Rachael paled around together for two years, both bar-hopping with wild dancing. That friendship ended when Rachael became a high-powered fashion model. Later on, in life, Rachael invited Jesus Christ into her heart and became a newborn-again-Christian. Shortly after accepting Jesus, Rachael became a fashion clothing line tycoon, eventually selling her business and becoming a billionaire.

Grace, along with her three friends, shunned the very thought of having Jesus in their life. Instead, they embezzled millions from the local church in Cedar Creek. Grace took her portion of the theft and escaped to Europe, living there for fifteen years, until she unexpectedly met the Vice-President, Ms. Firuzeh, in 2035.

Grace is magically taken from her hostess job at a Portugal restaurant and rises to the Washington D. C. hierarchy. The burning vendetta Grace has been harboring all these years will finally have the opportunity to show its ugly head.

That day arrived when Ms. Firuzeh invited Grace to join her for dinner at her mansion in D. C.

"Thank you for joining me, Grace. I'll get right to the point, and we can then discuss the details over dinner. Okay with you?'

"Yes, of course," replies Grace politely.

"It is my deepest concern that President Avci will never sign the D. C. Mandate into law, even after he wins re-election. He's intimidated by the power of congress, mostly women, and the Speaker of the House."

"Even while living in Portugal, I became curious about him and came to the same conclusion. Nevertheless, he did win the populous vote by a landslide."

"Yes, his ways of speech and oratory are blameless, but his inept handling of governing is no excuse. I don't pull any punches, so let me ask you a question, Grace. Would you be interested in being my VP and also living with me as my wife?"

"Ever since you brought me to Washington D. C., I was wondering how we would ever get together. The answer to that is, Yes! I am so enamored with you. I'd love to be your wife. But, how do you plan on getting to be President?"

"After he wins re-election, should he, out of the blue, die. I'll become President, and you, my Vice-President. We'll make history, becoming the first lesbian couple to occupy the White House!"

After dinner, Ms. Firuzeh goes into detail. "As director of the American Sheriff Squad, Grace, I want you to pick a city where the military goes into a church and arrests everyone. Don't burn the building. I prefer to tax churches heavily, but we need to make a statement. This show of action will boost my popularity with the New Reformed Communist Party, and hence, I will gain their support for the immediate and long-term future."

"I will gladly support your agenda, dear, and I choose the Jerusalem Tree Church in Cedar Creek to be the target," Grace proudly states.

Later that evening, Grace begins her new life with Ms. Firuzeh and spends the night at her mansion.

The following week, Grace requests the presence of Walter Smith in her office. "You're the manager of the Sheriff Squad for Cedar Creek County. Do I have that right?"

"Yes. Director, you do. How may I be of assistance to you?" Walter replies with military precision.

"I'm signing you an order to take as many military men and women as you need to arrest over 10,000 people in church next Sunday."

"Your command is my order. I never question the validity, but ma'am, is this a trial run or the real thing?"

"Only arrest. Use blank paper bullets if you need to. Scatter the people in jails throughout several counties and keep them there for five days."

"If the church leader or pastor asks what charge they are being arrested for, what do I state?"

"Declare! They are being arrested for preaching against same-sex marriage!"

The following Sunday, Walter had the command of over 5,000 military personnel. He discreetly placed several plainclothes officers inside to unlock the front doors after service began. No need to ram open a locked entrance at this time.

After the worship service concluded and Pastor Rachael began her message, the military rushed in and surrounded the entire sanctuary. No one was able to escape. Walter Smith approaches the stage where all the church leaders are congregated.

Before he could say a word, Rachael calmly states, "I see you have come to arrest me, the church leaders, and the congregation. Do I have that correct?"

"Yes, pastor. You have that correct."

"May I ask on what charge is the church being arrested and I?"

Walter answers as ordered by Grace. "You may. You and the church are being arrested on preaching that same-sex marriage is a sin against God."

Rachael replies calmly again, "Very well. May I ask unto who gave you the command to take this action?"

"Yes, you may. I believe, at one time in your life, you personally knew her. Ms. Grace Palmer, the new Director of the American Sheriff Squad."

"Yes, of course! Vendetta's revenge has come home to roost. Mr. Smith, if I and everyone in this sanctuary agree to calmy file out into your buses waiting for us, would you agree not to handcuff the congregation?"

"Sure! We can do that. But if anyone tries to make a run for it, they will be shot, regardless, if it's inside here or out in the parking lot."

"We understand. I assure you no shooting will be needed," Rachael confirms. "Now, go ahead and start the proceedings, Mr. Smith. You may handcuff me and my husband, Darrell, for starters."

Walter has his personnel handcuff all the members of the worship team and choir. Once completed, Walter escorts Rachael and Darrell, handcuffed with their hands behind their back, and walks them up the aisle.

During their arrested walk, the congregation is singing, 'Amazing Grace.'

Of course, the Reformed Communist Party didn't let an event like this evaporate and made certain every detail of this military action was telecast worldwide.

Before Rachael was placed on the prison bus, one lesbian reporter asked, "Do you now regret preaching against same-sex marriage?"

"Never! I will never back down preaching the truth from God's word-The Bible!"

"Do you have any idea on how long you'll be in jail?" asks the reporter.

"Duration of time in jail doesn't matter. Nor do these tight handcuffs. I will gladly suffer as did the Apostle Paul for Jesus Christ, my Lord."

"Well, Pastor Rachael, I wish you luck. From where I'm standing and looking at your bleak situation, you're going to need all the luck you can muster."

"I don't need luck. I live by faith in Jesus Christ and by the leading of the Holy Spirit. You have a good day, Ms. Reporter."

Walter had the 222 prison buses transport everyone arrested to Buffalo and Rochester jails and surrounding areas. Rachael was placed in a cell with fifty other women in Buffalo. While Darrell was in a Rochester cell with fifty other men.

To save face, President Avci holds a national news conference. "Good afternoon, Comrades and all Americans. Today, most of the nation witnessed an event that could occur more often after I sign the D. C. Mandate bill. I urge Congress not to delay any longer and get the job done. If not, shortly after my re-election, I will sign an executive order to place this bill into law. The arrest of an entire church this morning is a fair warning to all church leaders and pastors not to preach from the Bible nor speak the name of God, Jesus, or the Holy Spirit, nor preach that same-sex marriage is a sin. Failure to do so will be at your own peril. Thank you."

President Avci refused to answer any reporter questions as he walked back to the oval office and slammed the door shut. Sitting at his presidential desk, alone with only two female security guards in position, he calls the Vice-President.

"Ms. Firuzeh, may I see you and Ms. Palmer in the oval office immediately!" He shouts angrily.

As they walk in, President Avci screams at them, "What in the hell were you thinking pulling a stunt like that? You had no jurisdiction to evoke such an order. The D. C. Mandate bill hasn't passed yet, and you go ahead and pretend it has. What was your thinking?"

Ms. Firuzeh answers, "Mr. Avci, you are a timid president, afraid of your own shadow. What I did, sir, was to make you look good. You should win by another landslide now, easily."

"Maybe so. But what you did is nevertheless an embarrassment to me. I seriously should consider removing you from my ticket and selecting another running mate."

"Whatever you desire, sir. Keep in mind, the election is only three weeks away. A new face on the ticket may cause you to lose your seat in this magnificent oval office."

President Avci is reading in between the lines, he thinks. "Very well then, let's make a deal. I'll keep you on the ticket for the first one hundred days of my new term. For your trouble and loyalty, I'll pay you a million."

"Sure, for a million, I can play nice. No problem," declares Ms. Firuzeh.

Grace listening to the entire wrangling finally bursts out, "Mr. President, you look peaked. Here, have some water to cool you down a bit," Grace sincerely states as she reaches for a glass of water stationed by one of the security guards.

"Well, we best be going and let you rest, Mr. President," Ms. Firuzeh states as she and Grace walk out of the oval office.

Walking about a hundred yards down the hallway, the Vice-President places her hand on Grace's shoulder and states, "Stop! Let's pause here for a moment."

"Why? You don't want to return to your office? The Vice-Presidential Mansion?"

"I won't need to, but you will. The tainted water you gave the President was staged for the security guard to hand it to him. You inadvertently just killed the President!"

CHAPTER FORTY-SIX

HEADQUARTERS-SEPT 2036

Meanwhile, Mitch is sitting in his Buffalo office when his phone rings.

"You've reached the FBI, Mitch Kearney speaking."

"Mitch, this is Fred calling from the Washington D.C Bureau. I'm reassigning you to the West Coast Bureau. You've been with the division for over twenty-five years. So, consider this as a gift, getting you out of the cold wintery days in Buffalo. You can finish your last five years in the sunshine. Also, call in Brad and Nancy to give them their reassignment."

"Will do, boss, and thank you. When do I need to report?"

"One week. I'll touch base with you in about six months to see how you're doing. Enjoy."

Hardly having finished his talk with the big guy in D.C., Mitch receives a fax with the details of Brad's and Nancy's new assignments. He's thinking, *'I hope they'll like this?"*

Four days later, they arrive in Mitch's office.

"Thanks for coming in. Have a seat, please."

Brad catches on quickly. "I don't like the sound of this, Nancy. Usually, when your boss states ten words or less, it means trouble."

"It depends on how you define trouble, " Mitch continues. "I received a call and fax from my superior a few days ago. The bureau likes both of you working as a team. So much so, they want to offer you a full-time career as FBI agents."

Brad is working on all eight cylinders this day and states, "What I'm not hearing, Mitch, is that Nancy and I don't have a choice. It's a career with the bureau or a job in prison. Speaking for Nancy, we do appreciate the sugar coating and the offer."

"So, you'll each accept?"

Nancy shouts, "Yes! Brad and I accept. What's next?"

"Well, I've been assigned to the west coast bureau starting next week. You two are being transferred to our London Bureau. You'll be reporting to the Director of the United Kingdom, Gretta Huffstetter."

"Wow! When we received your call, Mitch, we figured something like this, but not London," Brad confesses.

Nancy states, "It's always foggy there, and they speak funny. Isn't there a Plan B or something else?"

"Sure, the Farm State Prison. You'll be milking cows, Nancy, and you'll be butchering them, Brad."

They both shout, "When does our flight leave?"

✶✶✶✶✶

Meanwhile, Donna, Leah, and Lucinda are busily setting up the new facilities in their first week and joyfully thought they had their first client walk in when they hear a voice.

"I was in the neighborhood and thought I'd stop by and see how you gals were doing."

Leah was the first to recognize the voice. "Mitch, what are you doing here?

"I brought you a cup of coffee, kind of returning the favor."

"Thank you, but I know there's more to this than you're sharing, Mitch."

"Well, I've been assigned to the west coast bureau for the remainder of my service years with the FBI. My boss states it's a gift to be in the sunshine. Anyway, I wondered if you'd be interested in going to lunch with me, and maybe a dinner or two. Maybe even a date."

"I thought you'd never ask. I would love to, Mitch," as she reaches over and gives him a soft kiss.

Another week goes by, and Lucinda gets ready to fly back to Cedar Creek when the clinic door opens, and she sees Sergio standing in the doorway.

"Sergio! What in heaven's name are you doing here?

"I thought it'd be a nice surprise to see my finance. I hope I'm not too late."

Lucinda replies, "No, I guess I can reschedule my flight. What did you have in mind?"

"Take you out to a romantic dinner, and afterward, we fly back home."

"That sounds so romantic. I love it."

"I found a lovely, quaint restaurant not far from here, and I have Richard waiting, flying his own six-seater plane to chauffeur us back."

She walks up to Sergio and softly gives him a hug and kiss. "I would love to be your forever companion wherever we go and do."

As they walk out, Lucinda whispers, '*Thank you, Lord.*"

A month goes by. Leah and Donna are busy consulting with pregnant girls and women. They've already had two adoptions, and their 180-room hotel is filling up to 25% capacity. The word of God and the adoption ministry is giving pro-choice a new lease on life.

Some six weeks into their new ministry, the doorbells chime as someone walks in and asks, "What do I need to do to adopt a baby?"

Donna picks up her head from staring at the computer screen, unaware that Connor is standing there.

"Oh, my goodness. What are you doing here? Are you really looking to adopting a baby?" Donna is caught off guard and stumbles over her thought process.

"No. Actually, I didn't renew my golf lease with Richard and decided to re-open my father's office here on the coast."

"Won't you miss playing golf?" Donna is trying to converse with small chatter but failing miserably.

"You have got to be kidding! There are hundreds of courses in the area; I'll never be lost for a round of links. Besides, I wanted to inspect my company's property out here."

"What property is that?" Donna inquires.

"This facility!" Connor firmly states.

"What?" Donna fully perplexed

"My father owned a real estate company here, and he had the bright idea to build this hotel. Remember when you and I met at the Edelweiss Café, and I mentioned we were getting resistance on the off-ramp? Well, this is the project. It would have worked, but my dad bribed the wrong politician and never got the exit ramp off the interstate."

"So, you're re-opening your dad's company, and our ministry is leasing this property from you. Do I have that correct?"

"Yes, you do, but I'm renting it for only 50% of what the market dictates."

"Why are you doing that, Connor?"

"Because I believe in this ministry, and I believe in you, Donna, and I believe in us. During the thirteen months, while I was under house arrest, there wasn't a day that went by that I didn't think of you."

"Well, I sort of thought of you and us also while I was milking cows. But when I first went in, my sentence was three years. Thinking and wishing at first didn't do much for me. Until Mitch shared that my sentence was reduced to thirteen months also. Then my wish got rekindled until I saw you at church. Knowing you were staying in Cedar Creek forever, and me, 2,500 miles away. I thought, what's the use. That's why I gave you the cold shoulder that Sunday."

Connor takes a chance and walks over to Donna, and begins to caress her shoulders.

"What are you doing?" Donna questions while she's giggling.

"You chirped that you had cold shoulders, so I thought I'd warm them up," he states as he continues kissing her shoulders and neck.

Donna wraps her arms around his neck and returns his kisses. "I miss you so much," as she continues to hug Connor tight.

"Let me ask you a question. How many hours can you run before overheating?"

Donna looks into his blue eyes and blonde wavey hair while they continue hugging each other and sharing kisses.

"For you, Mr. Bridgewater, it's still twenty seconds!"

CHAPTER FORTY-SEVEN

THE ELECTION-NOV 4, 2036

The Reformed Communist Party had rented the new 120,000 seat sports arena for the President's victory speech this evening, November 4, 2036.

"Thank you, thank you, thank you very much," states the newly elected President amidst the roaring noise of over one hundred thousand.

"I want to thank my loyal comrades and others all across the USA, and especially the nation of China. This victory would not have been possible without the unwavering help from both of you. Thank you."

The crowd cheers and chants, "Red, Red, Red. China, China, China!"

"I will not disappoint. I will keep my campaign promise and not sign the D. C. Mandate bill. You have my word! Instead, I will sign an executive order for all churches to pay an annual tax of one million. Also, all Bibles purchased will have an added tax of one hundred dollars. Lastly, a Sheriff Squad member will attend every church service throughout the nation. Whenever a pastor opens a Bible and preaches Jesus from it, they will be fined five thousand dollars, up to a million annually. "

The crowd roars with cheers. The stadium noise could be heard throughout the city. Everyone was celebrating, in the streets, in the bars-everywhere!

President Firuzeh continues her speech. "I want to thank Mayor Brady of Cedar Creek, New York, and his office for cooperating with the American Sheriff Squad on their raid of the Jerusalem Tree Church. Allow me to take a moment and celebrate another victory for our team., It is my pleasure and honor to appoint Mayor Brady as the new Director of the American Sheriff Squad. Congratulations, Mayor!"

The crowd goes stir crazy as President Firuzeh won the popular vote by over one hundred million against her four closest rivals. Indeed, along with her wife, Ms. Grace Palmer, as Vice-President, they won in a land-slide-a mandate to tax the churches to death!

Two months later Cedar Creek held a special election in January 2037 to fill the vacancy of Mayor. Lieutenant Kace won on a conservative Christian platform.

CHAPTER FORTY-EIGHT

EPILOGUE-JAN 2037

Rachael and Darrell are discussing their five-day jail time back in October over breakfast at their hotel café.

"My first blush when entering the women's cell of fifty was a shock, I have to admit," Rachael shares with her husband. "But soon, in a matter of minutes, the Holy Spirit touched every woman in that cell, enabling me to share the love of Jesus with them."

Darrell adds his experience over the breakfast conversation. "I, too, had a similar situation. One tough hombre asked me what I was in for, and when I shared that I had preached the truth from the Bible, he shouted back, "We haven't had church service for a month of Sundays in this jailhouse. Go ahead, preacher, show us what you have!"

"So, what happened?" Rachael asks.

"I preached the word and had an altar call. Five men gave their lives to Jesus Christ right there in the cell! Praise the Lord!"

"You know, Darrell, Since our new President has virtually shuttered all the small churches by her high taxes and unavoidable fines, we need to continue the fight and be sure to keep our doors open. I've asked Terri to calculate how much more each church member could give to cover our annual tax and fines. Surprisingly, it's only $11 monthly more for each member, and we'll be able to preach God's word-Hallelujah!"

"I was thinking along those same lines, honey. Let me ask you, what are your thoughts on asking our members to pledge, say, $44 monthly more so we could support three other smaller churches in the area that can't afford to pay the tax and fines?"

Rachael comes back, "Yes! Great idea, Darrell. Now, let me ask you a question. What's your take on a fund-raising campaign titled, 'Don't mess with my church doors.'"

"Very clever and witty, and sending a message of love, hope, and faith. I'm sure most members will pledge the extra monthly tithe to keep the doors open for our church and three others in the area," Darrell noted.

Rachael shouts, "Praise the Lord and Hallelujah!"

Darrell joins the celebration and also shouts, "Praise the Lord!"

About to finish breakfast, Rachael softly says, "Darrell, honey,"

"What is it, my dear Rachael?"

"You suppose, maybe, we could take a Spring vacation. After what we've been through, we deserve it. Don't you think?"

"You have anywhere in mind, sweetie?"

"Yes. How about London. I hear the sights are fabulous."

"London it is! Let's make reservations for April 2037!" Darrell shouts.

What to do now:

Be The First To Get My Next eBook,

"The Year 2037-The D.C. Scandal"

Go to: www.cedarcreekcounty.com

To buy my eBooks for Kindle.

Also Available, Personally Signed Autographed Paperback by your author,
Brandon J Rosenberg

What to do next:
Read the First Two Chapters of:

The Year 2037
The D. C. Scandal

Cedar Creek County, A Christian Thriller Series
Featuring Pastor Rachael & Friends

CHAPTER ONE

WED, APRIL 8, 2037
LONDON VACATION

Both husbands are nervously sitting behind the palatial desk, awaiting the next call from the kidnappers. The FBI and NCA joined forces to locate the kidnapper's hideout and free the two wives apprehended yesterday in broad daylight while shopping. Everyone in the hushed drawing-room, now designated as the war room, is anxiously pacing the thickly carpeted floor when suddenly, the phone rings. The FBI director nods her head for Erick to pick up the phone.

"This is Willowbend Manor, Erick speaking; how can I help you?"

Before marrying Cynthia, the Duchess of Willowbend, Eric was a drifter of sorts. Having served his country of England during the Desert Storm War, he became a vagabond doing odd jobs wherever needed. The late millionairess, Lucretia, manipulated him into action. Along with two of his gal friends, Grace and Sheila, they stole a historical relic, The Jerusalem Tree Picnic Table from Cedar Creek, New York, and brought it back to Italy.

The voice at the other end was grabbled, indistinguishable whether a woman or man's voice.

"Put this call on speakerphone so everyone, including the FBI and NCA, can hear our demands. Is Darrell in the room?"

"Yes, I am, Darrell shouts!"

"You and Erick listen carefully if you ever want to see your wives alive ever again. First, we demand that you release the thirteen Palestinian soldiers imprisoned in Israel. Secondly, we also demand one hundred million. You have one week to meet our first command." Caller hangs up abruptly.

✶✶✶✶✶

One day earlier, sitting in first class getting ready to land in an hour or so, Rachael brings up the dedication ceremonies to Darrell. "I'm delighted and honored to speak at Willowbend's new church, but I'm curious why I was chosen. You have any thoughts, Darrell?"

Darrell is basically no help but tries. "Ironic it is. We made plans to vacation in London, and two weeks later, you receive an invitation to be the headline speaker. I spoke with Dalton at the conservatory thinking, as a consultant to the President for American/Israel relations, he would have a clue, but no dice."

"Well, he's busy being a professor and a dad to his twelve-year-old daughter and eleven-year-old son. I doubt he had time to delve into my curious invite with any tenacity." Rachael shrugs off Dalton's lack of investigation as incidental with no harm done."

Out of the blue, Darrell remembers something Dalton mentioned. "Rachael, sweetheart, Dalton did state his counterpart in England, Garrison Anterra, could be some help to us."

"I believe he's the brother to Cynthia, the Duchess of Willowbend, and we'll be joining them for lunch tomorrow to review the ceremony's itinerary. I'm also curious to see their royal mansion," Rachael blurted.

"Do I detect a bit of jealousy, perhaps?" Darrell voiced.

"No, not really. Just wondering how a royal mansion compares to our royal hotel. Okay, maybe I'm a bit overly curious, but surely not jealous." They both laugh out loud at their silliness.

"This is the captain speaking. Please fasten your seat belts. We'll be landing shortly."

Rachael and Darrell land at London's Heathrow Airport early Tuesday morning and took a thirty-minute taxi ride to Hotel Park Lane.

Upon entering their hotel suite, Rachael shouts, "Darrell! Sweetheart! I love this place! The exquisite room and the location. Within walking distance to virtually everything in London."

Still early in the morning, they walk out to the balcony and happen to catch a glimpse of the Queen's horses riding out to Buckingham Palace. An everyday ritual morning and evening.

"That was breathtaking, honey. I'm so glad we're taking this vacation, "Darrell shares as they hug each other.

Rachael and Darrell have had a long history of dating each other and others in-between. Going back eighteen years to 2019, Rachael and Darrell were college roommates, but only for one year. She became an alcoholic to the point her addiction drove Darrell out of their relationship. In her last two years of college and eventual career as a pharmaceutical sales rep, Rachael became trapped into another addiction, a high-roller call-girl for the weekends. Her millionaire boss persuaded her to become his loyal mistress instead, and she obliged, lavishing in money and all the luxuries the world had to offer.

Rachael's fortune jettisoned into high fashion, and as fate happens, Darrell was the company's vice-president. They tried to resume their relationship, but Darrell took off with Abby, a fashion photographer, and Rachael flew off with Franz, a fashion choreographer, to Paris.

Before meeting Franz, Rachael had an earth-shattering experience in life. Her sugar daddy boss got killed in a robbery that devasted Rachael to the core of her humanity. Crying her heart out at a picnic table, she had a Jesus meeting and invited Him into her heart. As a newborn again Christian, Rachael believes and knows she is forgiven of all her sins and made new by the blood of Jesus.

Rachael was blessed beyond measure. She became the benefactor of her boss's will, receiving the entire fashion designer company, plus three hundred thousand. Soon after, she and Franz marry and honeymoon in Paris. Returning to Buffalo, New York, Rachael accepts an offer from an

Asian conglomerate for one billion dollars to sell her company. Unfortunately, Franz wasn't happy living in Buffalo, and desiring to return permanently to Paris, they divorce.

Subsequently, Rachael buys two abandoned casinos in the Buffalo area from the proceeds of her fashion company. She converts each casino into a church with restaurants, banquet rooms, and a hotel. Having taken an online Bible-College course, Rachael became a licensed pastor.

At Rachael's gala ball, New Year's Eve, 2019, she was surprised to see Darrell, who recently divorced Abby. While they were dancing, Darrell asked Rachael if they could start over as the clock struck midnight.

She replied, "I thought you'd never ask. I love you, Darrell, and yes, we can start all over again."

"I have always loved you, Rachael, and yes, I'll take a Bible College course and become a pastor with you."

Today, they are pastors of the Jerusalem Tree Church in Cedar Creek, New York, and finally taking a well-deserved overdue vacation.

CHAPTER TWO

TUE APRIL 7, 2037
AMERICAN TOURIST

In the five-hour difference between Buffalo and London, Rachael and Darrell didn't have a problem synchronizing their body clocks with the rest of the Londoners.

Rachael suggests, "Darrell, let's do a little sightseeing this afternoon. We have about ten hours to stay awake."

"Is that all! So, what do you have in mind?"

"Well, we're within walking distance to St James, one of London's exclusive neighborhoods. Let's browse around and get a feel for the area."

"Great idea, hon. But I'm getting a bit hungry. Let's do one of those posh food halls I've read about in the airline travel magazine first, and then do our part as the American tourist." Darrell gleans with pride.

Rachael agrees, and on their way to lunch, they pass by Her Majesty's Theatre and Christie's auction house. As they're walking, holding hands, Rachael nestles her shoulder closer to Darrell and softly states, "While we're here, we should attend as many functions as possible. It would be a shame not to."

"I agree, sweetheart, but I'm not doing anything until we have lunch. I'm starving! Upon entering the massive food hall, they quickly realize it's cafeteria-style. Darrell grabs a basket of London's infamous Fish n' Chips, while Rachael has its unique roasted chicken with Yorkshire pudding.

Leaving the food hall, they both look at each other and shout, "That was different!"

Darrell takes out his cell phone and calculates quickly, "Not bad. We have eighty-eight more days to get used to it!"

"We won't worry about the food; let's have fun, Darrell! Hey! Have you noticed how many bicycle couriers they have here? I bet it's more than New York City."

"I wouldn't be surprised, and by the different multiple-colored shirts, I'm guessing each color represents a company," Darrell conjectures.

"So, you suppose Royal Blue or Burgundy is affiliated with the palace?" Rachael throws out the question amusingly.

Darrell's answer, "Does it really matter? Come on, darling, let's check out Her Majesties Theatre."

Arriving at the box office, they were informed that Hamilton's world-famous stage play is sold out for the next five nights. The earliest seating availability was Monday evening in a private mezzanine box. Darrell's stomach churns at the outrageous ticket price, but he slides his card under the window anyway.

As they continue to stroll St. James arm in arm and casually window shop, Rachael softly shares, "That was mighty nice of you, Darrell. I love you."

"I love you too, honey."

The next day, Rachael and Darrell take a lunch riverboat cruise on the Thames River. Afterward, they stroll through Harrods Square, an elaborate shopping emporium. As they're about to enter the department store, a blue-shirted bicycle courier whisks by, slightly bumping Rachael enough to knock her down onto the sidewalk.

Darrell races over; he picks Rachael up by her right arm and inquires, "Are you okay?"

"Maybe? But I think I jarred or bruised my left shoulder when I fell."

"I'm calling 999 and getting an ambulance taking you to the hospital," Darrell commands.

Once arriving at St. James Hospital, emergency, Met's Police Chief, Walter Dowd, greets them.

"Please, don't be alarmed, Mr. and Mrs. Zellner. This is normal procedure, and I have to ask you a few questions since you arrived by ambulance."

Darrell flatly states, "We understand, but appreciate it if you could do this rather quickly. My wife is in a lot of pain."

"Of course. I'll get right to the first question. Do either of you remember anything unusual about the courier that caused the incident?"

Rachael replies, "He wore a blue shirt."

"Ah, yes. The infamous blue and burgundy shirt bicycle couriers. They ride for a company with an exclusive contract with Parliament."

"How many are there?" Darrell inquires.

"My guess the city of London has around two-thousand, with five-hundred riding for Parliament exclusively," states Walter.

Darrell sarcastically states, "Great! That certainly narrows it down! But, nevertheless, we need to catch the culprit." Chief Dowd, however, dismisses Darrell's sly ultimatum.

Even with her excruciating pain, Rachael still has some humor left. "The proverbial needle in the haystack conundrum. So, now what, Chief Dowd?"

Did either of you catch a glimpse of the bike rider?"

"Hardly. It happened so fast. The next thing I know, I was picking my wife off the sidewalk."

"Wait! Rachael shouts. "I believe the bike rider had an unusual tattoo on his left arm. Something like a lion with a rose stem in his mouth."

Those are the national symbols for England. By themselves, not so unusual, but a lion clenching a rose is rather very odd, I say. Should not be so difficult to find this individual and question him," states Chief Dowd reluctantly, having no desire to investigate.

Fortunately for Rachael, the nurse wheels her back for observation. While waiting, Darrell asks the chief, "When you locate the bike rider and say he admits to a hit and run, what are the consequences for him?"

"Sadly, not much. You'll have the option of suing for medical damages and other expenses, but unless your wife was killed in that incident, the police don't enforce the law of no bike riding on sidewalks."

"I figured as much. My wife and I are Christians and don't believe in suing. Prayerfully, he'll offer some compensation."

Meanwhile, Arda Demir is frantically yelling at Felix to remove the tattoo he inked on his left arm last year.

"Arda!" Shouts Felix, "Removal will take up to eight weeks. I can't do the procedure any faster. Why are you in such a hurry? Last year you loved my artistic approach. A brilliant picture of a lion with a rose in his mouth."

"I was running late delivering a package for Parliament and took to the sidewalk to avoid the snarled traffic jam in downtown, and accidentally brushed aside a woman knocking her down in the process."

"I take it you didn't stop."

"Remember, I was running late. No! I didn't stop. I'm afraid my tattoo will identify me if I get caught, and I certainly don't have funds to pay for medical expenses or anything else."

"Arda, the quick fix would be to give you a new tattoo over the old. Let's do England's national bird, the robin. I'll make it large enough, covering up the lion. No one will ever detect the old image."

"I like that idea. Let's do it!" Arda shouts with relief.

Suddenly, two men dressed in total black, shoes, slacks, shirt, jacket, and dark glasses, barge into the tattoo shop and briskly walk over to the bench where Felix was about to start the new tattoo. The first man states, "Do as we tell you, and you two won't be killed," while pointing two semi-automatics at them. "Our boss has earmarked each of you to kidnap two American tourists. When your job is completed, you'll each be paid ten thousand dollars."

Having served in the military, Felix maintained his composure and stated, "I'm not sure my buddy here knows how to steal someone. He's led a peaceful life, basically peddling a bicycle. You guys may have better success selecting two professional kidnappers."

At that moment, the second man dressed in black fires one shot onto the concrete floor with the bullet ricocheting into the wall and getting jammed.

"You have five days to teach your buddy. If you try to escape, you're both dead meat," the man shouts.

Felix doesn't give up, "After we do the job, how and when do we get paid, and how can we be assured you won't shot us anyway?"

"The second man dressed in black mutters, "We won't kill you if you do the job right."

Arda, patiently waiting for his tattoo cover-up, finally gets the courage to speak, "Why are you so anxious to kidnap the two American tourists?"

The second man answers again, "They're pastors of a mega-church in the USA. You two will be Europe's first operation in USA Church Down. With precision, every church in the USA will be shuttered in less than two years. Our group funnels the ransom money to continue the process. As an additional bonus, kidnapping these two pastors will be a warning for all church pastors to shut their church down-or else."

As the men dressed in black are quickly leaving the tattoo parlor, stepping outside, Bernard, the Angel of the Lord, shows up.

"Men in black, stop!" Bernard yells as loud as possible.

They hear a voice, stop in their tracks sharply, but turning around in all directions, they see no one.

"I'm over here, by the pole light. No one else sees or hears me but you two."

The first man in black inquires, "Who are you, and what do you want with us?"

"I'm the Angel of the Lord, Bernard, and I have come to help you stop your dastardly deeds."

The second man in black states, "We take orders from our boss only. You can't stop us from doing as commanded."

"Yes, you are correct. You take orders from your boss, Otto. But you do have a choice to do what is noble and true."

"And get us killed by his firing squad? No, Thanks, whatever your name is. Incidentally, how do you know our boss's name?"

"As I stated, I'm Bernard, the Angel of the Lord, and I know all things, including your two names. Bruno and Edzard."

The two men dressed in black were astonished by Bernard's knowledge. Bruno inquires, "If you're so smart, Bernard, then tell us how we get out alive not working for Otto?"

"I thought you'd never ask. First, confess your sins, asking Jesus to forgive you, and then inviting Him into your hearts. The Holy Spirit will guide you unto all things."

Edzard comes back, "That's easy for you to say. You haven't lived a life of dastardly deeds since the age of ten. Your Jesus could never forgive a scoundrel like Bruno and me."

"On the contrary, Jesus does and will forgive all sins. No matter how hideous. But listen, guys, I have other scoundrels to visit and chat with, but do yourselves a favor. If you don't have one, pick up a Bible and read the Book of Proverbs and Acts. Also, by the way, it may be best if Otto doesn't see you reading the Bible at this point in time. I will be in touch. Auf Wiedersehen!"

"He even knows German!" Bruno exclaims.

Meanwhile, after waiting what seemed like an hour, Darrell rejoiced to see the nurse wheel Rachael back and noticed she was wearing a sling.

"Are you alright, honey?"

"Sure am. The doctor says it'll be a few weeks for my left shoulder to heal. He gave me a few pain pills should I need them. But, no worries, Darrell, I can still play tourist with you. A banged-up shoulder isn't stopping this gal."

What to do next:

Made in the USA
Monee, IL
07 September 2021